THE FIANCÉ DILEMMA

ALSO BY ELENA ARMAS

The Spanish Love Deception

The American Roommate Experiment

The Long Game

THE FIANCÉ DILEMMA

ELENA ARMAS

ATRIA PAPERBACK

NEW YORK LONDON TORONTO SYDNEY NEW DELHI

An Imprint of Simon & Schuster, LLC
1230 Avenue of the Americas
New York, NY 10020

This book is a work of fiction. Any references to historical events, real people, or real places are used fictitiously. Other names, characters, places, and events are products of the author's imagination, and any resemblance to actual events or places or persons, living or dead, is entirely coincidental.

Copyright © 2024 by Elena Armas

All rights reserved, including the right to reproduce this book or portions thereof in any form whatsoever. For information, address Atria Books Subsidiary Rights Department, 1230 Avenue of the Americas, New York, NY 10020.

First Atria Paperback edition July 2024

ATRIA PAPERBACK and colophon are trademarks of Simon & Schuster, LLC

Simon & Schuster: Celebrating 100 Years of Publishing in 2024

For information about special discounts for bulk purchases, please contact Simon & Schuster Special Sales at 1-866-506-1949 or business@simonandschuster.com.

The Simon & Schuster Speakers Bureau can bring authors to your live event. For more information or to book an event, contact the Simon & Schuster Speakers Bureau at 1-866-248-3049 or visit our website at www.simonspeakers.com.

Manufactured in the United States of America

1 3 5 7 9 10 8 6 4 2

Library of Congress Cataloging-in-Publication Data has been applied for.

ISBN 978-1-6680-1134-8
ISBN 978-1-6680-1135-5 (ebook)

To my readers (yes, you. Hi, babe),
Your expectations are not impossibly high.
Never let anyone make you believe you're asking for too much.

THE FIANCÉ DILEMMA

PROLOGUE

A little over a year earlier . . .

Josie

The day you pick up the phone and a complete stranger says, *I'm your father*, you know your life is about to change.

I mean, look at Luke Skywalker. His existence turned all topsy-turvy after hearing those four words. And although I wasn't some guardian of justice about to be pushed to the very edge of evil and the man on the phone wasn't a heavy-breathing galactic villain in a mask, my world went a little off-kilter.

In the span of one call, I went from having a parent I'd known nothing of—except that his name was Andy—to entering the life of a man who happened to share *one of those nights* with my mother twenty-nine years ago. And by that, I obviously mean the *roll in the hay then never look back* kind of night. Which is fine, really. Mom never talked too much about that, or the man she went all *bam-bam in the ham* with, but she'd always told me enough so I wouldn't resent him or how I was conceived. That doesn't mean that a part of me never wondered. It did. But for the most part, I'd always been content with what I'd known. So what if it was just Mom and me? So what if that looked different from the other kids' families? So what if I had to fill the one side of my genealogy tree with my sea animal sticker collection, which led to being called *jellyfish* for all of fifth grade? They are stunning creatures, hugely underrated, and I owned it. Being brought up by a single parent wasn't that rare or strange. And like Mom always said, *normal is what you make of the cards fate hands you.*

It turned out, fate had been saving a couple of jokers up its sleeve.

Because after close to three decades of radio silence, my father was on the phone. And he had a first name (Andrew, *not Andy*, he insisted), a last name (Underwood), a zip code (Miami), and apparently, the mission to introduce me to a new family. A new world. A realm of life I never expected I'd belong to.

I also had a sister. *A sister.* And Andrew Underwood? He was a big deal.

And we're not talking *he's done well for himself* kind of deal. We're talking *business mogul, multimillion-dollar corporation, name in headlines, definitely has a chauffeur, probably a helicopter too* kind of big deal. He owned an MLS soccer club, for Pete's sake. Andrew Underwood had done more than well. He was thriving. And I knew, not because he'd just rattled that off as an introduction, but because I'd heard of this man before the call. Just like all of Green Oak, the county, and lately, most of the country.

That's why I laughed. After the longest period of silence, I laughed. It was either that or hang up, frankly. Because this man was telling *me*—Josie Moore, mayor of my hometown, proud coffee shop owner, collector of all things shiny, and enthusiastic fixer of broken pottery—that the man whose space I'd filled with a manta ray in my family tree was Andrew Underwood? Not only that, but that I was somehow also part of a complicated, wealthy world right out of an HBO drama centered on legacy? I didn't belong. I was a small-town girl. *Proudly so.* And sure, I'd been briefly engaged to a politician *and* technically almost became a WAG, but those were near misses. That was as close as I'd ever gotten. I couldn't be part of someone's legacy. Hence the laughing.

I don't joke, Josephine, Andrew replied in the same stern voice he had used to deliver the news. But undeterred, I chuckled some more. That's when he brought up Mom. I can't remember what he said exactly, just the words *Eloise,* and *I'm sorry for your loss,* or some other pleasantry.

Later, I realized I'd stopped listening right then and there. There was something about someone's assistant setting up a call. Some other thing about how Andrew would appreciate if I kept this conversation under wraps. And something about the press. But during the remainder of that call, everything slowed down and I went *poof,* nodding my head here and there, and eking out monosyllables when the line went quiet.

That night I didn't sleep a wink. The fact bothered me. So much that I—gently—let one of my flower vases slip through my fingers so I could spend hours putting it back together and . . . stop thinking. Or have the excuse to. I wasn't sure. I'd always thought of myself as someone who liked change. For the most part, change had been handed to me, but I could pinpoint a handful of instances when I'd chased it. I liked to be challenged. And change did that to you. I had no choice but to push through, and for a while, everything faded around the edges and all my energy went toward the one thing. Rising to the top. Overcoming.

Change spiced up life, in my opinion. It kept you on your toes.

But for the first time, faced with this new development, this new quest to embark upon, this new hand of cards fate had been saving for me, I didn't feel excited. It terrified me.

Because after I'd lost Mom, I'd lost all hope of ever finding out who *Andy* was. To find those missing puzzle pieces that made me the woman I was today. Or to simply have the choice to decide if I wanted to pursue that search.

There was not much of a choice now. Andrew had just landed smack bang in the middle of my simple life, throwing open a door right in front of me.

The million questions I'd kept bottled up were bubbling inside me. I felt like a different Josie.

Normal is what you make of the cards fate hands you.

I think I knew then that change was beginning.

CHAPTER ONE

Present day

I plunged my hand into the jam jar.

"Come on, come on, come on," I murmured, watching some of the jam spill as I pushed further in, strawberry-red goo covering my skin all the way up to my wrist. "Don't do this to me. *Please.* Come out. Nice and easy."

"*Moshie*?" Grandpa Moe's voice reached me from the living room.

I froze, the wiggling of my fingers coming to a sudden halt. Darn it. If Grandpa saw what was currently stuck around my finger I wouldn't hear the end of it. Furthermore, if he saw me using all the jam after I'd promised I'd bake him a cheesecake, he would—

"*Moshie,*" came again.

"Yes?"

"*Fhere's a moomaan in the yarhd.*"

I rolled my eyes. "What?" I asked, even though I'd caught some of that. I spoke toothless–Grandpa Moe.

"There's a woman in the yard," he repeated, his speech now clearer, indicating he'd put his dentures back in.

I sighed as I glanced down at my desperate attempt at getting that thing off my finger. I should have gone for butter. Or oil. And I needed him distracted and away from the kitchen. "How can you be sure she's not just passing by?"

"She's coming up the stairs of the porch. I don't like her."

Well, crap. There was someone coming? "What did I tell you about being a jeeper-creeper, huh?" I said, sticking my hand out and pulling at my finger with my other hand. "They can see you watching them like some"—I exerted a little more force—"weirdo in suspenders." The thing didn't move an inch. I went at it again. "I know you think you're on neighborhood watch or something, but—"

My fingers slipped, my hands sliding away from each other and knocking my elbow into the jar, sending it crashing to the floor with a loud, strawberry-red splash.

"But what?" Grandpa Moe asked. "And what was that?"

I silently cursed at the complete and absolute mess I'd made of the counter and floor and, well, me. Hands, robe, feet, all of it covered in jam while I stood surrounded by glass shards. "I just dropped something. It's all under control."

The doorbell rang.

Maybe not all. "Grandpa Moe?"

I heard the creaking his chair made when he plopped down.

"Moe Poe?" I called in my sweetest voice, wiping my hands on . . . Where were my kitchen towels? I used my robe. "Would you be a doll and get the door for me?"

"She ain't here for me," he said. "And I don't like strangers. Or how she looks. And," he added with a pause, "I'm old."

"Being old is not an excuse for everything, you know?" I picked up several pieces of glass before carefully padding to the sink and depositing them there. "You can't use it to get the last chocolate muffin and not the door."

A trail of angry mumbled words traveled from the living room as I collected more glass shards and waited for a sign that the man was on the move. None followed, pushing me closer and closer to the edge of . . . losing it.

"Moe Poe, are you—" The doorbell rang again, startling me. A sharp pang of pain in the middle of my palm made me wince. *"Shoot,"* I gasped. "Stupid silly glass and stupid silly—"

The sound of the doorbell came a third time. And a fourth. And a fifth.

I closed my eyes and let out a frustrated puff of air. *"Maurice Antonne Brown,"* I gritted between my teeth. "If you don't get that door, I swear I'm going to whoop your stubborn, stinkin' butt—"

"All right, all right," he croaked. His chair creaked. Slow and heavy steps followed. Then the sound of the front door opening, followed by a, *"Mhat can I help you wifh?"*

Son of a monkey. He made me want to scream sometimes.

A female voice answered, "I'm sorry?"

"Mhat can I help you wifh?" Grandpa Moe repeated like the absolutely insufferable man he could be. A part of me couldn't believe he'd popped those teeth out again, but why was I surprised? Grandpa was a certified grump, and ever since he'd had a mild stroke that had me immediately packing his things and moving him in with me, his grouchiness had been at max, even now that he'd recovered almost to a hundred.

"I . . ." the woman started again. "I'm looking for Josephine Moore. I'm certain this is the right address. Everyone in town I talked to confirmed it."

"And?" the old man had the nerve to say.

There was a beat of silence, then the woman said, "And I'm never wrong. And I'd hate to waste any more time, so if you don't mind getting Miss Moore for me, I would appreciate it. I've been standing here for a long time, watching you eye me from the window. I don't know if that was meant to intimidate me, but it didn't work."

A new pause. "I've dealt with a lot scarier than a toothless old man in suspenders."

I groaned. Last time someone had called him "old man," Grandpa Moe got us on the cover of the county gazette. The black-and-white shot of him fighting Otto Higgings over a pair of oversize shears—with me standing in the middle, arms outstretched and panicked expression on my face—still haunted my dreams some nights. I'd always wanted to make it to the front page of the gazette, I just wished it wasn't under the headline: *Pruning Warfare in Green Oak. Mayor Struggles to Keep Peace.*

As if on cue, Grandpa's chuckle drifted from the hallway. It wasn't a cute sound. It was his *I'm up to no good* chuckle, and jam and mess and robe—and yes, algae-extract face mask too—be damned, that chuckle kicked me right into action. I rubbed my hands as clean as I could on my already ruined robe and sprinted to the door.

Two pairs of eyes blinked at me. Grandpa's lips started to move around a question I didn't want to answer, so I smiled and—gently—pushed the old man aside. Only to realize that there was a darker shade of red covering my hand. Blood, definitely not jam.

I shoved both hands in the pockets of my robe and whirled to face the woman. "Hi," I greeted her, widening my smile. "I'm Josie. Josephine Moore. That's me. I'd shake your hand, but . . . germs. How about an elbow bump instead?" I stuck my elbow out. "I hear it's all the rage these days. With the kids and . . . young adults. Of the internet. Everywhere."

The woman blinked, her eyes traveling up and down my body a few times until a strange grimace formed. "Absolutely not. Nope." Her expression turned appalled. "What's . . ." She seemed to look for the right way to formulate the question. "Why do you look like you jumped out of a Pop-Tart?"

"Oh. I, ah, was just . . . baking," I explained with a laugh. I didn't want to laugh. I wanted this night to end and a new day where there was no ring stuck to my finger to start. "I'm messy. Messy bakers are common. I didn't catch your name, though. I'm Josie, but we've established that."

The woman's grimace dissipated. Slightly. "I'm Bobbi," she said with a shake of her head, her blond bob barely moving around her face. "Bobbi with an *i.* Bobbi Shark."

An awkward beat of silence followed. "Beautiful name," I offered. "Would you like to come in, Bobbi?"

Her eyebrow rose. "You're acting like this is the first time you've heard of me. You were supposed to be expecting me."

It was a good thing my face mask was hiding my frown because I'd remember if I was expecting someone with a last name like Shark. But then again, it wouldn't be the first time someone showed up at my door at an odd hour demanding something.

"Just like I tell everyone," I said, stepping aside and opening the door wider with my shoulder. My smile had never been bigger. "Come in and we can talk as long as you need about whatever you need." I shot a pointed look at the man to my left. "Grandpa Moe will head to the kitchen and get started on that little mess I left behind. Then he will prepare a cup of tea for us. *Right, Grandpa?*"

He grumbled something, but to his credit, he turned around and headed to the kitchen.

I returned my attention to Bobbi, finding a woman with no intention of stepping inside.

"Alternatively," I offered, suppressing a sigh. "We can chat here at the door. But in that case, we can forget about the tea. I don't think he's in the mood for delivery."

My joke didn't land. I didn't think it even registered, based on the way she was scowling. "You don't know who I am," Bobbi said. "And you're inviting me in?"

I considered my answer. "Well, I don't suppose you're a vampire so—"

"Nuh-uh," she interrupted. "Stop the cutesy routine." My mouth clamped down. "Okay, one? You need to immediately stop inviting strangers into your house from this point on," she instructed in a shockingly serious voice. "And two," she continued, sticking a hand out and waving it over my face and chest. "Whatever *this* is. It's not going to work. You won't open the door looking like this. You won't even glance out a window looking like this." She huffed out a breath. "Aren't you in politics?"

"I—" Was lost. And I had no idea what was going on. "I don't like to think of myself as a politician. Sure, I'm the mayor of town, but it's just a voluntary role in a place this small. Most days I don't need to do anything at all." Some other days, putting out a metaphorical fire shaved years off my life. Then something occurred to me. "Wait. Is this about Carmen?"

Bobbi's brows rose. "I'm sorry, who?"

I took in the woman in front of me—her silver-gray wool coat and leather boots peeking out from under the hem. The spotless makeup, the perfect bob, the barely concealed entitlement she spoke with.

Had the Clarksons taken the fence issue so far they'd hired some big-time city lawyer?

"You're wasting your time," I told her. "It was just an incident. The Clarksons are wasting good money on something that can be solved with a civil conversation. It's no one's fault that Carmen escaped. Cows aren't the lazy animals everyone paints them to be. They can be stealthy. And Robbie Vasquez had no way of knowing what she was doing until he installed the security cameras around the barn. He didn't expect Carmen to be sneaking out. Much less trespassing and getting a little frisky with the Clarksons' cattle. It's mother nature's call, if you ask me."

Bobbi *with an i* blinked at me like I'd just sprouted a second head. Or like she was thinking about how to chop it off and get rid of it.

Oh God, was I about to be sued? Was Robbie about to be sued? A knot formed in my stomach. "Please don't sue us. I swear the fence will be fixed."

Bobbi's eyes closed, then she muttered. "This is my worst nightmare."

"Is that a yes or a no? Because I promise you, Miss Shark, there's no need to—"

"You," she interjected. "This. Cattle. Cows named Carmen. Fences. Barns. This . . . weather. The fresh air. The fact that I haven't seen a Starbucks since leaving the airport. All of it." My lips fell open, but she stopped me with a finger. "You have no idea what's going on or why I'm here, and I was assured you'd been briefed and were on board with all of it. I have written confirmation of it. I can show you the emails, I could swear you're cc-d on all of them."

The emails?

The—

An image was triggered, flashing behind my eyelids. A memory.

Bobbi continued, "I thought my last relationship was toxic, but clients are worse than an egomaniac partner who thinks they're doing you a favor by gaslighting you." She pulled her phone out of her coat pocket and began tapping the screen. "He's going to hear about this. This is going to set us back a whole day, if not two. Such a waste of time."

He's going to hear about this.

He.

I swallowed a lump of dread. My words all but croaking out of me. "Who are you, exactly?"

The *tappety-tap* of her nails came to a stop. She gave me an impressed look. "I'm a PR strategist. An expensive one at that. You would know if you'd read the emails." She seemed to think of something. "You guys get internet here, right? Like, I know this is remote, and there's"—she looked around—"trees and mountains and nature and, you know, *cabincore* or whatever. But you guys get internet here. *Right?*"

I wished we didn't, if I were being completely honest.

That way I'd have an excuse to feed this PR strategist who could have only been sent by one man. *Him.*

Andrew Underwood.

It would excuse me for blatantly ignoring Andrew's latest attempts at communication. Something other than *I was hoping to work out the courage to read those eventually.* Or something other than *sorry, I can't sit through one more Zoom call with you and your assistant while he pretends to take notes because we're just awkwardly staring at each other.* Or—

". . . your father." Bobbi's words brought me back to the conversation.

Because I'd spaced out. And she'd been talking. Most likely about why she was here and who had sent her and why. A possibility crossed my mind. "Wait. Andrew's here?"

Bobbi waved a hand casually. "No. He's too busy to deal with stuff like this."

Stuff like this.

Stuff like what?

My head twirled with all the possible answers to that question and I—

"I don't think you're really listening to me, Josephine," Bobbi declared.

She wasn't wrong.

"So I guess I'm briefing you, then," she said with a sigh. "Again." She touched her temple for an instant. "There's a problem. Well, actually, you are the problem."

I flinched.

"You have a colorful past," she continued. "I'm not shaming you for all those engagements, believe me. It wouldn't matter if you weren't Andrew's daughter. Or if you hadn't showed up at the worst possible moment."

"He called me," I croaked. "I didn't show up. If anything—"

"Adalyn gave him no choice," Bobbi countered. My stomach dropped at the reminder of the ultimatum Adalyn gave Andrew when she found out we were sisters. No one had known, much less expected, that the woman he'd sent to Green Oak on a philanthropic assignment would turn out to be my sister. Not Adalyn, and certainly not me, as happy as I was to call Adalyn a friend by the time the news hit. "He handled it all poorly, in my professional opinion. And now, one year later, in an attempt at redemption or whatever he's intending, he's made everything worse by talking about you and this place to *Time* magazine."

The piece had come out last week. I wasn't sure how he'd made anything worse, but I did know my name was included in a four-page article dedicated to Andrew Underwood's life and business accomplishments. I also knew how the journalist who had penned it had referred to me.

A misstep.

Bobbi continued. "And just like I said it would happen, someone was curious enough to dig around about you and turn this whole affair into the soap opera no one needed. It's not reflecting well on Andrew. It's a threat to his image, his business, and everything that's at stake with his retirement around the corner." She paused. "*You* are the threat, by the way."

The words left me in a strange breath. "I am?"

"You *are* Andrew's misstep," Bobbi explained, repeating the term that journalist had used.

I paled under my algae mask, hearing those words spoken aloud.

"He swept you under the rug for decades, which is not unheard of. You'd be surprised to learn about the children big personalities keep under wraps. But he—"

"I'm—" I shook my head. "I'm no one's nothing. I'm just—his daughter."

"And now everyone knows he abandoned you, Josephine," Bobbi answered with a certainty that made me flinch back a step. "This sweet, small-town girl who lost her mother at seventeen and had to fend for herself while her dad made millions in Miami." Her hand rose in the air again, now drawing a wave in front of me. "This sweet, small-town girl whose father's absence damaged her so deeply she's been relentlessly and fruitlessly searching for that love somewhere else. This sweet, small-town girl, who's charmed not one, not two, not three, but four very distinct men, who she dropped like sad, lame, lukewarm potatoes. *On their wedding day.*" Her tone went dry. "It's like you were written in a room, really. I'm appalled at how such a clever man couldn't see how this would harm his image and threaten his legacy."

Threaten his legacy.

Now my cheeks flamed. My whole body did, the skin under my robe warming up by the second. "That couldn't be further from the truth."

"Can't it?" Bobbi asked with a shrug. "Maybe you should have a listen to a podcast called *Filthy Reali-Tea.* Season three, episode twelve, minute eighteen. They dissect the whole thing in detail. It's shockingly insightful. It's also the reason why I'm here."

I blinked. "What—" The gust of air that came out of me cut the words off. "What podcast?"

"One with two million weekly listeners," she said. "If you count all platforms, including video." My mouth fell open and she shot me a glance I didn't understand. "Would you move to Miami?" I swayed on my feet, starting to feel dizzy. "Seeing how tonight is going, I really think you should. You need me more than I thought you would. I won't help you pack, though. Unless that gets us on the first flight out of this place. It'd be temporary, and the old man could come, although I'd prefer he doesn't. We'll put you in a nice condo and have you attend events and public outings with Andrew. Weather the storm. Show a united front."

Bobbi's voice turned into a high-pitched buzz drilling my ears. I brought my hands to my head. My temples. I patted my cheeks, trying to feel whether my skin burned. But I felt nothing. Was I burning? Was this a fever dream? I felt so . . . overwhelmed. So . . . on the verge of doing something extremely stupid. Like . . . pulling at my robe with a scream and darting in the direction of the woods. Away from this conversation. Even if that would mean I'd be trail-running butt naked in the middle of the night. I—

"What's that?" Bobbi gasped, snapping back with a near shriek. "Why did no one tell me about that?"

I blinked the PR strategist back into focus, following the direction of her gaze straight to my hands. *Christ.* "It's just jam. Maybe some blood from a cut, but—"

"No," Bobbi huffed. "Not that." She pointed at my ring finger. "*That.*"

"Oh," I whispered. "That's just my engagement ring. It's not—"

"Why did no one tell me you're engaged again?"

Again? "Because—"

"Hold on," she interjected. "Shut up. Wait." Her eyes closed and then she did something I wasn't prepared for. Bobbi cackled. She laughed. It wasn't a nice sound. It sounded rusty, and slightly . . . evil. "This changes everything."

I was so tired. So done. So . . . "What does?"

"This," she said, lifting my hand. "Sucks for him, but this is excellent news. For us. You, me, Andrew, my job. This mess."

My mind searched for a way to explain to this woman that this was nothing but a misunderstanding. That this was one of my old engagement rings that was stuck on my finger. Not a new one. That sometimes I did silly things like trying them on again out of . . .

nostalgia? Loneliness? Stupidity? And that when I was stressed, my fingers and ankles swelled and, well, rings got accidentally stuck. But I was overwhelmed past my limit. I'd already been before she got here, if the jam was any indication of how bad my problem-solving was when I panicked.

And now this woman thought I was engaged? Again. For a fifth time. And that it somehow changed everything.

I . . . Oh God. I was going to be sick. I needed time to think. I—

My attention caught on something behind her.

Not something. Someone. A man. Standing at the end of the driveway.

We must have caught his attention too, because his head turned. His hair was a disarray of shades of dirty blond, and I could make out a pair of glasses resting on the bridge of his nose. He stepped forward, his face coming under the light from the street.

"Matthew?" I heard myself say.

Bobbi glanced over.

"Who's that? Your fiancé? Great. He should be here for this conversation anyway. How do you feel about a big wedding?" she continued, bending her mouth into a big smile. "We'll make a splashy announcement. No expense spared. Out of Andrew's pocket. Daddy to the rescue. There's nothing people love more than a wedding. A reformed villain walking the bride down the aisle straight to her happily ever after. And boom, PR bomb deactivated. Father-daughter bond strengthened. Reputations saved. Crisis averted. Irritating podcasters silenced. No relocation of anyone anywhere. Bobbi wins and returns to civilization undefeated."

Time seemed to stop for a second.

PR bomb deactivated. Father-daughter bond strengthened. Reputations saved. Crisis averted.

Then something in me clicked into place.

My hand rose in the air, and to everyone's surprise—mine,

Bobbi's, and definitely Matthew's—I yelled at the top of my lungs, "Hi, baby!"

Matthew's head reared back, and I prayed he'd just go along with it. He knew me. Who I was.

"Love of my life!" I called even louder. "You're finally back!"

As I said, I wasn't exactly great at problem-solving when under stress.

CHAPTER TWO

Matthew's eyes widened.

Crap.

Then he frowned.

Double crap.

Play along, I mouthed.

Matthew, who must have been caught in the storm that had just swept over Green Oak, based on his wet hair, glanced behind him. He pointed at himself.

Me? I read on his lips.

Okay, shit.

This wasn't going as I'd imagined. But what had I been expecting? I hadn't planned this. Matthew was my sister's best friend, and I'd known that he'd be arriving in Green Oak at some point this weekend. But I didn't even know why he was here, in my driveway. Had he decided to stop by on his way to Lazy Elk? Had Adalyn given him my address? Why was he carrying a duffel bag? Where was his car? I wished I had all those pieces of information, but he was

Adalyn's best friend, after all. Not mine. Matthew and I weren't good friends, we were acquaintances. Of sorts. If that's what you call two people who'd texted in a group chat but had never met in person.

And I'd just called him *love of my life*. Out loud. Really loud.

My eyes widened.

I'd just called him love of my life.

I swallowed, glancing back at Bobbi. Dark eyes met mine, expectant. Judging. Nope. I couldn't back down now. Absolutely not. She'd think I had issues. Real issues, not the ones she accused me of having. I returned my attention to Matthew Flanagan, Adalyn's best friend and, as of minutes ago, my doting fiancé. The thought made my head spin again, but I could work with this. He knew it was me. Josie. His best friend's sister. He'll know something's up.

Matthew moved. *Finally*. His foot rose in the air and . . . he took a step forward. In the direction of the porch.

I let out all the air I held in relief.

"Oh boy, have I missed you," I said, still loud. "Did you miss me too, sweet . . . baby . . . pie?"

Just like two light-brown flags of uncertainty would, his brows shot up.

"Oh, no need to answer that," I rushed out. "I already know the answer like it's tattooed on my heart. You've missed me a whole bunch, I'm sure. Because we love each other and people in love can't wait to, you know, canoodle. Smooch. Make sweet love."

Bobbi groaned behind me.

Matthew's step faltered for a moment.

I didn't blame either of them. I was appalled at myself too.

With a shake of my head, I walked down a couple of steps, closing some of the distance that was taking my impromptu fiancé ages to cover and ignoring the way my heart raced for all the wrong reasons.

He stopped at the bottom of the porch before looking up, his gaze swiping left and right. As if inspecting. Assessing. Then his eyes met mine. They were brown, big, and narrowed behind his glasses, still dripping with water. There was something in them, too. Something distracting that I couldn't read. Something that made me think he was still deciding what to do. I felt myself plead with him, even if silently. The quality of his gaze changed, and I held my breath again.

"That's me," he announced, setting his boot on the last step of the porch with a wet thump. *"Baby."* He cleared his throat. "And sweet baby pie. Which we'll talk about later. Right now, I'm just glad I'm finally . . . home. Ready for all that canoodling." There was a beat of silence. And Matthew must have mistaken my staggering relief for confusion, because he shot me a glance and said, "Now get your ass here and give me some sugar."

Bobbi sighed loudly before letting out an appalled ugh.

Not me though. Just as requested, I kicked into action, flying off the porch and landing on his chest like giving this man some sugar was something I knew how to do. I didn't, but my arms went around him either way, the top of my head locking right beneath his chin. And he . . . was soaking wet. Matthew's clothes were sopping, including his leather jacket, and I could feel my robe absorbing the moisture. My skin cooling. I could also feel his body tense and stiff against mine. Why?

A throat cleared.

Bobbi. Right.

I peeled myself off Matthew's chest with a murmured *thank you* that made him go even stiffer and turned to the woman standing on my porch. "Sorry," I said with a smile. "I got carried away there for a second. We're still in our honeymoon phase. Right, ah, *Mattsie . . . Boo?*"

Matthew remained silent, looking unsure again. Luckily, he shook it off quickly. "Right. Absolutely." His gaze shifted away, falling on Bobbi. "And I take full responsibility for that." A strange chuckle fell from his lips. "I'm Matthew. Flanagan. And this is my home. And this"—his arm swung over my shoulders—"is my woman."

"Bobbi," she said with a grimace. "Shark. I'm no one's property, nor do I own anything except perhaps too much cryptocurrency, thanks to questionable financial advice."

"*Yay,*" I squeaked. Loudly. "Now that that's out of the way, and introductions are made, how about—"

"How long have you been engaged?" Bobbi asked.

Matthew huffed out a strange sound that I had to cover with an obnoxious laugh before answering, "Six blissful days."

Bobbi's eyes narrowed.

"It was the most romantic proposal," I added. "My favorite, out of all of them." I felt Matthew's gaze falling on my profile, drilling two perfectly eye-shaped holes. "Why do you ask?"

"It's important information," Bobbi said with a shrug meant to be casual. It didn't fool me. She sauntered all the way to the banister and leaned right beside one of my flowerpots. "And how did he propose, if you don't mind me asking?"

"Romantic picnic," I immediately shot back, feeling Matthew's arm tense around my shoulders. Bobbi's brows arched. "At sunset," I offered, and the way she continued to look at me plucked every word that followed right out of my chest. "We drove to a sunflower field, an hour from Green Oak. I was wearing a sundress and he was wearing a white shirt. The flimsy kind that looks effortlessly great. It compliments his bone structure."

Bobbi's lips pursed. "I know the type."

"We were sipping rosé," I continued, unstoppable. "And eating cheese he'd cut into very thin slices, just how I like, and before I knew what was happening, he was kneeling in front of me, and a teacup pig emerged from the sunflowers, tiny legs jogging in our direction. The pig stopped at Matthew's feet, a letter attached to a bow around his neck. I unfolded the note, my heart racing with the question I knew was written there. Then he said the words, *Will you do me the honor of marrying me?*"

Silence followed my very elaborate proposal story, my heart racing in the middle of my chest.

"What a lucky, creative man I am," I heard very softly beside me.

Bobbi's head tilted to the side. "Agreed," she quipped, climbing down a step. "Let's circle back tomorrow. I can't believe I'm going to say this, but it looks like I might be acting as your wedding planner, too."

"Excuse me, our w— " Matthew started, his arm dropping off my shoulders.

I shot him a pointed look I covered with a smile. "You're tired. And need sleep. And there's all that sweet love, remember? So how about we let Bobbi go, and we go inside, and we sit down and chat? Alone."

"That's a great idea, Josephine," Bobbi commented, now right by our side. "You should explain everything to your fiancé. And remember not to forget the part about the big, fat, small-town wedding. Daddy's paying, no expense spared."

Words rose to my tongue, but the look on Matthew's face stopped them from coming out. His gaze took me in, up and down, quickly. Shock registered, then he paled.

I looked down at myself, understanding what he saw. "I keep forgetting about that. It's just jam," I explained.

Matthew, who seemed a little taller and wider now that he was standing in front of me like this, wavered. And to my surprise, all he said was, "*Josie?*"

I frowned at him, wondering why he was saying my name like that.

Bobbi patted Matthew's shoulder. "Congrats, champ. Let's just hope this ring sticks. At least long enough for me to work my magic and fix this mess. But we'll work on the details and the media angle. Tomorrow— *Oh,* maybe we should have the wedding in Miami? Hm, sleep on that. I will too. Now, it's been a pleasure, but bye."

Matthew looked at me, lips still pale, and expression miserable. Not shocked or baffled or even angry. But just . . . crestfallen.

My lips parted, but before I could speak, his hand was reaching out and clasping my wrist. He brought my left hand up, gently, slowly, his skin cold and clammy against mine as he turned my palm around.

"Matthew," I started.

But that was all I managed to get out before Grandpa Moe burst through the door, hands clad in pink cleaning gloves, and an apron lined with tiny yellow stars around his waist.

"Absolutely not!" he exclaimed, arms in the air, effectively drawing the attention of every human and every animal currently residing within a thirty-foot radius of us. "My Josie is not leaving for Miami. And I'm not leaving either." Grandpa's eyes bore into the man who was still holding my hand. "Josie, why is that wet-looking shallot holding your hand like that? Yes, you. The one flapping his lips like some trout swimming upstream. You're not taking nobody to Miami!"

"Jesus, Grandpa," I warned, looking around for Bobbi, but she'd . . . vanished. "Could you—"

"Do not *Jesus, Grandpa* me," he countered, moving to the banister. "Do you—" He stopped himself, his gaze moving behind us. "Otto Higgings!" he yelled. "Get your ass back into your house! This is nothing of your concern, you nosy, wilted prune."

A silent curse left me under my breath. I didn't need to turn to check if my neighbor—and Grandpa's nemesis—was across the yard, sticking his nose in our business. Because of course he was. Of course—

Something tugged at my hand.

I refocused on Matthew, who was looking down, the little color left in his face draining. I followed the direction of his gaze with mine. My hand was still in his, upturned, and a cut was on my palm. It was barely bleeding, but some of my skin was smudged with a darker red than the one from the strawberry jam.

"Josie," Matthew whispered. "You're bleeding."

"Oh," I said, retrieving my hand and wiping the cut with the sleeve of my robe. "Don't worry, it's just a . . ." I trailed off. "Matthew?"

His eyelids were at half-mast, and before I could do anything about it, he dropped to the ground.

CHAPTER THREE

When Matthew came to, he did so with a startled gasp.

I pushed a mug in his direction and forced myself to give him my warmest, most welcoming smile.

He blinked at me.

My lips fell. "Please drink this? I'll be right back. I'm a fast changer, and Grandpa Moe will keep an eye on you."

I couldn't blame Matthew for his confusion or reluctance to accept the mug. I couldn't blame Grandpa Moe for the complaint that left him either. But beggars couldn't be choosers, so the moment the tea was in Matthew's hand, I whirled around and sprinted upstairs. And the second I closed the door to my bedroom, I sank to the ground.

My eyes closed, shoulders resting against the wooden surface.

All the air in my lungs left me in a hissed, "Shit."

No, I corrected myself. This wasn't a *shit* situation. It was a *truckload of cow dung clogging all five of your senses* kind of situation.

Because tonight . . . had been *a lot*. There were comedy

sketches less far-fetched than what had gone down. Grandpa Moe screaming like a wolf had just sneaked into the coop and slaughtered half his chickens had only been the cherry on top. I still wondered how I'd managed to keep cool when Matthew had plummeted to the ground. How we—and yes, I was bringing the old man with me on this—had made a six-foot-something adult man collapse. Just like it happened to my clay when it didn't hold its shape. One second he was there, strong and solid and seemingly safe between my hands, and the next turn of the wheel he was smudged all over the floor.

Only, Matthew wasn't clay. Or a project I could mold into the shape I wanted. He was my sister's best friend. A person with a life, who I'd pulled into my mess. This wasn't something I could fix by stiffening him with a blow-dryer, as much as I wished I could. Actually, forget that. I shouldn't even be thinking of stiffening or blowing Matthew dry.

I reopened my eyes, stood back up, straightened my back, and refocused on my task. Change. Not digress. So I slipped into my en suite to clean the algae mask off my face, making a mental note to throw the rest of the can away. It had bad juju, I decided. Once that was off, I scrubbed at my hands, put a Band-Aid over the cut on my palm, and slipped into the first thing I found lying around. Leggings, tank top, and a cardigan. Brushing my hair with my hands only once I was trotting my way downstairs.

"Is the tea okay?" I asked, not even completely through the kitchen threshold.

The man sitting on my pink easy chair remained silent, his eyes meeting mine as I came to a stop in front of him.

"It's chamomile," I commented to fill in the silence. "My mom used to prepare it for me when I felt sick or I had a bad day. I figured you'd had one of those. So I thought it'd help. Comfort you. It makes me feel like new."

Matthew seemed to ponder his answer before giving me a curt, "Thanks."

It wasn't exactly reassuring, but at least the color had returned to his face. It was a nice face, now that I could see it under proper lighting. Square jaw, straight nose, full lips, and brown eyes hiding behind glasses. I'd cleaned them up for him during the couple minutes he'd been out of it. They'd been a little stained from the rain and it was the least I could do, all things considered. I . . . liked them. His glasses. I'd never seen him wear them in pictures. Or whenever Adalyn had FaceTimed him and I'd been around to steal a glance or exchange a hello.

They made him look . . . different. More . . . I didn't know. I supposed that hardly mattered anyway.

"Your hand okay?" Matthew asked in a deep, raspy voice.

"Yes," I admitted, relieved at the fact he was talking. I grabbed a stool and placed it in front of him before plopping down on it. "It was nothing. Just a tiny cut," I lied. It hadn't been that tiny.

"You were bleeding, Josie."

"I was, yup. But let's not talk about that. I'm okay, and I'd hate for you to . . . go all ghoulish again."

"It's fine," he commented, dragging the mug to his mouth. "I can't remember the last time that happened. I think being caught in the rain didn't help matters, and my body just gave out for a moment there." His hands lowered the tea to his lap. Brown eyes roamed across my face, then down, taking me in slowly, or lazily, or maybe tiredly, before returning back to mine. "You really are a quick changer."

"It's one of my superpowers," I said with a chuckle. But it was short-lived. I hadn't been the only one in need of a change of clothes and I hated the reminder. I eyed the damp jeans and even damper sweater on him. "We took off your leather jacket when we moved you inside. You muttered something under your breath, and I supposed it was about that." There was a new, awkward beat of silence. "It's going to take some miracle to bring it back to life. Sorry. Probably your boots, too, if I'm being honest. I didn't take those off you, but I wanted to. Ideally, I should have removed every item of clothing off you. But Grandpa Moe didn't let me."

Matthew's eyebrows rose.

"I obviously mean it in a practical, medical way," I explained. "Not in a *let's strip you to your underwear* kind of way."

The corner of his mouth tipped up.

"I wouldn't undress an unconscious man," I assured him. "Not unless I was sure his life depended on being, you know, naked. And yours didn't. You were mumbling stuff. So you were mostly fine. And it would have been really awkward to carry you inside naked."

Matthew's lips fell flat.

"Don't worry." I gave him a big smile. "Grandpa and I cart heavy stuff around on the regular. Well, mostly me, because I don't really let him do that anymore. Although I'm starting to believe those Pilates classes I've been taking are not toning my muscles as much as I was promised. Maybe I should have gone with my gut and given Krav Maga a try." I shrugged a shoulder. "Oh. Want to hear something funny?"

His only answer was a strange look.

"Adalyn also fainted the day she arrived in town last year," I told him anyway. "Under different circumstances, of course. Although I'm pretty sure you know all about that already. But hey, isn't that a fun coincidence? The two of you just losing consciousness the moment you step foot in Green Oak?"

Based on the way Matthew continued to look at me, I didn't think he found it exactly funny. In fact, I noticed he hadn't said a word in a little bit, and I'd arguably said too many of them.

"I tend to ramble when I'm nervous," I muttered. "So it would be nice if you said something. Just, anything, really."

"You're not what I expected." He huffed out a laugh. It was short. A little tired. But it was one, so I'd take it. "And at the same time, you are."

A small smile bent my lips. A genuine one, for a change, tonight. Even if I had no idea what Matthew meant by that.

"He doesn't deserve that," Grandpa Moe grunted, suddenly there beside us. He dropped a plate on Matthew's lap. "He hasn't earned a smile."

I rolled my eyes. "Well, I believe he has earned more than a smile after tonight. Plus, I'll give my smiles to whoever I want to, Moe Poe."

Grandpa Moe ignored that, pointing a finger at Matthew. "Grilled cheese. Eat. You were looking like some stale leek a few minutes ago. Something tells me you've skipped a meal today. So *eat*."

"Grandpa means well," I told the blond man crowding my favorite chair in the house. Mathew chewed diligently. "And I promise he'll stop calling you silly names. I don't know what's gotten into him tonight. He's being extra grumpy."

"I won't stop calling him nothing," Grandpa countered. "And I don't mean well. I want him healthy and strong for selfish reasons. I still don't know if I'll have to whoop his ass."

I scoffed at the old man before turning back to Matthew. "He doesn't mean that."

"I do," Grandpa Moe insisted, taking the plate off Matthew's hands just as he gobbled the last bite down. "That was fast. Still hungry?"

"No, sir," Matthew answered, passing his mouthful down. "But thank you, sir."

I snorted at the two *sirs*. "You can call him Grandpa Moe, just like everyone else in town does. Or at the very least Moe. There's no need for formalities, I promise—"

"My name is Maurice," Grandpa Moe interjected. "And how about he keeps calling me *sir* until I decide what to do with him? This is my home and he's not a guest."

I turned to look at my suspenders-wearing roommate. "*Your* home? You're lucky I like you, or else I'd be kicking your butt and shipping you to Fairhill's nursing home, Mr. *Nursing Homes Make Me Feel Ancient.*" Grandpa gasped, even though he knew I didn't mean it. He wasn't getting rid of me that easily. Not after his stroke, even if he had made a good recovery. I shifted my focus back to Matthew. "I'm so sorry, I—"

"He's right," he said, the light brown in his eyes shining with a reassurance I probably didn't deserve. "He just met me and he's your grandfather. I did skip lunch today. And dinner, seeing the time. That wasn't smart, and I'm sure it had something to do with me going down like that. So thanks for the food and the tea and for taking that wet jacket off me and dragging my ass here. Thank you for not stripping me down to my underwear, too. As comfortable as I am naked, you're right, it'd make everything twice as awkward."

Twice as awkward. I'd used the word myself, but it bothered me that it was his choice to describe this too.

Grandpa Moe grumbled something unintelligible before turning around and shuffling back to the stove, where I knew he'd be preparing more food for Matthew. He really was more bark than bite.

"Grandpa Moe is not really my grandfather," I felt the need to say. "I . . ." Thought this was something Adalyn might have told Matthew. "I don't think it hurts that I clarify it. Grandpa lives—used to live next door. Right beside Otto Higgings. Not sure if you remember him—"

"I do," Matthew said. "*Nosy, wilted prune.*"

I nodded with a light chuckle. "Grandpa would help around the house when I was little. Apparently, one day I decided that he was *my* Grandpa Moe, and not just Moe, and wouldn't call him anything else. It stuck, and somehow all of Green Oak calls him that now." I summoned a small smile. "So please, do that too. I promise he won't mind."

Matthew's eyes took me in for a few seconds. Contemplating. Then he leaned slightly forward, lowering his voice. "I think I'd like to be on the safe side and keep my balls intact," he said with a wink.

A wink.

The curve of my lips turned genuine. Happy, even. This was a lot more like the Matthew I'd heard about. The Matthew I'd expected. From everything Adalyn had said about her best friend, but also from the interactions we'd had. A while ago, Adalyn had added both of us to a group chat with her and Cameron, her boyfriend and my friend, and it was impossible not to form an idea of Matthew based on his texts. Funny, clever, often playful, brutally honest. Matthew typed the most outrageous things, and I'd found myself laughing out loud reading his messages more than once.

Which reminded me of the last conversation we'd had on there. "So . . ." I trailed off, tugging at the sleeves of my cardigan. "How was the trip?"

He sighed. "Long. Tedious. Necessary."

"Well, Chicago is not exactly around the corner," I commented. "I knew you were coming, but I didn't know you were getting here tonight."

His shoulders dropped, and he let his whole body fall back on the seat. "My lease wasn't up until Monday, but I couldn't sleep one more night surrounded by boxes."

"You're staying at the lodge, right?" I continued. It was vacant now that Adalyn and Cameron had found a home closer to Charlotte, and the soccer youth club they had founded and now dedicated all their time to. "Lazy Elk is great. You'll love it there, I promise. It's super cozy, stylish, and has the best views in town."

It made it twice as hard for Adalyn and Cameron to leave

Green Oak. Maybe that was why they hadn't rented it out yet. Maybe a part of them didn't want to fully let go. Or maybe they just thought it would be good to keep it vacant in case someone visited. Or needed it, like Matthew did. Neither my sister nor Cameron required the extra income from a potential lease anyway. Perks of being a hardworking boss lady and a retired professional soccer player.

"I've heard," Matthew said. "Adalyn warned me it was shockingly hard to find, too, but I wasn't expecting my maps app to keep rerouting me for a whole hour. I still don't understand how I ended up on some dirt road and drove right into a pothole."

"So that's what happened?" I felt my brows knot with concern. I knew I had no right to lecture him—especially not tonight—but . . . "You should have stayed in the car, Matthew. You shouldn't venture out into a storm. And please, do not ever wander into the woods. In fact, next time just call—" I stopped myself. I'd been about to say *me*. "Just call someone. Help. A tow."

His eyes did a strange swipe over my face, as if surprised by my reaction. Then a light roll of laughter left him. "Battery was out after all that rerouting. I know how much of a cliché that is. But my Prius doesn't have a USB port, and I was supposed to be a mile away from the lodge. I didn't think I'd be soaking wet within a few minutes and get lost. By the time I realized my mistake, I just hoped the lodge was closer than the car."

I frowned at him. I didn't *want* to say it, but . . . "You're such a man."

He snorted. "Fair assessment. But you're right. It was dumb and I . . . It's been a long day, Josie. A long fucking week, if I'm honest."

My stomach dropped at his words. The reason why he probably said that, besides his unfortunate arrival into town.

"I'm sorry," I said. "I can't imagine how incredibly hard that has been. Adalyn told me what happened with your job. And I'm sorry.

It wasn't fair, I'm sure, and it sucks that you were laid off like that. I'm just—sorry."

Matthew stiffened with every word that left my mouth. "There's nothing for you to be sorry for."

But there was. Because he'd been fired, and he'd had to leave Chicago, and was moving—temporarily, according to Adalyn—into Lazy Elk, and . . . tonight had happened.

We stayed like that, looking at each other in not an uncomfortable silence, but still not an easy one either. A plate clattered behind us, and I wondered whether I should excuse myself and go help Grandpa, whether I should continue to make small talk with Matthew, or whether I should address the topic I'd been avoiding.

Matthew's head must have been in the same place, because I watched his gaze dip, falling on my lap, where my hands were clasped.

"I'm not really engaged," I finally said, showing him the back of my left hand. I had a Band-Aid over the cut on my palm, but I still made sure to keep that facing me. Just in case. "Not to you, obviously. Not to anyone else, either. Not now, at least."

"So I didn't imagine all of that, huh?" His expression turned pensive. "I kind of hoped I had."

That stung a little.

But I couldn't say I didn't deserve it. I made myself smile. "You didn't. Every bizarre event you remember happened." I glanced down, bringing my hands back to my lap. "The ring is from a previous relationship and it's . . . stuck. I tried to lubricate my skin with jam, which wasn't the smartest idea. But soap wasn't working, and I didn't want to wait around for butter to melt." I shook my head. "So strawberry jam seemed like a good, sensible option."

Matthew was quiet again, enough to make me look back at him. His expression was now blank. As if he was trying to keep whatever he thought of me off his face.

So I continued. "Bobbi Shark was also real, I'm afraid. She, ah. Well. She was the reason I went into full panic mode, if you want to call it that. She . . . works for Andrew, my father. And her showing up caught me off guard. And before I could process that, she was rattling off all these things about me, and a PR crisis, and moving to Miami and . . . suddenly she was talking about the ring, and you were there, and I wanted her gone, and I really didn't want to move to Miami, so I—I didn't think. I acted."

Silence followed my very poor account of the facts.

I grew even more restless. "I know how hard that is to believe but—"

"No," he interjected. "It was clear that Bobbi was a threat from where I was standing."

A gulp of air escaped my lips. So he understood, then. Kind of. "I wouldn't call her a threat," I said with what I hoped was a reassuring smile. It was a real one, too. "But she's a little scary. Enough for me to see you and think, or hope, really, that you would help. I am your best friend's sister, anyway, so it's not like I was asking a complete stranger—"

"I didn't know."

My brow burrowed.

"I didn't know," he repeated. "I was trying to help, you're right." He rubbed the side of his neck with his hand. His voice went down. "But I didn't know it was you, Josie."

My smile faltered.

I didn't know it was you, Josie.

"That's all right," I croaked with a wave of my hand. Surely, I couldn't be hurt by that. I was being ridiculous and the sinking in my stomach meant nothing. "It took me all of three seconds to know it was you," I continued, watching his face fall. "Which is okay. It really is. I'm just really good with faces. Plus there was all the . . ." I pointed at myself. "You know. Algae extract and jam situation going on. So I wouldn't expect you to spot me in the distance, with only a streetlamp around, and be like, hey, that's Josie Moore right there. We don't even know each other that well. I mean, who does that?"

Me, that was who.

But that didn't matter now.

Matthew hesitated, as if at a loss, but then he said, "I'm sorry."

I let out a snort. "What for? There's nothing to be sorry about." I blinked at the new emotion entering his face and decided it was time. Now. Time to stop tiptoeing around this thing. I inhaled. Exhaled. Then said, *"Ithinkweshouldjustdoit."*

Matthew frowned.

"We should finish what we started and pretend it's you," I explained, lifting my hand. "The one who put this on my finger."

Matthew's mouth hung open for an instant. Then he said, *"What?"*

"Let's pretend we're engaged," I told him, my skin heating under the cardigan. "Just like we did at the porch. Bobbi bought it. She thought it was real. Real enough to leave. Which was the goal. She said it would fix the problem. The PR crisis that I was telling you about? I can get into the details, but your face is doing a really weird thing." It wasn't moving. Not a muscle in his body was. "Are you going to faint again?"

"No."

"Good. Great." I smiled a little, relieved. "So—"

"No," he repeated. His Adam's apple bobbed. *"No."*

"No?" I asked. "Those are a lot of nos and I only asked one question."

A strange sound left his throat. "We're not doing anything. We're not—" He stopped himself. "We're not pretending we're engaged. No." His back straightened, face serious. "Absolutely not, sweetheart."

I frowned. *"Sweetheart?"*

He shot me a look.

"But—"

"No," he said a fourth time. His voice softened. "I can't do it."

I squared my shoulders too. "We could talk about it. Discuss. Do a pros and cons list. Whatever you need to—"

"I can't," he interjected.

My shoulders sunk. "You can't or you won't?"

"Does it matter? Point is: what you're suggesting is crazy. Tonight was a fun anecdote I'm sure will make Cam and Adalyn holler with laughter. But we're not . . ." His throat worked. "Playing engaged. I've just gotten here."

That quick, albeit sharp, pang of hurt returned. "It'd be for a little while, I'm sure. Just to weather the storm. She only mentioned a splashy announcement. So we could hear Bobbi out and then, we reassess."

He laughed again but it was dark. Humorless. Bitter. "Do you realize how crazy this thing you're suggesting is? How ludicrous?"

Now that actually stung. "Well, from every single story Adalyn has told me about you, it wouldn't be the craziest thing you've done. You're pretty ludicrous yourself, you know that?"

Matthew didn't seem bothered by the accusation. "Well, this is not a college party where you're daring me to stroll naked down campus, sweetheart. This is marriage. A wedding. The ring of some man on your finger."

Again with the nakedness. And the sweetheart. "It's not marriage. It's an engagement," I corrected. "And it's fake. We're not getting married-married."

Matthew's mouth bent in a . . . disbelieving smile. It wasn't a nice smile, and I didn't think he realized the face he was making at me. "I can't believe we're having this conversation. I . . . can't even think straight." He stood up, and I had to tip my head back to look at him. "I should probably get to the lodge. I—"

A truck-like sound filled the kitchen, bringing Matthew's words to a stop.

We both turned toward the source, finding Grandpa Moe sitting at the kitchen table a few feet away. His head dangled back, mouth wide open, a tower of grilled sandwiches on a plate in front of him. He was snoring.

Cranky, sweet old man. He must have been exhausted from all that yelling.

I turned to study Matthew's profile as he stared at Grandpa. My hand reached out before I could stop it. Matthew's eyes plunged downward, landing on my fingers as they wrapped around his forearm. His clothes were still so damp.

"Stay," I told him. "You can have more food. Grab a shower and borrow some dry clothes. Then crash on the couch. It's comfortable and it's late. I'd feel a little better if you stayed the night. Grandpa will too."

Matthew hesitated, brown eyes still fastened around my hand. It was my left, I realized. He was probably inspecting Ricky's ring, thinking how *crazy* and *ludicrous* I was. "All right," he finally said.

I released him and stood up, the tip of my nose almost brushing his throat with the motion. Warmth rose to my cheeks as I stepped aside. "I'll get some blankets and a towel for you. You can get started on the sandwiches if you want."

Then I whirled on my heels, deciding that what I felt in my gut wasn't rejection.

Matthew couldn't reject someone he didn't have.

It was just guilt. And disappointment. And exhaustion. Matthew was probably right. I was a little crazy, and my plans always were a little ludicrous.

And we couldn't do this.

An engagement wasn't a quick patch over a flat tire. It wasn't something you faked for the sake of a narrative, or for a relationship with a parent that I didn't even know how to navigate. It was a commitment. A promise.

A walk down the aisle.

Although that had never been the case for me.

CHAPTER FOUR

Matthew slept like the dead.

Which didn't justify me watching him sleep for what had to be close to fifteen minutes now. But what was I supposed to do? My living room stood between the stairs and the kitchen. And he was currently occupying my couch. And I liked to do something while I had my morning coffee—gallons of it, after the night I'd had. So although I would have loved to give Matthew some privacy, it had been practically impossible to do so.

He looked . . . like a truck had run him over, frankly. His dirty-blond strands were a tangled mess. One of his arms was thrown over his head, while the other hung over the edge of the couch. And I could see a socked foot peeking out of the blanket. It was cute. If not for the fact that Matthew was bare chested under the blanket, and Grandpa's borrowed pajama top laid on the floor in a heap of checkered flannel.

I sipped at the tiny mug containing my fourth espresso. "I'm a creep," I murmured, tilting my head from my post at the armchair.

And this needed to stop. He was a guest. And I was ogling him. Like a weirdo with nothing better to do.

I cleared my throat. "Matthew?" I called, and when he didn't react, I said a little louder, "Matthew Flanagan?"

I watched him for a few moments, but he didn't even stir.

He left me no choice, really.

"MATTHEW!" I exclaimed.

The man sprung upward, producing his glasses from somewhere and slipping them right on. Wide brown eyes met mine.

I smiled at him. "Good morning, sunshine."

He blinked, sleep still tugging at his features and hair pointing in all directions. Also? The blanket had come down to his waist and I could see . . . his very glorious chest. Golden skin. Pecs. What had to be a seriously hard stomach. Holy shrimp. Matthew was . . .

"Ripped."

"Thanks," he said, his hand landing over his collarbone and scratching a spot. He yawned lazily. "What time is it?"

My eyes widened a little as I tried to keep them on his face. I had really said that out loud. "It's a little after nine," I answered. "And you're welcome. And also, can you please cover yourself? That's . . . a lot of man boob you're flashing."

It was slow, but a smirk took shape around his mouth. "That's why you were watching me sleep?"

A scoff left me. "I was not."

"Okay." He shrugged. "But I wouldn't mind if you were."

I tipped my chin up like the liar I was. "Okay, Bella Swan, but I wasn't." I leaned down, snagged the checkered pajama shirt on the floor, and threw it at him. "I need to talk to you and your *nippies* are staring into my eyes, like two beacons of manhood asking to be acknowledged. So if you don't mind?"

Matthew caught the shirt with a laugh. The sound warmed my chest. Just a little. "Never thought I'd have my nipples being called *nippies*," he said, slipping his arms into the sleeves. "Or beacons of manhood." He buttoned up. "I can't wait to hear what you say when you realize I'm wearing no pants."

My brows shot up, so high and so fast, they probably left a mark on my scalp.

"I . . ."

I'd just lost my focus. My nerve too.

Because I'd had a plan, I knew I had one. That was why I'd been waiting for Matthew to wake up before I left to open Josie's Joint, the coffee shop whose doors should have already been welcoming customers. I'd wanted to talk to him. Yes. But it was a little hard to do that now. Why wasn't he wearing the pajama bottoms he'd borrowed? Did I leave the heating too high? Did he simply sleep in the nude? Was Matthew not wearing any underwear? God. How was I supposed to think, much less sound convincing now?

I really couldn't catch a break, could I?

All I'd wanted was to pick things up where we'd left them last night. To give him the full picture I had now, after researching instead of sleeping, which is exactly why I was on my way to a fifth espresso.

The moment my head hit the pillow, Bobbi's words had returned to haunt me.

Maybe you should have a listen to a podcast called Filthy Reali-Tea. *Season three, episode twelve, minute eighteen. They dissect the whole thing in detail. It's shockingly insightful.*

It would have been really stupid—or naïve—not to check. So I did. Together with every single entry Google had offered about Andrew Underwood. Even the ones I hadn't fully understood. The ones about stock value and personal scandals affecting business. As if hearing—and watching—two strangers who really had *millions* of listeners dissect my existence in a five-minute section where they discussed unrelated A-list gossip wasn't enough of a blow.

The memory brought goose bumps to my skin. As if I were somehow thrust back in time and I was lying in bed all over again. Headphones plugged in and wide eyes blankly staring at the wall in front of me while the voices of two strangers curled around insecurities I didn't know I had.

INTERIOR—*FILTHY REALI-TEA* STUDIO—DAY

SAM: Wait up, wait up. You're telling me this is the same man whose daughter got into a brawl with that Miami team's mascot last year? The one who's with that retired soccer player from Europe?

NICK: (clicks tongue) That's exactly what I'm telling you, Sam. He's Andrew Underwood. From Underwood Enterprises or Holdings or something like that. He owns stuff like real estate and corporations? You know that if it's not tech no one really cares.

SAM: More like you don't, but fair I guess. Real estate is not as exciting—unless it's being sold by hot people in full glam, and unless I can peruse the properties from the comfort of my couch.

NICK: We like what we like. Thankfully, the Underwood family is just as deliciously layered. Like . . . a real-life *Succession* episode you're seeing unfold before your eyes. With the drama, the money, the orphan who happens to be an heiress, the secret past, and all the trauma.

SAM: Which reminds me that I should really reschedule my therapy session.

NICK: Do that, Sam. Therapy is crucial. But you should also stop sidetracking me. Because this family has issues, as I was telling you. It really is like they're growing them on demand. Rich Daddy, for example: kept his origins a secret for decades. There's this piece in *Time* magazine where he admits being ashamed of coming from some tiny place in North Carolina, and letting everyone believe he was in fact from Miami.

SAM: Ew. That's a big waving red flag.

NICK: And that's only the tip of the iceberg. This newly discovered daughter, Josephine something-something, who he also kept under wraps for decades, is from—brace yourself—that same tiny place.

SAM: The plot thickens. A nostalgic rendezvous?

NICK: It seems. And it more than thickens because she . . . whoa. (laughs) I can't even say it with a straight face. I swear, I'm not making it up.

SAM: Spill it. I spend way too much time on the internet to be shocked.

NICK: She's a serial runner.

SAM: (disappointed sigh)

NICK: No, no. Wait. This girl runs on men. On grooms. Her fiancés. She gets engaged and abandons the dudes AT THE ALTAR. (pause) On their wedding day.

SAM: Wait, what? But how many are we talking about?

NICK: FOUR. For now.

SAM: (gasps, then laughs) Like that rom-com from ages ago?

NICK: The nineties was not that long ago, Sammy. Stop talking about millennials like we're ancient. But yes, just like Julia Roberts in that movie. And I swear I'm not answering who Julia Roberts is. I'm also not making this up. We've hunted for pictures of her and found one, in some local newspaper, and as expected, she's a stunner. She also happens to be this wholesome, small-town girl with big blue eyes and cowboy boots. I didn't even know they wore those in North Carolina. But anyway. Four times!

SAM: (chokes out a laugh) Whoa. (slow clap) Listen, I applaud. We love a bad bish who can and will say no. Even if it's giving trauma and I'm low-key a little worried about her.

NICK: (chuckles) I mean, I can't blame her, really. I would have big, fat daddy issues if my father had ditched me in some town in the middle of nowhere to live it up in a mansion in Miami. Do you have any idea how nice my tan would be if I lived in Miami? (loud exhale) Now seriously, you know I occasionally have a heart. So drama aside, it's no wonder the girl is messed-up. She apparently lost her mother young—we didn't find out when exactly—and Rich Daddy did nothing. Small-Town Heiress didn't even know she was an Underwood until very recently.

SAM: (groans) Now that's truly disgusting behavior. I feel sick, really. That's why I never get past a situationship. It's so hard to . . . trust. The lengths some men will go to hide who they are. And this guy is the proof. (ponders with a hum) I wonder if we could do something in solidarity. You know I'm a girls' girl.

NICK: I don't know about that. We are just two people on a podcast. BUT we could ask our audience whether they want to hear more. So, Reali-tiers? Let us know in the comments if you'd like that. It's been a while since we did a *Reali-tea* series and I feel this one's layered.

The answer to Nick's question had been a resounding yes. I'd seen the comments myself. I also wished I hadn't just based it on the amount of unfiltered thoughts, opinions, and judgments some people felt the need to put into the universe. But regardless, I didn't need to be Bobbi Shark to know this wasn't good. I could already tell that it probably didn't register in the spectrum of *acceptable* or *manageable*.

"Josie?" Matthew tried. "You good, sweetheart?"

I swallowed, refocusing on him. "Ah . . . sure," I said. "I was just thinking. Thoughts. Of various types. Did Grandpa's bottoms not fit? Is that why you're not wearing them?"

Matthew tilted his head. "I'd rather talk about what's bothering you." His gaze dipped in the direction of my hands. "What is it?"

I knew what he'd just done. Checked for the ring. It was back in the box after it came off in the shower. But that didn't change or fix much now. "I was just wondering whether you had any time to think about last night. Our conversation. Because I have, and I'd like to pick up where we left it, if you don't mind."

A strange sigh left him as he rearranged his body, moving

slightly forward and bracing his elbows on the blanket covering his knees. "Yes," he admitted. "And I owe you an apology." My whole body perked up. "I was a little harsh in my delivery. I was dead on my feet, and cranky, and I . . . wasn't myself. So I'm sorry. You were right. If anyone would be jumping headfirst, no questions asked, into something like what happened back at the porch, it'd be me."

My chest tightened with . . . relief? Hope? "Seriously?"

"Yeah," he admitted with a nod. "That's why I want to be there next time you talk to this Bobbi person. I involved myself in this when I went along with the lie anyway, so I'll be there." I felt the corners of my mouth twitch, climbing up my face with a smile. "We'll tell her it was all a misunderstanding. Together."

And down it came.

"Oh," escaped me with a weak puff of air. "A misunderstanding. That's what you meant."

His chuckle was strained, as if he'd forced it out. "What else did you think I was going to say?"

Every new piece of information I'd learned last night, every single thing that had been said about me and Andrew, swirled in my head, making me feel a little dizzy.

It's no wonder the girl is messed-up.

How could I even explain everything to this man? Should I just hit play on the podcast and make him listen? Watch his face fill up with . . . pity, in the best of cases? I'd always considered myself a strong, independent woman. But based on everything being said, I had never been. Not really. Not even remotely.

I shook off that thought and stood up. I'd really lost my nerve. And that was fine. I'd be fine. "Or you know what? I think I'll just tell her myself. I'll say it was all a mistake. It'll be like ripping off a really feisty and uptight Band-Aid."

"You sure?" Matthew hesitated. "I could—"

"Oh no," I said, standing up from the armchair. "I should really go open Josie's now. Grandpa Moe will drive you to Lazy Elk while we sort out your car situation." Matthew's lips thinned and I averted my gaze, already moving. "You're right about everything, so I'll fix the mess I started. Plus, it's just Bobbi. It really isn't like I have to make some public statement, or worse, tell the whole town we're not . . . you know. A thing. It's just a woman I barely even know."

"So when's the wedding?" I was asked for the *fourth* time today.

I'd been counting. Together with *fifth time's the charm*—delivered a total of three times—and *who's the lucky man*—a chilling total of eight. Eight.

Because as it turned out, it wasn't just Bobbi who thought I was engaged again. It was all of Green Oak. Or at the very least, every customer who had strolled into Josie's Joint buzzing with the news of a new engagement.

They always, *always* buzzed. With any news, but engagement news was the worst—or buzziest. And when you were allegedly engaged to a mystery man you'd kept a secret, the buzz escalated to an angry buzzing beehive.

All thanks to snoopy and meddlesome Otto Higgings.

News traveled fast in Green Oak, but this fast? Not even when one of the kids discovered the video of Adalyn ripping the head off the Miami Flames' mascot with her bare hands did the news spread overnight. It took at least a day for everyone to start theorizing.

Not this time. It was barely lunchtime and I'd already heard that I was engaged to some guy named Marcus. Or Maddox. Or Maverick, a cowboy from Tennessee. *No, a wanderer named Martin,* someone claimed. They'd spotted him roaming around the edge of town with a duffel bag and a cloak.

A cloak.

Sometimes I wondered how we, as a community, had survived this long without going absolutely insane.

"We totally support you, you know?" Gabriel said, bringing me back to the conversation. "I know you must have your reasons for keeping this from everyone. We're all a bunch of gossips, although we mean well. But now that it's out . . . I want to hear everything." He smiled. "And see the ring. Let's see where this one ranks."

I loved Gabriel. We'd known each other since we were kids, and were still good friends, even if we didn't hang out like we used to. He was a family man now. A dad to Juniper, a husband to Isaac. I knew all of this came from a place of warmth, but boy, if he squeezed me for any more details, I was pretty sure I was going to scream. "Ring's not here," I said with a tight bend of my lips.

"What do you mean the ring's not here?" Gabriel's brows arched. "Where is it?"

"At the . . . cleaners. It needed a polish." All of them did, so I wasn't technically lying.

"If you say so," he said with an incredulous shrug. "So what about my other questions? Who is he? How did you meet? What wedding theme are we going with this time?"

Wedding theme. "Does any of that matter? Why can't we talk about Isaac? Or Juni. How is fifth grade treating her? Is Isaac coming to the Warriors game on Sunday or is he stuck somewhere traveling?"

Gabriel frowned. "Of course it matters. You're engaged, Josie. Again. After, you know, Duncan. Who by the way I've heard is, and I quote, *facing some important challenges.* My cousin Martha, the one who lives in South Carolina, told me she was keeping an eye on him, to keep us in the loop. And some lady in her book club is somehow related to one of Duncan's campaign managers and is feeding her top-notch information. Anyway." He pursed his lips. "Can't say I'm affected by the news. If he was running for state senator here, I sure as hell wouldn't—"

"That's kind of Martha," I interjected. "And you. But you know that whole anti-Duncan stuff never sat well with me. He isn't a bad man. He has principles, which is rare in politics. Things just didn't work out for us, and that's not a good reason for anyone in town to judge his work or want to cancel him."

Gabriel's eyes rolled behind his red-rimmed glasses. "You're too honorable, Josie girl. A true unicorn."

I wasn't. I was a *messed-up girl* who was *giving trauma.*

"So anyway," I said, readjusting my apron. "This is still a coffee shop, you know? You guys are going to run me out of business if all you want to do is chat."

"You know that couldn't be further from the truth," he answered with a snort. "Green Oak would cave into itself without this place. Or your baked goods. Or you. But okay. Point made. I'll wait until you decide to open up about this Maverick guy."

"His name's not—" I shot him a glance.

Gabriel's smile was sly. "Ugh, so close." Another shrug. "Alas. How about you get me something special today? To make up for not telling me a single detail about this man. Does he have abs? Is he a generous lover? Is he really from Tennessee? Nobody knows. Not even me. Which I'm fine with, by the way."

I got to work on an extra-large, extra-sweet *Josephino,* decidedly ignoring Gabriel as he debated the merits of dating a cowboy like Maverick and continued to prod at my barely standing patience.

"Cinnamon or cocoa?" I hit the metallic jug against the rack—hard—just as he said something about pitching bales of hay. *Shirtless.*

"Cocoa," he answered with a roll of his eyes. "If you please."

"Great," I said with a smile that I was sure wasn't reaching my eyes. Then I bent my knees and kneeled behind the counter with the excuse of reaching for a new cocoa powder shaker. But all I did was close my eyes, giving myself a moment and a pat on the chest. God, I was sweating. Rivers. I lifted my knit sweater and let some air get in, only springing up to my feet when I felt slightly better.

"Here's your— *Mothercracker.*"

Otto Higgings's—and his pug, Coco's—faces greeted me. "Don't know who you're talking about, but I don't think I can take more foreigners in town. Green Oak's small enough."

"Good morning, neighbor," I said, hearing the unease in my voice. And the grudge I so wanted to hold against him. But that wasn't who I was. So I decidedly ignored that and glanced down at where Coco was sitting. "You know the rules. Furry companions are welcome, but no stinky butts on my counter."

"That's what I said," Gabriel muttered. "That's not the place for a dog's ass, Otto."

Otto grumbled something, reluctantly snatching Coco off the counter and holding her in his arms. "My Coco doesn't stink."

I inhaled very slowly, then grabbed my disinfectant bottle and started wiping at the surface. "What can I get you, my sweet and cheery Otto?"

"So where's this Mario?" my neighbor asked in return. "The blond one. You sure made some ruckus in the middle of the night. Woke me and Coco up. You know she needs her rest."

"Oh?" Gabriel perked up. "Mario, huh? Blond. And *a ruckus*?" My so-called friend shot me an inquisitive glance. "Color me interested, Otto Higgings. On a scale from one to ten, how . . . *ardent* would you care to rate this ruckus?"

"Well," Otto started with a thinking face. "I'd say—"

"There wasn't any ruckus," I intervened. "It was a normal, ordinary, customary night."

"There was quite a commotion on your porch, though," Otto muttered, readjusting Coco's pink collar. "Can I get one of those puppy drinks you do? Coco loves them. I'll have a glass of water. They're both on the house, aren't they?"

"Of course," I gritted between a toothy smile. Both things were supposed to be complimentary with an actual order. But I'd give him anything to stop talking. "Here," I added, grabbing two brownies from the display and placing them in front of the men. "These are on the house too. And they're warm, so I wouldn't waste any time if I were you. I'll be right over with the puppuccino and the glass of water."

I turned, looking for the plain yogurt I got solely for the puppuccinos. Once located, I grabbed a container of pumpkin puree. Despite how warm it's been, it was fall, after all. Pumpkin season was in full swing, and that meant pumpkin beverages. Pups included. I returned to my spot at the front, eyes cast down as I balanced everything in my arms. "All right, so—"

A new face had joined the group.

"*Bobbi,*" I said, hearing the sheer exhaustion in my voice now too. "Hi. You're here. Great. Welcome to Josie's Joint."

"Don't sound so excited," she deadpanned. "Why is this so busy? Oh wait, don't answer that. There's no Starbucks around."

I suppressed an eye roll and smiled. "So you've said. And isn't that wonderful? Local businesses have the space to thrive."

"I didn't think you were listening all that closely last night," she answered, looking around with a strange grimace. "And thrive away for all I care, but do it beside a place where I can order from my phone. This is my only vice, Josephine. This and late-night shopping. If you tell me there's no one-day-delivery either, I might have a tiny stroke." She paused. "You guys get one-day-delivery here, right?"

Gabriel snorted.

I opted not to answer.

Otto frowned at our newcomer. "You were there too. Last night. In the ruckus."

The two men seemed to perk up. But I'd had enough questions. I'd had enough everything. So I clapped my hands, grabbing everyone's attention.

"Otto? Here's your water, and a puppuccino for Coco." I placed the two cups in front of him. "And Gabriel? Let's catch up later, yeah? Give Isaac and little Juni a hug. Now, bye. Auf Wiedersehen. Sayonara. Adiós. Toodles. Have a good day, and remember to bring your JJ loyalty cards next time, yes?"

I watched the two men—and dog—shuffle away, even if reluctantly, with a tight smile, before returning my attention to the PR strategist.

"Okay, Small-Town Heiress," Bobbi said in a seemingly impressed tone. "You have a backbone. Good."

Small-Town Heiress. That was what the podcast had called me.

"What can I get you, Bobbi?" *A flight back to Miami?* I thought. *A shovel so you can help me dig the hole I want to disappear into right now?*

Her bright red lips pursed in thought, giving me enough time to ponder while acknowledging her attire. That beautiful coat from last night was long gone, and she wore something that looked a lot like a corset over a black flimsy blouse, paired with leather leggings. She looked stunning. And terrifying. She cleared her throat. "Venti iced white chocolate mocha, no whip, sweet cream foam, extra caramel drizzle."

"I . . ." Wasn't an establishment prepared to serve that kind of drink. I smiled. "Coming right up."

"Good news. Finally," she said, throwing her hands up dramatically. I returned to my station and got to work on . . . my Sharkie, I'd decided to call it. "So how's Blondie?" Bobbi asked. "Good night's rest?"

"Matthew's okay," I muttered. "And he slept well. Like the dead, in fact."

"I think I prefer Blondie," Bobbi replied. My shoulders stiffened. "Don't get your panties in a bunch, I have nothing against him. I just can't take blonds seriously. I know I'm one before you point that out. But that's different. I'm a woman, and I'm me. I take myself—and women—very seriously." She braced her hands on the counter, right at the spot where Coco's butt had been. I felt the tiniest smirk appear on my face. "We should move quickly with the wedding planning."

Whatever smugness I'd been feeling disappeared.

Bobbi continued, "Did you have a look online? Listen to the podcast perhaps? You don't need to answer, I know you did by the way you're scrunching your face. Not so flattering, huh?"

I occupied myself with my convoluted Sharkie, trying to figure out a way to emulate the stuff I didn't have. "I'm not scrunching my face."

"You are," Bobbi pressed in a casual tone. "Naturally so. Having your dirty laundry and reputation aired like that would do that to you. I'm shocked you're here at all. I thought I'd have to pick up the pieces and put them together so we could talk. This stuff would break anyone. Maybe even me."

Dirty laundry. Reputation.

I swallowed. Hard. "I'm not breaking. That's just gossip."

"Is it gossip when they're speaking facts?" Bobbi answered. I felt myself go cold. In an instant. "Good thing you have a way to prove them wrong. You've found love. Again. And I hear everyone in town just found out about your happy news. Color me surprised." She waited, and I was sure the pause was very intentional. "Hey. I'm not here to pass judgment. I would be reticent to share that, too. If I'd been engaged half a dozen times."

My cheeks heated. "It was only four."

"Five," she corrected before tutting. "Poor Blondie. You're leaving him out this early in the game?"

"That's not what I meant."

"Not judging," she repeated, inspecting her nails. "I have daddy issues too. Half the world does, and the other half deals with a partner who has them."

"Well, that's not an issue I have. I don't belong to any of those groups."

"Tell that to pro soccer player Ricky Richardson," Bobbi countered. "Or senator wannabe Duncan Aguirre. Or Shawn or Greg, whose last names and occupations are irrelevant. Wasn't Ricky so affected by you leaving him at the altar that his performance turned to shit and he was transferred to some team in Canada? Yikes."

My spine went as stiff as a stick. "Canada is great. And he loves it there."

"Wasn't Duncan close to ending his campaign because he was so heartbroken? Didn't Greg flee to Thailand after you hit the road?"

My jaw clamped. "I thought Greg didn't matter. And how do you know any of that?"

"I'd be doing a bad job if I hadn't researched you before coming out here, Josephine. And if I found out, don't you think Page Nine will? That podcast belongs to the main source of gossip in the country. Sam and Nick would *love* to pick apart such a varied collection of grooms-that-never-were."

"That's not at all intrusive," I commented. I shook my head, returning to the counter with the final product. "And I don't collect them. Also, Greg now goes by Astro. Which you would know if you dug deep enough. I also didn't exactly leave Ricky at the altar. And Duncan is fine, believe me. I'm also not the only woman on the face of the earth who's been engaged a handful of times. I don't know why everyone's making it such a big deal."

"Four times. Five now. And under the age of thirty," Bobbi offered in a final tone. "It's a big deal when paired with who your father is. And please, don't tell me you're *good friends* with your exes. I thought you were smarter than that."

"What if I am friends with them? How is that bad?"

Bobbi blinked at me, her expression one of pure and utter outrage. "This is not a sitcom, girlie. Wake up." She let out a scoff. "This whole thing is giving unresolved childhood drama. It's giving off nineties rom-com vibes that haven't aged well. It's giving Ross Geller."

"Ross Geller is a divorcé," I argued, trying really hard not to let her words affect me.

As if at a loss, Bobbi picked up her cup with a sigh and brought it to her lips. A moan left her. "You know what? I'll marry you if you decide to give Blondie the boot."

I was flattered, but I took that for what it was. An opening. An exit, hopefully. "So about Matthew—"

"Look around you, Josephine," Bobbi said, dark gaze sharpening as it held mine. "Everyone's ecstatic with the news. I haven't seen this many smiles since my unfortunate visit to Barcelona's wax museum years ago. And these are not even that creepy."

I swallowed the strange lump in my throat and did as she asked as much as I didn't need to. Bobbi wasn't wrong. The atmosphere in the small café I considered my second home hadn't been this animated since the Green Warriors made it to last year's Little League final.

"Your father extends his best wishes, too," Bobbi continued.

My head whirled in the woman's direction. I braced myself on the counter. "Andrew knows?"

"He does now," she confirmed after a beat. "And he's thrilled you're open to letting him have a significant role in your life. He thinks the least he can do is pay for the wedding, all things considered. He's obviously thankful you'll do this at such a critical moment, too. This might give us the angle we need to fix this whole thing. *Unless,* you'd rather consider the move to Miami. Blondie could come, too, I suppose."

My stomach twisted, that sudden urge to scream, or run, or do something really silly, rising again.

He's thrilled you're open to letting him have a significant role in your life.

I would have big, fat daddy issues if my father had ditched me in some town in the middle of nowhere.

He thinks the least he can do is pay for the wedding.

I'd told myself I'd never go through that again. A wedding. Not after Duncan. Not after four. I would have been happy to help organize Adalyn and Cameron's, whenever they decided to tie the knot, but not mine. Definitely not a *fifth* wedding. And definitely not if I already knew I wouldn't make it down the aisle. Absolutely not to a man I barely knew, either.

But . . . that wasn't very different from any other time I'd told myself I wouldn't jump into a new engagement and had done it regardless.

It was Bobbi who spoke, as if she was somewhat aware of my internal struggle. "I really am not here to pass judgment, Josephine. I'm here to help. It's Andrew's and *your* image being trashed. And I'm incredible at my job." A pause. A tilt of her head. "I'm a good judge of character, too. I think you believe in second chances. I *know* you're a team player." Her arm rose, pointing at all the tables brimming with people behind her. "I can see you care about your community, so I know you care about your family, too. Andrew is your family now. Families look out for each other, so I encourage you to put your pride aside and accept his help."

My gaze shifted behind Bobbi, but I wasn't really looking at my patrons.

Andrew is your family now.

Families look out for each other.

It was all I'd wanted for a long time. A family. Someone to stuff the gaping hole Mom had left in the middle of my chest when I'd lost her. I knew Adalyn had somehow helped to do that, and I loved that. Having a sister. But a sister wasn't a parent, and my relationship with Andrew had been . . . unexpectedly different. Not as easy. Confusing in ways that made my stomach knot with the possibility that it might never work.

It wasn't about pride, like Bobbi had implied.

When I'd promised Matthew I'd fix this, I only had to face Bobbi. But it wasn't just Bobbi now. It was everyone. The whole town knew. Andrew knew, too. He thought I had the key to fix an issue I was responsible for in some twisted way I couldn't refute. I had also lied. It had been me making up a story last night.

Without really knowing how, I now faced a dilemma.

I had two choices: Tell everyone my engagement was a lie and snuff out all that excitement and hope. Or move with what I'd set into motion and break things off later, when the dust settled, and inform everyone of something they might already expect: that another engagement was no more.

Both were equally terrible.

The first one made me look like a liar. It cemented Bobbi's and Nick's and Sam's and everyone else's accusations. That Andrew had messed me up. That on top of being a misstep on an incredible résumé, I was also deeply troubled. A liar.

The second choice did that too in a way. But it fixed the problem for now. It gave me a chance to salvage something.

Andrew is your family now.

It gave *us* a chance.

"Coffee's on the house," I heard myself say. "My treat to first-time customers."

Bobbi's smile was slow, and when it fully formed, I noticed it was the first one to reach her eyes. "Excellent. Thank you."

I cleared my throat. "Of course."

The PR strategist tapped the counter before stepping back.

"Now go get your man. We have plans to make, and a little birdie told me that Blondie and Andrew have a past. Which explains why your fiancé was . . . somewhat reluctant to accept Andrew's help when I mentioned it last night. So, item number one on your list is prepping your doting fiancé. I want everyone on their best behavior. And that means Blondie, not my employer." She whirled around, and right before walking away, she looked over her shoulder one last time. "Oh, and I think your ring might have slipped off your finger at some point last night?" She *tsk*ed. "Hope you retrieve it soon, Josephine. Details are important in PR."

I looked down at my naked finger, wondering if a part of me had known last night, when Ricky's ring had gotten stuck. It hadn't been the first time this had happened with one of the four rings I kept in that box atop my dresser, but it had been the one time dread had filled me so overwhelmingly instantly.

I supposed it didn't matter.

Bobbi was wrong either way.

I had something more important than a ring to retrieve.

A fiancé.

CHAPTER FIVE

I pounded my fist on my fiancé's door.

Yup, that was what I was calling him in my head. Because for all practical purposes, he was. He just needed to be informed of that fact.

There was noise on the other side. A sort of bang. And a thump. Then steps. I leaned back and waited, relieved that Matthew was, frankly, alive. Grandpa Moe had joked about ditching him somewhere in the woods when I'd asked if he'd safely deposited our guest in Lazy Elk. I hadn't laughed. I didn't have the time to retrieve a man from the forest at the moment.

The door to Lazy Elk Lodge opened, revealing a messy-haired, half-asleep Matthew. He was in sweatpants and a hoodie. No glasses, I noticed. He looked nice. A *right out of bed, I'm hot without trying* kind of nice. Which was . . . unimportant.

"*Whattookyousolong,*" I asked in single rush of words, stepping under his arm and coming inside. Looked like I was not waiting to be let in. "I've been banging on the door for five whole minutes."

Matthew turned around slowly, blinking at me. "Josie?"

A strange sound left me. I wished it hadn't, but I hadn't been able to do a single thing to stop it. "Not this again," I whispered. He opened his mouth, but honestly? Now I was irked. I stomped in his direction, dropped the bags at our feet and whacked him in the stomach—*hard* stomach, by the way, just like I'd guessed, based on that peek I'd gotten this morning.

"*Christ,*" Matthew complained, barely flinching. "What was that for?"

I huffed. "Something memorable enough for you to remember me, Dory."

Matthew's lips twitched. The corners of his mouth went up momentarily. Then he shook his head, as if wanting to stop the smile from sprouting. It didn't work. He was grinning like some . . . I didn't know. Like a blond guy who had just rolled out of bed and was smiling for no reason.

"My glasses," he finally said. "I fell asleep on the couch and couldn't find them in time to get the door. Couldn't be sure it was you until you were close enough to punch me."

A strange wave of relief hit me.

Of course. His glasses. I'd noticed the absence of them on his face but hadn't put two and two together. "I'm sorry. I don't know what got into me. I'm usually more thoughtful than that."

He tilted his head. "You're memorable enough already. You don't need to resort to violence."

A part of me wanted to remind him he'd thought I was some strange woman on a porch the night before. "You sleep a lot. And you should have said so before." I snagged the bags off the ground, then pushed them against his chest. "You bring these to the kitchen. Or, wait. You stay here until I find your glasses. And then we talk." I turned around, ignoring the question on his face. "I'd really like you to see my face for this conversation."

Matthew's smile fell, but I scurried into the living room before I could discover why and got started with the search.

"I know Lazy Elk like the palm of my hand, you know?" I called loudly, lifting up one of the cream-colored pillows before dropping it on the carpet. "Before Adalyn and Cameron left town, I was spending a lot of time here. And before you ask, I didn't mind third-wheeling. I've always been confident in my singlehood, as much as you might think the opposite, considering . . . everything that has transpired."

I stared at the pillowless couch, bringing my hands to my hips and calculating my next move.

"Anyway," I said, carefully unfolding and shaking blanket number one. "I think they'll want babies soon," I added, discarding the burgundy wool cover aside. "They're spending New Years in Italy, and that's a pretty romantic country to be . . . you know." I kneeled, going down on my knees and checking under the couch. "Have a *li'l cheeky shag,* like Cam would say. Not that he'd ever— Found them!"

I jumped back to my feet, glasses in hand, and a proud smile on my face. Matthew's tall shape was there, right between the living and kitchen areas in the cabin's open space, no bags in his arms. His expression was . . . strange. Pensive with a touch of something I couldn't put a name to.

"Got your glasses," I told him. And because he didn't answer, I strode in his direction.

His gaze seemed to follow me as I made it all the way to where he stood. When I reached him, that thinking face didn't go away. "Not sure if I should do this," I told him, gently swiping the lenses with the cotton tee I wore under my sweater. "But they were laying on the carpet, so."

My gaze returned to his face, finding his chin tipped down to look at me. Matthew was tall. A few inches taller than me, which had me tilting my head back. Silence seemed to lazily settle around us now that I wasn't filling it, and he seemed to be waiting for something. Without thinking too much of it, I lifted my hands, the glasses rising in the small space between us with them. Gently, I touched the tips to the sides of his head. And when Matthew didn't complain, I pushed them forward, slipping the temples into his hair.

His eyelids fluttered closed. In reflex or reaction, I couldn't tell. I only knew it made me a little bolder. Before I could stop myself, my pinkies were brushing him. The sides of his neck. It was nothing but a soft, featherlike brush of my skin against his. But I was close enough to see his pulse jump.

He swallowed.

A shiver curled its way down my arms in response.

Matthew's eyes reopened, the quality of his gaze changing, the brown in his eyes sharpening. He glimpsed down, at me, my face, my mouth.

Something between my belly and chest took notice. And I—

I stepped back.

Matthew blinked, as if spat right out of a turning wheel.

"Coffee," I said, clearing my throat. "Let's have coffee." My hand rose to my face, unconsciously patting my cheeks. They were burning. "And snacks. Fruit. I've brought everything. What do you say?"

"You lead the way," Matthew answered, moving to the side. Was his voice strange? "I have no idea where anything is here."

He didn't need to tell me twice. In a matter of minutes we were seated across from each other with twin mugs of freshly made cappuccinos and everything I'd brought with me displayed between us.

"I hate to be that person who looks a gift horse in the mouth," Matthew said, gaze swiping every single container currently on the kitchen island. "But last time someone showered me with this many sweets, I was being bribed into taking my two sisters and three little cousins to Funtown Splashtown for a whole weekend."

Well, shoot. *"I'm not bribing you,"* I exclaimed with a slightly high-pitched laugh. "No one's bribing anyone. This is just coffee."

Matthew momentarily arched a brow but brought his mug to his mouth. Unlike last night—or this morning—he seemed a little more . . . easy. Comfortable, even. Not so drained and perplexed. Good. That hopefully meant he'd be more willing, too.

"Holy shit," he said, looking down at his coffee. "This is . . . wow. This is fantastic."

"You know I run a very popular coffee shop, right? I know it's fantastic."

"My apologies," he said in a joking tone. "I should have expected no less." He eyed Cameron's coffee machine on the counter. "I guess I was fooled with my own experience. I bought my dad one of those last year for Christmas, and whatever we did with it, coffee never tasted like this. Not even remotely close. And there was an embarrassing number of YouTube tutorials involved, trust me."

"It takes some practice," I pointed out with a shrug. "And I started years ago, if it makes you feel any better. With an older and less sophisticated model than the one Cam has here." My smile turned a little smug, but I couldn't help it. I was proud of myself. "There's always a trick for the foamer," I explained. "And the roast of the beans has to be right for milk-based brews. You have to go dark so you can still taste the richness of the coffee. And of course, the blend is also super important. One-hundred-percent Arabica, naturally, but the origin? Now there—" I stopped myself. "Sorry. I got carried away."

"So you're a coffee snob," Matthew said, ignoring my apology. "Besides being a barista, and coffee shop owner, you're also a nerd." His hand reached out over the island, settling on one of my mini eclairs. "Born or made?"

"Made," I answered easily, watching him chew and let out a tiny moan of appreciation. I was sure it'd been unconscious. My smile widened. "Someone taught me the basics and introduced me into the world. I went from there."

"Someone?" He asked, taking a carrot cake square this time.

"An old friend," I said, studying his reaction as he chewed once again. "He always dreamed of owning a coffee roaster with a small bar where customers could enjoy a cup while they're shopping or waiting for their beans order." Matthew licked the frosting off his thumb, a new sound of appreciation leaving his throat. "When we broke up, I was too deep into coffee culture to quit it."

"When you broke up?" Matthew asked.

My eyes bounced up, leaving his mouth. "Sorry?"

"You said an old friend got you into it."

I entertained the idea of making something up. But if I really wanted Matthew to do this big thing for me, and if he agreed, this would eventually come up. My exes.

"Shawn," I explained. "He was a friend first. Then my first love. Then my fiancé. Then an ex."

Shawn and I had been high school sweethearts. We'd dated through our teens, and he'd proposed soon after graduation. Unlike me, he decided not to go to college. So I'd lived in Chapel Hill while attending UNC and I'd go visit him up in Fairhill on the weekends. That didn't last as long as I'd hoped. Out of all my failed attempts at a successful walk down the aisle, this one had been the easiest to explain. We'd simply been too young. Too naïve. Stuffed with too many dreams. Too green and far from the people we were supposed to be. No one had judged me for leaving Shawn the way I did. Not with Mom's passing so relatively recent, and us being so young.

I didn't know if it was my wording that made Matthew ponder my words for so long, but he seemed as lost in thought as me. Only difference was, my stomach had closed at the memory, and he kept snagging more sweets. A second eclair. A lime mini tart. A white chocolate brownie. Then a pistachio one. Then raspberry. Macadamia.

"Whoa," I decided to say. "You're stress eating my rainbow brownies like your life depends on it."

"Fhey're really goohd," he admitted through a mouthful.

"Anything on your mind?"

His throat bobbed as he swallowed. "Nothing worth discussing."

Ouch. I couldn't explain exactly why, but that stung. "So . . ." I ventured, brushing whatever that was aside and focusing on what had brought me here. Our conversation. My dilemma. "Bobbi showed up at Josie's Joint earlier today. And before I say more, I want you to know that she promised—"

"Don't trust a single promise that woman makes you," Matthew said with a shake of his head.

I sighed. I was getting really tired of being interrupted by everyone anytime I summoned the nerve to say something. "Why not?"

Matthew averted his gaze, searching around the island that separated us. I hoped he wasn't considering going back to stress eating instead of elaborating. I was desperate and I'd take the food away from him. "The short version is because she works for Andrew Underwood."

"And the long one?"

"Because she works for your father."

"That's the same answer, Matthew."

His face hardened, that glimpse of the more playful, relaxed Matthew disappearing. "It's not," he said. "Andrew Underwood is a powerful businessman with a multimillion-dollar portfolio. Your father is a selfish man who has his own interests at heart. You can have your pick, but Bobbi doesn't work for you."

"Bobbi also said you'd be reluctant," I commented. "She seems to be right about that."

"There's nothing to be reluctant about," he answered. "Because I thought you were clearing this up with her. Telling her the truth."

"Plans change."

Matthew stiffened on his stool. "What changed?"

Everything, I should have said. But I went with a simple, "Everyone in town already thinks we're engaged."

"What?" he sputtered. "How?"

"My neighbor Otto Higgings. People have been coming by Josie's all day, extending their congratulations and theorizing who the mystery man is. Bets are on some guy named Maverick." Matthew's eyes turned to plates. "Believe me, I had no idea this would happen. I wanted to come clean, but I think that given the circumstances, the best course of action is that we do it."

"That we do what?"

I shot him a look. "That we pretend we're engaged. That we let the town, and everyone, think we actually are, and let Bobbi do her thing. Andrew knows now, too, apparently. He wants to be involved in the wedding like Bobbi said. Pay for it, show up . . ." I shook my head. I didn't want to think of what that meant right now. Not yet. "That's supposed to appease the gossip. Bobbi's good at her job. She has to be if she was hired by Andrew, so I'm sure she'll fix everything before you have to wear a bow tie. I don't think we'll even get into the thick of wedding preparations. Just . . . long-term, surface planning. We'll just let them believe Andrew's part of it and act like we want to get married, while Bobbi works her magic. I trust that she will do that quickly."

"Josie," he said. Just that. My name. He shook his head, a strange sound leaving him. "That's not pretending we're engaged. That's *being* engaged."

My cheeks flamed. "Then pretend you're in love with me. While we're engaged. Temporarily. Out of convenience. I'm not asking you to marry me. We'll break things off when all this PR stuff goes away."

He laughed then, but it dripped with . . . disbelief? Bitterness? "Out of convenience for whom? Because this is not just posing for a couple of pictures with Andrew. Believe me, I know. I was there, with Adalyn. I've seen a version of this PR crisis happen already. You have, too, when he shipped her here to shove her out of the way. So tell me, to what lengths are you willing to go to protect him just because some asshole with a bitchy attitude tells you to?"

I flinched. "This is different. It's not a silly viral video that will blow over. It's my life. Andrew's. Adalyn's." My . . . family's lives. One I thought I'd never have after Mom passed away, and I never seem to get a relationship right. "I've thought about this. I'm not just jumping on it because I'm told to."

His voice softened, his tone almost turning careful. "Aren't you, sweetheart?"

Sweetheart. It wasn't the word that bothered me. It was the way he said it. Like someone who wanted to protect me. To spare me the heartbreak. "Give me some credit, Matthew. I'm not some simpleton who's being tricked by the city folk."

He immediately paled, and I saw on his face that he hadn't meant it that way. I also realized I probably shouldn't have said that, but it had to be said.

"I'm protecting myself," I insisted.

"Josie," he warned. Apologetic. Honest. "I did not mean it like that. I'm trying to look out for you. You don't need to do this. You don't need me, or a fiancé, or anybody."

"Maybe I don't," I said, done with warnings. Apologies. Honesty, too. I hopped off my stool. "But that's unimportant. Because if you really want to look out for me, then you'll help me. I might not need to do this. But I want to. Do you want to hear why?"

I rounded the island, slowly crossing the distance to where he sat, his eyes not leaving me as I moved. "Why?"

"Because," I said, reaching his side and coming to a stop. Without breaking eye contact, I placed my hands on his knees. Matthew exhaled as I turned his body in the swiveling stool so he'd fully face me, ignoring the way his eyes widened slightly. "Because the idea of being a liability," I continued, stepping into his outstretched thighs, lowering my voice so it was nothing but a murmur. "The idea of becoming a problem," I added, feeling his body start to gravitate toward mine. Only a little. Only enough. "The idea of being a thorn in a man's side, or anyone's flaw or weakness, much less my father's, makes me sick to my stomach."

My words felt like a confession. And I didn't know what to do with that. I didn't know what to do with the way Matthew hadn't moved an inch, besides his hands dropping to his sides in fists. Or the way I was standing so, so, so, so close to him. So much that I could smell things like his shampoo or some faded traces of cologne on him. I didn't know what to do with how enraptured he seemed by my nearness and how that made me feel.

"I'm doing this for myself, Matthew," I whispered. His eyes dipped down. To my mouth, making me notice I was biting my bottom lip. "Not because anyone is telling me to. I want to do this because I started it, and it's *you* I need." My hand reached up, but I stopped myself before it made contact with his arm. Chest. Him. "Not anyone else. *You.* So be my fiancé, Matthew. Please."

Brown eyes softened and flared, all at once. My stomach started to constrict, but I pushed that down. I didn't know what I was doing, but whatever that was, it was working. Hope swelled inside me as I watched him. A muscle in his jaw jumped.

"Okay," he finally said.

My eyes widened, and I was sure they had to be sparking with surprise, because just then, Matthew seemed to realize what he'd said.

"Perfect!" I squeaked, stepping back from a confused Matthew. I started walking backward, making my way to the door. "Meet me tomorrow at the Warriors Park, okay? Eleven sharp. It's right across from Josie's, at the end of Main Street. You'll find it on Google, too;

I made sure it's there." I turned around, closing my eyes. *Oh boy. Oh man. What the hell had just happened?* "All right, toodles!"

It was only when I closed the lodge's entrance door behind me that the answer to my question seemed to form.

I'd just . . . proposed to Matthew.

And for someone who had been engaged four times, I really sucked at it.

CHAPTER SIX

It was eleven sharp and Matthew wasn't here for his hard launch.

Not that he knew he was being hard launched. The man had no idea, which I solidly believed was the best way to go about it. If he showed up at all, that was.

I waved a gloved hand at Gabriel, who met my gaze from across the bleachers. He returned my tense smile with a frown, and I pretended to get a call before he could approach and ask what had me looking like I'd sucked a lemon.

See you around, I mouthed at him, pointing at my phone before bringing it to my ear.

I dragged myself all the way down the bleachers, disconnecting my fake call and landing on the grass with a little jump. I greeted a couple of people here, and smiled and nodded to a few others there, but for the most part I was a girl on a mission. Scrutinizing my surroundings for my fiancé. It was game day, and everyone currently filling the stands in Warriors Park—the new name for our local sports facilities—had showed up this Sunday with more than just an interest in the Green Warriors, our girls ragtag soccer team turned Little League champions. They were here to be a part of the mayor's fiancé's entry into Green Oak society.

And I'd been here, in these exact shoes, four times before. The end of summer lake barbecue with Greg. Green Oak's Christmas tree lighting party with Ricky. Or our most recent tradition, the Easter Eggstravaganza, with Duncan. Even Shawn, who is from town, had to go through the motions.

I, Josie Moore, might act as mayor around here, but I didn't make the rules. And the longer I went without a man off my arm, the more restless every expectant Green Oak resident grew. It didn't exactly make the feminist in me sing, but one didn't blame a rabbit for wanting to chase a carrot you dangled in its face.

"So where's Marty?" Otto Higgings asked from my side.

"I was just thinking of you," I muttered, keeping my gaze forward and my smile firm. "And not here. Yet. That's also not his name."

Chances were he wasn't coming at all, but being delusional enough to think I could manifest things was something I loved to do. Plus, I had no alternative. It wasn't like I could drive down to Tennessee and find some cowboy named Maverick to tangle in my mess. Believe me, I'd researched last night.

"They're all the same to me," Otto grumbled. "It's hard to keep up anyway."

Well, ouch. "Excited for the game?" I asked, keeping an eye on the entrance gate as people poured in. "I haven't seen this many people since the Six Hills final last year. Do you think we'll win?"

"Can't say I care if we do," Otto commented. "So how long is Marshall staying? And what's with the gloves? It's scorching today. One could say we're in the middle of summer."

I chuckled, but it came out all strangled. "Cold hands," I lied. "Circulation problems. My hands and feet? Always cold. That's completely normal stuff that happens to everyone." I cleared my throat, sparing him a glance. Coco was, as always, astride his hip. "How about you go look for a spot, huh? The stands are filling up quick, and the game will start in a few minutes."

Otto scoffed. "And miss this now that he's here? Absolutely not."

He's here?

Matthew's here?

Heart suddenly racing, I turned, following Otto's gaze.

Matthew stood at the far end of the pitch, boots firmly set on the green grass, legs clad in dark denim, and shoulders covered in a long-sleeve baseball shirt. Brown eyes—no glasses, I noticed—met mine in the distance.

My thoughts stumbled.

He'd shown up. Matthew was here. And that meant he was really doing this. We were really doing this. We were about to confirm the engagement, and as much as this was just Green Oak and in the big scheme of things, it didn't matter all that much, the notion still had something in my stomach mirroring the strange discord in my head.

"Man looks like this is the last place he wants to be," Otto pointed out from my side, making me realize I was not moving. "Can't say I blame him, with all this fuss. He's not even wearing his hat. Isn't he a cowboy? Oh, isn't that Diane?" He tutted. "I wonder when she returned from her retreat. She doesn't look all that rejuvenated to me, if I'm allowed to say. Did you know that—"

"No time for gossip," I rushed out, finally leaving my neighbor and his pug behind.

Diane was not only back, but she was also on the move. Toward Matthew. And that meant I needed to get to him first. Intercept my fiancé before she could. Otto Higgings was *child's play* compared to that woman. She was a human lie detector. And persistent, too. So I jogged, stealing glances at her.

Diane did the same, picking up her pace the moment she spotted me.

I broke into a sprint.

Matthew's brown eyes widened, but he remained in position, his stance widening and his arms stretching slightly, as if readying himself for whatever was coming his way.

He'd better. Because Diane was close. And I hadn't run toward something this desperately since a raccoon broke into Josie's Joint, trashed the pie of the month display, and refused to leave.

"HELLO!" Diane started.

But Matthew's gaze didn't leave me in favor of the other woman. Good. *Great.* My legs ate away the last of the distance and I said, just as loud as Diane, "CATCH ME!"

Matthew's brows shot up.

I lunged at him.

It wasn't a swift, delicate lunge. Not even remotely close to the way I'd embraced him on my porch the disastrous night that put all of this in motion. It was a tackle. One that should have sent both of us tumbling to the ground. If not for Matthew's arms, that closed around my waist in a strong vise; and my legs, that wrapped around his hips.

He muttered something that sounded a lot like *motherfucker* under his breath.

My lips popped open with an explanation, but it was forgotten the moment Matthew moved. One of his palms landed at the center of my back, and the other shifted under my leg. My thigh. He rearranged me around him. And I . . . I realized then I hadn't thought this through well enough, because there were body parts. On body parts. Of various types.

"You caught me," I pointed out. *Clever.*

A quick but deep chuckle left Matthew, falling right on my cheek. "You didn't leave me any choice." Some warmth traveled to my face, but for the most part, I was concerned with the spider-monkey hold I had on the man. "Josie?"

"Yes?" I croaked.

Matthew's chest rose and fell with a sigh against mine. "What's going on?"

I extricated my head from his neck and finally looked at his face. Boy, he was close. So much so that I could see the brown of his eyes had tiny specks of green. How had I missed that before? It must be the sunlight, making them shine and—

"Josie," Matthew murmured, bringing me back.

I summoned an innocent smile. "Oopsie?"

Those eyes I'd been so caught on a moment ago dipped to my mouth. Briefly. "Oopsie?" His gaze returned to mine. "That's your answer?"

It was a little hard to think when I could feel the imprint of his palm on the back of my thigh, even through my jeans. "Yes?" I cleared my throat. "Sorry. What was the question? And do you, ah, want me to jump off? I could. Just say the word."

His arms didn't loosen their hold around me. "Tell me who the woman you were racing is first. The one who's still circling us like she's waiting for something."

Was that why he wasn't dropping me on the ground? "That'd be Diane," I explained. "She . . . Let's say she's very enthusiastic when it comes to newcomers. That's why"—I glanced down at the small gap between our chests—"I did this. I'm protecting you from her. But don't worry too much. It's just Diane. Ignore her and she'll go away. Just let me know when you're ready for me to stop . . . protecting you."

His eyes shifted behind me for a moment. "I don't think it's just her."

"What do you mean?"

"Every single person in the stands is staring. Do you have any idea why?"

"Oh. Right. So about that . . ." I made myself smile. "That's because this is your hard launch. As my fiancé. Yay!"

We sat in the stands with equally stiff backs, pretending to watch the game.

"On a scale from zero being a golden retriever to ten being a rabid raccoon with a taste for pie, how mad about the surprise intro into society are you?" I ventured. "Be honest, please. I can take it."

A long sigh left Matthew. He looked more resigned than mad to me. But for all I knew, he might have been secretly seething. "Do you think we should talk about this here?"

I looked around. The stands were packed. And everyone's attention, as much as it had slowly shifted to the game, was still on us. Except for Grandpa Moe's. He'd shown up just as my boots touched the ground and grumbled something unintelligible about a beetroot before heading for his usual spot in the front row. Since then, the cranky old man I loved to bits had gone to great lengths to pretend we didn't exist.

It was my turn to sigh. "That's a good point. We wouldn't want anyone to think this wasn't planned, or a trap to lock up my new man before he gets cold feet and flees town." I glanced to my right, where a head full of permed curls I knew well protruded from the sea of people. I'd always had my suspicions the perm gave Diane her super-hearing powers, so I turned back to my newly and officially appointed fiancé and I scooted a little closer to him. "So . . . What do you want to talk about?"

"How about we watch the game?" Matthew offered. "The Grovesville Bears' defense is starting to struggle."

My brows arched. "So you're not just pretending to watch?"

"They're disorganized," Matthew commented, his eyes on the grass. "Communication is off, and they're giving the Warriors too much space."

I returned my gaze to the game and watched, like really watched, for the first time. He was right. "Wow. It really is like they've left the back door wide open." I stole a glance at the score. "And that explains the 4–0. Oh my God." I clapped. "Go Warriors!"

"Exactly right," he agreed. "Bears' coach is more concerned about yelling than tightening them up."

I could see as much. "You know," I started, lowering my voice. "That woman, the Bears' coach, she got into a little altercation with Cameron and Adalyn last year. During a game, while Cam was coaching the Warriors and Adalyn supervised the team." Matthew glanced quickly at me, brows up. And I whispered, "She called Cam *a little bitch,* and Adalyn got all worked up." I chuckled. "I swear, I knew then that she had it bad for him."

Matthew let out a laugh with a shake of his head. "Unbelievable. Who calls Cameron Caldani *a little bitch*?"

I watched him return his attention to the pitch as if he didn't want to miss too much of it, but my eyes stayed on his profile. So what I'd heard about Matthew was true. Baseball shirt. Defense talk. Man-crush on former soccer star Cameron Caldani. He really was a sports nerd.

"So . . . Why are you not working in something like this?" I asked. And the question must have felt just as out of the blue for him as it did for me, because it stole his attention from the ball. "Sports," I explained. "Most journalists who are *also* sports nerds end up following a team around the country or landing some kind of position as a correspondent or anchor."

But not Matthew. He worked for an entertainment and celebrity news outlet. Or had worked, up until a few weeks ago. Neither Adalyn nor Cameron had ever gone into much detail about his departure, and it hadn't been broached in our group chat. All Adalyn had told me was that Matthew had been asked to write about Andrew after the *Time* article that had attracted so much attention, and that Matthew had refused. Adalyn never said it had been to protect her and Cameron, but it seemed like it. Why else would he refuse?

When he didn't say anything, I felt the need to fill the silence. "I always wondered, that's all. But we don't need to talk about it. I can see it's not a topic you want to discuss. And that's fine."

"Exactly how much time do you and Adalyn spend discussing me?"

Some warmth rushed to my cheeks, but I tipped my chin up. "Don't let it get to your head. We talk about everyone. In detail." And we really did. "I was simply curious because you were analyzing the defense strategy of some local team that consists of sixth graders like we're sitting at Wembley and the Spurs are playing a Premier League final."

"*Spurs*, huh?" he repeated with a smile. It was really small, and lopsided, but at least it wasn't a frown.

"Tottenham Hotspurs, of course. Not the San Antonio basketball team. No offense to the NBA, but European *football* is where it's at."

That slightly bent corner of his mouth twitched. "Sounding like Cam there for a second."

"Pssh," I let out. "A girl can know about the English league, you know." A girl who had also been briefly engaged to a professional soccer player. But I didn't say that, and I threw Matthew a wink. The brown of his eyes twinkled with surprise. "But yes. I could sound exactly like Cam if I wanted to. He grumbles a lot at games, and I've picked up some things."

"Mind demonstrating?"

I cleared my throat lightly, then shot to my feet. *"Oi, Tony!"* I shouted in my best English accent. *"Bloody get Rashford in. Can't you see the Bears' defense's going to shite?"* A few heads turned my way, the referee's included. "Sorry, hon!" I told Tony, switching back to my voice. "Please carry on and make sure to swing by Josie's Joint for the aftergame. You're doing amazing, thank you!"

Matthew's whole expression filled with amusement. "The resemblance is uncanny," he said. To which I responded with a little bow before sitting back down. "In fact . . ." His eyelids fluttered shut. "Oh yeah, I think I can smell shortbread and stale beer if I close my eyes."

"You *did* ask me to demonstrate," I said with a snort. "And that's what you think they eat at games? Shortbread?"

"I would," he said, returning his gaze to the game. "Shortbread is great. I could eat it anywhere, at any time. My sister smuggled a box in her suitcase last Christmas, and it was a life-changing experience."

I perked up with interest. *Finally* a piece of information I hadn't been handed by Adalyn. "Was she visiting?"

"She lives there," he answered easily. And his profile softened so much it made me pause. "Tay's in London on a tennis scholarship. It isn't a full ride, but it was her dream. Fell in love with the sport when we were kids and my dad somehow won tickets to the US Open. She's been obsessed ever since. It's a good thing she's incredible at it."

I ignored the warmth flooding my chest at the affection in Matthew's voice. Oversharing was one of my love languages. It wasn't the best love language to have, but it was the way I was wired. I overshared, and in turn, consumed and filed all and any information that fell into my hands. This was the first thing I'd added to my Matthew binder on my own, and I liked that it had been about his sister and that he'd looked like that while telling me.

"Those are the best things to fall in love with," I heard myself say. "The ones we find accidentally."

Matthew's eyes found mine. That softness was still there, but something else had emerged. It made me . . . nervous. And it made me feel comfortable, too. Like I could say that kind of thing around him, but at the same time, like he wasn't just hearing the words.

"Anyway," I said, averting my gaze. "It's good to know. This is the kind of stuff I should know if we . . . you know. Do this."

"If?" I heard him ask from my side. "I was under the impression the deal was already sealed. Hard launch and all."

"Otto said that you looked like this was the last place on earth you wanted to be. And you were a little late, after all. So it crossed my mind that you were on the first flight out of Charlotte. You did look a little like you were entering one of those creepy mirror houses they have at fairs." I paused. "Even though you agreed to this whole thing."

A strange hum left him.

It made me want to turn. But I wanted to be casual about what I was saying. So I stayed put, even when I felt his eyes intent on my profile.

"Did I?" he asked.

"Did you what?" I was holding the fort so well, I was proud of myself. "Agree or look terrified?"

"Either. All I remember from those two instances is being immediately and thoroughly sidetracked. By you."

My stance broke. I glanced back at him. Matthew's expression was serious in a way that made heat rush up my neck, bathing my whole face. I'd done that. Sidetracked him. I had used my double gaze stare on him yesterday, and I'd climbed him like a tree today.

"Well, that's not my fault, is it?" I feigned indifference with a shrug. "That's your prerogative as an easily *sidetrackable* man."

"It really is," he said.

I frowned at him, my façade quickly dissolving. Why wasn't he joking? My stomach dropped with dread at the logical answer to that: I had done a little more than sidetrack Matthew. I had *pushed* him to do this. I had beguiled him into it, even. And that didn't make me a monster as much as it made me a desperate woman with only one way out of a mess she'd started, but I hated the idea of him feeling trapped all the same. Was that why his expression was so closed-off and stern-looking?

"You can jump ship and say no," I told him. "At any moment."

Matthew tilted his head in question. Which kind, I couldn't know.

I insisted, "I'm not planning to shackle you to my wrist and drag you around town. It'd be a little awkward to do it here, but we could break up. Today. It wouldn't be my first public breakup, and it wouldn't be the first time a man dumped me, even though some podcaster believes I'm a heartless, damaged, evil witch with issues and a penchant for weddings."

"They said that about you?" Matthew asked. "When?"

I opened my mouth to answer, but he was pulling out his phone. His fingers swiped with a determination that drove me to peek at the screen. Page Nine's Instagram was open. "Matthew," I called, feeling a little apprehensive now. My hand crossed the few inches separating us, landing on his arm. The sleeves of his baseball tee were pushed up and I immediately regretted having gloves on. "Why are you checking—" It locked into place then. "You've listened to it. *Filthy Reali-Tea,* Page Nine's podcast. I didn't tell you the specifics. That's why you're checking their page?"

A muscle in his jaw jumped when he looked up at me. "Yes."

I had wondered if making Matthew listen to it would have been a quicker way to have him agree, but a part of me hadn't wanted his pity. Judgment. And it didn't matter how or when he found out about my past. It just bothered me a little that he had listened to it before . . . I could tell him myself? I could prepare?

"And what were you planning to do right now?" I asked him, pushing all of that aside. "Comment on some post like an outraged Karen?"

"I can be a great Karen."

I gave him a half-hearted smile. "That's sweet."

It was also unnecessary.

Matthew hesitated, as if he was going to say something important. But I stopped him with a hand. Out of the corner of my eye I saw a perm moving in the crowd of heads, going one, two, three stands up. Right above us, but to the left. Pug ears popped up too. Then Otto's cap. Jesus. Those two were like the Avengers of None of Their Business, assembling the moment anything important was picked up by the wind.

"Put your arm around me," I instructed in a low voice. All Matthew did was frown. "Or do something. Anything you'd do to your fiancée if you were watching a game with her and she asked you something silly like 'would you love me if I were a worm?' Anything that's PDA and would keep people from interrupting us. Anything that—" My eyes widened. "No lips or mouth," I rushed out, realizing what I was asking might imply Matthew kissing me. But we'd eventually have to do that, right? Right? Oh God. And that— Focus, Josie. "Just do something. Now. Please?"

His hand met mine in a swift motion. Warmth wrapped around my wrist, and before I could so much as process the gentle touch, my gloved fingers were being brought up to the height of his chest. Matthew's eyes met mine as he lowered his chin, his teeth closing slowly around the extra fabric around my pinky. He gave the glove a quick, gentle tug, and a breath seemed to get stuck somewhere between my throat and lungs. Then he replaced his mouth with his own expert hand, peeling the pink wool off my skin.

Wide-eyed—and frankly boiling hot despite the missing layer—I could do nothing but watch Matthew as he sandwiched my hand in his big palms and blew air into it. A warmth, soft like melted butter, spread, chased away by goose bumps breaking across my skin. My whole body tingled. *Tingled.*

The corners of his lips tipped up, his gaze roaming all over my face in a way that told me he knew exactly what he was doing. "This," he finally said, rubbing my skin with his thumbs. "If my woman has cold hands, I'm going to keep them nice and warm."

My woman.

Nice and warm.

I—

Shoot. I'd just been uno-reversed.

No words rose to my tongue, so I cleared my throat. All right. This was fine. I'd asked for *this*. It just caught me off guard, that's all. That is what the wobble in my belly meant. Surprise.

"But sweetheart," he said a lot louder. "Of course I would love you if you were a worm." He winked. "I'd build you a tiny box and carry you in my pocket anywhere I'd go."

"That's . . . cute," I muttered. Although it really was. It also felt incredibly nice to have my hand held like this. I dragged my eyes behind him. "The Gossip Brigade is down. For now."

Matthew didn't seem to care as much as I did. He was now preoccupied with turning my hand and inspecting my palm. His thumb caressed the skin, sending more tingles up my wrist. "The cut is healing." He lifted his gaze to meet mine. "Do you still want me to kiss it and make it better?"

My brain tripped. *Kiss it and make it better?* "That's—" My voice broke. "No lips or mouth. I think I—I think I said that."

He shrugged. Casually. Way too much. "Sorry. I really thought I mentioned having excellent selective hearing."

I narrowed my eyes at him, seeing the start of a smile tugging at his mouth. My lips opened, but before I could say anything, both our phones started buzzing.

We frowned at each other, letting go of the other's hands to fish out our devices.

"It's Adalyn," I said.

"Cam's calling me," Matthew said at the same time.

We both paused, and then it all clicked together. "Have you—"

"No," he answered with a shake of his head. He declined the call.

"Whoa. Did you just hang up on Cameron Caldani?" I asked him in disbelief. "Do you not know the man?"

Before Matthew could respond, our phones started ringing again. Only the ID-callers were switched. Matthew declined his best friend's call, too.

"You're ballsy," I breathed out, letting my call go to voicemail. "And they are insistent, which can only mean one thing." I studied Matthew, gauging how this made him feel. "A part of me expected you to call Adalyn yesterday. After I left. It's really okay if you did."

"I didn't," he said, brows knotting. "You didn't tell them anything?"

I shook my head. "I was waiting for today. In case you . . . called it off. And it would really be okay if you wanted to check with Adalyn to see if she's comfortable with this. You've been best friends for years. And I'm Adalyn's sister, but I'm new to her life. You get shotgun on the conversation if you want to reassure her, and them, first. Or make sure I'm trustworthy. Or—"

"Do you really believe that?"

I didn't want to ask him for clarification, so I didn't. Luckily, the perfect distraction came in the shape of a trail of notifications making my hands ping.

ADALYN: We're not mad, just surprised. And happy!! Why are you not picking up? We know you're together. Someone texted me a picture to say congrats.

CAM: Oh. I'm actually mad.

ADALYN: Ignore him. There's nothing to be mad about. Except maybe you guys not telling us earlier? BUT WE ARE

HAPPY. My best friend and my sister (!). I have so many questions. But please know, there was no need to hide your relationship. Or your engagement.

CAM: That's exactly why I'm mad.

CAM: Also, congrats. Happy for you. Now answer the bloody phone.

ADALYN: Please 🙂

I stared at the screen, all kinds of emotions rioting in my stomach. They were all mixed, and they took up all the space in there. Probably more than that, judging on how heavy my whole body felt.

"They . . . They're not questioning if it's real," I heard myself say. "They're not asking us if we're together. Just assuming we hid it. Do you think that's good? Or bad? I wasn't expecting someone to text them. I thought I'd have a little time to think about how to tell them. And what to tell them. If you hadn't already, of course. God, they must be so hurt. Disappointed. Although Adalyn doesn't sound super hurt or disappointed. Do you think that's weird? We need to tell them the truth. Unless you think they'll . . . freak out. Convince us not to do it. I mean, let's face it, Cameron hates anything that has to do with the press or media, and Adalyn will go all overprotective on you. You're her best friend. She'll probably get into a fight with Andrew over this. And Bobbi. Maybe even me. The whole PR drama is already bad enough. And they've been under so much stress with the Club. It's only one year old, and I know they're getting a lot more attention after Andrew mentioned it in that *Time* article. So how— God. I—I think I'm getting a little sweaty. Dizzy? Do you think they're on their way here? I don't know if I can face them. Or tell them the truth. Oh God, just the idea is making me—"

Matthew's hand fell on my forearm, bringing my gaze up. "Deep breath."

I inhaled deeply, holding his gaze. Immediately realizing I hadn't done that in a minute or two.

"We don't need to tell them," Matthew said.

"We don't?"

"Not if the thought of it is giving you a goddamn panic attack, no."

"I'm okay," I whispered. I wasn't, but the noise in my head had quieted with that deep breath. Or Matthew's words. "I'm fine. And this shouldn't be my call. You shouldn't be pushed to lie to your best friend just because I'm a wreck. It should be your call."

"You're wrong."

My only answer was a frown.

"It's not my call," he insisted simply. Matter-of-factly. "And I don't get shotgun on anything. Me getting that based on some strange seniority of friendship, it's bullshit, Josie. She's your sister." He paused, as if to make a point. "You get to make the call. Or at the very least *we* do. Together."

My head worked out his words, but it was all chaos upstairs again. I didn't know if I could trust myself. My decision-making capabilities had been really off lately. It was . . . selfless of Matthew to say that. It made me feel . . . good. Worse. Relieved. Shook up. My voice came out weird. "You're talking like we're in a relationship."

"Are we not?" Then, a little louder. "We're engaged."

My eyes widened at first, but then I realized. We were in the stands. Still. I swallowed, trying to get ahold of my thoughts. "We are."

Matthew nodded, as if that was all he needed as confirmation. "I'll return their call after the game. I'll handle most of the initial heat on why we kept it hidden from them. Or why I proposed so fast. You have enough on your plate with Bobbi, and I was planning on bringing this up with you anyway."

My throat worked around the air stuck in my throat. Matthew had . . . thought of this. It didn't matter if for a day or a few hours. He was far better than me at problem-solving, and that . . . made me feel a way I wasn't able to fully grasp. Guilty? Selfish? Grateful? Relieved. Maybe all of those things.

Before I could look too much into it, he was slipping the phone back into the pocket of his jeans and plucking something else out, distracting me.

Everything inside me halted at the sight.

"You should have this," Matthew said.

With a shaky breath, my eyes inspected what was held between his fingers. A moss-green pouch. My heart resumed, whipping about, thrashing against the walls of my chest. My words were a whisper, "Have what?"

"This," Matthew said, sending the struggling organ to my feet. "Your hands weren't cold," he added. "Makes no sense in the seventy-degree weather. You were hiding them, weren't you? You can't wear the ring from the other night. From your ex. So have this one instead."

Every word had sent me further into shock. I couldn't find my thoughts, or words, or reason. I couldn't find . . . anything.

So I asked again, "Have what instead?"

"My ring."

CHAPTER SEVEN

Bobbi Shark drummed her nails against her arm as she stood in front of us.

She was making my ass cheeks sweat, frankly.

The flush covering my body like frosting over a birthday cake had nothing to do with the strange heat wave hitting Green Oak in the middle of October. I'd been sweating since last night, when Bobbi had called for a meeting to *strategize.*

The woman appraised us some more. Gaze bouncing from me to Matthew, then returning to me. We were sitting shoulder to shoulder on twin chairs, lined up right in the middle of Josie's Joint—which I'd closed at noon just for this. On a weekday, by the way. So not only was Bobbi making me lose precious bodily fluids, but also, good rush-hour income.

"Fine," she finally said.

"Fine," I repeated. Carefully, and feeling like I was talking back to the principal after being called to her office. "But what do you mean exactly? Is it a fine *fine* or a fine *not fine*?"

"Fine means fine," she countered.

"I know what it means," I said. "But what do *you* mean?"

"I mean fine," Bobbi said again.

"But a fi—" I started.

Matthew's palm fell on my leg, the contact severing my speech. The warmth of his skin seeped through the thin fabric of my silk skirt. "Neither of us are mind readers," he said. "Thankfully. So how about you explain to us what exactly is fine? Or why we're here? Or the objective of this impromptu meeting you've called?"

"You two," Bobbi deadpanned. "You look okay together. I'd make some changes, but not many. Would you consider Botox?"

Oh God. "I don't think—" I started, but stopped myself. Why was I so freaking nervous? And were my wrinkles so bad? "That's not really—"

"Neither of us needs Botox," Matthew interjected. "Next topic."

I all but slumped in my chair, relieved he'd taken the lead. Matthew tapped my leg with a thumb, in some kind of reflex or code I couldn't crack, and then he retrieved his hand. The patch of skin where it had been felt strangely cold, but that was good. Great. For the best.

Bobbi resumed talking and I crossed my legs and arms in an attempt at giving her the impression I was chill and not a nervous wreck. But it was hard to pay her any attention when I felt so off, so fidgety, as if I couldn't stop turning and twisting in my seat. I returned my two feet to the floor and clasped my hands in my lap.

Something sparkled under the light, and I immediately glanced down.

The ring.

Matthew's ring.

Mine now, for all intents and purposes. The ring was on a strange loan whose length hadn't been discussed yet. Or terms.

Which reminded me we should, after this, and which didn't change the fact there was a ring on my finger.

It wasn't the first time I'd worn one, or the second, or even the third. It was my fifth. And yet it felt like all that experience counted for nothing. Matthew's ring was, without a doubt, beautiful. Unique, and so different from any other engagement ring I'd ever been given. Distinct in that way only a piece of jewelry with personality and soul could be. I wasn't a fool, I'd known the moment I'd pulled it out of the pouch—after recovering from the shock and saying a very loud *thank you for picking it up from the cleaners, baby*—that it was a Claddagh ring. It bore some modifications to the original design, but it had been obvious enough for me to recognize the crown and hands clasped around a heart whose space was replaced by a stone. And topped by a crown lined with much smaller ones. Even if the detailing was minimal, and the elegant band was thinner than the typical one.

The ring begged too many questions. Starting with: Why did Matthew have one around in the first place? Or, in what way was Matthew connected to Irish symbology and tradition? And ending with a long list of other unresolved mysteries that revolved around him giving me his ring instead of getting a new one. Which was what I'd been planning. Eventually.

Bobbi cleared her throat.

Cheeks flushing, I ripped my eyes off my finger.

"Earth to Josie," Bobbi said with an unimpressed grimace. "I know all you want to do is stare at your hand, show the girlfriends, daydream of Blondie in a tux, handwrite your vows into perfection, or I don't know, scroll down Pinterest to create the perfect wedding board. But we have ground to cover. *And* I'm going to need your full attention."

"I scrapbook," I countered, out of anything better to say. "*Scrapbooked*, for my other, ah, projects. I like manual labor far more than staring at a screen, in case you're wondering."

"I wasn't." Bobbi's lip curled. "And you won't need a scrapbook for this." Bobbi produced an iPad. "You're going digital. That's why I need both your iCloud addresses. I'm syncing you to Bobbi Shark's Ultimate Wedding Planner. You need to treat this as your new Bible. And before you ask, no, there's no printable. And yes, you're welcome for bringing you into the twenty-first century. Just remember this moment when I give you that last push down the aisle and you think, *Damn, I wish I could marry Bobbi instead.*" She frowned. "Although with your track record, you better not think of any such thing. You walk down that aisle, not up."

A shout came from behind us.

"For the last time, there's no pushing nobody down nowhere. Matter of fact, there won't be any aisle at all if I have a say in it!"

I didn't need to turn to know that Grandpa Moe, who had insisted on fixing a nonexistent problem with the window lighting while I was closed, was holding some tool he didn't need and glaring at us.

"Does he need to be here?" Bobbi asked me.

"I'm changing a bulb," Grandpa Moe complained.

"With a hammer?" Bobbi said.

"I'll change bulbs however I please to," he huffed out. "And this is my Josie, and this is her shop, so I'll stay if I want to. And there won't be any aisle-pushing unless she wants it. Is that understood?"

We all stared at the man, face serious and chest heaving.

Guilt and concern surged deep in my belly. Grandpa had lived through all my previous engagements, and it hadn't been fun for him to watch me . . . navigate my way out of them. This was in many ways worse than a conventional engagement, because he knew the truth about Matthew and me. He was the only person who did. And he was doing a poor job concealing it.

I summoned a reassuring smile. "How about you go back to work, Moe Poe? I promise we have it handled over here. And if at any point we don't, I'll call out for you."

That seemed to appease him enough to give me a nod and return to his alleged work.

"Back to iCloud details," Bobbi continued. "You can give them to me or I'll get them myself. I have my ways and asking is just the polite approach."

Out of the corner of my eye, I saw Matthew shake his head. A whiff of his cologne hit me in the nose. Cedar and a touch of something I couldn't catch. It was nice. And I liked it. It was also unimportant that I did, so I rattled my details off before I was sidetracked again, and Matthew followed my lead.

In seconds, our phones pinged with twin notifications.

"Excellent," Bobbi said. "Now, this is not just any calendar, this is B.S.'s Ultimate W.P., which is what I prefer to call it. I know it's unusual for a PR strategist, but I'm also your wedding planner." She grimaced. "Apparently. Everything is linked to a checklist, log, diary, record, budget—which is only a reference, we can go higher—and everything you need to know." She flipped the screen, tapping quickly in different spots. "Here. Here. Here. Here. Here. And here. Your homework is to go through it, read it, process it, assimilate it, and embrace it. You'll have to sign an agreement to confirm you understand and concur with everything disclosed. Nothing strange, considering I suggested an NDA that Andrew immediately shot down. So. Questions?"

Huh. All of them. "Why do we need a—"

"Awesome, no questions," she cut me off, her fingers decidedly flying over the device again. "Now that that's out of the way. Have you settled on a date?"

Matthew grunted something unintelligible, shifting in his seat.

Something clattered to the ground from Grandpa's corner.

"A date?" I repeated, my stomach swooping.

"For the big day," she countered. "I've set a temporary one in the planner. One that suits us. But I'm open to discussion."

My body turned to, well, stone. Not ice, because I was still sweating. Either way, I went very, very still. It really amazed me how I'd jumped into this without thinking things like rings or wedding dates would obviously be discussed. "No date," I croaked. Bent my lips upward. "Let's stick to the temporary one for now, please."

"Music to my ears," Bobbi declared. Crisis averted. "That's December first."

And back to crisis land. "That's less than two months away," I rushed out. My ears started ringing and I was almost sure I was between one and three seconds from dropping to the floor. Bobbi's eyes narrowed, and suddenly Matthew's arm was there. Resting on my back. "You'll fix it, right? The press situation? The . . . narrative." I found enough strength to say. "Before we get to that day. I'd . . . rather avoid rushing this. It's supposed to be a special day."

Although the truth was that I couldn't chicken out. Not after convincing Matthew it was all fine and having us lie to everyone.

"That's what I said, isn't it?" Bobbi countered. Her head tilted to the side. "You can stop panicking. The news that you're happily engaged *and* Andrew is part of it will probably put out most of the fire."

I let out some of the air that had been squeezed in my lungs. "Okay," I said, focusing on the slight reprieve and not on the fact that Matthew wasn't speaking. He was probably fuming. This wasn't what we'd talked about.

Bobbi continued, unbothered. "Now, speaking of putting out fires, I'm going to need you to set your socials to private, and I want access to all the pictures you two have together. Dates, weekend trips, mirror selfies, domestic shots . . . anything but nudes. And most importantly, your proposal shots."

Well, crap.

"No, no," she tutted. "I don't like that face. Please, don't tell me all you have is mirror selfies. No one actually wants to see that."

I blinked at the woman, realizing with urgency that I'd definitely miscalculated and underestimated this whole thing. Anxiety blossomed, and I did what I do when that happens. I smiled. Big and wide.

"What is your mouth doing?" she asked me.

Matthew's hand returned to my leg, which was bouncing. But before I could begin to process the weight or the warmth of his palm, or how the fidgeting had stopped under it, he said, "No."

Bobbi's brows arched. "Pardon me?"

The tension thickened in an unexpected way, and I didn't think, I just acted. It was time to get the control back. "We lost them," I said. "To hackers. We were hacked. You know as careful as one tries to be, they're sneaky. They tricked me and before I knew it, my gallery was poof. Gone. It happens to the best of us. All the hard copies were lost, too. In a fire. It was horrible and—"

"And we're private," Matthew said, fingers squeezing my knee. "We're not giving you access to our memories just because you ask. That's what *no* means. We don't want to and it's our decision. The only reason Josie was not telling you this is because she has manners. I don't. I say shit like it is."

Bobbi's expression was . . . strange. As if she wanted to fling her iPad at Matthew, but she was also impressed. "All right, Blondie. But don't forget Andrew's putting a lot into this and you're getting a free ride on the wedding of your dreams. So you get to draw some lines, but I'm still in charge." A pause. "You'll take new pictures. That's my compromise, and I'll forget about that hacking story or why Josephine has been looking like a deer in headlights since taking a seat."

Had I?

I turned to look at my fiancé, as if looking for the answer to that. But Matthew was busy holding the woman's eyes. For a long time.

He squeezed my knee.

Oh. "Yeah, okay." I let my hand rest on top of his. Sandwiching his fingers against my thigh. They twitched. Tapped. "New pictures sound like a reasonable compromise."

The atmosphere in the coffee shop relaxed with my words. And when Bobbi's phone rang and she excused herself with a, "I'll be right back," before moving to the back, it improved exponentially where tension was concerned.

"Ugh," I said, turning to look at Matthew. "Thank you for that."

He sat back on his chair, letting his shoulders fall but keeping his hand exactly where it was. On my thigh. Under my palm "Place is cute," he said. "Really charming and cozy," he added with the tiniest smirk. "Very Josie."

Very Josie. Did that mean he found me cute? Charming? Cozy? They weren't the worst things to be. "Of course it is," I muttered. "I'm in charge and I have excellent taste."

His lips twitched. "Cocky. I like that too."

Too. I tipped my chin up. "Not cocky. Just confident. Cute and charming decor is in my skills repertoire."

He dipped his head, only slightly. His voice lowered. "Unlike lying. Hackers? A fire? I feel like I should have been warned about this."

The tips of my ears warmed. Those green specks in his eyes were there again. Flicking under the fluorescent light and staring right back at me. Our faces were once again too close. Our shoulders touched, and the gentle pressure his palm exerted on my leg, as it remained in place, seemed to scream at me.

"I feel like I should have been warned about this too," I murmured.

I glanced down at the ring on my finger. The stones around the crown reminded me of the beautiful specks of green.

Matthew's voice was nothing but a hush. "You don't like it? You didn't say."

His thumb moved from beneath my hand to swipe at the ring. It was merely a brush, but the small gesture sent a truckload of memories cascading down my head. Flashes of men's faces, first dates, proposals, bouquets of roses, candlelit dinners, rings that were now stored in a box atop my dresser. They all seemed to belong to a past life. Like they were never really mine.

"It doesn't matter if I like it," I heard myself say. Because it was this ring, the one that didn't belong to me. Even when it seemed to occupy all the space in my head after wearing it all of one day. "But it's beautiful."

I glanced back at Matthew, a question at the tip of my tongue. There was a question in his eyes, too.

But before we could voice any of that, Bobbi was back, face grim and words even grimmer.

"We have a problem."

INTERIOR—*FILTHY REALI-TEA* STUDIO—DAY

SAM: Why are you vibrating with excitement? (laughs)

NICK: (screeches) That's because I'm in a complete tizzy.

SAM: I can't wait to hear what you brought us today, then.

NICK: (pause, then rushes out) Everyone has been blowing up our comment section—on all platforms—demanding to know more about a certain girlie and her daddy. SO . . .

without further ado, I am pleased to bring you, Sammy, and our Reali-tiers, our new *Filthy* series, the one, the— Oh wait. Can I please get a drumroll? Do we have audio effects? Is that a—

(Drumroll sound)

NICK: Oh wow. (chuckles) I didn't know we had that. Look at us being so fancy. Or the opposite maybe, that was a little too radio for me. All right, anyway, let me get back on track. Drumroll please? (drumroll sound) (pitch increases) I'm honored to present you and our listeners our new series: *THE UNDERWOOD AFFAIR.*

SAM: Shocker! (claps) And you didn't tell me any of this? Rude.

NICK: Keeping the secret almost unalived me, believe me. But it was so worth it. Because we've got lots of new-sies and I get to see your face while I tell you about them. (calculated pause) And you do, too, by the way. Remember to check our pod recordings in vid format on any platform if you haven't. And subscribe, for the love of Harry Styles. Click that button.

SAM: Thanks for that Nick. BUT. For context . . . We're talking about Small-Town Princess, right? Abandoned by Rich Daddy, on her quest to serve revenge, one heart at a time—tally is high. Which we support, by the way. We support women's rights and we cheer for women's wrongs. We don't support men, for the most part. Specifically Andrew Underwood. And excluding all our short kings.

NICK: That was an excellent summary. And yes to short kings. But we were calling her Small-Town Heiress, not princess. Which brings me to . . . The new-sies. It's taken us a lot of work, BUT: one of our little birdies has confirmed that—brace yourself—our babygirl is . . . ENGAGED. AGAIN.

SAM: Shut up. This makes it . . . the fifth.

NICK: That we know of. (chuckles) And apparently, in a shocking turn of events, Rich Daddy is paying for the wedding? We don't have all the deets, but our source said there seems to be a rekindlement of the relationship and both are (lowers voice) blessed to plan and celebrate such a special event together.

SAM: Sounds like PR BS to me (clicks tongue). And rekindlement of what? Was there a relationship?

NICK: I know, right? That's what I thought too.

SAM: Huh. I wonder how she feels about this. I wonder if he'll just throw money at it from his mansion or actually get involved. Have we—

NICK: Found her socials and messaged her? Yes. No response. But we're persistent. And you know what was the strangest thing?

SAM: That it wasn't set to private? (incredulous chortle)

NICK: Besides that. I mean, someone should have advised her a little better, I guess. But the strangest thing was that there was no trace of her new man. Just farm animals, pottery, shots of sunsets, and a really cool picture of her doing yoga. Girlie has the moves, FYI. What I suspect she doesn't have is . . . a lot of interest for this new man if she hasn't posted him at all.

SAM: Are you thinking the same thing I am?

NICK: You know I like conventionally ugly men. They put in the work. I'd show them off. And the bigger the nose, the better the man, by the way.

SAM: (hums) You aren't wrong. But I was thinking . . . why would she have him up anyway? It must be so annoying to delete old posts that include the fiancé of the year. Messes with the aesthetic. Oh, speaking of that: Do we have names? Of the fiancé and the exes? Besides the one we talked to. Derek? Dawson? And— Oh my God, could we bring them to the pod? That would be—

NICK: Wouldn't that be ah-mazing, sweet Sammy? (secretive chuckle) For now, I'll just say that you and our listeners will have to wait until the first episode in *The Underwood Affair* to find out. This was just a teaser. And as always, let us know in the comments what you think—not that you need any encouragement to speak up, you *Filthy* creatures.

For the fifth time in my life, there was a man on his knee in front of me.

It was like the sickest kind of déjà vu. Because he wasn't proposing. He never had. But we were engaged. Officially. To the town of Green Oak, but also to the world now. The internet. The gossip-sphere. Something I never thought I'd be part of. Not even when I was with Ricky or Duncan, and they both led lifestyles that related to the public eye.

Apparently it had taken a little more than professional soccer or politics to launch this *small-town heiress, not princess* into the gossip-sphere. It had taken a different kind of man. My father.

"AND CUT!"

The two words echoed through the Vasquezes' property, startling me and the man at my feet. Bobbi stomped in our direction, moving gravel as she went.

"WHAT ARE YOU DOING?" she asked when she reached us.

Matthew released my hand and went up on his feet. "Do you need to hold that? You're standing right here."

Bobbi put down the bullhorn she'd been using to order everyone around. "Happy?"

"Elated," Matthew deadpanned. "Thank you."

Bobbi rolled her eyes. "So? What exactly are you doing? Discussing the weather? Talking about the economy? The real estate market? All of the above? Because that would explain why all the pictures are giving off funeral, instead of *happily engaged, yay.*"

"Maybe—" Matthew started.

But Bobbi tsked. "Nuh-uh. We're not postponing, and if we want to catch the sunset—and we do—you need to start acting more *lovey-dovey* and less *the milk in my Pumpkin Spice Latte went sour.*" She seemed to think of something. "Is that what's happening? Do you need caffeine?" The bullhorn rose in the air. "ROBERTO. ROBERTO VASQUEZ?" She turned around in her heels. "THE ANGRY— OH, THERE YOU ARE. COFFEE. AND A MATCHA LATTE . PRONTO. THANK YOU."

If looks could kill, Bobbi would already be six feet under Robbie Vasquez's land.

She faced us. "WHERE WERE WE?"

Matthew snatched the bullhorn out of the woman's hands and crossed his arms.

"Hey," she complained. "That's mine."

"I'm doing you a favor," he told her. "Believe me."

"God, why is everyone in this town so touchy?" Bobbi huffed. "All right. Let's regroup while Roberto gets to work on those drinks. The kneeling is not working, so . . . You, Josephine. You are going to stand there." A perfectly manicured finger pointed at a fence. "And you, Matthew, are going to . . . Hm. Let me think."

Bobbi pulled her phone out of the chest pocket of her tweed vest, as if that's what *thinking* equated to, and started tapping away.

Matthew shifted by my side, his head and voice lowering. "Can't wait to see the matcha latte Robbie brings her."

His voice was amused, and that made me purse my lips in question. "Why?"

"If I were him, I'd definitely get creative with the ingredients."

I snorted. "I don't think he was *that* irked. He's also a dad of two. A stand-up family man. A widower. He wouldn't go around pranking anyone with drinks."

"She told him how she loved that farmers would just *wear anything,*" Matthew countered, brows up. "And then proceeded to order him around his farm. With a bullhorn. That drink is arriving contaminated, sweetheart."

Sweetheart. I no longer knew how I felt about the way he let that "sweetheart" out so often. I wondered if he called everyone that. Usually people who used it like Matthew had did. "I think you need to call me something else," I told him in a low voice. "Something other than 'sweetheart.' And should I be concerned about you going around town corrupting beverages? You do seem an expert on the topic."

Matthew's lips twitched, and for some reason, a mental image of a younger version of him, blond hair and mischievous smile, popped into my mind. I bet he was so much trouble. I bet he'd broken many hearts with those sweet brown eyes that made the hard angles in his face look soft. I wondered why he didn't wear his glasses more often, too. His head went even lower, his chin almost reaching my shoulder. When he spoke, his voice was nothing but a rumble. "I hope to corrupt far more than beverages, *sweetcheeks*."

"Sweetcheeks?" I whispered, my focus flicking between the sudden closeness of his face and his words. "Is that meant to . . . compliment my butt or my face?"

The chuckle that left him fell against my cheek. "I'm—"

"YAWN."

We turned to look at Bobbi.

Her brows were bunched up in disbelief. "I was letting that go on in the hopes that the flirting would turn into dirty talk, so you'd get a little worked up and make this photoshoot a little less painful. But I'm bored out of my mind."

Flirting. Flirting?

"We weren't flirting," I huffed out. A scoff left Matthew, and I decided to take that as a sign of agreement. Bobbi's lips, however, tipped down in question. "I know what flirting looks like. Or how to flirt. I'm excellent at it. And that wasn't it. Plus, if we were flirting, we wouldn't do it with you right there."

"I would," Matthew said. I turned toward him, slowly, arching my brows. "I would." He shrugged. "Even if my game seems to be a little off."

I also decided to ignore how that sent a tiny flutter down my belly and returned my attention to Bobbi, whose lips were pursed in thought. She tapped her chin with a fingernail. "Are you open to something a little less country, alpine, outdoorsy, et cetera, and a little more boudoir?"

"No," I croaked. "*Why?*"

"One, because you ignored my request, left your socials public, and now there's nothing to do about that except act normal," she answered, and my cheeks flushed. "The fact that Blondie doesn't have any is a blessing in disguise." Her gaze sharpened on Matthew. "Unless you tell me there's a burner account with boy shit. And if that's going to come up, it better come up now."

"What is 'boy shit,' exactly?" he asked nonchalantly.

Bobbi's jaw clenched in a way that had me intervening before she could speak. "How is a boudoir picture going to fix that? Not that I'm not open to that kind of thing. But maybe for something else." I felt Matthew's gaze on my profile. "Not for this." Not with Matthew. Not if it's all insincere. Not if—

"Breasts have the power to fix almost every issue," Bobbi countered, bringing my thoughts to a stop. "I don't make the rules. If I did, we wouldn't be here, on this farm, breathing in the scent of manure, trying to show two random prattlers with a podcast that you're actually in love with this man."

Ouch. Nick and Sam had pointed out that I had no pictures of Matthew anywhere, and while that was a good point, it was also dangerous enough for me not to resist Bobbi's impromptu photoshoot. "I don't even post that much. That's why I haven't shared pictures of us. And—"

"You're a private couple. The hackers. Yeah, whatever." Bobbi shook her head. "At least, thanks to that, the focus seems to be shifting away from Andrew being . . . rich and selfish. As if those were bad things to be. Either way, that whole *Underwood Affair* thing needs to be contained. Andrew is concerned." I stiffened at the mention. "He doesn't—"

Matthew interjected. "How about you just tell us where you want us? You don't need to brief us on Andrew's feelings, yeah?"

Her hands braced on her hips. "The fence. Stand by the fence.

And look like you're in love this time around. It can't be *that* hard." She met my gaze. "You've done it a few times, yes?"

I smiled at her, giving her my best accommodating face before walking toward the fence. But I kept thinking about that comment she'd made about Andrew. Matthew was right, I didn't need to be briefed. The idea of being informed about how concerned my father was made me want to crawl out of my skin. Even when a part of me wondered why he hadn't gotten in touch. Directly, not through Bobbi. Was it because I'd ignored his latest attempts? That seemed a logical explanation. I'd be irked, too.

Before I could really notice how, I was turning around and Matthew was there, right in front of me. His lips parted, but whatever he was going to say was silenced by Bobbi's annoyingly amplified voice.

"WILL YOU CONSIDER WEARING A COWBOY HAT?"

"Christ," I murmured. "Not the bullhorn again."

Matthew's head turned slightly over his shoulder. "No."

I leaned my back on one of the posts, arms crossed a little awkwardly over my chest. "I hate to side with Bobbi, but you might break a few hearts by not wearing one."

"I'm from Boston," he countered, stepping closer. The tips of his boots—Chelsea boots, not cowboy ones—brushed the tips of mine. "And how would I break any hearts?"

I thought of how half of Green Oak was still convinced I was engaged to Tennessee's Maverick. "Just a hunch."

There was a glint of interest in Matthew's eyes, as if he wanted to ask more. But once again, Bobbi's voice was filling the Vasquezes' property. "LESS CHATTING. MORE TOUCHING."

"I swear I'm going to—"

Matthew's hands braced on the wooden rails, his arms suddenly caging me in. "You're going to do what?"

I cleared my throat, telling my brain to chill. Telling the pounding in my chest to calm the heck down too. These were just arms.

And Matthew was just . . . a man. Blond. Tall. A little more built than I'd expected. But still a man. Only now, it seemed very important to find out whether he worked out regularly. Or what he did as a workout. Strength of some kind. Weights? Pull-ups? The image of him lifting himself up to a bar—I stopped myself. This wasn't helping. It was also terribly inappropriate. I wanted to keep this as practical as possible.

"SUN IS SETTING," Bobbi warned. "TICK TOCK."

That wasn't helping either.

I blew some air out my nose. "I'm going to have very vivid dreams of me and that bullhorn in one of those rage rooms where you can smash stuff with a bat."

The corners of Matthew's lips tipped up. "Mmh, do I get to be there too?"

"In the smash room? Of course."

Matthew leaned forward, his head coming to the side of mine. I went very, very still. His breath tickled my ear. "Anywhere in those very vivid dreams you're telling me about."

Somewhere in my head a bell went off. But both my brain and nervous system were busy, all of me tingling with . . . awareness. The closeness of him. The waves of body heat his arms and chest gave off, feeling like a blanket over me. The brush of his chin on my cheek. "Matthew?" I whispered. "Are you flirting with me?"

The chuckle that rumbled out of the man's throat was brief and deep and extremely inconvenient. I was genuinely trying to figure out if he was. "Yes," he answered. Simply.

"Why?"

Matthew's arms closed in on me, his stance widening and his boots moving until his legs enclosed mine. "Sun is setting," he repeated. "Less chatting. More touching."

"Oh, okay. Good." Because that was . . . good. Yes. "So, ah, where do you want me?"

Another of those short-lived chuckles toppled on my skin. My temple this time. "You tell me, sweetheart." One of his hands left the fence, landing on my waist. My breath hitched. "I have never done this before."

"Pictures?" I asked him. My voice came out husky. Off. His palm over the waistband of my dress was all I could focus on. "And I thought we were past the sweetheart."

I felt him start to say something, but the contact of my hand on his shoulder brought that to a halt. His whole body stiffened for just a moment, so brief that I would have missed it if we weren't standing this close, or I wasn't this determined to notice this much. He eased into my touch. "Engagement shoots," he said. And to my surprise, he grasped my wrist softly, then rearranged my palm so it'd rest higher up. My hand wrapped around the back of his neck, fingertips tingling against his skin. "Sweetpea."

The word was nothing but a breath, yet it made my belly flop. *Flutter.* "I . . . I don't think that's working either," I admitted, the strange quality of my voice even more prominent. "I think . . ." My left arm rose, my hands meeting behind his neck. "I think you should look at me." I swallowed, tongue feeling like sandpaper. That blanket of awareness covering my skin thickened. "I think we should look at each other. Gaze into each other's eyes while we touch. It's what engagement shoots are about. What people in love do."

Matthew's eyes were immediately on me. "What else?"

"Maybe lean a little closer," I instructed.

He did, and boy it was really hard to focus on anything but him with his face so very close. Matthew's expression grew serious, the line of his brows determined, and I swore I could feel the tension hanging off that pair of shoulders I seemed so caught on. "Now?"

"Maybe smile a little," I told him, whatever control I was grasping at in the situation slipping with every inch lost between our chests. "You have a handsome smile."

Matthew's hand at my waist flexed, his thumb pushing softly into the purple fabric. "Enough to make you proud? Enough to make you want to show me off?"

I immediately knew what he was referring to. Sam and Nick's speculation about why I didn't show my new fiancé anywhere. "They aren't wrong," I whispered. And I didn't know why I said what I did, but the words simply came out. "It's a little tedious to clean up your life when something ends. Social posts included."

His hand shifted, sliding across my waist and resting at the small of my back. "Good thing we're a private couple," he said, letting more of the weight of his body fall on me. Our hips clashed. Matthew swallowed. "And you can have all this for yourself."

Breath officially lost to the heaving of my chest, I tried my best to speak. "I thought the purpose of this was the opposite." My voice came out hoarse. "And your game's not off. If you're . . ." My fingertips stumbled upon those short strands at the nape of his neck, the feel of them making me lose my focus for an instant. "If you're flirting with me."

His gaze roamed over my face for an instant. A muscle in his jaw ticked. "I could still do a little better. A little more. If you need me to." His tongue made a pass of his lower lip. "Do you need me to?"

Yes, I thought. *Please.* But I said, "Only if you're comfortable. Are you comfortable with this?" My fingernails grazed his scalp as if to make a point of what I meant.

Matthew's weight fell a little heavier, a little . . . nicer. "Do I look uncomfortable to you?"

He didn't. But I was pretty sure it was a rhetorical question. "I always liked this part," I heard myself say. "Of a relationship. It's what I miss the most."

"That's a dangerous green light you're giving me."

I watched him, waiting for more of . . . more of anything. But Matthew didn't say how or move to show me, and with the press of his thighs against mine, and the heat of his palm on my back, and the cocoon of intimacy that had somehow formed around us, I felt the need to speak. "I would post you. Everywhere. If this was real." The brown in Matthew's eyes sharpened as his gaze held mine. "I'd be very happy to show you off. Just so you know."

Matthew continued to watch me, and I continued to study his face in return. He seemed to be thinking of something. Hard. As if he was trying to make up his mind. It intrigued me, what he was debating or what conclusion he would reach.

His lips finally popped open, and I wasn't going to lie, I held my breath a little. "Josie—"

"AND THAT'S A WRAP!" Bobbi hollered through the bullhorn. Again. "HALLELLUJAH. FINALLY SOMETHING WE CAN USE. GOOD WORK. YOU'RE GIVING HORNY. AMERICA IS GOING TO LOVE THAT."

That breath I'd been holding left me, and I suddenly felt . . . dazed. Matthew must have, too, because it took him a beat to step back.

"Hallelujah," he repeated.

I frowned at that, a little lost as to what the stiffness with which he'd said that came from. Matthew wasn't Bobbi's biggest fan, which would explain it. But a part of me wanted to ask. And I would have if I hadn't seen the woman turning around and walking away. With her phone. That contained the pictures we hadn't even seen.

"Bobbi!" I called, walking around Matthew. "Wait up!"

I didn't like leaving Matthew behind like that, but there was something a little more pressing than dissecting why my fiancé was still frowning down at me, lost in thought.

Why was America going to love us?

And how horny exactly did we look?

CHAPTER EIGHT

"You look incredible."

We did.

We also looked horny. Like two people who had incredible chemistry and who were ready to jump each other's bones, simply put. Which was a little funny, in a way. Under normal circumstances I would have totally framed that picture and had it displayed somewhere in the house. But these weren't normal circumstances, and it was hard to laugh at how my sister's best friend had put that aroused look on my face when I felt so horrible for actively lying to her. Face-to-face. Even if through my phone.

"You don't think so?" Adalyn asked. "Is that why you're frowning? Or is it because the picture is on a page with two million followers?"

I forced my eyebrows to chill. "Well, seeing our picture on Page Nine makes me a little woozy. But it's fine." That wasn't a lie. I wasn't all that rattled by the photo. It was a great photo, even though it was a hoax. "I just . . . wish I'd thought out my outfit better, I guess.

Am I showing too much cleavage? Grandpa Moe said I should have worn a scarf."

"He's sweet," she answered with a chuckle that made her dark eyes spark with amusement. "But absolutely not. Your outfit is perfect and you are glowing. What did Matthew think? I'm sure he had plenty to say about that dress. Or the fence, really."

Once more, I felt that gut instinct to switch topics. Deflect. And once again, I suppressed it. A week had passed since the game, and Adalyn and Cameron finding out. We'd talked to them separately, Matthew going first like he insisted. So this . . . feeling of betrayal would surely go away. I still believed it was best for Adalyn and Cameron not to know the truth. Adalyn would go bananas on the whole thing if she knew, and she'd probably try to become my personal bodyguard. Less involvement meant less stuff shoved on their plates. Her plate. Bobbi had been sent to deal with me, anyway. Not Adalyn. She'd had enough. Plus, neither Adalyn nor Cameron questioned my supposed relationship with Matthew anyway. I guessed that was based on my track record with relatively quick engagements and my tendency to get carried away by the moment.

"He . . . said we look great," I lied. Lies, lies, lies. He hadn't. Matthew hadn't said anything about the picture. Nothing specific when Bobbi shared it with us. And nothing when I posted it to my socials. I didn't even know for sure if he'd seen Page Nine using it too.

Adalyn's brows arched for a moment. Then she sighed. "You can tell me what he really said. Even if it'll gross me out, because you're my sister and he's . . . very unfiltered and inappropriate."

I racked my head for a Matthew thing to say but came up empty.

Adalyn shook her head. "Is this why you thought you had to keep your relationship a secret? These kind of things? I won't react in a weird way. We can talk about . . . private stuff." She made a face. "Like sex, or . . . dirty talk."

"Can we?" I asked her, genuinely surprised.

"Maybe not," she said. "Not yet? Ugh, I don't know."

We both laughed, even if a little awkwardly.

"You . . ." she trailed off for an instant. "You make an incredible couple. And I love you both. I think I've already said that, but I don't know how else I can reassure you that I'm okay with you two being together." Her expression sobered and it was so hard to keep my arm up, holding the phone in place, when I felt there was a *but* coming. "But I'm still disappointed that you felt the need to hide it. It's not just directed at you or Matthew. I—" She sighed, and the sound was so sad it broke my heart a little more. "I'm sorry, I know we've gone through this already. It's the stress of everything. Life has been a lot lately. Building the youth club from the ground up hasn't been easy, and I think I need a vacation."

That felt like a punch to the gut. All of it. Several punches I deserved. "I'm so sorry, Adalyn. It was never my—our—intention to hurt you. Or Cam. Do you believe me when I say that all I did and do is with the best of intentions? So you wouldn't worry about unnecessary stuff?"

"Of course," she said quickly. "I know that. And Cameron knows too. Even if he still gave Matthew the third degree."

"He did?" I croaked. "When?"

"Matthew drove down here and came by the club the other day. He was dying to see the facilities after hearing us going on about it for months. We showed him around and before I knew what was happening, Cam had him sitting down in one of the meeting rooms." She huffed out a laugh. "He got really graphic about how well he knew every muscle and bone in a body and all the ways he could inflict damage on them." A snort left her. "With only a boot. Or a ball. *He wouldn't even need to get his hands dirty.*" More laughter followed. "Wait. Matthew didn't tell you?"

I blinked at the screen for a second before groaning, "Oh God. No. He didn't, and now I feel . . . horrible. Awful."

"Don't," Adalyn reassured me. "I'm sure Matthew was trying to spare you feeling bad. And honestly? I think he secretly enjoyed it. He kept trying not to smile, and Cam kept trying not to be aggravated by that. It was cute."

I didn't think it was. I also didn't understand how Matthew hadn't said a word. "Is Cam . . . angry at me?"

Her head tilted, shoulder-length dark waves moving with the gesture. "Cam's just protective of you. I think because he was there when you were engaged to Ricky and because he knows enough of the rest. You're also the reason he moved to Green Oak, and therefore, the reason why we met. So I think you'll just have to deal with the fact he's not going to back down. Once he makes up his mind, he's immovable. And in this case, that's promising retribution if you're hurt."

"Right," I said, feeling my throat work around a lump. "I'm so . . ." Lucky to have them. So scared to lose them. So determined to spare them any unnecessary hardships. "Flattered. And I think I deserve the third degree too."

"Are you going to break his heart?" Adalyn asked.

The question caught me so off guard I stumbled. "No." Because no hearts were on the line. Only an engagement that wasn't meant to last.

"Okay."

Okay. That was it? "I'm . . ."

"You're overwhelmed," Adalyn finished for me. "And I get it. The attention is a lot. If anyone gets it, it's me, I swear. I've been a meme in the past. And Cam has been in the spotlight enough time to get it too. That's why we're offering our support, from any distance you're comfortable with, and in any way we can." I frowned at her choice of words, but she was quick to add, "I just hope this doesn't ruin the excitement of the engagement?"

"It doesn't. I'm just a little overwhelmed, you're right. And no, if anything, I just hope the timing of the news has the opposite effect and it makes everything a little less bad." Or makes them go away. "Like Bobbi said."

"I don't like that she's putting that pressure on you. And I could take Bobbi Shark," Adalyn offered. Her expression was serious. Very bodyguard-ish, just like I'd feared. "If she gives you trouble. You know I could. I can take Dad, too. I know he's talking about being part of the wedding, but if you—"

"It's okay," I interjected. "I swear. You already have so much on your plate." And I really didn't want to discuss Andrew. Or Bobbi. Or any of this. "Are you still struggling with the development programs?"

Adalyn pursed her lips. "We are. It's hard to cater to so many different age brackets with the workforce we currently have. We had a big influx of sign-ups from out of state since Dad's *Time* piece. Dad gave us a shout-out we didn't expect to get, and it's a blessing and a little bit of a curse. We're trying to accommodate as many—" She tapped on her phone screen. "One sec. It's Cam."

"Go," I told her. "I'm sure it's important. And I need to take these." I lifted the basket I'd placed on the copilot seat. "Muffins. To Robbie, as an apology. And tomorrow, I'll give another basket to Bobbi. Also as an apology." Adalyn arched her brows in question, dark eyes filled with curiosity. "There was an incident with a matcha latte. I'll tell you some other day. I'm running a goat yoga class in ten minutes anyway."

"Okay," she said with a small smile. "I would press for that story, but I really do need to go. Cam only texts when it's important." I nodded my head, already throwing the driver's door open, when Adalyn said, "Hey Josie?"

"Yeah?"

"I'm really happy about the two of you. And I get it. Why you hid it from me. It hurts a little, but this whole sister thing is new for me too. I've never had a sibling before, and some days I don't know how to have one. I would have definitely freaked out at the possibility of ruining things with you."

A weight seemed to lift off my shoulders, though for the wrong reasons. Adalyn didn't mean it the way I wished. But I chose to believe that when the time came, she'd remember her words. "I love you. Give Cam a hug. Good luck!"

"You didn't have to," Robbie said, taking the basket off my hands.

I learned early in life that a basket of freshly baked mini muffins would always smooth out the sharpest of edges. Liz Moore's had been known across all the county, and mine weren't that far from Mom's. Or at the very least, they'd never failed me. "I think I really do."

"I should be the one apologizing. I lost it for a second there." He shook his head. "I swear I didn't do anything to the latte. I did consider it, though, which is just as bad. That woman . . . She's something else. And María has been picking up on everything lately. She's no longer my baby girl, I'm afraid."

She really wasn't. The kid had always been sharp and mature for her age in her own way. Which I *knew* was a product of losing her mom so early in life. The weight of which I could see right now in Robbie's gaze.

"You know María is her own person," I countered with an easy smile. "Even if she is eleven years old. There's nothing you could have done to stop her if she thought Bobbi deserved a matcha latte with a pinch of tabasco. We all but invaded your property. So the muffins are the least I could do. Bobbi's my responsibility."

He sighed. "You're not responsible for her actions. Don't put that on yourself, Josie." He stole a glance at the group of people behind me. "Anyway. How was the class? Did any of the goats give you a hard time? The new kids have been a complete nightmare, and I was hesitant to have them out today."

"No hardships to report," I said with a little salute. "I love those furry monsters rolling around the mats." I threw him a wink. "And the baby goats, too."

Robbie laughed in response, and I felt an ease, a sense of normalcy I'd been missing these past few days. This was one of the things I loved about my life in Green Oak. The apparent simplicity I was always working on spicing up. I ran activities like goat yoga—or Green Oak's Goat Happy Hour, as it was advertised in our pamphlet—pottery night; pre- and postgame get-togethers, no matter if the Warriors won or lost; and seasonal fun events like the haunted pumpkin patch, the star of our Fall Fest. Mayor or not, I adored doing all of that. It was my way to show up for my community. Just like I had today with the muffins for the Vasquezes after Bobbi hijacked their farm. Change, as I loved to think, challenged you in a way not much else would. But I'd had enough of that this week. A girl still needed something to hold on to when the road bent and turned a little too much. Yoga, muffins, baby goats.

"All right." I tugged at the towel around my neck. "I should probably let you get back to it and throw a hoodie on before I cool off. I'm so swea—"

Lips brushed against my cheek, just as a warm and solid body gently eased against my back.

My spine stiffened with surprise.

"Hi, *babycakes*," was murmured in my ear.

Matthew, my mind screamed. Fiancé. Engagement. Ring.

"Hi," I croaked. "Mattsie-Boo?"

Matthew laughed easily, and before I could grimace at myself, his arm snaked around my front, palm slipping under the towel and setting up camp over my collarbone. I felt myself flush. Toes to the roots of my hair.

"Robbie," Matthew said in acknowledgment before switching his voice back to . . . his fiancé voice? "Did I miss the class? Damn, I was hoping to make at least the last few minutes. Mmh, I would have loved to watch."

My lips twitched a few times, dazed by everything, really. That mmh. That voice. The feel of . . . Matthew, suddenly there. Everywhere. Much like during the photoshoot, when we'd been against a fence, and he'd been—I stopped myself.

"Boy," I said with an awkward-sounding chuckle. "You missed nothing. Just me, sweating like a glassblower's *arse,* like Cameron would say."

I really did grimace then. Cameron had never said that.

"Cute," Matthew said, and I swore I could hear the smile on that word. "And sweaty. Just how I like."

A laugh seemed to be strangled out of me before I blurted out a "Yummy."

Yummy?

Robbie shot me a worried glance.

Fair. I couldn't understand how, but that kiss on the cheek had made me short-circuit. Which wasn't good. I loved PDA, and everyone in town knew that. Under normal circumstances, I would have lit up and turned in Matthew's arms, planting a kiss on his mouth. But I was pretty sure I'd collapse to the ground if I did that. Which . . . was worse than bad. Maybe we needed rules. Guidelines. A . . . plan, too, after Adalyn asked me if I was going to break his heart, and Matthew getting the third degree from Cameron. This engagement needed a Terms and Conditions. Yes.

"Do you mind if I steal my fiancée?" Matthew asked the other man, snagging my attention back. "She's been out all day and I'm a needy man."

"Absolutely," Robbie said with a smile, already walking off. "I'll put these in a safe place before María runs through them in the blink of an eye."

I nodded my head, watching the man leave in the direction of the house.

"Hi," Matthew said after a beat. As if he hadn't done all that cheek-kissing and arm wrapping and suggestive commenting about my sweat. He moved, coming around to face me. "Was that a basket of muffins?"

The sight of the sun shining on him, surrounded by the greenery of the farm and slopes beyond, disarmed me. "You're wearing your glasses," I heard myself point out. Surprise registered in Matthew's expression. Okay. That had been a little out of the blue. "You hardly ever wear them. They're nice. And they momentarily distracted me, I guess."

Matthew's smile was hesitant at first, but big and smug once it fully parted his face. "You're wearing a pretty distracting workout set yourself, *shortcake*."

I hoped the slight flush that his words brought back to my skin wasn't as obvious as it felt. "I don't think the cake thing is going to work," I commented with a shrug. "And thanks. I'm feeling exactly how tight my clothes are." I also knew he could be referring to the blinding shade of pink of the leggings and top, and not the way my body looked in it, but what did that matter in the big scheme of things? "Those were my apology muffins in Robbie's hands. And you kissed me on the cheek. I think we need rules for things like that."

"Things like you calling me 'Mattsie-Boo'?"

"It was the best I could do," I countered. "You caught me off guard."

"With my kiss. On the cheek. That we need rules for."

I could see the amusement in his eyes, so I shot him a glance.

"With your presence. But yes. Did Bobbi send you or are you here to talk about Page Nine?"

His brows arched. "I'm your fiancé. I'm here to walk you home."

My chest did a weird thing. Odd enough for me to know that it wasn't only about the nice gesture. Strong enough for me to know we really needed that conversation about rules and a plan. "A walk home sounds great," I said. "I'll just have to let Robbie know that I'm leaving. Goat Happy Hour runs for another hour, and I usually hang around. It's mostly the kids petting them and hanging out, but baby goats can be a bit of a handful."

"Let's stay, then," Matthew offered.

I glanced at his clothes. Worn jeans, those Chelsea boots I'd seen a few times on him, and a basic tee under a corduroy overshirt. "I'd hate for you to get all messy or your clothes covered in goat hair." I never minded having to do a little extra laundry, but the last time I'd brought a man to something like this had taught me that not everyone did.

"You underestimate how much I love a good mess."

My silly mind took in that glint in his eyes and ran with the implications of it. A different part of me too, based on the questions that rose to the tip of my tongue.

"Let's go," Matthew insisted. Was that genuine excitement in his voice? He nodded his head toward the group gathered around the furry little monsters, setting his palm at the small of my back. "Let's hang out with the goats, then I'll walk you home."

Matthew hadn't lied.

He loved a good mess.

He hadn't even blinked at the mud stains on his white tee, or the grass and goat hair scattered all over his jeans. Even when María had approached with Pedro—a teacup pig and the newest addition to the Vasquez family that had inspired my proposal story that night on the porch—Matthew hadn't hesitated to snatch him up in his arms.

Based on how my lower belly had perked up at the sight, I seemed to be into glasses-wearing men holding tiny farm animals. Which shouldn't be surprising. I loved tiny farm animals. I'd just never felt this invested in a pair of arms holding them. Much less, arms belonging to a blond man.

I didn't think I'd ever date a blond. Not that I was dating one now. I—

I was probably ovulating. That had to be the explanation for why I couldn't stop gaping at Matthew like I would at a celebrity doing one of those puppy interviews. Only this wasn't a celeb. This was my fiancé. Matthew Flanagan, who was blond and who I was not technically dating. Sitting on the grass with a mini pig called Pedro Pigscal.

"You should snap a picture."

My gaze bounced from Pedro's pink snout to Matthew's eyes. "What?"

"Just saying," he offered, rearranging Pedro in his arms. "That way you could stare at it. Me. And little Pedro. Whenever you please." He winked. "And whenever you need."

I snorted. Or tried to. He really was good at this whole flirting thing. I shook my head. "I think I've had enough staring at a picture to last me a few weeks."

Matthew sobered up. "How do you feel about that?"

That. Page Nine. Us on it. "It's a good picture. It could have been a lot worse." I brushed back a lock of hair that had come out of my ponytail, tucking it behind my ear. "It's very believable."

And I wondered what his family, friends, anyone who knew him thought of it. But the question was getting stuck every time I tried to summon it.

"You looked beautiful."

My breath left me, and I had to get my head in check with the way my heart had skipped a beat. "We looked flustered. And horny. Like Bobbi said. I wouldn't exactly call that beautiful."

His head tilted. "It's a beautiful look on you."

Another beat was skipped, and then there was a beat in which we just looked at each other. Me, flushed. Again. And Matthew, easy. Casual. As if he hadn't just complimented me again.

"Thanks," I finally answered.

"You haven't told me how you feel."

"You didn't tell me Cameron gave you the third degree," I threw back at him. "Over this. Us."

His smile was slow and bashful. A nice surprise. "That's because it wasn't a big deal. And I kind of enjoyed it."

"That's what Adalyn said," I admitted. And God, there were so many things I could or should have said then, but I didn't. I didn't jump straight to the conversation we should have been having, either. "Smile bigger for me?" I asked, and before he knew what was coming, my phone was on his face and I was snapping those pictures he'd mentioned.

Matthew pursed his lips. "I thought you were done with that?"

"Bobbi would love this," I said with a shrug. I went up on my knees and scooted closer, pointing the camera at him from a new angle. I schooled my face into a blank expression, trying to imitate her. "Domestic pictures. Chop chop. Tick tock. More stroking, less chatting. And can you look more hot and less depressed?"

Matthew narrowed his eyes at me.

"Not hot enough," I reported after checking some of them. "You look like Pedro peed in your—"

"Get over here," he said. And suddenly, I was dragged down onto the grass by a strong arm and planted right beside Pedro Pigscal.

On Matthew's lap.

I swallowed at the unforeseen change, at what I felt at my back, at the fact I was sharing a lap—my fiancé's—with a teacup pig. Giggling came from our left. María Vasquez and a few kids. A few people stared, too. Robbie, who was back, smirked to himself.

I cleared my throat. "I hope you don't try this with Bobbi."

"Jealous?" Matthew asked. But I could hear the amusement in his words. I could also *feel* those words rumbling in his chest.

Bracing my hands on his legs, I rearranged myself and snatched Pedro so he'd rest more comfortably on my lap. "More like intrigued at the idea of whether she would snap you in two like a twig if you did," I said. At which he chuckled. "Now, if you don't mind telling me why I'm sitting on you?"

"Domestic pictures." One of his arms came around my waist, his hand latching on to my side. I went very still, only my chest moving with the breath I took. "Is this okay, Josie?"

It wasn't. Not really. But it was in the way he meant. "Yeah."

"I wanted to make sure," he offered. His head came down a little, his voice growing closer. "You didn't seem to appreciate that kiss on the cheek."

Thing was, I had. "How do you want to do this?" I asked, decidedly ignoring that. I felt Matthew's hum against my back, and I realized in that instant that I was spending a lot of time in this man's arms lately, and a lot more was to come. So maybe it was time for me to stop acting surprised. "Hold on," I said before Matthew could suggest how to approach the task at hand. I tugged at my hoodie, slipping it off over my head. "Now. I didn't splurge on these yoga clothes for nothing."

Two things happened at the same time. Matthew's hand went back to its place on my waist, only now, thanks to my crop top and the missing layer, that was my skin. His fingers spread, and a murmured word I couldn't make out dropped from his lips.

My belly fluttered, then dipped. And I had no choice but to

bring my phone up in the air just so I wouldn't think of that. Matthew's free hand wrapped around my smaller one. The warmth of his palm, his skin against mine, once more overwhelming me.

I watched as his thumb changed the settings of the camera and he turned around the phone. He snapped a couple of photos. And not satisfied with that, he shifted the angle of our arms and took some more.

When he brought both our arms down, I felt so warm—sandwiched between the animal in my arms and the man at my back—and so dazed—by how nice, how natural, how confusing—the last minute had felt, that I didn't even know if I'd smiled at all.

"I think those will do," Matthew murmured, his voice deep and almost startling in a way I didn't even mind.

I took the opportunity to elegantly slip out and return to a spot on the grass. At a safe distance. I tapped on my gallery and studied the results.

Hot freaking damn.

We looked . . . so hot. So absolutely real, too, with Matthew's eyes peeking down at me, and the corners of my lips parting my flushed cheeks. There were also a couple of shots of him looking up at the camera while my gaze stayed cast down on Pedro. And one where he was openly checking me out.

My cleavage.

I pursed my lips to hide my delight. I had been very serious about splurging on athleisure, this was the least he could do.

"Bobbi would be proud," I told him. As casually as I could. "You really seem to know what you're doing, too. With the selfies. Should Bobbi be worried a Hinge account is going to pop up?" *Should I?*

A strange chuckle left him as he placed Pedro back on the grass and patted his jeans with his hands. "I've never been a big fan of dating apps. I'm a little too blunt for them." He braced his arms on his knees and met my gaze. "I managed socials at work. Just for a while. It's a savage world that makes you learn fast. I picked up a few tricks from the guy they brought in, though. And it was from watching him take the selfies, definitely not me."

I wanted to ask him so many different things about that that I didn't even know where to start. What exactly had he been doing? What was his plan now that he was unemployed? How long had he managed socials? I'd been sure he'd been doing something else. Something that had to do with writing. Was he applying to anything now? And if so, where?

But how did any of that concern me? How much prodding could I do without intruding or him closing off? Could I help him in any way? Make up for everything else? And why had he shut down the two times I asked?

"I could pay you, you know?" I blurted out.

Matthew frowned.

"For this," I said. "For what we're doing."

He seemed as surprised by the offer as I was appalled by my poor delivery. A strange laugh left him. "What are we doing exactly?"

I shot him a bland look.

"Why would you want to pay me?" he asked, sobering. "What happened to *it's you I need to do this. Be my fiancé. Oh Matthew, please.*"

My cheeks warmed. I knew what he was doing, as serious as he looked or sounded. "I never said *Oh Matthew, please* like that." I swallowed, and the quality of his gaze changed. "And I'm offering because you deserve to get something out of it. I didn't think of that when I asked you for help, but it's the least I can do. You should get something in exchange. I'm asking a lot of you. Having your picture on the internet. Your time and energy. That must have a cost."

"You're making me feel like an escort, sweetheart," he told me, but his tone wasn't harsh, or hurt. His words seemed resigned more than anything. "I can freelance until I find something else. From here. That was the plan, anyway." His jaw clenched for an instant. "It's sweet of you to offer compensation for the hardship of touching you, kissing your cheek, or pretending I have the right to pull you on my lap just because I want to. All of which I agreed to do, by the way."

"Okay," I said with a nod. "That's fair. I just wanted to make sure you didn't think I was taking advantage of you."

"You aren't, Josie."

"Do you . . . want help with the job hunt?"

"It's all right."

"I could really help."

His only response was a small smile. A bitter one. Or a sad one. I wasn't sure. I was scared to push him for more and of him saying something I didn't want to hear. Like how he might have already found something and already had a departure date. Or how I couldn't be taking advantage of him when it was me who needed his help.

"We should talk about the terms, then," I told him, lowering my voice. "The plan. The rules of engagement. We never did with how . . . fast everything unraveled, and I think we should."

"What about them?"

The brown in his eyes flared, so I averted my gaze. My eyes fell on one of my hands as they rested on my thighs. "We're not getting married," I said. The ring caught the light of the sun, making it impossible for me not to look at it while I spoke. "I just want to appease whatever fear you might have. There won't be a wedding on December first. That date just serves whatever narrative Bobbi wants to create. We're more than a month away, and a professional is handling things. Gossip is fickle. That stuff dies out quickly. People can't possibly be invested in someone like me for long."

"Why not?"

I glanced back at him. "Because there are more important or scandalous things in the world than some small-town girl who happens to share DNA with a powerful man, and who never gathered the courage to say I do."

"Is that what happened? With your exes?"

Yes. But also, no. It was a complicated and convoluted answer I didn't have the heart to give him right now. Or the courage. "We'll wait a sensible amount of time and break things off," I said, noticing the way he sighed when I deflected. "It'll be a clean, friendly breakup that will allow us to continue to coexist. We're both in Adalyn's and Cameron's lives for the long run and neither of us wants to hurt them. So we do that, and soon enough it'll be like nothing ever happened." I remembered Adalyn's words. "No hearts will be broken anyway. So it'll be fine."

"Okay," he said with a nod.

My brows furrowed. No remarks? "I know it'll be a little awkward to be friends after that, but we'll be fine. I'm friends with all—almost all of my exes."

Matthew clasped his hands as they hung between his knees, glancing at me over them. "All right. What else?"

"Kissing," I croaked. "It's obvious we're bound to kiss, eventually, so let's not fight it. On the cheek, like earlier, should be fine." I straightened my back. Squared my shoulders. "On the mouth only if we must. No one died over lips on lips, but unless it is really necessary . . ."

He huffed out a chuckle I didn't understand. "Next rule?"

"We're obviously handsy." My face heated up, leaving my exposed arms and section of my belly running a little colder. "I know I am. And I think you are too, from what I've seen. It's working in our favor so . . . I don't think we need rules about this. Touching is not like kissing. It doesn't need to mean anything. Unless you're . . . groping my ass or something. You could, but that needs a reason and a warning, maybe? We've touched plenty already and we're fine." A strange shiver ran down my arms. "Right?"

"Right. We're fine."

I waited for him to elaborate, and when he didn't, I shifted in my spot. I waited, crossing my legs and giving Matthew time if that was what he needed.

He didn't add anything.

"You are awfully agreeable for someone I had to seduce and trick into this. No remarks? No demands? No rules that you want to add?"

A gust of wind picked up, hitting my skin and making me wince a little, just as he finally looked like he wanted to add something. He came up on his knees. "Arms up," he said.

I frowned at him, and he moved, coming closer and snatching up the hoodie I discarded when we'd taken the pictures. He held it in his hands, positioning it above me before I could take it from him. The gesture was sweet, and exactly what everyone around us would expect him to do. Without complaining, I raised my arms and met his gaze, waiting for him to slip the sleeves around them. He did, and in one gentle and determined tug of pink fabric, it was going over my head.

"That's all?" Matthew asked, only when the hoodie was secured around me. I noticed how he didn't deny that I had to seduce and trick him into this. But that was fine. I could own that bit. "Those are your three rules? We don't get married but stay friends. We kiss if we must. We can touch."

That was a very condensed version of them but . . . "Except uncalled-for-ass-groping."

"We touch. Except uncalled-for-ass-groping," he repeated.

"Yes," I said, tempted to correct him again. We *can* touch. Not *we touch*. But I didn't. "All right. Great. I feel a little better now that we've talked about this. Phew."

Matthew didn't say anything for a few moments, then one of those chuckles left him with a breath. "I'm happy to hear you feel better." A pause. "My . . . *ladybug*?"

I wrinkled my nose at him, hiding how *relieved* I was that he'd said that. "Nope," I told him. "You're going to have to keep trying."

It was slow, maybe a little too small, but Matthew gave me a smile. "I will persist, then."

And just as my lips were bending to return it, my phone chimed with a message.

BOBBI: Urgent. Call me.

"She can wait," Matthew said. I looked back at him and found that smile gone. "Let me walk you home first."

Let me walk you home first.

First . . . before what? I should have asked. But I didn't.

It didn't matter.

So I ignored the message and let Matthew bring me to my feet after he stood up. I could deal with Bobbi later. Now I wanted to bask in the little normalcy today had brought, and the way things seemed a little clearer between us. Plus, I'd been looking forward to that walk back home with him.

Even though my truck was parked outside the farm.

CHAPTER NINE

The Sharkie I'd been drinking almost left me through my nose.

"Josie?" Gabriel asked from the other side of the counter. "You good, honey?"

I patted my chest, then appeased both my friend and the concerned glances from my customers with a wave. "Yes," I rushed. "Sure. I just got a text from Adalyn."

"Oh, nice." Gabriel smiled. "What did she say?"

I glanced down at the notification.

ADALYN: Did you know Dad is coming?

"She . . ." I trailed off. "Just some random stuff. About the club."

Gabriel's brows arched. "That's exactly what I mean. You were never this guarded and . . . secretive, Josie. And I'm starting to get a little worried. Not about having to read—or hear—all the details about your life on some gossip page, but about whether this whole thing is starting to get to you."

I nodded my head slowly, my brain still hung up on that text. "Can you give me a sec?"

My friend huffed out a "Sure," and I tapped on Adalyn's message.

JOSIE: What do you mean Andrew's coming?

ADALYN: He's on his way to NC. His assistant just emailed.

My knees buckled under my weight for a second, making me stumble against the counter of Josie's Joint.

"Whoa," Gabriel called. "Are you okay? What was that? Josie—"

I stopped him with a big, bright smile. "I'm perfect. Just tripped over a milk carton. You know I get clumsy when I'm hungry, and it's almost lunchtime. Do you want something to eat? I think I'm going to switch on the jumbo sandwich grill. Get us two nice, big sandwiches."

Gabriel stared at me for a long moment. "Okay?"

"Awesome!" I chirped. "Now just give me a sec."

His lips popped open, but I was already turning around, phone in hand.

JOSIE: On his way now? As in today? Or on his way as in, maybe soon/eventually?

ADALYN: He's already boarded the flight and will land at some point this afternoon in Charlotte.

A strange sound escaped me. Or maybe it didn't. I was almost sure I had stopped breathing. I . . . Shit. Shoot. Crap. I brought my hand to my forehead, feeling a little faint. Andrew was on his way. To North Carolina. To Green Oak. And I—

I switched chats, purely on automatic. Matthew's opened.

There weren't any texts. My fingers moved over the keyboard. I didn't know why or how Matthew could help, but a very specific part of my brain was in charge and it was the one typing away. I hit send.

A new notification popped up. My sister. I switched back to her chat.

ADALYN: Are you okay? Do you want me to call you?

ADALYN: Do you want me to drive up to Green Oak? I can be there in an hour. I'll stay with you.

JOSIE: No.

Shoot. I'd hit send too fast. It sounded so harsh. I took a deep breath and told myself to chill. This was just Andrew. My father. Coming to my state and my town. I didn't need to make a big deal out of it.

JOSIE: I'm good, I promise. 🙂

JOSIE: It just caught me off guard. I had no idea he was coming.

Just as I typed that, I realized the reason why I probably didn't. Bobbi's text. I'd never answered or called her back. Not last night after Matthew walked me home, or this morning. I'd been meaning to, I'd just . . . put it off a little longer. Last time there'd been an emergency, I'd found out I was a chess piece in some new internet series two strangers were recounting to the country.

JOSIE: I'll talk to Bobbi.

ADALYN: How about you call Matthew instead? He should be with you right now. Promise me to lean on him when things get heavy with Dad.

There was so much weight behind Adalyn's text. Unsaid things. Like how we both knew this was the first time Andrew was returning to Green Oak since he'd . . . conceived me. Since that trip almost three decades ago. We both knew this would be the first time I'd see him in the flesh and not through the screen of my laptop.

My belly felt like it had just filled with wasps.

JOSIE: Already done. 🙂 I'll catch you later, okay? Josie's is packed.

I stared at the screen of my phone, debating whether to call Matthew or leave it at that text I'd sent. I swapped chats. My message had been read. He'd seen it, but he hadn't answered. That was fine. It was a little jumbly. It contained stuff like exclamation points, question marks, a few words, and an SOS. He probably thought I was being dramatic, and what I felt in my chest probably wasn't disappointment. Or hurt. It was . . . concern.

Because Andrew was on his way. To Green Oak.

"Josie?" Gabriel called from behind the counter. "You've been standing there for a few minutes, and I'm wondering if I should come get you or just give you more time to sieve through whatever you're going through. Can you let me know so we avoid having to get Grandpa Moe? His grumpy ass is unbearable lately."

I squared my shoulders, and when I turned around, it was with a smile. "Wedding drama," I said as an explanation. I knew from experience that could excuse almost anything. "Adalyn was checking some things for me. Things that have to do with the guest list."

"I thought you said it was club stuff," he countered with a frown.

Shit. "Well, I can't have the entirety of a youth soccer club sitting at my wedding, now, can I?"

"I guess not," Gabriel commented. His face transformed, and he was suddenly beaming at me. "Wait. Does that mean you guys have a date?"

I thought of Bobbi's temporary date. December first. I also thought of our new rules. We don't get married. "Nope," I quipped. "Oh hey, that's our Green Warriors coming into the café. You know what that means: after-game smoothies."

The group of kids in green and black training gear made their way to their usual spot, all but María and Juniper taking a seat at the table. The two kids approached us.

"Hi, Miss Josie!" María quipped. "Hi, Mr. Gabriel!"

"Hi, Dad," Juniper said, planting a kiss on Gabriel's cheek. "Hi, Miss Josie."

I pushed away from the counter, welcoming the distraction. "Hi, girls. I was just texting Adalyn, and she says to give the two of you a hug. She misses you and the team a whole lot."

María beamed at the mention of my sister. "Oh, I miss her too! I'll make sure to send her a selfie of me and Pedro Pigscal. And all the photos I have of him with Brandy." She scrunched her face. "I can't wait to introduce her and Coach Cam to Pedro." She pointed at my cup. "Oh. Can I get one of those?"

"That's going to be a no," I answered with a laugh. "Way too much caffeine in it. And other . . . stuff that's not good for you. You guys need to rehydrate."

"I'm eleven," she complained, as Gabriel and I shared a glance. "I'm not a kid anymore. And Dad lets me have a sip of coffee every once in a while."

I arched my brows.

"Fine," she relented. "When he's not looking. It tastes like monkey butt, honestly, so I thought yours would be nicer. Adults are weird." She shrugged a shoulder. "So how's Mr. Matthew? You know what I was thinking the other day? That you should get married at the farm! Wouldn't that be amazing? We could have a petting zoo for the guests. And all the space in the world to dance. Dad keeps all the things from the fairs and markets in the old barn, so we could even hang the Christmas lights. Oh, and use the turkey float from last year's Thanksgiving parade."

Gabriel braced an elbow on the counter. "That would be amazing actually. I always wondered why you never tried to get married here in Green Oak."

Tried to get married, my brain seemed to get hung up on those words.

"I don't think the petting zoo is a good idea," Juniper commented, earning a glance from María. "But we could have a tournament." The two kids beamed at each other. "That way I wouldn't need to wear a dress."

The two girls then launched into a debate about whether one could play soccer in a dress, while at a wedding.

I cleared my throat. "How about I get the smoothies going and throw in a chocolate chip cookie for everyone? Deal?"

Both their faces told me we had a deal.

"Perfect," I concluded. "Give me a min—"

My words were brought to a halt by someone bursting into the coffee shop, shoving the door open so hard that it almost sent the bell atop it flying.

Everyone in Josie's Joint froze. Silence, thick and heavy, settled around the place.

"Matthew?" I croaked.

My fiancé's saucer-sized eyes caught on mine.

He didn't say a word. I didn't think he could, with how heavy he was breathing.

Concern surged, and my gaze dipped, as if searching for whatever was wrong instead of asking. It was a reflex. Something one does when alert. First inspect, then ask. Look for any signs of bodily harm. Last time someone had burst into Josie's like that, they'd had a garter snake hanging off their calf.

Only there was no snake.

There was . . . skin. So much golden, smooth-looking skin. Arms. Big, toned. And . . . muscles that peeked out of one of those sleeveless tees you saw men working out in, in gym vlogs. I knew those well. And Matthew was standing there, at the entrance of my café, looking like one of the men whose thirst traps I pretended not to save.

I blinked, or maybe I didn't. I couldn't be sure. I didn't think I'd ever been this dazed by a shirt whose sleeves had been ripped off.

"Now I get it," Gabriel whispered from my side. I turned my wide eyes to him. He was smirking. "I would want to keep that just for myself too."

A gurgly-sounding scoff left me.

"Good afternoon," Matthew said, snatching my attention away from the other man . . . Just in time to catch his arm drawing a wave in the air. Every barely concealed muscle moved. "I apologize for the dramatic entrance. I was in what seems like an obvious rush to see my . . . Josie. My fiancée, Josie. Who's standing there, looking beautiful and definitely not in distress or in any kind of life-threatening emergency that would have me sprinting here in slightly inappropriate workout attire, based on the looks on everyone's faces." He met my gaze. "Can we have a word, *sugar snap*?"

Every head turned in my direction in one single joined motion.

I should have cared. Probably. But it was funny how my brain was very selectively picking apart Matthew's words and focusing on very specific ones. *My Josie. My fiancée, Josie.*

Who's standing there looking beautiful.

Beautiful.

Some measure of heat climbed to my face. And those rounded shoulders he was flashing half the town must have done some damage to my brain cells because all I could think of was that I couldn't recall what I'd thrown on this morning. Or if I'd done my makeup. I only remembered braiding my hair. I glanced down to check myself. Right. My palazzo pants and silk blouse. My ass looked very nice in these. But I was standing behind the counter so he couldn't possibly know that. I dragged my attention back to the front, somewhat aware that it was my turn to say something.

"I—"

"So love really makes you silly, huh?" María observed. "Should I tell Mr. Matthew everyone can see his *boobies,* or will you do that, Miss Josie?"

My eyes widened for a second at the kid's words. Boobies. It wasn't very different from the man boobs I'd used to describe his pecs the morning he'd woken up on my couch. But there hadn't been dozens of people around. Just us. And now everyone's attention was back on Matthew. On his kinda visible chest as he threw his head back and laughed. Laughed.

I pushed aside how very good his reaction made me feel. How much it warmed my heart that he didn't care or find offense. "All right, everyone," I said, clapping my hands. "How about we all stop ogling my fiancé's pectoral muscles and continue about our business? We have things we'd like to discuss. In private."

The usual murmur of chatter picked up, but not even half the heads in the sitting area turned away as Matthew crossed the shop to where I was.

Gabriel sent María and Juniper away to rejoin the group of girls, and then leaned his elbows on the counter. His chin rested on his fists. I arched my brows in question. "Oh, I'm not going anywhere."

"Please?"

He made a show of thinking. "No. I'd rather ask for forgiveness tomorrow. Sorry. You love me enough."

"What is that supposed to mean?"

Matthew reached us, coming to a stop beside Gabriel. "Hi, I'm M—"

"Matthew, Josie's new man. Hi, hello. We missed each other at the game. I'm Gabriel. Your newest best friend." Gabriel winked. I panicked. "Whatever you need to know about our Josie, you ask me. Any story, detail, or anecdote. No matter how crazy or intrusive. I'm your man. I know all the stuff, like that time she got so drunk she got her house confused with Otto's and fell asleep in his tub, or when she lost her v—"

I croaked out a loud, squeaky laugh. "Let's take this into the back room," I rushed out, walking around the counter. "Matthew? *Please.* And Gabriel, I'll see you later."

My so-called friend sent me a dirty look. And when my eyes turned to my fiancé, he sent me an amused one. I wasn't amused, but I was standing close enough for my gaze to hopelessly dip down to his arms. Again. Ugh. They were very nice. I whirled on my heels with a silent curse and led my fiancé away, vowing to stop objectifying him.

I stopped at the door we'd been headed for, took one deep inhale, closed my hand around the knob, twisted it open, and shoved Matthew inside.

His back hit one of the shelves I knew stood between three and four feet from the door. "What the . . ." Matthew started. I shut the door behind me and raised my hand; the one lightbulb above us lit up with a click. Matthew's frown materialized. He blinked. "Did you bring me into a supply closet?"

Yes.

And it seemed awfully small with Matthew in it.

"So . . . you wanted to talk?"

Matthew stared at me. For one, two, three, ten seconds. At least. Then he released a long exhale, making some of my hair move. That was how close we were standing. I decided to ignore space and focused on how minty his breath was.

"So there's no back shop," he finally said.

"I do have a back supply closet, though," I countered. "And a nosy friend who is no longer my friend. And very nosy customers. You wanted to have a word. So what is it?"

Matthew's brows furrowed even more. It wasn't a scowl, but he still didn't look satisfied with any of the explaining I'd just done.

"Listen," I said, shifting on my feet. My hip hit something, a shelf, making me move away. Warmth hit my other side. *Matthew's warmth.* "You made a very dramatic entrance into a packed establishment. It threw me off and I did my best to handle the situation. I improvised with the back room comment to give ourselves some privacy. Away from them, and especially Gabriel. To talk. Does it really matter that I don't have one? Everyone knows that anyway."

He held his breath for like a second, then huffed out a laugh. "Everyone knows that anyway?" he repeated, and I gave him a nod. "Do you really believe they'll think you brought me into a dark closet to talk?"

My lips parted with the realization. "Oh." That was a very good point. I was terribly off my game lately. "We're engaged," I whispered loudly. "To be married. So it wouldn't be that strange for us to, you know, want to sneak out and *get each other's kettle meddled with,* if you know what I—"

His finger fell gently on my lips, sending my whole body into shock. "No cute euphemisms for sex, please. I'm trying my goddamn best here, Josie, but I don't think I'll be able to stay mad at you if you get all sugary-sweet."

Shock melted away, giving way to a strange kind of warmth. And as much as I tried to ignore it, it only got worse when Matthew's hand shuffled to the side, his finger leaving my mouth and his palm settling on the side of my neck. "You're mad?" I breathed out.

"You sent me an SOS," Matthew explained, his brow knotting again. The urgency with which he'd stormed in returned to his eyes. "You can't text me an SOS when there's no real emergency. Do you have any idea how—" He shook his head. "I *ran* down here. From the lodge. I thought something was wrong. You wrote *I need you.*"

The sensation in my stomach skipped, realization rippling. "So that's why you're wearing a slutty shirt and slutty sweats?" My voice turned to a whisper. "You were working out? You didn't leave me on read?"

My heart plunked to the ground at my own words. I hadn't meant to say that, and hearing it left me a little off-balance. Glass clinked together behind me, and our bodies drew closer together. Mine, to move away from the rack. And Matthew's, to stabilize me.

"Why are you so surprised?" he asked, the heat coming off him, and the palm still at the base of my neck making me warm.

"I don't know," I said, immediately realizing it was a lie. I did know. "I guess I assumed you were done with my dramatics. Most people don't take an all-caps message from me very seriously. So I assumed you'd . . . call. Or text. Later." The breath he let out hit my cheek, and I shivered a little, even when it felt so incredibly hot in the tiny room. "You didn't need to drop what you were doing and come rescue me. Next time I text an SOS just . . . maybe put on a hoodie and calmly make your way down to me instead?"

His thumb moved, grazing the underside of my jaw. "You can't send me an SOS, then, Josie. An SOS means I fucking run."

My heart skipped a beat. "You're being very rigid about this," I told him, and boy, did my voice come out rocky. "It was just a text."

"I am rigid when it comes to important things," he conceded. And when he stepped even closer, I could feel more than his breath falling on my skin. I could scent the perspiration on him. The proof of the exertion. I could touch his skin, too. If I dared to. I could see how it felt under my fingertips. Damp? Dry? Sticky? As smooth as it looked? "There are rules for this, Josie. It's the first thing I taught my little sisters when they started going out. I don't take this shit lightly, and no one else should either."

His little sisters. Did he see me as such? Not as a sibling, but as someone whose protection he was responsible for? The thought both chilled and warmed my skin. "Is that why you didn't hesitate to help me that first night on my porch?" *When you didn't know who I was.*

"Oh, I hesitated," he answered, and I knew he was being sincere. His voice always went down. "Believe me, I was tempted to turn around and run."

But he didn't. Because I seemed like I was in trouble, and he had sisters and took SOS texts very seriously. God, he was such a good guy. I wished . . . we were under different circumstances. Normal ones. Circumstances that would allow us to . . . to what, Josie?

I shook my head. "If it makes you any less mad, there is an emergency of sorts," I murmured, my chest suddenly feeling . . . tender. Soft to the touch. Vulnerable. *He'd run down here. Run. For me.* "It's not exactly life-threatening. But it's almost as bad: Andrew's coming."

"Of course he is," he muttered under his breath. "Is that what Bobbi wanted last night?"

"I wouldn't know," I admitted. "I kind of ignored her text. Yesterday was a good day, and I wanted that to last a little longer."

Matthew's expression softened, and I didn't want to read too much into it, but I swore I could see a hint of smugness, as if he was proud of me for making Bobbi wait.

"Adalyn offered to drive to Green Oak," I added. "To be with me."

Matthew seemed to consider my words, then he said, "Is she going to?"

"I told her she didn't have to." I bit my lip, musing over whether to admit I'd texted him before she offered. "That I had you," I whispered. "That I'd already called you. And here we are."

His brows met. In concentration or determination, I couldn't know, because his thumb brushed my chin next, distracting me and sending a wave of awareness cascading down my body. It was strange that we'd had this conversation with his palm resting on the side of my neck, and my body had eased right into his touch. Now that peace had been broken by the way he was looking down at me. It was broken by the reminder that all that expanse of skin was a hair-thin distance from my hands. I wanted to reach out. And according to our rules, I could. Touching was fine. And I would have, if I was sure that wouldn't make me a little selfish, or a bad liar. Because me not being affected if I set my palms on his arms right now? It didn't seem possible.

I flexed my hands at my sides. Then asked, "What are we going to do about this?"

"Can I be honest?" Matthew asked.

I nodded my head, and he let out a little grunt. The sound hit me right in my belly.

"I'm talking real honest," he insisted, head dipping lower, body coming even closer. My back hit the rack behind me, and he regained the distance. "Blunt. Do you think you can take that, Josie?"

"Yes," I breathed out.

"If this were my hometown," he said, words tickling my temple. His hands rose, leaving me and bracing on the rack at my back. "We'd ruffle your hair and come out of this closet pretending I've just fucked you against this shelf right here."

Whoa.

I— My stomach dove right to my feet.

An intense wave of heat climbed up my body before swooshing back down immediately. Images, many of them, bombarded my mind. Of Matthew, hands on the backs of my thighs, rack rattling, me—

A shaky breath exploded out of me. "That seems . . . unnecessary."

His chuckle was amused and dark. Sultry. He knew exactly what was crossing my mind. "Depends on who you ask," he said. "We're sneaking off, aren't we? You're my fiancée. I would want to make use of the opportunity. You said so yourself."

I had. I really had. I was also envisioning it now. And my body was invested in the specifics. My mouth parted, and his eyes jumped to my lips before leaping back up. "I meant what are we going to do about my father. He's getting here today. For all we know, he could be waiting outside when we come out." I shook my head, slowly bringing my thoughts back to the real matter at hand. "I never thought he'd show up so soon." *Or at all,* but I didn't say that.

Matthew leaned back. To have a better look at me if I had to guess. I watched his smile dim but not disappear. "We could still ruffle your hair, and come out of here—"

"Be serious," I told him with a soft pat to his chest. He snatched my wrist with his hand, and I swallowed at the soft contact of his fingers on my skin.

His voice dropped. "I'm always serious."

"You're really not," I countered. "What are we going to do? He thinks we're—" My voice cracked. "Organizing a wedding. What if he wants to get *really* involved. While here? What if he realizes we have no intention of getting married at all? Did you see that planner Bobbi sent us? It's absolutely terrifying. And it's filled with links and stuff, and who knows what else. What if Andrew wants us to actually organize a wedding? *Now?*"

Matthew's words took a moment to come out, but when he finally spoke, they made my heart speed up. "Then we give him that."

CHAPTER TEN

Andrew Underwood didn't show up in Green Oak alone.

He'd arrived with a journalist named Willa Wang, who had done Andrew's piece for *Time,* and who dressed in a range of beiges and carried a little leather notepad she'd been tapping her pen on for the last ten minutes.

She was the woman who called me a *misstep* in a renowned magazine.

Andrew Underwood was also late. To a meeting he'd set up.

But he belonged to a world where certain things couldn't wait. That had to be why the call he was taking in the room next to the living area in the elegant house he was renting outside Green Oak was more important than the four people waiting.

I fidgeted with my fingers in my lap, trying to ignore the sound of both Bobbi's nails tipping and tapping away at her phone, and Willa's pen as it rapped against her notepad. I wondered if she actually scribbled in it or if it was just for show. Maybe it was some kind of trick journalists used to intimidate the truth out of their subjects. Although that sounded more like an interrogation and not the *casual chat* Bobbi had mentioned we were having whenever Andrew got here.

Warmth enveloped my hand, making my breath hitch. Matthew. Obviously. I turned my head, brown eyes meeting mine from his spot beside me on the burgundy couch. He held my gaze, a question in his eyes.

Sorry, I mouthed, deciding he was referring to the fidgeting.

He frowned and shook his head slightly, a soft smile parting his face. He had such a handsome smile. My shoulders eased slightly. "You look beautiful in this dress." His gaze dipped briefly. "Is this tulle?"

"It is," I admitted. My face was flaming. I didn't even know why, just that apparently I wasn't in control of simple bodily functions when this man called me beautiful. "And you . . . look beautiful too." Matthew's brows arched, then a smirk took shape. I lowered my voice a little. "But not too beautiful. You're presentable. The right amount of attractive. And I actually prefer you in your glasses."

The brown in his eyes sparked with interest. His voice went down, and he must have been on a quest to distract me because he said, "I know that now. *Sugarplum.*"

I wrinkled my nose at him before turning toward the other two women with a tense smile. *Sugarplum* wasn't a winner either.

Bobbi's eyes found mine from the settee she was perched on. Her lips were pressed in a line. She was still a little mad at me for ignoring her. And she probably thought my and Matthew's exchange was cringy. I gave her a nod and she answered with more glaring.

"So, Josephine," Willa said, snatching my attention. "How far along are the wedding preparations?"

"They're . . . far enough to be along."

"She means that everything's under control," Bobbi explained. "Especially now that the father of the bride is here."

I couldn't help but stiffen in the plush cushion I was sitting on. Was that why Andrew was here? Gosh, I wished I could pull out my phone and see one more time if I could find the answers in Bobbi's magic W.P. of Hell, or whatever she called it.

"I bet," Willa commented, eyes still on me. "I hope that's not being tainted by all that is being said online." My breath caught on its way in, and I felt Matthew's arm coming around my waist. "I hear planning can be daunting."

"Daunting is one way to put it," I repeated with a smile. "So how long have you been writing for *Time* magazine? Any reason in particular why you've decided to visit the beautiful state of North Carolina?"

"I've worked in the field long enough to know it can't be easy for you to be roped into something like this," Willa answered. She flung her pad open and scribbled a word. "The public eye can be vicious, as I'm sure you've seen with your father. Then your sister. Now you." Her gaze bounced to the man by my side. "Or the two of you, better said."

I wondered what she'd just written down. I wondered if I could see if I squinted my eyes. "That's nothing I—or my fiancé—can't handle," I quipped. Matthew's hand at my hip squeezed as if in confirmation. "We know how to keep busy, block the noise, and stay focused on what's important."

"Like the wedding," Willa concluded, making me think that Bobbi wasn't the only person who believed that a wedding was the solution to every problem. A drop of sweat clung to the nape of my neck, and Willa scribbled some more in her pad. She lifted her head. "Do you mind telling me a little about that?"

Sheesh. For such an aesthetically pleasing–looking woman, she was like a dog with a bone. Reminded me of Bobbi, and we were only ten minutes into this. "What about it?"

"Anything you're comfortable sharing." She shrugged an elegant shoulder, her poise casual. "Returning to your question, that's why I'm here. To learn everything there is about Andrew. We're working on a book, as I'm sure he's told you. I wouldn't call it a biography but more of a recollection of all his accomplishments and failures. We're still finessing the details. For now, all I want is to gain an understanding of his life. That includes you, Josephine. It also includes things like your fiancé, the wedding, Andrew's role in that, or the hometown you two share."

I blinked at the woman. For a long moment.

A book? A . . . memoir, from what she'd described. She was wrong. I was hearing about it for the first time. And the fact that the woman who had called me a misstep was writing it led me to believe she might consider me one of those failures she'd mentioned.

I pushed out an awkward-sounding laugh. "Well, if you're looking for the story of how I was conceived, I don't think I'm the person to ask. I wasn't really there that night, Willa."

Bobbi's jaw hit the floor.

Matthew covered a snort with a cough.

And I would have felt a prickle of pride if I wasn't busy trying not to be intimidated by the way Willa was looking at me.

"I'd like for you to show me around, Josephine," Willa said. "Spend some time with you while I'm here. Besides shadowing Andrew."

"Sure, of course," the people pleaser in me started, but I saw Bobbi's head shaking. "Or maybe not. Maybe . . ." Bobbi lifted a finger and signaled something I didn't understand. "Maybe Bobbi should? Yes. She's been here long enough to know her way around town. And I know she's been dying to socialize with someone who can relate to being away from home. So she should take you."

Bobbi's eyes narrowed. "Thank you, Josephine," she deadpanned. "I'm truly ecstatic to show Willa around this wonderful place."

Matthew's hand moved at my hip, what had to be his thumb brushing my skin over the tulle, the gesture tickling and warming my skin. It felt like a tiny reward, a distraction I deserved, and a strange sound left my throat in response. He continued, awareness bubbling in the most inappropriate way and moment.

"I wonder what's taking Andrew so long," Willa commented.

"He'll be here in a minute," Bobbi answered.

That thumb got a little adventurous, trailing up, tickling me further, and driving me even more distracted. "I guess only Andrew would be late to the first meeting with his child, huh?"

Matthew's hand went still. His body, too.

Bobbi gave her head one disapproving shake. Willa returned to her notes, adding something else.

"Sorry," I said, flustered. "That came out worse than it sounded in my head. We've been face-to-face. Through a screen. In the monthly Zoom calls. It's really not like he didn't want to come here. He's a busy man. And I get it. I'm mayor of town and I own a business. I could have flown to Miami if I wanted to, but I was busy." I swallowed, my excuse feeling silly. Had I really compared those two things to Andrew's responsibilities? "Anyone else struggling with this heat wave? Because this time last year, I wouldn't have been wearing this dress. I can tell you that much."

Bobbi chuckled, the sound as stiff as it was brief. "Andrew has plenty of time for his children," she said before turning to the other woman. "There's barely been a second to breathe with the news of his retirement and everything that it entails, much less to fly around the country. That's why we have the internet. I FaceTime everyone in my life." Her eyes landed back on me. "That's completely normal."

Despite the smile I gave her, a heaviness I'd more than gotten acquainted with had settled in my belly. "Absolutely. Hundred percent. I'm sorry I phrased it that way."

With a long, worn-out-sounding sigh, as if he'd just lost some secret inner battle, Matthew dragged me closer to his side with his arm. Right against him. And I couldn't know what it was about the gesture, or the way he felt against me in that moment, but if he offered me a cuddle—even with Willa and Bobbi right there—I'd take him up on the offer.

"Hey," he said, low, so low. Almost hushed. And I didn't want to look at him, because I was clearly on the verge of doing something silly. But I did. I watched his eyes as they roamed all over my face, searching for something. Then I felt his fingers close softly—yet tightly—around the tulle of my dress. He looked away. "He'd better get here in the next thirty seconds."

I rolled my eyes at the muttered words. Even if for myself.

But all I could think about was how glad I was that Matthew was here. How absolutely relieved I was to have him with me. Even if all of this was nothing but an arrangement, and the ring on my finger was on loan, and we weren't celebrating that wedding everyone was so hyper-focused on. Even if I'd cornered him into helping me. Matthew had managed to be someone I could escape to for a second of respite, for support, just like Adalyn had encouraged. Right this moment, I really was leaning on Matthew like I would on my partner, my fiancé. Using him to bear some, if not most, of the weight I couldn't hold myself. And I didn't think he was aware how much I was doing that.

"Josephine," a new voice sounded.

I sprang to my feet.

I didn't have the slightest idea why, only that I did.

My eyes landed on a sixty-something man with striking blue eyes I knew well. They were my own. Unlike all the previous times I'd seen him, Andrew wasn't wearing a suit. Instead, he wore a collared sweater over a dark shirt that matched the color of his pants. Oddly enough, it somehow seemed even more formal than the suit.

"Sorry to make you wait," he said, looking straight at me. As if I was the only person in the room with him.

I realized I hadn't yet spoken then. Not even a hi.

I also realized how strange it felt to hear those words coming out of his mouth. *Sorry to make you wait.* What a natural yet intricate thing to say for someone who is always making me wait. I knew he meant those fifteen or twenty minutes that we'd been sitting here. But what about the twelve months since the day he called me to inform me he was my father? What about the lifetime I'd gone without knowing about him? Was he sorry about those waits too?

"No problem," I said. I willed my mouth to give him a smile, ignoring the way the gesture made me off-balance. "So how was the trip? Tedious, I bet."

"It's a two-hour flight," Andrew countered in the same deep voice he'd use during those scattered Zoom calls we'd had. "So it wasn't too bad."

It's *just* a two-hour flight, I thought, and not for the first time.

A two-hour flight, but so much distance between us.

"Right." I chuckled, the sound matching the tightness in my chest. "I knew that. It would be a different thing if you were on the West Coast, huh? Now that would be a hassle to come all the way over here for this. Changing time zones is one of my least favorite things in the world."

Andrew's jaw clenched in response, something changing in his gaze. I waited for him to voice whatever that was, engrossed by how much the color of his eyes resembled mine. Or the other way around, perhaps. He moved, striding in my direction, and with those first steps, I felt my whole body go into high alert. Would he go for a hug? A handshake? A kiss on the cheek? I didn't know what I preferred.

My father came to a stop before reaching me. Right on the other side of the coffee table that had been separating Bobbi and Willa from me and Matthew. Andrew hesitated, and it was as if an invisible line was drawn.

I felt a weight, soft but solid, at the small of my back. It was what made me notice I'd taken a small step back myself.

"You look just like her," Andrew said. "Eloise."

I changed my mind. I no longer cared about whether I wanted a hug, or a handshake, or a kiss on the cheek from this man. I wanted him to take that back. To start this over. Not because it was untrue. But because I didn't think I could have this conversation right now. Not right off the bat. Not when we could have talked about Mom on any of those calls his assistant had scheduled for us. This was not how I'd ever pictured meeting him. We were supposed to make some small talk. Maybe I'd tell a joke and break through that hard façade. Maybe he'd laugh. Maybe we'd awkwardly hug each other goodbye. I'd been ready to try that, not this.

"Liz," Andrew explained, as if my silence could possibly mean I didn't know. "Your mother."

Both my thoughts and emotions scrambled. Liz. Mom. God, I wondered what she thought of this moment. I wondered what she'd like me to do, too. Or what she'd seen in a man like him. I wondered if she'd go off on that woman for calling me Andrew's misstep. No. She wouldn't do that.

She would have laughed at how awkwardly I was smiling and said something funny to lighten the mood. "I think you knew how I looked before entering this room," I told him, shoving everything aside. Clean slate, Josie. Second chances can't bloom without water. I pushed out a light laugh. "And I do have your eyes. Mom's were dark, just like her sense of humor."

"Right," my father said. He cleared his throat. "Congratulations are in order." His gaze shifted to my side, making me notice Matthew was right there. Solid. Silent. His palm at my back. "Matthew. Happy to see you."

"Andrew," my fiancé replied in a voice I'd never heard him use. "Wish I could say the same."

Unlike me, or Bobbi, or Willa, who I could see turning a page in her notepad, my father's face didn't register shock at Matthew's words. Especially when he said, "Can't say I'm surprised."

"About what, exactly?" Matthew asked.

Andrew huffed out what I supposed was a laugh. "You. Laying hold of one of my daughters after tagging along with this family for so long. I see you didn't waste time."

Bobbi's eyes widened. Willa scribbled some more on her pad.

I just watched, taken aback, as something passed between the two men, something I didn't like. Almost as little as what Andrew had implied. My lips parted with a complaint, a defense, but Matthew clasped my hand in his. He squeezed.

"Funny you should say that, Andrew," he said, brown eyes flickering to the side to meet mine. He brought my fingers to his lips. Laid a kiss on my skin. "Only a fool would wait when there's something so precious to be claimed."

My heart stopped in my chest.

To anyone else, I was sure that sounded like a confirmation of Andrew's accusation that my fiancé was after his money. But to me . . . to me it meant him having my back. It meant he didn't care what anyone thought. It meant being seen, too. Because Andrew had waited a long time to reach out. And Matthew had called him a fool for it. To his face. And from the way he was looking at me right now, I could tell that it wasn't out of spite, but because he understood exactly how that made me feel. Because he could see what I hadn't told him. Was this part of the reason why he was helping me?

"Well, this was wonderful," Bobbi intervened, snatching the attention from everyone in the room. "Great first meeting. Very insightful for Willa, I'm sure. Let's cut it short for now and pick this back up on Friday. During the welcome party Green Oak is throwing for Andrew. Josie is organizing it."

The what? I mouthed at Bobbi, shock cascading down my back.

Bobbi sent me a look before turning her attention to a frowning Willa. "Yes, please make sure to write that down, because we'd love to have you there. Actually, do you mind if I have a look at what you've been scribbling? I'm a great fact-checker."

Willa threw the thing inside her bag. "I mind, yes."

Bobbi glared at her before murmuring an, "Okay, fine." She turned toward my father. "Andrew, there are a couple of issues we should discuss. But before we leave, we should . . . take care of that little thing we need."

Andrew Underwood shifted on his feet, looking uncomfortable. "I already told you it won't be necessary. I don't want Josephine to feel pressured into it."

Matthew seemed to go on alert again, as if he was hearing something I didn't.

"Nonsense." Bobbi's attention jumped to me. Her arm stretched in Andrew's direction. "Josephine, I'm sure you don't mind?"

"I don't mind what?" I asked, genuinely confused.

Matthew grumbled something under his breath before speaking in that voice he'd used with my father, "Don't test me, Shark. Josie's not a prop you can—"

"Now, now," Bobbi interjected, smiling. "Everyone loves a family picture." My blood swooshed to my feet. "And I think Josephine can decide whether she wants one on her own. So, Josephine? I have the perfect backdrop for a father-daughter shot."

CHAPTER ELEVEN

INTERIOR—*FILTHY REALI-TEA* STUDIO—DAY

NICK: I don't know, Sam, the picture feels a little forced.

SAM: She's a stunner, though. And that dress? An absolute slay.

NICK: Yeah, you're right. And I guess it's the timing of it all that's forced. But hey, at least we've gotten confirmation. Rich Daddy has packed his things and returned home.

SAM: Unless he chartered a private jet to snap a picture and is planning to fly right back to Miami. You know how much I hate celebs who do that. If my carbon footprint matters, why shouldn't theirs, huh?

NICK: Amen. Although word on the street is that Andrew Underwood is there to stay. Our little birdies managed to narrow the suitable properties available to rent in the area to three. We made some calls and one of them won't be back on the market for a long while. And before you ask: I'm talking long-long, not just a few weeks. This smells like wedding stuff if you ask me, yum. So we shall keep an eye on that, but until then . . . we've got plenty to discuss.

SAM: Oh?

NICK: Oh indeed. Because we've fi-nal-ly put together a TIMELINE. (chuckles) Oops, sorry. That came out a little loud.

SAM: You're forgiven. Now gimme. Are we talking about THE timeline? Of the exes? The infamous list of grooms that never were? The hearts that were smashed and stomped?

NICK: (laughs) You sound like an Olivia Rodrigo song. And I love that, because yes. Yes, we are. (clears throat) Okay, so first came Shawn—and before you point it out, no, he wasn't a match. There's a Ricky, too, just like in the Ariana Grande song.

SAM: Damn. I do love that song. (sings: *Thank you, next)* Although I'm not thankful for my exes. Neither is Small-Town Heiress, probs. Now, focus. Shawn?

NICK: I always loved your voice. (chuckles) Right. So, Shawn. Nothing special. Normal guy. Cute. Coffee barista, which we love. Runs a roaster. Still lives in North Carolina. They were young. Source said the engagement lasted throughout freshman year of college. Didn't make it to senior year.

SAM: I think it's a reasonable run. I couldn't see myself getting married so young.

NICK: You're in your midtwenties, Sam.

SAM: Exactly. And do you see a hubby by my side? So, next?

NICK: (short-lived sigh) Okay. Here things start getting interesting . . . Number two is Greg. Happened between two and three years after Shawn. Former yoga instructor. And I say former because apparently—and brace yourself—he was so absolutely devastated after the breakup—or well, being left at the altar, I should say—that he fled. Not the place. Or the state. The country.

SAM: Stop.

NICK: I'm serious. (chuckles) He's in Thailand now. And he runs a retreat. We've checked and it exists. These are facts.

SAM: Oh my God. You're telling me the guy went full *Eat, Pray, Love*? I . . . (huffs with disbelief) This is amazing. Addictive. I want more.

NICK: Ricky. That's number three. And boy, is he a good number three.

SAM: (laughs) What does that even mean, and why are you making that face?

NICK: Because he's a professional athlete, duh.

SAM: STOP. WH—

NICK: (clicks tongue) Don't get too excited. It's not football. Or hockey. It's soccer. But the big leagues, MLS, I think it's called. Last name is Richardson, for those who want to google him. (lowers voice) That means that you totally should.

SAM: (pause) Dang. He's . . . whoa. He's hot. Reminds me of like a European version of Joe Burrow? Does that make sense? Doesn't matter, I'm switching to soccer. Officially a soccer girlie. How could she leave this? Wait—important question: Are soccer wives considered WAGs?

NICK: I think they might be the OG WAGs. And I would have definitely put a ring on that, too. Something must have been amiss. Our source told us the engagement was fast and short. Who knows. Doesn't matter anyway, result was the same.

SAM: No, but seriously. Ricky Richardson, I'll marry you with paper rings. Unless . . . Do we not have any dirt on them? It's hard to believe that she'll run without them doing anything. I'm a girls' girl and I need to point that out.

NICK: You always do point it out, Sam. But before tackling that, let's touch base on Duncan. Aguirre. He's number four, and the timeline places him a little less than two years ago. So recent. He's a politician. (laughs with disbelief) Who has gone all quiet on us after being so chatty the first time we reached out. He's running for senator in South Carolina, and that's probably why. This story has blown up, after all.

SAM: (snaps fingers three times) Yes, it has.

NICK: His office keeps declining any comment, but we'll persist. Hey Duncan? If you're listening, pick up the phone. Answer our DMs. We know you want to. (pause) Until that happens . . . You can tell us in the comments what you thought of this ep in *The Underwood Affair.* Because girlie has surely been busy collecting them like Pokémon. (chuckles) Reminds me of a certain pop singer and songwriter I shall not bring into this because I'd like to avoid getting canceled.

SAM: Hey. No TS slander, you know the rules.

NICK: And if anyone's noticing, we've skipped number five. That's because we're saving the best for last.

"*Hypothetically* . . . What do you think is our aesthetic?"

Matthew considered my question. "That depends."

I shot him a bland look over the dozens of papers, trays of snacks, and empty glasses covering my kitchen table. "On what?"

"On how *hypothetical* the hypothetical aesthetic is."

I pondered his answer while I cringed at the mess. Ugh, I'd tried so badly to channel Adalyn. I even had color-coded binders and plastic sleeves with sticky labels. It wasn't working. "Are you deflecting so you don't need to ask me what an aesthetic is?"

"Give me a little credit," he said before popping a kale chip into his mouth. "I'm a little better than weaponized incompetence, *snuggle bear.*"

I narrowed my eyes at him, feigning that I wasn't impressed by his answer. Or distracted by his basic white T-shirt, the short sleeves slightly rolled up mid-bicep. "That's the worst one yet. We haven't even snuggled. I could be horrible at it for all you know."

Something sparked in his eyes. I wondered if he'd ask me to show him. It would—technically—be within the rules. And a part of me I was struggling to keep quiet was very aware of that.

"Our aesthetic should reflect who we are as a couple," he continued.

I considered that, pretending once again I didn't love that answer. For someone who had organized so many weddings and been in this exact position so many times, none of the men who had preceded Matthew had ever given me an answer like that. "That's correct," I conceded. "And that's probably why I'm struggling with it. I can't envision something that doesn't exactly exist."

His fingers brought an apricot slice to his mouth. "Walk me through your thought process," Matthew instructed, before chewing on it. A little too hard. "Dump it all on me. And don't leave whatever has you frowning like that out. I want every messy thought."

I snorted. "You don't know what you're asking. Have you met me?"

"I have." He crunched on a new chunk of fruit. "And I know what I'm asking."

The determination in his voice made me pause. Hesitate. I knew he was trying to help, and I knew I had asked him. But . . . Why was he looking so sullen all of a sudden? Was this about what they'd said about me on the last episode of *Filthy Reali-Tea*? The idea made me a little more than uneasy. They hadn't talked about Matthew, but they had about me. In detail.

I smiled at him. "My, my, it's getting late and you must be about done with all of this." I stacked some of the sleeves in a neat pile. "I'll move this to my room and just pick whatever. Andrew's welcome dinner doesn't need to match the wedding aesthetic anyway, like

Bobbi is preaching. Mostly, because there is no wedding." I collected some of the labels and set them in a pile too. "It'd be ridiculous to match anything to it. I just went into autopilot and forgot for a second." I made my smile even wider. "I can handle Andrew's party on my own."

Matthew occupied himself with the task of unearthing a tray with roasted nuts that had been buried in the mess. "I know you can," he said nonchalantly, placing the nuts in front of him and falling back on the chair. "But you won't."

"I won't . . . what exactly?"

"Handle it yourself," he pointed out. Simply. "You won't handle shit on your own. We will. And we're finding an aesthetic if that's what you need."

"I'm used to it," I countered, eyes narrowing. "I do it all the time. I'm the mayor of town. A business owner. I run multiple activities. I've . . . organized a few of these." I swallowed. "It's fine. And you can go."

He threw a couple nuts into his mouth. "I have full confidence in your skills to handle anything that comes your way."

"Then it's settled. I'll—"

"You're my fiancée," Matthew said.

My stomach dropped. Heart skipped.

Matthew's eyes met mine, as if daring me to negate that. "There's a ring on your finger. I don't care about the specifics, for all practical purposes, it means we're a team. We handle shit together. I don't care if you can do it on your own. You shouldn't have to."

I . . . wasn't used to this. Usually, people let me take the issue off their hands. And yes, that had included my exes. I didn't resent them for it, I'd been glad to handle things. It was something I did well. It just . . . was a lot sometimes.

"Okay," I let out with a breath. "Thank you. We'll settle on a wedding aesthetic so Andrew's party can match it, Snack Man. Together. Even when there's no need. But don't say I didn't try to save you from this. Your window to escape is now closed."

Matthew switched back to the kale chips, popping one into his mouth with a smile. "You love that I'm munching away at your food. I can see it in your face."

I did.

"So . . ." I started. "I usually make a list of favorite things. To pick an aesthetic. It's what represents a couple best." My determination to proceed with this wavered, but I persisted. "Like for example: Shawn was obsessed with 1920s jazz, so we planned a vintage ceremony and a very laid-back cocktail party accompanied by the Hilly Jazzers, who were a little overrated but very popular back then, and it took me a great deal of bribing to book them on the wedding anniversary of the lead singer."

Matthew kept popping in chips, not saying a thing.

"The gig was canceled, as you know. And I sent the singer a voucher for a romantic night at a spa for the trouble."

The crunching came to a stop. "And what about that wedding fit your aesthetic? I think we should focus on that."

"Everything, duh. My dress was beautiful. It was a very pale shade of gold, and so simple and elegant I could still wear it if I wanted to."

Matthew considered that for a moment. "What about your wedding to Greg, then?" Some measure of surprise must have shown on my face, because Matthew sighed. "I can remember a handful of names after hearing them a couple times. What details about that wedding were yours?"

Yes, he could. The whole country could now. "It was woodland wonderland. Towering trees, mossy detailing. It was important that we were connected to the earth, so we went with an outdoor ceremony in the woods. And Greg goes by Astro now. Ever since he became a yogi master."

"I want to hear about you now."

"You're hearing about me," I countered. "I'm telling you about me right now. My previous aesthetics."

"You're really not." He patted his hands over his jeans, as if he was done snacking and it was time to get down to business. "You're telling me about them. I want to hear about you. Likes, dislikes, passions, fears, what makes you smile, and what makes you sad. Then I'll do the same. That's what we should know about each other, and that's what we should be focusing on if we want to find an aesthetic. And we're going to. Tonight."

I pursed my lips. Trying not to give him anything. Not the big smile tugging at my mouth, or the happy laugh tickling my throat. Because, damn. The man was cute. And sweet. And that determination was unexpectedly hot.

"Wildflowers," I announced. "They make me smile. They grow free. They're beauty and defiance, and the fact that no matter what goes on in the world, they still continue to bloom, makes me happy."

He gave one solemn nod. "Favorite one?"

"Pinkshell azaleas or blue thimbles. But I'm not picky. I love them all, and I won't normally pluck them unless they're already starting to wither."

When Matthew spoke, his voice sounded twice as low. Intimate. "A fear?"

"Waterfalls," I answered easily. "It's called katarraktiphobia, if you're wondering." A shiver ran down my arms. "I'd rather jump into the open ocean and venture being eaten by a shark than walk under one."

"It's clowns for me," Matthew offered. "They terrify me."

A small smile touched my lips. "They can be very scary."

"What makes you sad, Josie?"

"Saying goodbye," I said. "Throwing away leftover cake. Lonely people. Broken things shoved aside."

There was a strange pause, then something in the brown of his eyes changed. "Why didn't you tell me that it was your first time meeting Andrew?"

"I do recall sending an SOS text."

"Josie."

I sighed, and all the questions I hadn't asked left me with the exhale. "Why are you not freaking out over this? Page Nine posted our picture, that podcast is apparently saving you for last—whatever that means. Are you not scared? What is your family saying? Are *they* scared?"

"Would me worrying about any of that change anything? Would my family knowing what we're doing change a thing?"

His answer made me sad. For many different reasons I didn't want to explain. So I didn't speak.

"You should have told me, Josie," he said. "About Andrew."

I shrugged a shoulder. "Maybe. But it doesn't change anything either, now, does it?"

"Andrew and I have never gotten along," Matthew told me, that easy and intimate atmosphere around us wilting. "I shouldn't say this, not again, but I just don't trust him. That's not going to change, even if I step back while you decide whether you want to give him a chance."

He talked like it was my decision to make. Or like I was his to protect. But were any of those things true? The truth was that my relationship with my father hung by a thread, and I didn't think Matthew could do more than he already did.

"I'm done talking about myself," I said. "I'm also done with me being the topic of conversation. I want to hear about Matthew Flanagan." A sigh escaped me. "At least before everyone else does first. Let's start with exes. Past relationships? You know all of mine. So what should I know?"

"I've had fun," he answered. "Fucked around. Got my heart broken a couple times. Nothing worth discussing, really. I made work a priority during the last years."

Fucked around. He said it so coarsely, as if the word didn't trigger images he'd planted there during those moments we'd shared in the supply closet at Josie's. "You had a ring, though," I observed, my gaze falling on my hand. I moved my fingers and watched the stone catch the light. I really loved when that happened. "That usually means something."

"A man can coexist with jewelry without imploding," he said, his hand suddenly there. With mine. On the table. His fingers touched the ornamented band. "So how do you want to play this out, then?"

My gaze lifted, falling back on him. "What do you mean *how*?"

"Your exes." Matthew's fingers skimmed over my skin now, his eyes still cast down. "You wanted to talk about me. So am I on good terms with the idea of them, or do I want to rip their heads off?"

My mouth parted in surprise. Or maybe it was the way the pad of his thumb was still playing around with the ring, my finger, my hand, sending waves of goose bumps up and down my arms. "I don't know, Matthew. Are you the jealous, possessive type?"

"Yes." His brows met in thought. "I can be. But I'm easily swayed to be nice and proper." He interlaced our fingers, and my heart tripped, tumbling down. "Do you have me wrapped around your pinky, Josie?"

The skin under my blouse flushed. Belly. Back. Arms. It all lit up as a red-hot sensation climbed up my wrist and traveled all the way to the tips of my ears.

We were holding hands.

Which we already had. Many times. Too often, for what we were, perhaps. But we could touch. Touching was part of the rules. Touching was fine. "Yes." I swallowed. "You're wrapped around my pinky all right. Tangled up in there like a—"

Matthew moved, bringing our joined hands down, under my

chair. He pulled at it—with me on it—and dragged it all the way to his side in one swift motion. "Like a what," he said, his words now falling on my temple.

My lips fell open wordlessly, the awareness—the sudden closeness of his body, in that basic white tee that didn't have any business looking as good as it did on him—robbing me of the capability of speech for an instant. "Like . . ." I finally managed to say, my voice rocky and bouncy and all wrong. "Like grandma's yarn?"

Matthew chuckled, a smile splitting that serious face he'd been sporting for most of the night. As if he hadn't been able to stop it and, *ugh.* It was such a handsome smile, and it was so devastatingly close, so within my reach that I had to physically stop myself from reaching out and feeling those creases that weren't quite dimples with the tips of my fingers. I wondered how soft his lips were. How they would feel against mine.

A record scratched in my head.

Against mine.

Against mine?

Nope. No, no, no. Absolutely not, Josie.

"We should go back to . . . the checklist," I told him, realizing my hand was still in his grasp. Resting on the colorful chair cushion, right beside my ass. *While I'd been thinking of his mouth. On mine.* I wrenched my hand from his hold, setting it back on the table. "There's so much to do." I fumbled with my phone, opening and closing apps until I found the right one. I made a show out of scrolling down and busying myself with all the work we were neglecting by playing *handsies.*

"Here." I swallowed. "Let's do something easy. I wrote down some housekeeping stuff I came up with while I listened to that god-awful podcast. Things I don't know or things that should be done to cover all fronts." My finger tapped my Notes app open. "All right, what's your middle name?"

The man whose chair was still solidly planted right by mine didn't move an inch when he said, "Eugene."

Something in my chest immediately thawed. Dear God. "Like Flynn Rider? From *Tangled*?"

Matthew's chuckle matched the feeling inside me. "Exactly like that."

"That's . . ." Ugh. I couldn't be going all squishy like this. "Great. Amazing middle name. Please congratulate your parents on my behalf. Oh wait. What are your parents' names? I think I should know that. Your sisters', too, besides Tay."

"Patrick and Pam," he answered simply. Curtly. Straight to the point. "Dad would have you calling him Paddy, though. And my sisters are Taylor—or Tay, who's the youngest—and Eve. They're constantly giving me shit, you'd love them."

I jotted that down in my notes, just to keep my mind from wandering and picturing stuff like meeting Matthew's family, or joking with his dad about those obvious Irish roots, or sitting down with them for Thanksgiving, or deciding where to spend Christmas. Boston or Green Oak? Should we have Paddy and Pam come visit during the spring? It's my favorite time of the year and they'd love it here. I—

I was being so silly.

No wedding, but we stay friends.

"Emergency contact," I murmured. Then said a little louder. "Mine has always been Grandpa Moe. But do you think we should change them? I think we should change them. Let's change them."

"Josie—" Matthew started.

"Okay, done!" I squealed. I wasn't proud of how my voice sounded. "You're set to my emergency contact. It makes sense. What if someone sneaks into our phones and checks? They could start asking questions. So better safe than sorry."

"Sweetheart," Matthew said, sounding so sweet, so unaware of my current state, that I wondered if I wasn't that bad of a liar after all. "I don't think anyone's going to check."

"So we're back to the sweetheart stuff," I murmured. And when he didn't comment, I reached for his phone, which had been somewhere to the right. I held it out to him. "It'd make me feel better if you set me as your emergency contact too. I promise I'll be very respectful of the Flanagan SOS Code and memorize all the rules you have for it."

Matthew breathed out a laugh that hit me right on the cheek. My belly too. "One, zero, two, seven, zero, four."

"What's that?"

"My passcode," he explained nonchalantly. "Change it. If it's going to make you feel better, I won't stand in the way."

"You're giving me your passcode. Why?"

"You're my fiancée," he pointed out. Again. And one more time, my heart skipped a crazy, stupid beat. "And my emergency contact."

"What if I find something on here?" I said, reluctantly entering the code and tapping on his contacts. "Something like bad mirror selfies, or an embarrassing playlist or worse, nudes from someone who— *You have me as Josephine Moore*?"

"I don't keep nudes from women I'm not seeing," he stated.

And my restraint broke. I looked at him then. "Which means you've gotten them." My cheeks flushed with my words, but I ignored it. I wasn't shy or prudish, I never was. It just seemed like Matthew managed to alter my brain chemistry in a way I was unprepared for. "Which is totally fine."

"It also usually means I've sent them," he offered.

My whole body flushed. Properly this time. "Sure," I breathed out. "I mean, who hasn't?" I hadn't, but he didn't need to know that. "I have plenty of experience under my belt. And I've had very physical relationships, you know?"

Matthew's expression hardened and there was a moment there.

Something that passed between us. Some glint in the brown of his eyes that I couldn't quite understand. Was he wondering about that? Was he thinking of the nudes I never sent? Was his mind going through my exes, wondering who I was talking about? It had been Ricky.

"I'm sure you have," he finally said.

I cleared my throat, glancing down at the phone. "You only save your banker under their full name. Or your accountant. I can't be Josephine Moore." There was an underlying disappointment that I ignored too. "I had you as Adalyn's former BFF, because I became her new best friend when she met me. Then changed it to . . . something else."

If Matthew was interested in knowing that, he didn't say. I was glad, because I didn't think he'd like that he was *Mattsie-Boo* on my phone. I also wanted to put off him seeing the picture that would light up my screen if he called me.

It was the brush of his fingers against mine that made me notice that he was taking his phone from my grasp. One-handed, he tapped at it. Then returned it to me.

My contact was open on the screen.

He'd changed it to Baby Blue.

With a butterfly emoji.

And I . . . Ah shit. This was too much. Because I shouldn't feel the way I did over it, but I did, and I absolutely loved it. "Because of my blue eyes?" I asked, making every emotion inside me obvious in my voice.

"I don't know why I didn't think of it before."

"What do you mean?"

His voice grew closer, as if he was leaning forward. "It's what I called you. In my head. That night."

All that happy bubbling dwindled. "When you thought I was some strange woman in a robe covered in jam?"

A gulp of air left the man by my side. "Hey. Look at me, please."

I didn't want to, but I'd also been putting this man through the wringer since that night, so the least I could do was turn if he asked. "Yes?"

Brown eyes bore into mine through the lenses of that pair of glasses I was growing so obsessed with. And then he said, serious, concerned, "Why are you disappointed? That I couldn't tell it was you right away?"

My heart halted for a second. I had not expected that. Not the direct question or him noticing what I had felt that night. "The answer to that makes me somewhat of a monster," I whispered. "You won't like it."

"Try me."

"It made me a little sad," I let out with a sigh. "You, not being able to tell it was me right away. But also realizing that you were helping a stranger. I love that you're kind and good and just . . . a great man." My voice almost left me then. "But a part of me wished you'd be helping me, Josie, not just anyone. That's it."

Matthew was taken aback by my answer for a long moment. So long I was sure I'd just ruined things I wasn't supposed to ruin. But then he moved. Body turning in his chair, he scooted forward, close, closer, until his legs sandwiched mine. His eyes did that thing, bouncing around my face until setting camp on mine. When he spoke, his voice was low, and his words sounded like a confession. Just like mine. "Maybe I would help any stranger. But it's you I'm going this far for. It's you. Josie."

The tension that had just taken shape thickened, filling the space around us.

It's you.

Josie.

My mind was stuck. My chest filling with . . . things. Stuff that had nothing to do with being *relieved* or *glad* to have him by my side. Stuff that shouldn't be there. Not this fast and certainly not when we were the main characters in a PR hoax I'd asked him to be a part of. "It doesn't matter, anyway," I lied. "It's not important now." More lies. "It wasn't like I was dying to meet you or anything."

"It'd be so easy to prove you wrong."

His answer surprised me. It also excited me. Irked me. Defied me. I made no sense. We didn't. "There's nothing to prove wrong."

"You thought about me," Matthew pressed. Determined. His gaze dipped down, I didn't know where—mouth, chin, neck, a stain on my blouse, I had no idea. But when it returned, there was a challenge in the glint of his eyes. "Before I got here, to Green Oak. You'd given me shit in the group chat, or whenever you were around when I called Adalyn, but you liked me."

I snorted, but Matthew's body moved. His legs pushed forward, my knees almost coming in contact with his crotch, and his hands braced on both sides of my seat, caging me. My cheeks flamed, rivers of awareness flowing down my body. "I like everyone," I whispered. "Ask anyone in town."

The corner of his mouth tipped up in a smile that should have sent me running for the hills. "Yet I'm the one sitting here."

My first impulse was to argue. I hadn't pulled Matthew into this arrangement out of some selfish plot to get him naked. But I knew he knew that. He was baiting me, he was trying to prove a point only because I refused to admit it. Because I'd opened up, taken a step outside my cocoon of safety, and then gone right back into it. But didn't he understand? How terrifying it was for me to peek my head out? Especially when it was him on the other side. Especially when he saw so much, knew so much, was so deep into the tangle I was. Especially when he was a little right.

Thing was, every step I walked forward could be run right back. I was excellent at that.

"So what if you are?" I told him, raising my hands and watching them cross the space between our chests. Two could play this game, and he should have known that. Softly, I placed my palms on his shoulders. Then dragged them down his arms, slowly, deliberately, my fingernails grazing first the fabric, then his skin, making him shudder under them. "Maybe I wanted you to help me. But I would have asked any stranger walking by." My tongue peeked out, wetting my bottom lip. "Are you not familiar with my track record?"

Matthew's brows came down in thought, but his gaze was unfocused, distracted. "Stop talking about yourself like that."

I let my fingers slip inside his sleeves, then dragged my hands up, basking in the way Matthew's breath caught. "Like what?"

"Like you're some selfish monster," he said, voice deep and rocky. My determination wobbled, and Matthew took the chance. His hands moved from their spot on the chair to my sides. He pulled my body closer. Our noses almost brushed. "I know what you're doing."

My heart raced, the closeness of his face, our bodies, too much too soon and too little all at once. "And what is that?"

"Distracting me," he said. "Hiding." And in response, in rebellion, my hands moved against his skin, rounding his arms, holding on to him, as if he was going to stand up and leave now that he'd called me out. The quality of his gaze changed, the sharpness softening. "But that's all right, isn't it?" he whispered, voice tender, the hands at my waist trailing up gently. As if he was soothing me. "We'll hide behind your rules. I won't break any until you ask me."

That deafening flutter in my belly rioted at his words. Ask him? My chest heaved. The feel of his skin under my hands, the feeling of him filling the space, the weight of his words, overwhelming me. I—

A throat cleared.

We both froze.

"Your hands cold, Josie?" Grandpa Moe grumbled. "Because you can wear mittens, if that's the case. You don't need to probe him like you're searching for lice."

I snatched my hands back with a sigh. Then turned to look at Grandpa. He was standing under the doorframe, in a robe, holding an empty bottle of rosé. "Lice?" I deadpanned. "Really?"

"Yes, really," he answered, before shooting Matthew a warning glance. Matthew's hands fell off my waist. "Smart choice, kiddo."

Matthew nodded his head, but not with shame or reluctance. "I'll be better next time, sir."

Both Grandpa and I arched our brows, the same two words causing the same reaction for vastly different reasons. *Next time.* As if me sitting on a chair in the cradle of his legs while having my hands all over him would happen again.

"You walked here?" Grandpa asked Matthew. He nodded. "I'll drive you home, then. If you're done with whatever you were doing." He shot me a pointed glance. "I'm done with my show and my rosé doesn't have any alcohol in it anyway. She's been sneaking me fizzy pink watered-down juice."

"Gee," I let out. "And here I thought the fact you run through it like we have it on tap meant you liked it."

Matthew stood up, his body unfolding before me, sidetracking me. I leaned my head back to look at him, finding his eyes on me.

"We wouldn't have an aesthetic," he announced. "Beautiful things shouldn't be boxed. It eventually dims their light."

My lips parted with a hundred questions, and in the same heartbeat, Matthew's head dipped.

He brushed a kiss against my jaw. "I really had to," he whispered. "In case I don't survive the drive."

And then he was off, joining Grandpa at the door.

I . . . I should have been concerned with so many things, really. Like how I'd wanted to grab his arm and stop him from leaving.

How I'd wanted to ask him to kiss my cheek again. Stay a little longer. But I couldn't. Not when I was trying to decipher what he'd just said.

Beautiful things shouldn't be boxed. It eventually dims their light.

Had he meant me? Or us?

CHAPTER TWELVE

The hammer slipped out of my hand and hit me on the foot before dropping to the ground.

"Fudgenuggets," I muttered, climbing down the ladder and picking the tool up off the ground.

With a sigh, I walked back to the bench Robbie had set outside the barn. Then I sat on top of it with a little jump. I'd done enough of these to know when it was time to take a break. Being perched on a ladder for an hour straight, hanging string after string of lights until my fingers were numb, usually was a hint.

I snagged the apple I'd brought as a snack from the corner of the bench and pulled out my phone to check my notifications.

There were a few messages from Bobbi, all of them different variations of *are things handled for Andrew's welcome dinner.*

The answer was: duh. Although not in the way she imagined. So I replied with a thumbs-up and moved on.

Next was a message from Grandpa. He'd sent me a link earlier today, after he'd been alerted of a new post from Page Nine. It was a *Filthy Reali-Tea* teaser, announcing something was dropping tonight. At midnight. The drama of the internet never ceased to amaze me. Almost as much as how quick of a study Grandpa was with new technology. He was asking me how to create a burner account. I snorted at the screen and typed an answer.

JOSIE: You don't need one of those. You're already anonymous. And where did you learn that?

His answer was immediate.

GRANDPA MOE: 👍

Ugh.

I should have never taught him how to create, let alone use, an Instagram account. God knew what he was plotting now. I brought the apple to my mouth, taking a bite and debating whether I should be worried or at the very least press Grandpa for more details than that thumbs-up, but a message came in the group chat.

CAMERON: Adalyn's feeling under the weather. Won't be able to make it to Andrew's thing tonight. Sorry.

JOSIE: Omg, is she okay?? And don't even worry about it. It's nothing special. Just our midnight farmers' market at the barn, but repurposed. The only thing you'll miss is a banner that says WELCOME HOME.

The thought of the banner made it a little hard to swallow the apple I was chewing on. But just like I'd told myself when I pulled out the paint can: *tough shit, Josie.* This was still Andrew's town, much as it was mine. And I was mayor of it, besides being his daughter, so how could I not make him a sign?

MATTHEW: Shit. Is it the stomach bug she'd mentioned the other day?

CAMERON: Yes. It's gotten a little worse, so I've made the executive decision to sit this one out. She's sleeping, otherwise she wouldn't let me cancel. We're sorry, but she needs to rest.

JOSIE: Ugh. I'm so sorry. That sucks. Please give her a hug? And stop saying you're sorry. Tonight's thing is not that special.

The only one who needed to learn that was Bobbi. But I'd take one battle at a time. I'd thought about this long and hard. I knew my town, and no one would have attended a stiff, fancy dinner. The midnight farmers' market on the other hand? It was a hit ever since we'd hosted the first one. And I couldn't think of a better way to welcome anyone than this.

Matthew's words from a couple of nights ago in my kitchen returned.

We wouldn't have an aesthetic. Beautiful things shouldn't be boxed. It eventually dims their light.

They'd been stuck in my mind since then. Together with everything that had preceded them. *Together with Matthew, his eyes, the feel of his skin under my hands, the way he made me feel. Want.* It had all inspired me. Inspired me to . . . go rogue. To escape the cage of control that Bobbi had snapped around my life.

She wanted a welcome party for Andrew to impress Willa Wang, and so I was giving her my version of one.

My phone buzzed, recapturing my attention.

MATTHEW: Tonight will be special, though.

MATTHEW: Because you'll be there @BabyBlue

My cheeks flushed. I . . . He . . . I snorted.

JOSIE: Did you really just text that?

MATTHEW: Too much?

CAMERON: Yes. And I'm leaving. Bye.

JOSIE: Let me know if you need us to help with anything, though! I could drive down later, check in on Adalyn and help with whatever. Grandpa opened Josie's today. I have time.

CAMERON: Absolutely not. And you don't have time. You have enough on your hands.

JOSIE: Maybe soup? I can send Matthew down there while I handle things up here.

MATTHEW: Yes, she can.

MATTHEW: Boss me around, @BabyBlue 🔥

CAMERON: We're fine. And I'm really leaving if you don't stop that. I'm still pissed.

My face fell. Together with my stomach that had just dropped to my feet. A message immediately popped up in Matthew's chat.

MATTHEW: He's fine. He's just being Cam. He's not mad at you, and he shouldn't have said that.

JOSIE: It's okay.

It really was. And I deserved that. I was lying to them, after all. We were. I couldn't pretend like everything was fine and we were two couples texting in a group chat. Matthew and I weren't really one.

MATTHEW: Where are you?

JOSIE: At the Vasquezes'.

MATTHEW: Why are you already there? It's not even ten in the morning. Is that why Maurice opened Josie's today?

JOSIE: Grandpa Moe opens for me when I can't. I won't be here all day. I was taking care of last-minute stuff for the midnight market. We have it handled.

MATTHEW: We?

JOSIE: The special events and parades committee. It's still a town event.

MATTHEW: I'm calling you. Don't let it ring and then text. Pick up.

My eyes widened. Wait, what? He was—

My phone rang.

With a puff of air, I brought it to my ear. "Yes, dear?"

"I thought I was clear last night."

I suppressed a smile. "You're not the only one with excellent selective hearing, *ya* know."

He huffed out a surprised laugh. "Why am I not with you? Jog my memory."

His words made my stomach flip-flop. But they were just that, words. "I dunno," I said. "The laws of physics? Time? Space? It was something about all of it being relative, and depending on who you ask. But I can't be sure."

There was a pause, then an "I'm coming over."

My chest filled with crazy, stupid butterflies. "Almost everything is done."

"Then I'll keep you company. Bring you snacks. Don't make me beg, Baby Blue. Because I will."

Baby Blue. The flutter multiplied, pulling at all the strings tangled around my heart. I considered what to say. How to say it. Whether I should be stubborn and say no, or naïve and believe none of this meant a single thing. But then something occurred to me. Maybe Matthew was lonely. A rug had been swept out from under his feet and he was in a new place. Alone. And I'd been so set on what we were doing, and on bothering him as little as I could, that I'd overlooked that.

"I could use anything fuzzy and fruity." I jumped off the bench. "No blueberry though."

"You got it." His voice was happy, and that made me feel . . . good. Like I wanted more. "What else?"

"Maybe something sweet?"

"All right."

"And something savory too. A pretzel would be nice; it's today's special at Josie's."

The rumble of laughter that left him felt like butter against my ear. It also made me smile in return.

"You asked," I told him. "You brought this on yourself."

"I guess I did, yes."

There was beat, a moment of silence in which neither of us spoke.

"Hey Matthew?" I asked.

"Yeah?"

"How's the job hunt going?" I ventured. "Is there anything I can do to help? If you're busy with whatever you're doing, you don't need to come. I know you're freelancing from home, so—"

"I'm not busy," he said. "I'm never too busy for important things." There was a pause. Some of the color returned to my face. *Important things.* "And I haven't found anything yet."

"Okay," I answered. "Okay. Yes. Will you . . . tell me? When you do?"

"Yes." The pause that followed that was longer still. Then he asked, "Hey Josie?"

But before he could say more, Robbie's shape materialized in the distance. He was walking toward the barn with a face I knew well. One that was never—ever—good news.

"Uh-oh," I murmured into the line, distracted by the intensity of Robbie's scowling at the ground. "Robbie's walking over. I think there's some kind of issue. I gotta go. Talk to you later, 'kay? And don't worry about the pretzels!"

A muttered curse made me look down from the ladder I was once again perched on.

I lowered the banner I'd been nailing to the outside wall of the barn and glanced down.

Matthew.

He was standing at the foot of the ladder, his hands braced on the side rails. The terra-cotta shirt he wore was again rolled up, as if he loved those sleeves to strain around his forearms.

"You're here," I said, realizing only then that my mouth had parted with a smile. My eyes trailed up his arms, chest, neck, chin, searching for . . . "Oh my God. What's wrong?"

"What's wrong?" he repeated, sounding as displeased as he looked, right as his own gaze found mine. The frown that had been knotting his brows dissolved. His lips parted. He hesitated.

"Matthew?" I tilted my head. "Are you okay?"

He swallowed, as if needing a minute. Then he grumbled, "Do you know how unstable these things are?" I arched my brows in surprise. "Can't anyone spare a minute to do whatever you're doing up there? Or at the very least, spot you while you work? Where is Robbie? I could have come earlier if you needed me. You should have just said."

I blinked at him for a moment, taken a little aback.

But then a fizzy feeling tickled my rib cage. He was all growly and grouchy over me being up here. Over something I could do with my eyes closed, I'd done it so many times. I bit back a smile.

"Gee, you're grumpy." I slipped my hammer back into the tool belt. "I can't decide if you have a problem with ladders or me," I continued, turning around on the step I was perched on. Matthew's jaw clenched. "Did you drink enough water today? One gallon a day keeps the grouchiness away, you know."

His face scrunched down. I knew he'd found that funny, I knew he had. But he was trying to stay mad. "Will you come down now?" he pleaded with a sigh. "There's something I want to ask you and I can't do it with you up there."

"But I'm not done," I complained, using my sweetest voice. "And I can talk while I work. Today I've spent more time up a ladder than on the ground."

That didn't seem to reassure him.

"It's fine, I promise," I insisted. "I can multitask. You ask me while I nail this sign. Oh, and then I need to check on the orange slices we're hanging off one beam. I have Robbie sewing them together on a string. It's going to look ah-mazing." I braced a hand at the top and stretched my body so I could peek inside the barn. "He was right there, inside. You can go check. I'll be here."

Matthew cursed.

I leaned back and glanced down at Matthew. He looked like he was about to climb the ladder and join me up here. Or . . . I don't know, lift the thing—with me on it—and run into the forest circling the property. It was so cute. "You're looking so cute right now."

"Oh yeah?" he grumbled.

"Ah-ha."

"So you like watching me suffer?" he asked, still as grouchy. "That it, huh?"

I shrugged a casual shoulder. "Not necessarily. Did you bring the snacks?"

"They're in the car," he said, sounding miserable. My lips popped open. "No. I'm not going to grab them and leave you up there because you're fine." I rolled my eyes, and a disbelieving laugh huffed out of him. "You're not risking your neck for a goddamn welcome sign. So tough shit, but I'm not leaving your side. Period."

I pursed my lips in thought, debating whether that had been hot, coddling, or sweet. "Period?" I repeated.

His nostrils flared. "Period."

"Okay." I shrugged. His expression relaxed. "I guess that's a good thing, then. When I'm about to do this."

"Do wh—"

I jumped off the ladder with a squeal, incapable of keeping the expression of pure joy off my face. Matthew stiffened, and sure, maybe his soul left his body for like a second, but just like I'd anticipated, his reaction was immediate.

His arms captured me in the air, easing me against a hard chest with an ease that made the flutter in my belly even more prominent.

Warmth replaced adrenaline as my body acknowledged all the ways I was pressed against him. My chest heaved against his, my legs hiked around his waist, while two strong arms held me in place. Much like the day at the game, only there wasn't shock this time. There wasn't reticence or hesitation. Just butterflies.

"I've always wanted to do that," I whispered, my words falling on his lips. Awareness danced in the brown of Matthew's eyes in response as he rearranged me in his arms with a little bounce. The daisy I'd slipped in the front pocket of my overalls brushed his chin. Our faces were so, so very close, and he looked so, so very handsome in this moment, that the words toppled from my lips, "You're wearing your glasses."

The corner of his mouth twitched. "You're a reckless woman. You almost gave me a heart attack."

"Well, you lied," I murmured, officially distracted by the glint in his eyes.

"Remind me about what."

"It's not clowns that terrify you the most." I lowered my voice to a hush. "It's clearly ladders."

Matthew's chuckle was a deep and rich sound, and it grazed my lips. "Maybe it is," he said, that frown knotting his brow again. "Or maybe it's seeing you hurt."

Whatever amusement I'd been feeling vanished, the little space between us filling up with something else. Something a little somber, but something sincere.

Matthew lowered me to the ground slowly, a muscle in his jaw jumping when my feet touched the ground. One of his hands left my waist, coming to pluck the daisy out of the front pocket of my overalls. He slipped the wildflower into my hair. Right above my ear. And when he said, "Beauty and defiance," a breath caught in my chest.

He remembered what I'd said that night in my kitchen, a few days ago. When he'd asked me what made me smile. *Wildflowers. They're beauty and defiance.*

"It was lying on the ground," I murmured. "It must have been dragged all the way here by one of the wheelbarrows. It's far from perfect, with so many petals missing, but it made me sad to see it lying there, so I picked it up."

Matthew's smile was soft. "Perfection is subjective."

"That's a beautiful thing to say." And I loved that he thought so. I loved that I did too. "You can be so articulate for someone who occasionally sounds like a caveman." I lowered my voice to imitate a masculine tone. *"Me, Matthew. Me, protect. Ladder, bad."*

"Can you blame me?" he asked, tilting his head. "You mentioned Robbie and dropped my call."

"What does that have to do with—" I stopped myself. My brows arched. "You can't be jealous of Robbie."

Matthew's lips thinned. "He gets your muffins."

"Everyone does," I told him. But what my mind was blasting at max volume was, *he's not denying it. Matthew is jealous and he's not denying it.*

"Not me." A shoulder was shrugged. "I don't."

I laughed. Like properly threw my head back and laughed. Matthew's expression went lax for a second before puzzling itself right back. "You've gone through most of my pantry. Several times. All my kale chips? Gone."

"Does that mean only I get them?"

More laughter left me. "Are you for real?" His face said no. His eyes said yes. "Yes, *Mattsie-Boo,* you're the only one who gets my kale chips." He smiled. "No one else likes them though."

"Fools. All of them," he said, his expression filling up with . . . something that told me he was about to do something crazy. Something—

He wouldn't do now.

Bobbi's unmistakable blond bob jutted out from one of the stands already assembled around the barn. She was on her phone, her hand slicing through the air.

"Bobbi's here," I said just as she spotted us. "Ugh. She's also coming this way."

Matthew's expression hardened, and he stepped back just as the woman in question appeared in front of us.

"This is chaos," Bobbi announced, locking her phone. "You should fire your event planner."

I sighed and adjusted my blouse sleeves in an attempt at not appearing as bothered as I was by the comment. "It's *organized* chaos. And there's no event planner to be fired. Our midnight farmers' market is organized by Green Oak's Special Events and Parades Committee."

Bobbi arched her brows. "Excuse me, what?"

"Our Midnight—"

"No," Bobbi interjected. "This is supposed to be a dinner. A welcome party. For Andrew. Why am I hearing the words *Midnight* and *Farmers'* and *Market*?"

Out of the corner of my eye, I felt Matthew stiffening, so I made sure to sound appeasing. "Because you asked me to organize it. And this is Green Oak's welcome party for Andrew. And there's nothing more Green Oak than our famous midnight farmers' market. So . . ."

"So this is not what we talked about," Bobbi scoffed. "Did you not read the description I added to the planner?" She pitched her voice down as if reciting something from memory. *"Casual dinner to celebrate Andrew's return and launch wedding preparations. Ide-*

ally, should match wedding theme. Preferably in a local restaurant. Alternatively, with catering service that showcases the town's cuisine. Objectively, a smooth reintroduction of father of the bride into community with mingling potential. It's clear enough."

I swallowed. "Well, I'm afraid I've gone a little rogue."

Dark scowling eyes held mine for a tense moment. "Is this rogue thing supposed to explain why the barn looks like a rainbow hurled all over the place? Who runs this committee? I need to talk to them." Her expression hardened. "Is it Roberto?"

"I'm in charge," I told her with a smile. "I'm chair, deputy chair, secretary, and treasurer of the committee. And I think the barn looks fantastic. And hey," I added, pointing at the spot above the ladder. "We'll have a welcome sign for Andrew. And a sitting area for whoever wants to eat any of the amazing local produce, so technically, almost everything you asked for is here. It's all a matter of perspective."

"You played me," Bobbi stated.

"You played me first," I countered with a little scoff. "You sprung this thing on me. In front of Willa Wang. And I'm a little done with being ordered around. Maybe it's time you see how we do things in Green Oak, you know?"

Bobbi's eyes narrowed. "I'd be annoyed if I weren't a little impressed." She tilted her head. "No. I'm definitely annoyed. You don't play Bobbi Shark." She glanced at the man to my right. "And what are you smirking about, Blondie?"

"Just quietly happy. Seeing my woman handing you your ass, is all."

My brows shot up. "That is not what I'm doing. I'm not handing anyone any ass. I promise."

Bobbi appraised us—or maybe me—for a few seconds. "Okay," she finally said. "Do it your way." She turned around. "I can do the same."

CHAPTER THIRTEEN

I would never dare to call myself witchy, but I had a way of knowing when something was about to go awry.

It usually started with a sign. A freshly done nail that split right before an important event, or a pull on a dress minutes before leaving the house for a date. Silly things that could happen to anyone. Things that are objectively fixable but made you pause to ask: *Ugh, why tonight of all nights? Why right now?*

Tonight, it had been the zipper of one of my ankle boots. They were lilac, and new, and I was pairing them with jeans and a matching cardigan covered in daisies. I'd been saving these boots for a special occasion and decided they'd be my lucky pair. But one didn't snap the zipper of their new lucky charm. That's why I'd shook my head, determined to deny this was one of those signs. And then my tummy dropped.

And I was talking a *roller coaster, takes your breath away for a sec* kind of drop. Exactly the one that always, always followed these little omens.

"Penny for your thoughts," Matthew said, offering me a raspberry from the box he'd just bought at one of the midnight farmers' market stands.

I declined with a sigh. "Do you believe in magic? Juju? Premonitions? Ghosts? Fate? The power of manifestation? The yeti?"

Matthew pondered the question. "Oh, absolutely."

I watched him, gauging how serious he was about his answer. To be completely frank, I'd only added all those things to make light of the gloomy feeling in my gut. "You do?"

He gave a serious nod.

"That's all? No remarks? No comments about how out of the blue that was? Not even about the yeti?"

"I asked you for your thoughts," he said matter-of-factly. One raspberry went flying into his mouth. "Why would I complain about your sharing with me?" Another one. "And if you want the remarks," he continued, meticulously closing the bag and pinning me with a glance as if he was about to get down to business. "The world would be boring without magic, so I choose to believe it exists. Regarding the juju matter, well, I'm fully convinced I was cursed at least once in my life. Premonitions are tricky, but there have to be people with a direct line to all those things we normies can't really see. Ghosts are objectively probable. Fate explains things that would go unanswered otherwise. Manifestation is scientifically proven. And the yeti just makes sense."

I blinked at the man who had just called himself a *normie* with a serious face. I was many things right now. I was surprised, for one. I was also determined to ignore that fluffiness I felt in the middle of my chest, as if my heart were about to start levitating and float out of my mouth. I was also a little—

"You're incredibly turned on," he pointed out with a knowing smile. My cheeks flushed. "Do you want to grab my ass?"

A strange-sounding laugh left me. "*What?* I—Wh—I'm not

grabbing your ass." I looked around, spotting Willa Wang's set of cold eyes right on us. She was standing next to Andrew, and although she hadn't approached tonight, she'd been watching us. I cleared my throat. "Sorry to bring you down from whatever cloud you're on right now, but talking about the yeti doesn't exactly do it for me."

"Oh yeah?" Matthew leaned a little closer, until all I could see was him.

I swallowed at his nearness, then tried to stay in the game with a cold face. "Yup," I said, going up on my tiptoes to glance over Matthew's shoulder. Willa was murmuring something to Andrew, and he was nodding his head. God, he looked so out of place. So foreign. As if he was crashing a party instead of attending his own. As if—

"You're breaking my heart," Matthew murmured, his nose almost brushing my temple.

My body stilled, my mind quieting. "Why?" I whispered.

"Because I'm trying to flirt and you're not paying attention to me."

I tipped my head back so I could look at him. His smile was a contrast to the deep, hushed tone those words had been whispered in. "You're smiling too much for someone heartbroken," I told him, feeling that fluffiness return. Expand. "And is that what you want to do? Right in the middle of my father's slightly awkward welcome party? Flirt? For me to grab your ass?"

"Of course," he said, lips inching even higher. "I'm your fiancé. Isn't that my role here?"

I licked my lips. Everybody was watching. Almost the entirety of Green Oak was here. Our midnight farmers' market was popular, but it had never attracted this kind of crowd. Maybe my assessment of the dinner we were supposed to be having instead of this had been wrong. Even Diane, who had always complained about this event being held on a school night, and Otto, who claimed Coco's bedtime was more important than *some market*—had showed up.

The only people missing were Gabriel and Isaac, who were down in Charlotte for the night.

As if manifested into reality by my own mind, Diane's high-pitched voice grew closer. Anxiety started bubbling inside me.

"Eyes on me," Matthew instructed. That silky sensation in my chest thickened when my gaze obeyed, meeting his. And I quivered when he grasped my hand. He tugged at my arm, bringing it around him. I arched my brows in question, wondering what he was doing, and why. He arched his own suggestively in return, in that goofy way that always managed to make me smile. Then he slipped my hand into the back pocket of his jeans. "Mmh," he hummed. "So much better now."

I huffed out a laugh, and his eyes sparked with amusement and . . . something a little huskier than that. "For you or me?"

"Hopefully both."

Definitely both. "If Grandpa Moe catches us, he'll get us that huge box of hand warmers he threatened me with. It's already in his cart. He showed me. You're reckless doing this."

A chuckle rumbled out of Matthew's chest. "I'm not breaking any rules."

Our rules. Not Grandpa's.

We don't get married but stay friends. We kiss if we must. We can touch.

I swallowed. "I guess you're not. This can't be uncalled-for-ass-groping if it's you moving my hand to your butt."

"I have a great butt too," he told me, eyes glinting with something I really liked. "Some might say it's a magical one. I think you should touch it more often. As often as you can, in fact. It's something we can do."

It was so hard not to smile. So hard not to notice what he was doing and how much I loved that he was doing it. "You're distracting me."

He nodded his head and took one step closer, keeping my hand in his back pocket. To anyone looking, we were an engaged couple having a moment. He was joking. She was smiling. There were hushed words. The memory of the last time they danced and stood like this, so close together, noses almost touching.

To me, it was a story someone had fabricated. Me. It was a girl, standing in a barn, a bad feeling in her gut, and a man who was trying his best to keep ahold of the mess she always made of things.

"I'm so sorry, Matthew," I said.

His gaze filled with concern. Shock too. "For what?" he asked, and there was frustration in his voice. Well, I was frustrated too. And I did silly things when I was under stress. Perhaps this was one of them. Saying more than I should. "Josie—" He stopped himself, his eyes shifting behind me. "We'll talk about this later."

I turned, finding what he was looking at just as the clinking of something metallic against glass sliced right through the chatter in the barn. The groups that had gathered around the stands quieted, the chairs of those who had taken a seat to eat or drink something scraped as they turned, and every head in Green Oak's midnight farmers' market twisted in the direction of the noise.

"What is Bobbi doing?" I whispered.

"Does it even matter?" Matthew answered. "She's standing on a stool and everyone's looking at her now."

Bobbi cleared her throat. Then waited a moment. A beam of light flickered to life, illuminating her from bob to combat boots. "A little off with the timing, but we'll talk about that later, Roberto," she muttered before a smile parted her face. Her voice rose. "Hello, people of Green Oak."

There was a pause, as if she expected the crowd to respond. No one did.

"I guess I can't blame you," she deadpanned. "It's one in the morning and we're here, in a barn, surrounded by . . . vegetables and goat cheese. It doesn't exactly scream party." There was another pause, smaller, judging by the way her lips parted to continue. A goat bleated. Brandy, if I had to guess. She sighed. "Okay, whatever. Thank you for giving Andrew Underwood your warmest welcome in his return to Green Oak. The town that saw him grow up as a young boy, and the place he's been looking after, and advocating for, even if from the shadows over the decades. Gasp, gasp. Applause, applause. Now I'll give the stage to a very special person to Andrew, and the town, who *I know* would love to say a few words—Josephine Underwood-Moore. Or future Mrs. Flanagan, as I'm sure many are already calling her."

Every head in the barn turned to look at me.

My whole body had gone slack. I felt like my name had just been picked out of a jar and I'd somehow been selected as tribute in some strange version of the Hunger Games. Only it wasn't my name. My name was Josephine Penelope Moore. No hyphen. No Underwood. And I wasn't the future Mrs. Flanagan. I was . . . in shock. Like proper, paralyzing, petrifying shock.

A gentle tug at my hand, followed by a weight at the small of my back, was the only warning I got before I started moving. Matthew's scent wrapped around my senses, the warmth of his shoulder against mine as we apparently navigated the sea of staring eyes.

Bobbi smiled tensely before leaning her head down. "Why does she look like that?" she whispered. "She doesn't have a speech? The planner—"

She was somehow shoved aside.

Matthew occupied my field of vision. "You want to do this? Yes or no?"

This. The speech. It took me a beat, but I nodded my head. What was the alternative? Looking like a fool? As suddenly terrified and intimidated as I was, this was my town. My community. They loved me, cared for me, looked up to me. I had a responsibility.

Matthew gave me a wink, and it wasn't a playful one. It was a reassuring one. *You got this,* it told me. *You can do anything.* My body moved toward the stool. My boot slipped. Hands seized me by the waist. Matthew picked me up and planted me on top of it.

"I . . ." I trailed off. Matthew stood below, head at the height of my hip, as if guarding me. But from what? This was Green Oak. I was their mayor. I could do this. I've faced much worse. "Phew," I said with a strange-sounding laugh. "I wasn't expecting that." Bobbi's scoff from the back was obvious. "I mean, I certainly wasn't expecting *that* wonderful speech from Bobbi; that'll be super hard to follow up."

I studied the crowd before me, looking for what, I didn't know. Not until I stumbled upon a set of blue eyes that looked exactly like mine. Andrew arched his brows, as if in question.

I squared my shoulders. "When I was tasked with organizing a welcome dinner for my father, a part of me rebelled at the thought." Some murmur picked up, but I pushed past it. "A dinner somehow didn't feel like the best fit for something like this. If you'll allow me to be blunt, I was a little scared that not many people would show up." Andrew's brows arched. "Let's be honest, the man is a stranger." My father's lips thinned. "But strangers can be turned into friends with a smile and the right amount of effort. And Andrew's efforts to preserve and improve the town he once called home can't be ignored. The farm we stand on tonight is an example of that. Although his support was always from the shadows, like Bobbi said, I believe it wasn't from a place of shame, but from deep in his heart. And that is why I thought there couldn't be a better way to welcome him than to show him what Green Oak has become in his absence. With his help. A piece of our soul. And potentially, a new beginning."

The hardness that always accompanied Andrew's features seemed to momentarily crumble. And for the first time in the short time I'd known him, I was pretty sure I was seeing who I suspected was the man behind the mask. A man capable of showing tenderness. Nostalgia. A man whose eyes glinted with emotion, and perhaps even hope, for just a few moments.

I tried to stop the satisfaction from swelling inside me. From advancing and eating away at everything—anything—else that had been there a second before. But I failed. I was never good at managing big feelings, no matter how good or bad they were.

Someone clapped. Quickly, more people followed, the resounding applause breaking through whatever I'd momentarily fallen into.

In the same breath, Matthew's hands were at my waist again, lifting me off the stool, and Andrew was stepping forward, effortlessly parting the crowd around him.

Matthew's hand clasped mine, just as Andrew reached us.

"Thank you, Josephine," my father said, voice booming across the barn ease. Out of the corner of my eye, I saw Bobbi approaching, doing something with her hands. But my father continued. "I don't think there's a better chance than this to share the good news: I'm happy to cordially invite everyone present to my daughter's and Matthew's union on December first, in a ceremony that will take place here, at the Vasquez Farm."

The blood in my whole body froze.

Andrew chuckled, as if happy with himself. "And to the joyful four weeks of celebration that will precede the wedding."

The barn blinked out of existence for a second. Every face, every moving hand as they clapped excitedly, every stand, every detail I'd personally decorated, even the WELCOME HOME banner I'd painted and hung outside, I was sure had disappeared. It all went poof, black, for a second or two.

Good, I thought. *Great.* I wanted everything to disappear.

The warmth at my hand squeezed. Tugged. *Matthew.*

But I didn't want to face him, I didn't want to have to explain or comfort. I couldn't. I was barely managing to do that myself. I wished . . . I wished there was a way everyone would just forget what my father had said.

And as if summoned, the whole place quieted. There were phones pinging, chirping, then Grandpa Moe was in front of me, granting me my wish.

"Josie," he said.

My stomach dropped. Just like when the zipper had snapped.

"There's a video," Grandpa explained. "Of your wedding." I noticed the smartphone in his hand. "To Greg."

He didn't need to say more.

I knew exactly what he meant.

CHAPTER FOURTEEN

As a teenager, I never smuggled alcohol out of Mom's cabinet. She'd sat me down at some point in my early teens and told me that if I ever felt the need to try or was curious about getting drunk, she'd rather be there with me. That Thanksgiving I tried wine and sipped Grandpa Moe's bourbon. I liked neither, and I remember thinking that day that some of my friends were crazy for risking getting grounded for something that left such a bad taste on your tongue.

Well, things had certainly changed since then.

At the ripe age of twenty-nine years old, I found myself risking something far worse than being grounded for drinking the only booze in the house: a bottle of rosé. The real stuff, not the placebo wine I gave Grandpa Moe after his stroke. I hadn't meant to hide it, but when I noticed it had somehow been misplaced after I did The Swap, I decided to keep it in the laundry room, right behind the big bottle of detergent. Because a secret stash, even if accidental, always came in handy.

"Josie?" Grandpa Moe called from his room, bringing me to a halt in the middle of the hallway, rosé behind my back.

"Yes?"

"You still up?"

"Yes."

"I can't sleep either," he admitted.

That ball of lead taking up all the space in my chest doubled in weight. "I know."

There was a pause, and I knew exactly what he was going to say next. "You sure you're okay?" Another careful pause. "We can talk. I can make you a grilled cheese."

My fingers tightened around the neck of the bottle. "I'm okay," I lied. "Plus, it's past two in the morning. That's a little late for grilled cheese."

Silence followed, long enough that I started moving. But then Grandpa said, "I love you, honey. So you holler if you need me, okay?"

It took me a second to speak through the lump in my throat. "Love you too! Good night."

Closing the door behind me, I didn't waste any time plopping down right in the middle of the bed and placing the bottle on my nightstand. I still hadn't decided if I wanted to open it, but I dragged it a little closer. Just in case.

I settled back against the headboard and blinked at the cream wallpaper in front of me. Then I glanced at the sun I'd painted one day, all these years ago, and never covered because it made me smile.

It didn't tonight. It made me the opposite, and I didn't have the heart to dissect why.

I didn't want to think. I wanted to be blank. To be numb. To turn into an inanimate object without overwhelming emotions. I could be a vase. Hold flowers. Bring joy into a room. Breathe that last wisp of life into something meant to sag and shrivel.

That thought had a dark aftertaste. I didn't like it, but sagging and shriveling seemed to be in the cards for me after all. A frame from the clip that half the country had seen now waltzed across my mind and I shook my head, shoving it away with a scoff.

I eyed the stack of books that had accidentally piled up at the foot of my bed. A spooky thriller, the autobiography of a pop star that promised all the 2000s goss, and a couple of spicy romance novels I'd been dying to read. None of that called out to me right now. I wasn't exactly in the mood for getting spooked, gossip was a definite nope, and romance . . . should be the last of my priorities right now.

My gaze flickered to my dresser. The top drawer, where I'd decided to lock my phone. It had been blowing up with so many messages, so many reminders of all the things I didn't want to think of, so many people asking if I was okay. I wasn't, and I didn't want to talk about it. I'd never done this. Ever. I wasn't the kind of person who needed to retreat after a blow. Not even after Mom's passing, and definitely not after I'd run away from any man I was supposed to marry.

In those instances, the people I loved brought me the comfort I needed. But not tonight. Tonight, I didn't want to see Grandpa's sadness. Or hear about Adalyn's and Cameron's concern. My father's—and Bobbi's—disappointment.

I was even struggling to face Matthew. Struggling with the concern and the protectiveness on his face after Grandpa had shown us the video. The absolute but silent refusal to go back to the Lazy Elk after we'd driven here. He'd wanted to stay, I'd seen it in his eyes. I'd seen all of that, all of this, overwhelming him too.

Matthew had waited for me to ask him. I wasn't a fool, but I'd let him leave. Why stay?

I didn't want to be checked in on tonight. I wasn't ashamed or embarrassed. I just felt . . . ugly. Inside. All wrong. Like I wanted to crawl out of my skin and hide under my bed until the world outside my door disappeared.

A sigh erupted out of me, my gaze drifting to the drawer again. Had Matthew texted? Called? Was he at home, watching the video of me making my way up an aisle in a wedding dress, leaving a gasping wedding party and a shocked groom behind, on repeat? Could he tell that I'd been losing it as I ran that velvety rug that separated a sea of chairs? Was he finally realizing that I had issues? That I was messed-up?

Who did that anyway? Sprint, as fast as one can, away from someone you were about to promise to love in sickness and in health. For the rest of your life.

I did. And he'd known. Matthew had. Everyone had known. But it was different to watch it happen. It became undeniable then. Written in stone.

Ugh. Was Venus in retrograde? Was that why I felt so yucky, why all my past relationships festered in a way they never had?

I should draw a bath. Yes. At two a.m. With a new surge of energy, I headed for my en suite and started the water. As hot as possible so the steam could purge all the bad thoughts. I snatched my bath box off the rack and started concocting the perfect recipe. Lavender bath bomb. Wild berry salts. Peppermint essential oil. The tub filled, and I basked in the delicious scents, the change in the atmosphere, the mirror steaming up.

Oh. The rosé.

I snatched the bottle from the nightstand. And a pink mug that would have to serve as a glass from the top of my dresser. I turned around.

My feet stopped me, rooted to the floor.

My phone was inside the dresser.

I told myself to leave. Get in the bath. But the temptation was too strong, and my willpower had always been so weak, so easily overthrown by curiosity. That was why I'd hidden my phone. I sighed. Squared my shoulders. Whirled back around. In a blink, the phone was in my hands.

My gaze fell on the one name in the sea of notifications. I tapped on it. I couldn't help myself.

MATTHEW: You up?

I chewed my lip in thought. He'd texted only a few minutes ago. Had he been trying to give me space? Was that why he'd only texted now? Was that why he wasn't asking if I was okay, like everybody else?

"God, Josie," I muttered, stopping that. I was giving myself a headache.

I could ignore the text. The reasonable thing to do right now was that. Then the bath, then sleep. Phone in hand, I padded back to the bath, set the bottle and phone on the side table I kept by the tub, and undressed. I slipped in, making up my mind: I wasn't going to reply. I'd soak in my scalding hot water and let all these essential oils melt everything away. Including Matthew's text.

The screen of my phone lit up. I peeked.

MATTHEW: Knock knock.

I stuck my hand out of the tub and snatched my phone.

JOSIE: Go to sleep.

MATTHEW: You go first.

This was ridiculous. He was ridiculous.

JOSIE: I'm busy.

MATTHEW: Doing what?

JOSIE: Taking a bath.

MATTHEW: I'm calling your bluff.

With a scoff, I snapped a picture, making sure to get my feet peeking out of the water so he'd know it wasn't a fake, and sent it.

The three dots danced on the screen for so long that I wondered if I was getting a whole paragraph in response. Or maybe nothing at all.

MATTHEW: I'm coming over.

I straightened, water splashing with my sudden move.

JOSIE: What? No. Why?

MATTHEW: Because you left me on read. Because you're drinking. Because I'm worried. Because you didn't ask "who's there?" and that tells me you're really not okay. Because you didn't ask me to stay with you tonight.

Everything in me softened, melted, broke. *Because you didn't ask me to stay with you tonight.* And I had no choice but to ease back into the water and take a deep breath.

JOSIE: I'm sorry.

JOSIE: I didn't want to leave you on read.

JOSIE: But you can drop the car keys and slip back into bed. If Grandpa catches a boy sneaking into the house at this hour, I can't be responsible for what he'll do.

MATTHEW: I'm your fiancé.

MATTHEW: Not a boy.

I didn't answer. Not right away. I didn't know how. Not when my eyes were caught on one specific word and I was feeling this . . . way.

JOSIE: Knock knock.

I held my breath, waiting. And when his text came, I smiled, a little relieved. It was a small one, probably a sad one too, but it still felt like a reprieve.

MATTHEW: Who's there?

JOSIE: Dwayne.

MATTHEW: Dwayne who?

JOSIE: Dwayne the wine and the bathtub, I'm drowning! Glug glug.

MATTHEW: That's not really reassuring me.

I chuckled. I thought it was pretty funny. But just as it came, it went away, both the sentiment and my smile dying off, leaving me . . . back in the same place.

JOSIE: Tonight was weird. I'm sorry.

MATTHEW: I don't want or need an apology, Josie.

JOSIE: What do you want or need, then?

MATTHEW: Don't ask for something you're not ready to hear.

JOSIE: That's a good line. 🙂 Kinda hot.

MATTHEW: I'm finally being noticed, yay.

JOSIE: I've always noticed you, Matthew.

When his response took a few moments to come, I shifted in the tub, wanting to take that back.

MATTHEW: Talk to me, Baby Blue. Please?

The nickname caught me off guard. It was almost as if I could see him, hear him saying those words. That concern shining in the brown of his eyes, making it darken, just like it had earlier tonight. I started to type, and suddenly I couldn't stop.

JOSIE: I don't want to talk. I locked my phone in a drawer when I got home because I was scared you'd ask me to explain myself. Ask if I was fine. How I felt. But how I feel right now isn't important. Not in the big scheme of things. So it's not what I want to be thinking about right now. Because then I'll think of everything else. Like the reason why I ran that day, or all the other times I was a coward and ruined things, just like I might be ruining everything now, and I'll be left with nothing. With no one.

So no. I don't want to talk. We'll dissect the absolute wreck that I am tomorrow. You can fix me some other day. But not today. Not tonight. And not after you called me Baby Blue like that.

MATTHEW: Josie.

MATTHEW: You're important.

MATTHEW: You have me.

MATTHEW: And there's nothing about you I want to fix.

MATTHEW: There's nothing about you that needs fixing.

I stared at the screen. My heart now pounding. Drumming in my ears. Making my chest rise and fall. *Heaving.* I was heaving, and I couldn't believe he'd just told me that.

JOSIE: Stop that. Don't be nice to me.

MATTHEW: Do you want me to be mad? Because I am, but not at you. You don't need to hide from me. Give me everything that's making you feel this way. I meant it when I said we would talk later. And I said that before anything happened. That video doesn't matter.

JOSIE: Of course it matters.

MATTHEW: It doesn't to me. The only thing that matters right now is you.

The only thing that matters right now is you.

I blinked at the phone, incapable of making sense of the ruckus he was causing in my head, the wreck in my chest. And once more, my fingers were flying over the screen and I was once again talking, just like he wanted. Just like he asked.

JOSIE: I wish you wouldn't have said that. I wish . . . we could go back to what we were doing. To what we know how to do. Our rules. Meaningless jokes. Touching and it not meaning anything. You, talking about magic or demanding that I grope your ass. I wish you'd wanted to flirt and distract me, say those things that made me blush, or I don't know, ask for something outrageous like a nude, just because it'd take my mind off things.

MATTHEW: Nudes. Jokes. A distraction. My dirty mouth. Is that all you want from me, then?

No. I didn't. Not even close. I didn't even know why I'd typed that, only that I needed him. Matthew. Not because he was goofy or flirty, but because I desperately needed him in a way I couldn't explain. In a way that made me scared of losing him if I got too close. Too fast. If I gave him a little too much. If he saw me on that stupid video in such a low moment. But he'd been right. There were things I wasn't ready to hear. Or perhaps, I simply wasn't brave enough to admit any of this.

JOSIE: Maybe I do.

MATTHEW: You mean that?

The air was sawing in and out of my lungs now. My skin burning for a reason that had nothing to do with the temperature of the water, or the steam clinging everywhere.

MATTHEW: Do you mean that, Josie?

My heart doubled, tripled its pace.

JOSIE: Yes.

My phone buzzed in my hand. Matthew was calling. I picked up. "Hi," I breathed into the line.

Matthew's answer was immediate, his voice deep, intimate in the silence of the night. "I'll give you what you need."

I swallowed. "Matthew—"

"How much wine did you have?"

My laugh was strange. Strangled. Not really a laugh. "None."

His sigh was deep and relieved. Also a little sad.

"I'm so—" I started.

But he cut me off. "Stop apologizing. I'm not sorry. Not with you." My lips parted with a question, but he beat me to it again. "Ask me what I'm wearing, Josie."

My skin flushed warmer still. I hesitated. Just for an instant. But this is what I had asked for, hadn't I? I'd all but begged him to distract me. Guilt sprouted. He'd already given me so much, and I kept—

"Ask me what I'm wearing, Baby Blue," he repeated. His voice had changed. Turned a little lighter. Easier. "You'll like my answer, I promise."

The guilt started to recede. "What are you wearing?"

"Sweats. No shirt," he answered. Fast. Diligently. My pulse sped up. "Ask me more."

"Are you in bed?"

"Yes. More."

A soft puff of air left me. "Tucked inside or over the covers?"

"I'm sitting, back against my headboard, covers at my feet."

I hummed. That was a nice visual. I liked it. A little too much. "Are your glasses on?"

Matthew's husky laugh came through the line, the sound curling around my ears, easing me and awakening a specific part of me. "Is this a kink I should know about?"

"Maybe," I told him, voice soft.

There was a pause, and an audible swallow. "Tell me what you see."

"My knees," I answered. "They're peeking out of the water. Which is pink. And there're bubbles."

"And what do you smell, huh? I'm sure something nice."

"Essential oils. Lavender, berries, and peppermint."

He hummed, the sound appreciative and . . . something else. Something that made me shift in the tub. Anticipation starting to climb up my spine. "What can you feel against your skin, Josie?"

"I . . ." I wetted my lips. "I can feel everything." He let out another hum, encouraging me. "The steam and sweat clinging to my shoulders and face. The bubbles, bursting against my arms and chest. My . . . legs, slippery when I move."

"Does it feel nice?" he asked, voice tickling my ear it was so deep. "When you move inside that tub you've filled with all those wonderful things?"

"Yes," I answered, and God, I could feel my blood pumping at an increasing rhythm, rising to my face, dropping to my feet.

"Where are your hands, Josie?"

My stomach dipped. "One holding the phone. The other one in the water."

"Where exactly? Describe it to me. Is it on your thigh? Belly? Chest?"

I swallowed, my eyelids fluttering shut. We were really doing this. He was doing what I'd asked for, and the knowledge, the close approach of the line we were about to cross, made me . . . breathless.

Heady. Hesitate. "Matthew," I whispered. That's it. That was all. His name.

"Where," he repeated. A demand. It made all that doubt melt away. Almost completely. It also made me want to ask him to please bark more demands. Take the reins I didn't know how to hold. "Close your eyes," he said, and the way he'd somehow guessed. Known. Read me. Even through the phone, almost made me want to weep. Laugh. "Now."

My eyelids shut, and I leaned my head back onto the tub rest.

He let out a strained sound as if he could see me. Obedient. Eyes shut. "Now tell me, where's your hand, Baby Blue?"

Baby Blue. "On my thigh."

"I want you to bring it up," he instructed, pulling an exhale out of me. "Can you do that?"

"Yes," I whispered. "Where?" Another broken breath left me. "How? I—"

"Drag it slowly up your body, letting the tips of your fingers draw a line on your skin. All the way up to your hip, belly, stopping at the swells of your breasts."

My blood swirled at the clarity of his instructions, the hardness in his voice, how much I loved hearing it. I moved, dragging my hand impossibly slow, every touch, shiver, and caress feeling twice as powerful with my eyes closed and Matthew's breath in my ear.

"Is it there?" Matthew asked, and I nodded my head with a soft hum. "Good. Now, I want you to take your breast in your hand and do whatever makes you feel good, Josie. I want to hear a little moan. Think you can give me that?"

"I want to. I can try," I murmured, but when I did I just . . .

"What's wrong?" Matthew asked.

"I think we should skip this part," I said, unsure of what to do or how to do it. "It's not—"

"Do you want to hear what I'd do? If I was there with you? If it was my hand and not yours?"

"Yes."

A low grunt left him. "I'd start with my mouth on your jaw. Just a quick nip. A graze of my teeth." A pause. "That's not really breaking any rule."

My lips parted with a yes, a no, I wasn't sure.

"Then I'd drag it down," he continued, a shiver curling down the imaginary line. "Right along your neck, nipping at your collarbone, right until every inch of skin on your chest tingled and those nipples hardened under my gaze."

My blood swooshed down, gathering, pooling, flooding me with need. My thighs pressed. "I'd like that."

"Like, huh?" he asked with a strange sound. "What if I'd close my lips over that glorious peak? Just a little. Just enough. Just until you're shaking. Would you like that too?"

My hand moved up, following his lead. Imagining it was him. "Yes."

"That *yes* right there, only when you said that would I lift my head and watch your face." A strangled breath left me at the thought. "Rewarding every one of those with a soft pinch, wanting a little more."

The words, what they painted in my mind, the sensation of my hand, extricated a whimper from my throat.

Matthew rasped out a laugh. "The idea is killing me too, sweetheart. It's making me mad with need."

I wanted that, I realized. I wanted Matthew mad with need. My body, aching with that same urge. The hunger in his voice.

"Keep going," he grumbled, rustling of clothing in the background. "Don't stop making it feel good, Josie. That's what I'd do. Drive you closer and closer to the edge. Drive us both desperate for more."

My lungs expelled a rough breath, my motions obedient, my need growing. "Matthew?"

"I'm here."

He wasn't, though. And that felt so unfair. "I'm—" Something coiled inside me. "I need more. I—"

"Pull your hand down."

A whimper escaped me.

"Right between your legs. Do that for me." The command in his voice had me moving, obedient, letting my hand glide down, right where all that pulsing need swirled and gathered. The tips of my fingers brushed the apex of my thighs, and a rocky breath broke out. "That's not the spot," Matthew said. "I want to hear you squirm with need. Try again for me."

Squirm with need. Without him here? Touching me? "I'll get there," I told him, moving my hand tentatively over my folds "I want to hear you—"

"You're going to be a good girl and let me work for those moans."

My belly cartwheeled, the pulsing under my fingers doubling. I moaned.

"That's a good fucking girl."

Oh God.

"Now a little faster," he instructed. His voice took on an edge, and I moved faster, hearing fabric ruffling. Matthew grunted. "I'm the one getting you off. Understand? My voice. The idea of my touch."

The motion of my fingers turned more confident, tracing one rough circle after the next. Moving quicker. Just the way I knew would walk me closer and closer. Just the way he wanted me to.

"Yes or no, Josie?"

"Yes."

"Now give me what I want," Matthew commanded, and boy, the way his voice broke tipped me a little closer to the edge. "Slip those fingers in," he instructed. "Make us both feel good."

My fingers glided right in, a loud moan toppling from my lips.

"That fucking sound," he all but growled. "The things I'd do for it. The things I'm doing, Josie. The things I'll do if you ask."

"Matthew?" I called, feeling my cheeks burn, my body heating impossibly high, the sound of water splashing. "Oh God. I—" My words cut off, need building up, climbing, rising, feeling like too much.

"Keep going," he rasped, a groan escaping between gulps of air. "Thrust a little deeper." Sweet baby Jesus, was he stroking himself? Oh God—Matthew grunted again. "Touching is good, isn't it, Josie? No rules are being broken, now give me what I need. Let go. Give your fiancé a little scream. Tell me who's making the fucking world disappear."

Give your fiancé a little scream.

Tell me who's making the fucking world disappear.

It was that, all of it, all at once, that made the tension gripping my body break. *Say my name.* My eyelids fluttered closed and that wave of heat I'd been riding crashed.

"Matthew," I expelled, spasms traveling through my body. Oh boy. Oh man. I was flying. Coming so desperately hard that I—

"Josie?" came with a knock.

My whole body flinched, my hands flying up.

The phone, loose in my hand, slipped, dropping into the water.

"No!" I yelped.

"Josie," Grandpa Moe repeated. "Is something wrong in there?"

Everything was. "Everything's good!" I shouted, fishing my phone out of the water. The screen was black. Shit. Crap. "I'm taking a bath," I explained, jumping out of the tub and wrapping the device in a towel. "I'm . . . relaxing?" I shook my head. "Affirmative. I am relaxing. Why?"

There was a beat of silence. "I heard you talking."

"I was talking to myself," I answered quickly. I squinted my eyes closed, silently cursing. "Rambling. Singing." *Singing?* "Did you need anything?"

Grandpa Moe grumbled. "Just checking on you is all. I saw light under the door."

I sagged with a breath. "I'm all right."

"You sure you're okay?" Grandpa Moe insisted.

"I will be," I admitted.

Maybe once I brought my phone back to life and texted Matthew, before he panicked and thought I'd died, victim of the incredible orgasm he'd just guided me through.

Or maybe I wouldn't be okay at all.

Not when it dawned on me what Matthew and I had just done.

CHAPTER FIFTEEN

"What's gotten into you, Josie Girl?"

I shifted my glaring from the bowl I had clasped against my chest to the man in suspenders. "My egg whites. They're not stiffening."

Grandpa Moe frowned at me. "That's what has you sounding like a grizzly?"

No. But also, yes. "Is your show done?" I gritted, restarting the whipping motions of my arm. "The tiramisu is, as you might be able to tell from the alleged growling, not ready *yet.* Now if you don't mind . . ." I pointed to the door with my head.

"Isn't it supposed to rest in the fridge overnight?"

I narrowed my eyes at him, the motions of my wrist turning aggressive. It was supposed to do that, yes. "I'll be the judge of that."

Grandpa looked unimpressed. "But—"

"No buts," I hissed.

"Josie—"

"I am fine. I am—"

He stomped his foot. "Put that whisk away before you hurt yourself, girl!"

My arm came to a stop. I was panting. Heaving. Much like three nights ago, in the tub, when— No. Absolutely not. I was not thinking of that. Not now and preferably not with Grandpa Moe present.

"I'm in perfect control of my whisk," I announced, bringing my breathing down. "And my life, by the way. Before you ask for the one thousandth three hundred and forty-eighth time if I'm okay. I am. I'm so okay and so in control that it's not even funny. And these egg whites are going to be subjected, dominated, and . . . fluffy as hell. In time. You'll see."

Grandpa Moe's expression softened. There was no pity in it, just concern. Which wasn't a relief, not really. It just made Grandpa one more person I was trying not to preoccupy and hurt with my doings. Or to show how I felt about Andrew's announcement. About December first. The wedding.

Only Grandpa I hadn't been able to avoid for the last three days.

"Look around you, honey," he said. I didn't. I knew exactly how *around me* looked. He continued anyway, "The kitchen is a mess. There's not an inch of any surface that's not covered in lady fingers, bowls of coffee, cocoa powder, or egg splatter. This is just tiramisu. You've done far more elaborate recipes and made it look easy. Remember the croquembouche?"

I inhaled. "This is not *just* tiramisu. I baked the lady fingers. From scratch. I brought special beans from Josie's Joint for the coffee. I'm using the best quality mascarpone I found available in the *county* and I'm whisking the whites manually. I'm—"

"It's still not croquembouche."

"Stop saying 'croquembouche.' "

Grandpa's nostrils flared. "Nah. Croquembouche."

"Grandpa—"

"Croquembouche," he repeated.

Jesus Christ. "You're unbearable."

"And you're cranky," he pointed out. "You're a *crankembouche.*"

My teeth gritted. "Are you five?"

"I wish," he grumbled.

And he reminded me so much of Matthew in that exact moment that I felt my irritation slip away. Because that was what thinking of Matthew did to me now. It made everything else melt away. Which wasn't good. Not right now. Not after that night.

Grandpa tutted. "You're acting like the fools in my show. Only it's no longer entertaining watching you. It's just painful at this point."

"Gee, thanks," I murmured. "And don't worry. I'm not about to go around giving away long-stem roses to random men." *I already did that in a way,* my brain filled in. And I had to shake my head, physically ridding myself of the thought.

He shrugged, unconvinced. "This thing's messing with your head. The tiramisu, but also the video and the goddamn wedding. I don't like it."

I put the bowl and whisk down and crossed my arms over my chest. "Nothing's messing with my head," I lied.

Except maybe orgasms. And fine, a wedding day that was less than a month away. And the internet going absolutely bananas over a ten-second clip. And Andrew, and Bobbi, and Willa Wang and—

Maybe Grandpa was right.

"What's in the pantry, then?"

I scoffed. "Pantry stuff."

"Oh yeah?"

I narrowed my eyes at him. I knew what was currently hanging from one of the racks in the pantry. I simply couldn't explain why they were there. Or how Grandpa found out they were there in the first place. Had he seen me carry them down the stairs?

Grandpa's lips thinned. "Just call Matthew already. It's been a hellish three days with that woman calling at all times and driving past the house. I've run out of excuses and I'm annoyed. At the very least she should be annoying Matthew *and* you. Not me."

"Well, that's mature and not at all selfish," I deadpanned.

"You're the one being a little selfish, honey."

Well, ouch. I leaned my hip on the counter and moved some of the ladyfingers around, pretending that hadn't affected me. Was I being selfish? "Am I being selfish?"

"Ghosting is always selfish."

A gasp escaped my throat. "How do you even know what ghosting is? And I'm not ghosting Matthew."

Grandpa Moe arched his brows. "I know plenty. And you got the boy wrapped into this whole thing and now, what? You're not talking to him?"

"My phone died. I had to put it in rice. It's a miracle it came back to life at all. And I'm sure he's fine. Maybe a little worried, but okay."

"I saw him yesterday, power walking through the edge of town while he glared at the ground much like you were at those egg whites."

My chest squeezed. He'd been power walking? While glaring at the ground? What did that mean? Was he—

Grandpa continued, "It's my duty to point out that you're not doing yourself any favors. Whatever reason you think you have is idiotic."

"I thought you didn't like him."

"I don't dislike him. And if I can cut the boy some slack, so can you. Now do that before he resorts to trespassing with some boom box on his shoulder and makes a fool out of himself."

I huffed out a laugh. But it was bitter. "As if he'd ever—"

The doorbell rang.

Grandpa Moe smirked. "He'd better not be bringing any music with him. I paused right at the rose ceremony and I'd like to watch who Emmanuelle leaves for last. In peace."

With that, he whirled around and left, giving me no choice but to get the door myself.

My insides played tug-of-war, a part of me hoping it'd be him, and another one dreading the idea that it would. It was so silly. *I* was being so silly.

Objectively, I knew nothing needed to change after our phone call. That I had asked him to distract me in the first place, and that there were plenty of things to prioritize before this. Like that stupid wedding announcement Andrew made at the midnight farmers' market and what that meant for me. Matthew. Us. Everything, really.

We don't get married but stay friends.

That was one of the rules.

And now . . . Now what? Could we even keep doing this, seeing each other, talking, without breaking any of those statements?

How did one stay *friends* after what had happened? How could we stay engaged and not get married but stay friends after the other night? Maybe Matthew had had casual relationships, casual sex, but I hadn't. Not ever. So I didn't know if I could put it all aside and act like he hadn't given me an orgasm. A mind-blowing, toe-curling orgasm at that. Like I hadn't moaned his name on the phone. Now I didn't know if I could see him and not think of that. All because I'd been upset and it seemed like the world had been crumbling on me.

You're important.

You have me.

And there's nothing about you I want to fix.

There's nothing about you that needs fixing.

You have me, my brain was stuck on. But did I? Not only did I not know what to do with that, but I no longer knew if I did have him.

He'd said all those things before I'd begged him to distract me. Before I'd let him believe that distraction was *all* I wanted from him. It wasn't, but what if I'd hurt him? Confused him? Annoyed him?

What if Matthew wanted out now that he'd had time to think? Now that everyone believed he'd be standing at an altar on December first, waiting for me? I'd understand, I really would. I was no longer sure if I could do this whole engagement thing myself. This silly fiancé dilemma on my hands that I'd taken way too far. I'd been so selfish. Just like Grandpa Moe accused me of being. Just like I'd done so many times, to so many men.

That was why I'd been hiding.

Because Sam and Nick were right, I was a runner, and therefore, this is what I did best.

Another knock on the door made me notice that I'd been standing there, staring into space.

I squared my shoulders. Clasped the knob. Turned it.

It'll all be fine. You'll say hi. He'll reply with a small smile, because that's the man Matthew is. Good, kind, no matter what. Would you like to come in? I think we should talk.

Matthew's eyes met mine.

My breath caught.

His mouth twitched. But it wasn't a smile. "Ah . . . fuck, Josie."

Ah fuck, Josie indeed.

He looked so handsome in front of me. At my door. Right here with me. Should I make small talk? Follow that with a joke? Oh, the plan had been to—

"You can't avoid me anymore," he said. "Please."

Straight to the point it was. I couldn't complain, really. It was one of the things I liked the most about him. "I wasn't trying to avoid you," I answered, voice weak, the lie rolling off my tongue. It was one of the things I liked the least about me. At least lately.

"I went on a mental health walk."

That chipped at the armor I was set on keeping around my chest. That was what Grandpa had meant, then. He'd seen Matthew on that walk. Hearing him say the words didn't sit well with me. It made the sour taste at the back of my mouth even more sour. Mental health was important. My kitchen covered in mascarpone cheese and egg splatter was proof of it. "Did it help?"

Matthew's jaw clenched. Then he pulled something I'd somehow missed from behind his back. "I made you a pie."

The armor clunked to the floor. "You did what?"

"I made you a pie."

My chest went warm and cold, soft and tender, exposed to everything he'd say now. My words were nothing but a whisper. "But no one ever bakes for me."

"I do."

He did.

Every ounce of fortitude and stubbornness in my body melted away with those two words. Every fear that had kept everything inside me so taut, so high-strung, as if ready to break, receded from view.

Matthew made me a pie. I'd been here, hiding, for three days, like the coward I was, letting him believe things I didn't really think, but that I couldn't put into words, and he'd showed up at my door with a pie he'd baked for me.

"Let me in?" he asked.

A broken breath left me, and I hoped to God that I wasn't going to cry, because it'd be so silly. This was just pie. Matthew stepped forward, as if in response to that thought. The side of the tray brushed my shoulder. It smelled like apples and cinnamon. He reached out with his hand, his thumb swiping across my cheek. When he brought it down, there was a splatter of what had to be egg white clinging to his finger.

"Tiramisu," I murmured. "That's my version of a mental health walk."

Matthew's eyes flashed with understanding. Something else too. "Let me in, Josie."

I *knew* that if I told him to leave, he would. I also wondered if the words meant more to him than just stepping inside my house. They probably did, and that was fair. I wouldn't turn him away, though. I didn't think I could, as scared as I'd been and was still.

"I think we should talk," I said, just like I'd rehearsed in my head. I moved to the side. "Take a seat in the living room, please. I'll bring the plates."

Matthew's apple pie was fantastic. A little too much lemon for many, but I liked my apple desserts more sour than sweet. Although maybe sitting down to eat hadn't been the best idea. Because now, dangling off a corner of Matthew's lips was a tiny crumb of caramelized pastry. So small I was only noticing it because I'd been fixated on his mouth.

The little moans he made while he cleaned off his plate.

It was truly unfair how much he loved to eat and how happy it made me to watch him.

"What's in the kitchen, Josie?"

My eyes flickered up his face. No glasses today. "Nothing special besides the mess left after a failed dessert." And the four hangers currently hooked to a rack in my pantry. "Why?"

"You're stealing glances at the kitchen door. And you asked me to wait here. You said 'please.' "

"Just manners." I stood up and walked to his end of the couch before retrieving the empty plate from him. "And the fact that I'm a thoughtful host who wants her guest to be comfy," I added, stacking it on top of mine.

Matthew tugged at the hem of my cardigan, and I glanced down at his face. "You were wearing this the night I got here. After you changed."

My heart skipped a beat. I made myself smile, but it was probably strained. "It's my cozy cardigan. I wear it when the mood hits."

"The mood," he murmured. His thumb and index fingers moved around the fabric. I watched him shake his head as if making up his mind about something. "So is that what I am now? A guest?"

Here it was, then, the moment I'd been avoiding. The conversation we'd been tiptoeing around while we had his pie. The topic that had been keeping me awake at night, filling me with just as much anxiety as the fact that the whole town—my community, my father, my sister and my friend, the world—believed we were getting married on December first. Or how my reputation was now set in stone. Online, thanks to Page Nine. Confirming what everyone thought of me. All thanks to an anonymous editor's submission.

"You should tell me what you are," I finally said.

His brows met for an instant. But it wasn't in confusion, I didn't think. It was determination. Unlike me, Matthew never shied away from saying things like they were. "I'm Matthew. I'm your fiancé."

Are those two things the same? I should have asked.

"Even after that night?" I said instead. "Even after everything that's changed?"

Matthew came to his feet. "What has changed?"

The nearness of his body overwhelmed me. Like it had never before. In a good way. A way that made me want more. To tug at his sweater. Flick my fingers across his cheek. Hear his voice close, words falling on my ear. This was what I'd feared. "There's a clip of me in a wedding dress, jaw slack and eyes crazy, as I run away from a beautiful yet packed winter wonderland ceremony." I averted my gaze. "I go so far as to stomp on the bouquet. Even if accidentally. It was a beautiful one, and those flowers didn't deserve that."

Soft fingers touched my chin, pushing up. I met his gaze. "There was a waterfall, Josie." His jaw clenched. "Right behind that fool. How could you *not* run away like that? He couldn't have known."

He had known. But so had I. "My phobia didn't fully kick in until that day. And I was convinced I could do it. Greg worked really hard at an eight-week plan to correct it with meditation. We were both sure it'd work."

"You don't correct a fear," Matthew countered with a frown. "You change the fucking venue."

"It was his dream to get married in a place like that."

"His dream should have been getting married to you."

I felt myself pale at his words, as if they had somehow opened my eyes to something I'd never seen. "Thank you," I murmured. All that *tenderness* in my chest expanding, eating away at every ounce of space. "That's a nice sentiment."

He stepped a little closer, boots moving forward until he was occupying all of my space. "I'm not being nice."

My eyelids fluttered shut at how good he felt standing so close. "Then what are you being? Because I thought you'd be in a panic, honestly. I thought—"

"I'm sorry, for one," he said. And when I reopened my eyes there was something I didn't like on his face. Something I hated seeing there. "I shouldn't have pushed you like I did when you were very clear about not wanting to talk."

I felt myself part my lips. "What? No. You have nothing to apologize for."

"Then answer my question, please." His Adam's apple bobbed. "What's changed? Because I need to know. I've given you space now, and I'm done doing that. I'm . . ." He let out a strange laugh. "I'm needy, I guess. I'm not cool enough to act like I don't care, when I've been moping around. No. Fuck that. I'm cool enough to admit I have. I made a playlist. For the walks. There was more than one. I watched all the seasons of *Bridgerton*. And Christ, that show is so goddamn good. It made me cry several times. I want to read the books now."

My lips twitched. I tried so hard to stop that, I really did, but I . . . God.

"You're smiling, Josie. It's beautiful."

A small puff of air left me. "You made me a pie."

No one baked for me. No one ever had. Not since Mom.

"A good fucking pie," he added.

My smile turned bigger. Sappier. Probably uglier. "You'll have to give me the recipe."

"No." He gave his head a shake. "I'll make you another one."

A strange wave of emotion rose, making my eyes . . . sting. And I—God. I couldn't cry. It didn't even make sense. *Focus, Josie. Focus.* I let out a shaky breath. "What do you want to do? Things have changed since we talked about our plan. There's . . . December first. And Andrew invited everyone in town. I . . . haven't talked to Bobbi, or been online, or answered my phone at all, but I guess the world knows about that now. Adalyn must hate me. Or think I hate her. Cam is probably furious." I shook my head. "I had Grandpa Moe check in on them to make sure she was feeling better. But I'm still a horrible sister."

"I talked to her," Matthew said. "To Cam too."

"You did?" My heart sped up. "To tell them what?"

Matthew's exhale was long and deep as the air left his nose. "That Andrew blindsided us."

Us. A breath caught. So he hadn't just talked to Adalyn and Cam. He had for the two of us.

As if sensing I needed to hear more, he continued, "That we never planned for the date to be so soon, but Bobbi went behind our back. That they're doing whatever serves the narrative, independently of what we want. That you were so caught off guard by that and the clip, that you needed a few days to unplug and recharge. That being in the spotlight is new for you, and you're overwhelmed. That you were barely even leaving the house, let alone talking to anyone, and that that's so out of character, I was scared and basically running circles around the place, making sure no one bothered you. And that unfortunately included them."

My voice barely came out. "Were you? Running circles around the house?"

"I wanted to."

But he hadn't. Yet, he'd still made sure to keep things under control. Everything I'd neglected by hiding and curling into a messy, egg-splattered ball.

A strange sound bubbled up my throat. It was relief, I realized. Plain and simple. Overpowering, eye-opening relief. "We're four days short of a month away. From December first," I said. "That would scare me." And it did.

There was a flash of surprise in the light brown of his eyes. The specks of green. "I agreed to this. I told you I'd do it. So give me some credit, yeah? I'm not going to have a change of heart and back down because Andrew makes some speech." An exhale left him. "I don't like or trust Bobbi, but she's good at what she does. She had the video taken down." His expression sobered, and he didn't need to say the words. *Although the damage has already been done.* "Let's give her room to act."

I thought about that for a brief moment, but . . . "You're right. I guess it doesn't make a difference whether we call things off now or four weeks from today."

Matthew's answer was a nod.

"What . . . What about the other night?"

"What about it?"

"We . . ."

His hand rose, the backs of his fingers grazing the side of my neck, brushing my hair back. His head dipped. "You came," he said in my ear. Just like I'd craved him doing minutes ago. Every night for three days straight. "Saying my name. It's all right, we say things like they are."

I stumbled over my words. Thoughts. The wave of heat washing over me. "Yes. It has to change something."

"Has to or you want it to?"

The way he'd asked me reminded me of that night too. He always managed to give me a choice, the choice, no matter how or what. "I don't want it to change anything."

"Then it won't." He leaned back a little, watching my face. "But I think I want a revision of the rules."

Grandpa's words returned, making a splash. *You got the boy wrapped into this whole thing.* I had. And now he was asking for some control.

"Of course."

"We add a new rule."

I nodded. "Okay."

"I distract you, Josie. From whatever's bothering you. Whatever's making you doubt who you really are and what we're doing. That'll be my job." His voice lowered. "Whenever you can't, I take control. I won't wait for you to ask. That's my rule."

Words from that night made it hard to answer him right away. *Nudes. Jokes. A distraction. My dirty mouth. Is that all you want from me, then?* I let him believe that. Of himself. But if I told him he was far more than that to me, he'd ask me what. What else am I, then? And I didn't know how to answer that. All I knew was that the idea of Matthew, here, so close all I could smell was him and apple and cinnamon from baking me a pie, would make me say anything so he'd stay. "Okay."

"Okay," he repeated. "Now, you show me what you're hiding in the kitchen."

I didn't even try pretending he meant the tiramisu. Clearly, he meant what I was really hiding. I was such a bad liar, truly. "Follow me, please. I guess that at this rate you were probably going to see them anyway."

Matthew followed me as I navigated the chaos that was my kitchen—that to his credit he ignored. And when I came to a stop, right in front of the pantry, he did too. Right behind me.

I took one deep breath, then threw the double doors open with a *ta-da.* Although the moment I turned around and looked at Matthew, I realized how much of an overkill that had been. This wasn't a fun, light ta-da moment.

"I was planning on donating them," I explained, glancing back at the pantry. "Today. That's why they're here. Although I think I chickened out at some point between hanging them here and getting wrapped up in my failed tiramisu."

It took Matthew a beat to speak, but when he did I knew, just by the way his voice changed, that his eyes were now on me. "These are your wedding gowns."

They were. They are. "You asked me to show you." I made myself smile. "Do you think it's strange I kept them?"

He frowned. "No. I—" A gulp of air left him. He shook his head. "It's not. I think it's something you would do."

"Are you saying my place is cluttered? That I might have a hoarding problem, perhaps?" I teased.

His chuckle was huffed out. And boy, did it alleviate some of the pressure in my chest at how out of sorts he'd just looked. Even if he didn't give me much of an answer.

I got it though. He didn't owe me one.

It was my turn to speak. "I've kept them," I said. "Because they're my wedding dresses. And as much as they're a reminder of bad or rash decisions, and hurt, and yes, also heartbreak, they're still memories of a time I was happy. Hopeful. In love, even if for a little while. That's also why I kept the rings. It's not like I have any of them on display or anything. I just like knowing they're here. Relationships end, and whether you're the one leaving or the one being left behind, the one thing that you can't run away from are the memories.

They're part of you; they deserve better than to disappear. These dresses are like a weird, twisted version of a photo album. That take up a lot of space."

Our eyes met, and I wondered what he saw. What was he thinking right at that instant? I was no longer insisting and asking whether he was spooked and wanted out. Not after we'd just talked about it. Not after he'd *showed* me I still had him.

"Will you give me a tour?" Matthew finally asked.

"Of my dresses?"

"Of your past. Your memories."

Matthew made something everyone seemed to see as a problem sound beautiful. Or maybe he reminded me that that was how I'd always seen it.

"Yes," I told him. "I think I can do that."

And in a strange way, I also wanted to. Not because it was the least I could do, but because I wanted to do it with him.

CHAPTER SIXTEEN

I snorted at my phone before typing a response.

JOSIE: It's the leg thing for me.

MATTHEW: I wanted to show you the shoes.

JOSIE: Oh. I just thought you wanted to brag about your foot pop.

MATTHEW: You asked me what I was wearing tonight.

JOSIE: And I love the effort and enthusiasm in your answer.

I also loved how those dark olive-green dress pants looked on him. And the cream-colored long-sleeved polo shirt. And oh, the glasses. I didn't dare ask him if he'd wear them tonight, but I wanted him to. I wanted to demand he would. My teeth caught my lip. I hit play again.

Matthew materialized on my screen, walking backward, away from the phone. His hands slipped into his pockets, gaze cast down. He spun, showcasing his side. Little pause. Then his back. A strange breath left me at the sight of those shoulders in that old-school-looking shirt. My fingers itched to pause and take a screenshot just so I could save that in my gallery, but my favorite part was coming. The one-, two-, three-second pause and . . . Foot pop.

Ugh.

I hadn't been expecting a fit-check video when I asked what he was wearing tonight, but I wasn't going to complain. Maybe I'd even demand one from him every day from this point on.

Fingers snapped right in front of my face, making me flinch.

"If you don't stop giggling at that screen, I'm going to regurgitate my A.B. and I'm not in the mood to wait for you to make a new one. It takes you the longest time."

I blinked at Bobbi. Specifically, the dark sunglasses she was wearing indoors. "What in the world is an *A.B.*?"

She raised the cup in front of her and gave it a quick shake, at which I frowned. "Christ, Josephine. Do you spend any time on the internet? Like at all?"

I rolled my eyes. "If you were referring to your coffee, I was calling that a *Sharkie*."

"Aw," Bobbi deadpanned. "You named a drink after me. I'd be moved if this was some Hallmark movie where the coffee shop owner teaches the badass boss bitch city lady—with amazing fashion sense—how to open her heart so she can start to live, laugh, love her life. But luckily, this is real life. And that's not on our meeting minutes."

It was easy to let that slide and not take offense, frankly. I felt like I'd lived exactly through that with Adalyn. "I'm not the Hallmark coffee shop owner you paint me to be." I smiled at her. "You know the mayor of town has power, right? I could make your job much harder if you cross me."

Bobbi studied me. "Wow, Blondie must have banged the shit out of you this week."

My jaw fell to the floor. Then I scoffed. "He did not." Bobbi's brows arched. "He just banged me the appropriate, normal amount engaged couples bang."

Her face turned into a grimace. And I . . . well, I laughed, even if still flushed a little. If Matthew had heard me saying that he would—

"Yikes," she said, feigning to shiver. "Noted. I won't bring that up again if you're going to get all starry-eyed. I really can't stomach more of that. Can we move on with our meeting?"

I tipped my chin up. "This is not a meeting. You ambushed me at work and demanded I tick boxes on some checklist."

"I'll write that in the minutes," she deadpanned.

"I have more suggestions if you're interested." I snatched the rag from my apron's pocket and folded it meticulously. "Like . . . *Annoying wedding planner had father of the bride invite county to wedding. Without telling her.* Or *annoying wedding planner demands coffee is prepared in under two minutes, claiming life-or-death situation.* Or *annoying wedding planner drives bride insane while wearing sunglasses indoors.*"

Bobbi gasped. "I'm not just a *wedding planner.*"

"If you say so."

She brought her sunglasses down her nose. Dark eyes narrowed at me. "I don't like this newfound surge of . . . defiance."

Defiance. The word now reminded me of Matthew too.

"God," Bobbi groaned. "People in love are too self-centered. I'm trying to have breakfast here, besides a meeting. Can you stop looking like that and focus?"

"Coffee is not a meal." I rolled my eyes at her, but a part of my brain lingered on a few specific words. "And I don't know if I can focus, honestly. I'm not happy about how things were handled. This is . . . my wedding. Not yours to announce on a whim."

"Listen," she said. And I couldn't tell exactly what it was about Bobbi, but I could tell something had just changed. "I'm sorry. I—" Her lips pursed. "Don't look so shocked. I really am sorry. But I had to act fast because I knew they were dropping something *bad* that night, all right. I have contacts at Page Nine. I was tipped off about that editor's submission. I knew it'd be a video, so it wasn't hard to put two and two together. Every wedding has a videographer. And you had four of those, so that makes four potential threats hanging over our heads."

"So you assumed the video had to be of me?"

"It couldn't be of Andrew. I have all of that under lock and key. You're my wild card, Josephine. You've always been. But you know that, and the reason why, so don't make me explain again why those two internet drama queens are so hyperfixated on you."

I did know why. Clout. Gossip. Drama. Entertainment. More to add to the Underwood saga. Bored people needing something to listen to so they wouldn't be alone with their own thoughts. It was funny, I supposed, that this had started as a problem for Andrew's image, and now, it seemed, was only a threat to mine. "It's three videographers, by the way," I said. "Duncan and I terminated our relationship weeks before the date we were supposed to get married."

"I know," Bobbi admitted. And at this point I wasn't even surprised by her knowing this. Her head tilted. "And I am sorry for blindsiding you, for what it's worth. Your little meltdown set us back almost a week."

A sigh escaped me. "Can you fix it, though? Can you fix any of this? Like you said you would?"

"I am Bobbi Shark, aren't I?" She pushed the iPad closer to me. "I had them take the video down in less than a day. A good way to continue that is by letting me *really* handle things now. I am your"—she shivered theatrically—"wedding planner, after all. So. Checklist?"

My gaze fell on the device, but I didn't reach out for it. Not yet. "On one condition."

Her eyes narrowed.

"No wedding dress," I said, to which she frowned. "I'll handle that."

I couldn't stomach looking at gowns. Not for this. Not when it felt like I was going to add a fifth memory to my already large collection. Not after I opened up like that to Matthew and showed him such a crucial part of who I was that no one else knew. And not when that'd mean I'd always have a reminder of something meant to break, hanging off a rack.

We don't get married but stay friends.

"I'm in charge of that," I finished. "It's something I want to pay for myself. And you can stop looking at me like I'd show up to my own wedding wearing a kitchen rag. I have experience with gowns, have I not? It'll be simple but elegant. I just don't need anyone to make a fuss. I'm tired of fusses at this point. And Andrew is already paying for . . . everything."

Bobbi considered my request for a long moment, then she said, "Works for me."

"Oh," I quipped. "And stop calling Grandpa Moe if I don't answer the phone. He's a little overwhelmed."

She shot me a glance. "Fine."

"Oh. And be nice to Robbie."

"I don't do nice," she deadpanned. "Certainly not to a man who wears a padded vest to a party. With pockets. That he stuffs with things."

"But—"

"I'll be reasonably agreeable." She gave a new push to the iPad. "Now check the list. I want you to mark your preferences on basic stuff so I can get an idea of what to do. Then Blondie will. I'll collate the two, and then we'll move to more important stuff. Like choice for the centerpieces. Florists. Catering. Seating chart for the rehearsal dinner and ceremony. It'll all take place on the farm, I've decided. So, is Roberto handling the lighting or should I bring a third party? And before you ask, no, your ring bearer is not going to be that pig. Last time I stepped foot on that farm, I caught him munching at my Hermès."

I blinked at her, watching her as she took a quick swig of her Sharkie. That bag Pedro Pigscal had been munching at, as she put it, was worth thousands of dollars.

But all right. Good. I could also exercise some reasonable agreeableness. So I took the iPad from her with a smile. And when she offered me a pen, I snatched it, too, my lips tipping even higher.

And I started checking random things off the multicategory lists. Tap-tap-tap-tap I went. Wickedly fast. Wooden accents, mason jars, centerpieces, hors d'oeuvres, Southern sweets, signature cocktails, a band, also a string quartet. Wedding favors? All of them. Types of flowers . . . tap. Caterer options, tap-tap. I swiped up and down and tapped some more. It took me all of a couple of minutes, and when I was done, I placed the pen beside the device and returned both things to her.

"Gee, thanks," Bobbi huffed.

I rested my chin on my fist. "I'm quick." And the wedding wasn't taking place anyway. So what did it matter what I chose? "Plenty of experience under my belt, huh?"

Bobbi collected the iPad and pen. "So I have heard," Bobbi muttered, glancing down. "Let's hope the Build Your Own Sundae station makes this one the charm, huh?"

I had no idea I'd ticked that off. "Nothing says wedding like a sundae."

Bobbi leaned away from the counter in one swift and elegant

motion. "Don't be late to tonight's party." Her lips pursed in thought. "Willa Wang will try to corner you and Blondie. Don't ask me how I know, but I know. So don't let her corner you. Understood? Say you're sick, or make the face from earlier and then pretend to sneak away to have sex. Engaged people get away with that. Or even better, you agree on a safe word with Blondie and use it. But you are, under no circumstances, talking to that woman unless I'm present. Got it?"

I swallowed. "Got it."

Bobbi whirled on her heels, then stopped herself.

She glanced back at me over her shoulder. "Oh, and please tell the maid of honor and best man to reach out. They didn't confirm attendance for tonight and I still don't know what kind of party they'll want to throw you, if any, but the good strippers will be booked on such short notice. And Andrew is not paying for the cheap ones, yeah?"

And with that she left.

Leaving me to deal with the implications of what she'd just said.

In my attempt at protecting Adalyn, I'd also kept her from things she should have been otherwise involved in. I hadn't even asked her to be my maid of honor. I . . . hadn't even known that they weren't coming to Andrew's wine tasting. I hadn't even talked to her in the past few days.

My heart sank.

God. Was I driving away my sister, too?

In a not-so-shocking turn of events, Willa Wang had cornered us.

Bobbi was going to give us so much crap for this. I'd been hoping she'd pop out of thin air like she always seemed to be doing, then whisk us away and save the night. But she was nowhere to be found.

This was bad. Worse than what I'd expected, or Bobbi had implied. Willa Wang had a recording device, the kind you saw in old movies. Did she know there was an app for that? The tiny charcoal-colored device she'd clicked the moment we'd taken a seat was making me feel like we were being interrogated.

That, and her questions.

Matthew had been batting those away as Willa pitched them. And there'd been many. We were just missing the little mound of sand beneath our feet at this point. Which was a strange thought considering I knew very little about baseball.

My fiancé shifted by my side, his arm coming up behind me and resting on the back of my chair. We were sitting on the patio, if I had to pick a name. I wasn't sure the kind of estate Andrew was renting had *a patio.* It felt more like a big expanse of greenery and gardens. Several. I was pretty sure there was a gazebo past the line of trees around the area where we were sitting, where most of the guests were gathered now, and I was betting all of Josie's revenue this month that there was a fountain somewhere.

The evening was warm, or warmer than it should have been, perhaps, much like the days preceding this one, but there was a bite to the air. The kind that had you keep a jacket at the ready. I'd left mine in the car just in case, and when Matthew's hand grazed the back of my shoulder blade with his thumb, I couldn't be more grateful for having left it there. I glanced at him, taking notice of how absolutely delectable he looked. His outfit looked even better in person, and when I'd come out the door to find him leaning on his car, I'd had to bite my tongue so I didn't beg him to wear those exact pants and that exact shirt every day of the week.

And by the way? I'd been right about the glasses. I—

Willa cleared her throat, snagging me back. "Thank you, Matthew," she said, even though she was looking at me. "That was another fascinating story about Boston-based sports. But I'm also interested in hearing about you, Josie."

So that's where the baseball metaphor had come from.

I snickered. "I think I'd like to hear more Boston trivia. It was really cool to hear that the sinking of the *Titanic* overshadowed the first big win the Red Sox ever had. I wonder if there's more Matthew can tell us about the Sox." The man beside me huffed out a surprised laugh. "Actually, I don't think he was done with the story about the wall. I'd love to hear why it's called the Green Monster. What came first, the fact that it was green or the name? I've been wondering since he mentioned it."

Willa let out a puff of air I interpreted as a sign of frustration.

The truth was that after Willa's first—and very personal—question directed at me, Matthew had been taking *all* of them. And the man possessed the ability to bring any topic of conversation to sports. Specifically, Boston-based sports. It was truly outstanding, really. Oh, and he was really bad at masking his clear distaste for the New York Yankees. Which I'd found . . . adorable. It was probably the only sports-related thing I could name that Matthew didn't *love.*

"It was very generous of Andrew," Willa said in that tone I was beginning to think she used when her patience slipped. "To extend the wedding invitation to everyone in town. Don't you think?"

"Yes," I answered, my back going ramrod straight. The soft weight of Matthew's hand disappeared, and I ignored the goose bumps its absence left. "It really is. We're so grateful that he's offering to cover all costs, too. As I'm sure you know. It's a big guest list now. Big catering effort. Lots of glasses to fill and skewers to have at hand. No one thinks of skewers, but they're important."

Willa blinked. "Your speech at the farmers' market was so moving," she said then, patting her chest. "One could tell it came right from the heart." Her eyes fluttered closed, as if she was remembering something. "Oh yes. *A piece of our soul. And potentially, the start of a new beginning.* That was my favorite part. Beautiful words, really."

I'd been trying not to think too much of it, but in hindsight, my words had probably been a little more revealing than I'd intended. I peeked down at the recorder, unease swelling in my gut. Matthew's hand fell on top of mine, engulfing it as it rested on the white linen covering the elegant garden table.

"Why, thank you, Willa," I said with a smile. Of sorts. "Mmh, you know what? I'm sorry, but I can't get that story about the wall out of my head." I turned to Matthew, brown eyes already on me. "I think I might be into baseball. Who would have thought?"

I knew from the way Matthew looked at me that he was gauging my words. The urgency behind them. The urgency I was sure was making my smile look wonky. Bobbi had been right: we needed a safe word. I would have used it right now.

Willa cleared her throat, just like she'd done the dozen times she'd been about to intercept a change in topic.

Without thinking too much of it, I brought Matthew's hand to my mouth, much like he'd done a time or two in the past. I brushed my lips over the back, widening my eyes at him with a wordless sign.

It didn't work.

Matthew was so taken aback for a second, the look in his eyes so . . . dazed, that my attempt backfired. For both of us.

"I—I'd love to take you home to Boston," Matthew said, voice rocky. We both realized Willa was talking. But we weren't looking at her. He brought our hands to his lap, and I would have probably flushed if I wasn't so surprised by his words. "All this talk about the Sox is making me a little homesick." He laughed, but it was strained, maybe even filled with longing. He turned to face Willa. My eyes remained on his profile. "I guess that's why I can't shake the idea of taking Josie to a game. Putting her in a jersey. Watching the sunset from the stands. Grabbing an Italian sausage from a cart outside

Fenway. And walking back home after the game to catch dinner at my folks'."

His eyes creased at the corners. My heart stopped.

"Ma would give us shit for snacking, but nothing has ever stopped me from polishing off her shepherd's pie." His thumb caressed the back of my hand. "She'd love to have someone to gang up on me with." His throat worked. Mine tightened, emotion sending the organ in my chest for a sprint. "She'd fall in love with Josie at first sight. Try to steal her away from me."

I started shaking. It wasn't cold; there wasn't a runaway gust of wind breaking through the evening and hitting my skin. It was longing. An intense kind of yearning. At his words. And God, I wanted them, I realized. I wanted that. To reach out and grasp it in my hands. Make it true.

Only I . . . I wasn't going to. I didn't even know how much of that he really did mean. And that was probably why I felt so rattled inside. Fenway, the Italian sausage, the shepherd's pie, it wouldn't be mine. Not in the way he meant, not now, and certainly not after this. Boston might have been in the cards, perhaps, at some point. In some strange and parallel reality where we weren't doing this.

We don't get married but stay friends.

"So they haven't met?" Willa asked. Matthew stiffened. I did too. "Josephine and your mother, they haven't met?"

Whatever I'd been so occupied yearning for vanished. This was exactly why we needed a safe word.

"Not in person," I rushed out. "We've met on FaceTime. Which is perfectly normal these days. As Bobbi said, remember? At least for me, it is. I love Pam and Paddy, they're wonderful."

"Do you have plans to meet soon?" Willa fired back before I could so much as relax after saying that. "Surely before the wedding, right?"

I blinked, my stomach sinking. I didn't have an answer for that.

I . . . Did Matthew's parents know about December first? Did they know the truth? Was he lying to them, too? God. I couldn't believe I didn't know that. I couldn't believe I hadn't asked or assured Matthew he didn't need to lie to them. I'd never want him to. And if he had, and they thought I was that person all over Page Nine, then I couldn't even begin to fathom what they thought about me. How had I not asked? How—

"They're on a trip," my fiancé answered, his voice stern. Dry. What did that mean? "They packed up all their stuff, sold the house, and are now traveling the country in an RV. A realization of their retirement dreams."

Willa pulled her notepad and pen out and scribbled something. "Tell me about your mother, Josephine."

My attention bounced back to the journalist.

"Liz," Willa insisted. "You must miss her at times like this."

"I miss her every day she's been gone," I heard myself say. My voice was strong, but only because I was used to switching that on when I talked about her. "I've been loved, though," I added. Long fingers interlaced with mine, and the comfort they brought me didn't help with how hard my next breath was. "I was very fortunate."

"Maurice took you in, if I'm correct?" Willa asked. "I assume he was the father figure you didn't have growing up."

He had and he hadn't. Grandpa Moe had been in my life long before then. He'd always been the grandparent figure I never had, helping Mom out when she needed a hand, although we weren't related. But I never considered him a replacement or a way to fill a void I had. Grandpa Moe was Grandpa Moe. When he took me in for those few months, things didn't really change except for the fact that Mom wasn't there. But none of that was relevant to Willa's job. Andrew was. "He did," I finally managed to get out.

"I can't imagine how hard that must have been," Willa commented.

"Luckily, I have Andrew now." My words felt funny as they left me, but this was the whole point of everything I'd put myself through. I'd put everyone through. "He's in Green Oak, generously paying for the wedding"—I took in a breath—"and ready to be a part of my life."

The hand engulfing mine tightened.

Willa continued, relentless. "Was it hard to go through the motions of four engagements, knowing he was out there?"

Her words bounced in the space between us for a few moments, and I became very still. So much so, I didn't speak.

Her dark eyes glinted with interest. "How did it feel to stand at the start of that aisle, not once, but multiple times, knowing your father didn't want to be there for you?"

Matthew stood up, my hand still clasped in his. "That's enough—"

I tugged at him, bringing his words to a stop. He was such a good, protective man. He made my heart squeeze and burst at the way he'd just jumped. I'd always wanted that. Someone like him. But I wasn't defenseless. I'd fended for myself for a long time. And as neurotic and naïve and people-pleasing as I might be, I also knew how to stand up for myself.

"Why is that relevant to you?" I asked Willa. "Aren't you supposed to focus on Andrew's achievements? His career? All the things he's accomplished? Why would I matter?"

"Maybe because Andrew hasn't worked out the courage to talk too much about you yet." She shrugged an elegant shoulder. But I could tell she was bothered. I could tell she was a woman who wasn't used to not getting the answers she searched for. "Or maybe because all this buzz online is making me curious about *the* infamous Josie Moore. *The Underwood Affair,* as some are calling it."

My teeth grated together for an instant. "You're not that different from them, then. Page Nine." Willa's easy poise broke. "And if you're looking for a new direction for my father's book, I'm not the person to run that by."

She clicked a button on the recorder with a tight smile, as if I'd just hit the nail on the head. "It's our pasts that forge the people we are today, Josephine. You're a piece in Andrew's puzzle. A fortunate accident, a phase, a misstep . . . It doesn't really matter what. I thought you could understand that much, considering you too hid a past."

I came to a slow, relaxed stand. Feeling my hands shake. "You're wrong about that." I moved around the chair and casually inserted myself at Matthew's side, as if that was something I did every day. As if it was something I was meant to do. I kept my eyes on Willa Wang. "Unlike my father, everything about me has always been out in the open. The only difference is that now people seem to care." I placed my hand on Matthew's chest. "And now, if you don't mind, I'd love to sneak away from everyone and have a *private moment* with my fiancé, if you know what I mean." I winked. "I need the kind of distraction only he can provide after this. And someone told me we might get away with that sort of *thing*."

In a matter of seconds, we were moving, something halfway between a laugh and a grunt rumbling out the chest my cheek and hand were still plastered to.

"Shit," I murmured. Feeling the weight of what I'd just said with every step we took away from Willa. "Crap. Ugh. *Shitballs.* No. *Hairy stinking* shitballs. That was soooo bad. So super bad. Bobbi is going to have both our heads."

Matthew's arm tightened around me. "That was incredibly hot."

"You get off on people being rude?" I muttered.

"I think you know what gets me off, sweetheart," he said. Proudly. Loudly, too, by the way.

"I thought we were not doing the *sweetheart* thing." I sighed, trying to ignore his answer. "That's a step backward."

"Direction is relative."

I frowned. "What does that even mean?"

"It means what it means." His hand splayed around my hip, the tips of his fingers catching on the bodice of the dress I wore. My breath hitched. He changed directions, swaying us left. "I'm just praying you were serious about what you said."

"About what?"

Matthew stopped at the bar. It was a lot less crowded now that most guests had drifted toward the trays of charcuterie near the house.

He faced me, and I didn't know if it was the adrenaline releasing or the fact we were somewhat alone, but I felt my whole body relax. The corners of his mouth twitched, satisfied.

"About what?" I repeated.

His smile turned sly. Dangerous. Enticing. "We're having that private moment I was promised."

CHAPTER SEVENTEEN

"I don't think we're supposed to do this if we've picked the wine selection," I murmured, watching the waiter fill up the first glass in a line of six.

Matthew stopped him with a hand. "I'll take it from here, thank you."

I ignored how surprisingly hot that had been and watched the waiter nodding and walking away, leaving the display of bottles in front of us.

"Wow," I observed. "He really left six bottles of very expensive wine unsupervised. They must know we're bride and groom."

There was no reason for me to freeze at the last three words, but I did. Maybe it was how easily they'd left me, or the familiarity of saying them, as if my mouth was used to working around them. Or the fact that it was the first time I acknowledged us as bride and groom. Out loud. Casually. Like nothing.

I gave myself a shake. "You know what I mean."

Matthew's eyes remained on me a second before returning to the bottle he held in his hand. "I do."

"Let's strategize," I offered quickly. "We should think what we're going to tell Bobbi when she finds out we had a sit-down with Willa. Let's think of exactly what we said and how we said it and when we said it. Yes. That way we'll know what's on that tape."

Matthew frowned at the glass he'd just filled. "All right," he conceded. "But we can do that while we drink."

I arched my brows. "Getting drunk is not going to help us strategize."

"Who said anything about getting drunk?" He turned back to me, leaning an elbow on the bar. "This is a wine tasting. For us." He pointed his head at the far end of the bar. "It says so on the—very classy—sign: *Andrew Underwood is pleased to welcome you into his home to celebrate the engagement of Josephine and Matthew with a local selection of wines for your tasting.*"

"Which we selected," I repeated with a light laugh. "You and me. We sat down at Josie's two days ago, in the evening, and picked six out of a long list. We know exactly how they taste."

"Thing is, I've totally forgotten," Matthew said with a shrug. "In fact, I can't remember a single thing from that day, except for something about a tiramisu and no longer feeling sad."

It was hard to ignore the way my chest constricted at that. "There was your pie too," I said, voice the slightest bit wobbly. "That I loved. Remember now?"

There was a moment in which we looked at each other. Just that. Just gazed into each other's eyes. Then he made a thinking face, looking so unbearably cute that it cost me a great deal of willpower to shoot him a warning glance. A reluctant sigh left him. "We should really act like bride and groom."

The wording—or the words, once again—made me frown.

Matthew continued, "Willa has been staring at us since we left the table," and I didn't need to turn to know it was true. I trusted Matthew. Unlike me, he wouldn't lie. Only thing was, now I wondered if this was the only reason why he insisted on us having that private moment. "If we strategize, as you suggested, it'll look like she got to us. And I don't trust her, or her intentions, after this afternoon."

I didn't either. Not completely. I knew she was doing her job, whatever that was at the end of the day, but . . . "We're running out of allies," I said with a sigh. "You never trusted Bobbi. Or Andrew. Now Willa. You don't trust anybody."

"Not around you, I don't." My lips parted with surprise, and his brows met, his expression turning intent. "Andrew's also been looking like he wants to approach but doesn't know how. I've waited all evening for him to do it, and I'm done with that, too."

I'm done with that, too.

He was done with what? Waiting? And what was whatever else he was done with?

Matthew's arms rose in the space between us, and he stepped closer, crowding my space in a way that had my heart skipping a beat or two. "Can I have this?" he asked, giving the handkerchief I had around my hair a soft tug. I nodded my head, overwhelmed by how nice he smelled and how good that sudden lack of space between us felt. "Thank you," he said, voice going low. I felt him make work of the already loose knot, then my hair cascaded down. Goose bumps erupted at my shoulder blades at the tickle of my hair against my skin. "Close your eyes."

My mouth parted with a shaky, "Matthew."

"Close them for me, Baby Blue," he insisted, as if my warning had worked. It hadn't been for him. It was for me. And yet my eyelids fluttered shut. He hummed with something that could only be described as delight. If delight could ever sound a little too deep and dark. "I'm going to tie this around your eyes," he explained softly, more of that cadence hugging his words. "You seem to know these so well that this is the only way to taste them."

The silk fell against my skin, anticipation surging deep inside me. His wrists grazed the sides of my head. I sensed his fingers moving around a knot. My heart thrummed. "We're doing a blind tasting?"

His words flickered across my temple. "You are."

The handkerchief must have been secured around my eyes, because I felt his hands and arms falling. I brought mine up, feeling the impromptu blindfold with the pads of my fingers.

Excitement, plain and simple, broke through, bubbling in my belly. I failed to push it down, so the best I could do was say, "But we're in the middle of a party."

"And you're my fiancée."

A helpless breath escaped me, together with something that should have remained a thought. "You say that like nothing."

"No," he murmured, voice low. "I say this like it's a reason to do with you whatever I want."

A new wave of anticipation poured down my body in response.

Matthew hummed. "I love that smile on you. It's a new one."

I pressed my lips together. I hadn't realized I'd been smiling. "I don't think I have more than one."

"You do." A caress brushed against my cheek. I shivered. "And I think I'm going to call this one your *please, Matthew* smile."

I huffed out a breath, giving my head a half-hearted shake.

"And that one right there is your *I'm going to pretend you're ridiculous, but I actually think you're ridiculously hot* smile."

My lips pursed. "I thought we were tasting wines. Not smiles, Boston Boy."

A deep chuckle coiled around me, making it twice as hard to keep my pout up. "My brain is very selective with the topics when I'm a little on edge. You were lucky my accent didn't come out with all that Fenway trivia."

I perked up with interest. "You have a Boston accent?"

"You're doing your *please, Matthew* smile again. Does that mean you want to hear it?"

The glug glug of a glass being filled crowded the silence. I wanted to. So badly. "No, I think I'm good." I leaned my elbow on the bar, regaining a little space and resting my hand on its surface. I drummed my nails. "When's my blind tasting starting?"

The tips of my fingers brushed the base of a glass. My lips parted with a question, but then Matthew was right there again. Reclaiming the room between us. His scent, woodsy, peppermint, clean, permeated my senses, the sudden closeness twice as intoxicating. "Josie," he said, voice grave, that Boston cadence clinging to my name. *"The Green Monstah's big, but I'm biggah."*

It was ridiculous how absolutely arousing I'd found that. Ri-dic-u-lous how my toes were all but curling, my cheeks most certainly flushing red.

I . . . was into Bostonians, it seemed. Or I simply was into him. I cleared my throat. "Is that a pickup line? Has it ever worked?"

Matthew's words fell right over the shell of my ear. "I might use it again"—the tip of his nose brushed my hair—"if you ask nicely. See how well it really does."

A shiver cascaded down my arms, his words triggering memories. Husky whispers and that hint of command in his voice. *You're going to be a good girl and let me work for those moans.* I was hardly able to shake that off now, so I released a breath, feeling it wobble as it came out.

"I'm . . . thirsty?"

The graze of Matthew's stubble over my jaw told me he was on the move again. Fingers wrapped around my wrist, gently turning the hand that had been resting on the bar. The neck of a glass pushed softly against my palm. "We're starting nice and easy," he said.

I closed my hand around it and brought it to my lips, biting down the disappointment that he wasn't going to raise the glass there himself. I inhaled softly, the crisp and floral notes telling me it had to be a white. Closing my lips around the rim, I tipped the glass slowly, just enough for a small sip. I ignored the weight of Matthew's attention on me. His gaze. Because it was silly that I could feel that with a blindfold on. I focused on the aftertaste, my tongue peeking out to clean off my lips. "Viognier," I said. "Old Stud Winery. Has a red horse on the label. Owned by a married couple. She's a biochemist, and I thought, who better than that to know what they're doing around wine? I also think a lady in STEM just kicks ass. The peach note is very nice. No shame to her husband, but it was probably her idea."

There was a pause that followed my words. A moment. Just a heartbeat. And then Matthew laughed, but it wasn't his usual happy, smug, or amused laughter. It was an abated sound. Helpless. As if he'd just received a punch. Or bad news.

I frowned. Then the glass was out of my grasp in one gentle swipe of his hand. Then there was a weight on my waist. His hand. He pulled me forward. Right against him. Warmth erupted from the point where our chests now touched, spreading across my body. There was a quick, brisk rumble in his rib cage. I felt it on my breasts.

"You need to stop that," he said, that huskiness surfacing once more.

My voice was nothing but a whisper. "Stop what?"

"Blowing me away like that," he answered immediately. I felt his palm splay across the small of my back. My body swayed in response. "You set rules and then make it impossible for me to follow them. Why?"

There it was again, that command in his voice. That rough . . . softness, if that could ever be a thing. "Rules are important," I told him, swallowing around the need to bring my hands to his chest and pull him closer. "They're not that hard to follow. You yourself made one."

"Part your lips," he said. And when I didn't, his hand moved up my body, reaching my face, cupping my jaw. "Everyone's watching us, Josie." His thumb brushed at my skin, grazing the corner of my mouth. "Seeing how I've blindfolded you in a sad excuse to spare you the sight of how I look right now."

My throat worked. *Everyone's watching us, Josie.* I could indulge in that. We could. "And how is that?"

"Like I want to throw you over my shoulder and run," he said, voice low, just for me. He swiped at my bottom lip. "Like I want to drag my fiancée to that gazebo in the back and fuck the anxiety out of her."

All the blood in my body swooshed to my feet. And the only reason I didn't slip to the ground was Matthew's body against mine.

"Now, part those lips, Baby Blue," Matthew ordered. "I'm bringing a glass to your mouth."

Ever so gently he did. Letting me go through the motions—smell, wet my lips, taste—although my brain was screaming at me to stop that and let him drag me to that gazebo. Drag him myself. All I wanted was to taste him, not the wine. Blindfolded was fine. Just this once. *Just this once?* "Chambourcin," I said. Voice almost gone. "You skipped two wines. No. You skipped three. You—"

"I'm impatient." His words sounded so strained, so very tense, that I wanted to take the handkerchief off my eyes. See him. Was that pain? Need? The urge I felt pooling down my body in overwhelming waves? "Greedy, too."

I shook my head. "No, you're not." And I felt it in the air that left him, the way he was ready to argue that, or distract me away from the point. "You're the opposite of those two things."

Warmth engulfed my waist, and then my hips were pushed against his. A breath hitched in my throat. He brushed his nose against mine before dragging it across my cheek, until it was deep in my hair. "Maybe I should kiss you, then," Matthew whispered in my ear. "If I'm not that impatient and not at all greedy."

My whole body shook. So much that I clasped his arms with my hands. I tried to make sense of this. I was blindfolded. In the middle of a party. Turned on like I had no business being. Pressed against Matthew's hips. I wanted to squirm. Search for more. Chase the feeling making my belly tight. I . . . I wanted him to kiss me. "If everyone's really watching."

He huffed out one of those strange laughs, his hold starting to loosen, as if I'd said the wrong thing.

I fisted the fabric of his shirt, stopping him before he could move away. "Maybe you should kiss me, then." He went still against me. "Maybe it's what my fiancé would do."

"Take the blindfold off," Matthew said. Barked. His fingers digging into the fabric of my dress. "I want you to look at me."

All that need and anticipation, and yes, urgency, rioting inside me came to a halt. Everything paused as I dragged the silky handkerchief down my face, letting it pool at my neck.

There was thunder in Matthew's eyes. The brown behind the glasses I loved so much mingled with an emotion I swore I could feel swirling deep in my gut. Lower, too. He looked so on the edge, so absolutely on the verge of doing what he'd been stopping himself from doing. Was that kissing me? He could. It looked like he would. I wanted him to. Now. So badly.

"If you don't wipe that *please, Matthew* smile off your mouth, I swear I'm going to kiss it away myself, Josie."

His words made my ears ring. A sense of triumph tightened my chest, making me blind. Forgetful. Careless. *God, yes. Matthew's mouth. On mine.*

Matthew's gaze dipped, desperately returning to mine. I was still smiling. Then his hands were climbing up my spine, the roughness in the motion making everything in me rise, thicken. Where were we? What were we doing? I didn't care. My chest heaved, and I moved into him, as if I could cling to him, speed things up. Matthew's grunt was brief but telling, making me grow even more impatient, coming even closer. I felt him at my belly, hard. My breath caught. I—

A throat was cleared.

Loudly.

And whatever bubble we'd been in burst.

"Go. Away. Shark," Matthew said, eyes on me, voice hoarse.

"Believe me," Bobbi answered. "I wish I could. Because PDA I can deal with. But you crossed that line a while ago. You're . . . edging each other with wine and blindfolds. And I wouldn't mind watching *if* we didn't have something of an emergency on our hands."

Matthew's nostrils flared, unwavering brown eyes not leaving me. I knew how that felt. I couldn't look away myself, as if those minutes without the sight of him had me greedy for his face.

"Still not interested," Matthew said, his jaw now bunching up.

"I don't care," Bobbi answered. "Because that senator wannabe, Josephine's ex, is here. And we're going to have to deal with that."

My head spun then.

Reality finally seeped in.

"Duncan's here?"

The one man I had once been *sure* I'd marry materialized in the distance.

My brain threw a memory at me. Blue dress shirt tucked in jeans, suit jacket hanging off wide shoulders. All of it paired with brown loafers. Turning around and walking away. Slipping through the door.

He'd been dressed a lot like he was right now, standing at the edge of the garden, talking to Andrew. I remembered looking at a loose thread on the shoulder of his jacket that day, as he told me that he couldn't do it.

That he couldn't marry me.

He'd been so polite about it, so nice. Even smiled encouragingly, as if saying *don't worry, honey. You'll get over me.* Ever the Southern gentleman, Duncan. Born and raised in Charleston. I always wondered what brought him to North Carolina during that time we were engaged. What would have tied him here. Couldn't have been me.

"Josie, sweetheart."

Those two words, uttered with a cadence I was starting to crave, pulled me back to the present.

"I'm over him," I heard myself say. Warmth rose to my cheeks. Or perhaps it had been already there. Matthew tipped my chin in the direction of his face. Brown eyes met mine. A handsome face. I'd been about to kiss him, and it had nothing to do with where we were, or who we pretended to be. "I'm not just saying this to reassure anyone. I'm over him. And I wanted you to know that."

"I believe you," he said. And I knew he did. "Is he over you, though?"

I scoffed. But it wasn't with outrage or disbelief. "He left me."

Something registered on Matthew's face, quick and subtle. Understanding? Surprise? No. It was none of those things.

"Ah, hello?" Bobbi said from our side. "I'm still here. And you're still ignoring me. I shouldn't be ignored right now."

Matthew set his jaw. He seemed to make a decision. "We know you're still there, Shark." He stepped away from me, leaving me all . . . unbalanced and cold. I wish we could go back in time. Have that blindfold back on. Push for that kiss when I could. "You're making yourself impossible to ignore." My hand was clasped. Fingers interlaced. "What's the real problem? Can't be just him."

"You assume right," Bobbi answered. She moved closer to me, hands reaching out in the direction of my head. Matthew didn't let go of my hand. "*He* hasn't come alone," she explained, gently but nimbly rearranging my hair. "There's an entourage of sorts." Her fingers fumbled with the handkerchief loosely dangling off my neck. She turned it, tightened it slightly. Made what I supposed was a knot. Her head leaned back, dark eyes assessing. "It'll do." She met my gaze. "And you will too. Whatever you do, don't let him break you."

Her words caught me so off guard that I stumbled for something to say. "What—"

"Does it mean?" Bobbi finished for me. "It means you two approach him while he poaches your father for God knows what. You say hi. Let Blondie scowl at him like he wants to do bodily harm but *won't.* Just like he is looking at him now, but a little less teeth, maybe. Meanwhile, I deal with the cameras he showed up with. They all slipped past security somehow."

"You had security for this? Here?"

She rolled her eyes. "Do you know who your father is?" A sigh. "Hired locally, though. Too friendly and trusting. They are now fired and— You're distracting me, Josephine. Security is not my job. You are." Her expression hardened. "So you go there, and I handle the press. I'm extremely unhappy about this. I'm not wearing the right shoes to make anyone cry today but—"

"He won't let you," I said. Matthew let out a concerned grunt from my side, the hold of his hand tightening. Bobbi's brows arched. "No. You don't understand. I'm not saying he'll do anything, but he'll turn it around. Duncan is— Let the press stay. It'll be worse if you kick them out. He'll manage to make himself look like the victim here."

Bobbi huffed, but I could see understanding starting to seep in. "I'm not about to throw a hapless client into this."

"I'm not hapless," I countered. "I . . . know him, all right? He's here for a reason. And the press, too. He'll spin it against us if he doesn't get away with it. I can handle this." I swallowed. "I have Matthew. Let the press stay."

Bobbi looked like that was the last thing she wanted to do. "Okay, let's go. But I'll contain them. I say when and where a flash goes off."

Matthew tugged at my arm, moving us forward. He arranged his body around mine, the curve of my shoulder locking into place against his side, his right arm snaking around my back, his left hand grasping my wrist and bringing my palm to his stomach. It was scary how safe I felt. How confident I grew with every step I took in his embrace. How *right* he felt against me.

"I'm over him," I repeated, just for him. It seemed important that he knew.

His answer was immediate. "I know you are."

"It hurt me when he broke the engagement. But it didn't break my heart as much as it hurt my pride. He made me feel like I wasn't worth it. Worth the trouble."

There was a miss in Matthew's step, as if a part of him had wanted to stop, but the rest was determined to move forward. "Give me a safe word."

I glanced up, finding his profile. "Did Bobbi also tell you we should have one?" He gave a nod, bending his lips in a smile. But it was a weird one. Odd. A little scary, too. It wasn't like Matthew, and I wanted to change that. Make it more like himself. Handsome. Nice. Happy. "*Bootylicious.* And if you don't relax, I'll break into song. Start rapping. Popping. Locking. I know how to."

Some of the tension around his mouth eased. His gaze flickered down, meeting mine with a brow arched. I summoned a smile of my own, and I was as surprised as I was relieved to see how easy it was.

His throat bobbed. "If we weren't currently making our way

toward your father and your ex, and they hadn't already seen us, I'd turn us around right now." His eyes returned forward. Mine didn't. "I should have taken you to that fucking gazebo when I had my chance."

My pulse thrummed. "You say that like my going with you was a given," I lied. I would have gone, no questions asked. I was pretty sure Matthew knew. "I might consider it, after this. I could use some distraction."

My words were teasing, referring to Matthew's new rule. *I distract you, from whatever's bothering you. Whatever's making you doubt who you really are and what we're doing.* And they had the effect I expected, because his mouth finally relaxed. He smiled. Proudly. Smugly. It made that thrumming double.

I looked forward, then. Out of pure survival, because I really wanted to see that glint in his eye. Tonight had unlocked . . . something that I realized I'd done a poor job at containing. But we were mere steps away from them. Andrew and Duncan. They hadn't so much as acknowledged our approach. They were too deep in a conversation that looked more important than whatever was happening around them. It was in the stern set of both their profiles while they talked and nodded. I used to call it the *sober muttering.* And it was always done at parties like this one, always by groups of men.

I'd been so ready to marry right into that, I thought. Parties like these. Watching stern-looking men having stern-looking conversations while I fluttered around the grass in a pretty dress, introducing myself as Mrs. Someone. It didn't seem like something I wanted now. It didn't seem like something I wanted, period.

Matthew's head dipped as we came to a stop, and I felt his mouth press over the skin on my temple before brushing my ear. "He has five minutes."

I couldn't know if he meant Andrew or Duncan. I couldn't know what would happen after those five minutes either, but the tug at my lower belly told me it had to do with the gazebo.

"Josephine," the two men said at the same time.

Duncan laughed lightly. Andrew gave a tight smile.

Matthew's hand climbed up my spine, fingers slipping into my hair. He brushed the back of my neck with his thumb. Encouraging. Distracting.

I cleared my throat. "Sorry, ah, for not making our way here before," I told them, assembling my face into a polite, friendly, happy mask. I'd done this a hundred times. "We were a little caught up in the moment." I glanced to my side. Matthew smiled. "Matthew, this is Duncan Aguirre." My eyes returned to the other man. "Duncan, this is Matthew Flanagan." I swallowed. "My fiancé."

Matthew let out a hum that to anyone else would seem pleasant agreement. But I knew it wasn't, not when he accompanied it with another happy brush of his thumb. It felt like a promise of a reward. One that I had no business wanting when—

Duncan stretched his hand in Matthew's direction. "It's a pleasure, Matthew."

Matthew stared back at Duncan for one, two, three seconds. Letting him wait, with his arm in the air. "Oh," he said in an easy, surprised tone, making a show out of glancing down at Duncan's offering. "Sorry, Duncan," he said, finally taking it. "I didn't see that there. Nice to meet you too. I would love to pretend I haven't heard anything about you, but I'm a little better than that."

Duncan's frown came as quickly as he batted it away. "Congratulations on the engagement. To both of you." He retrieved his hand and let it fall to his side. "Can't say I am surprised to see Josie being snatched away so quickly. She's a great catch, as tricky as the catch is."

"I am, if nothing else, persistent." Matthew said. "Some say like a dog with a bone. Once I decide something's mine, there's no stopping me."

Was there malice in my ex's words? Maybe.

But I didn't find it in me to care. Not when Matthew had just said that *mine,* and not when his thumb skipped up and down the back of my neck like that.

"The wine is excellent," I expelled with a breath. "Andrew was so generous. With everything, really. But this party takes the cake so far." I met my father's eyes. "The estate is gorgeous, and I'm sure it makes you miss Florida a little less?"

There was a moment of silence before my father spoke. "It's not a problem," he said. Curtly. Just like he always did. "Duncan was just telling me about a similar property one of his friends owns. Not far from here, in fact."

I blinked at my father, trying to make sense of what that meant. Or waiting for him to elaborate. He didn't.

"The wedding preparations are going great," Matthew offered, and I knew from his voice he was smiling at the two men. I knew what smile he was using, too. "Just pointing it out in case you were wondering, Andrew. I'm not sure I recall you personally checking in and I can't be sure of what Bobbi reports." My father's expression strained. Matthew continued, his tone easy, casual, "We're a little stressed with the time crunch, but hey, it won't be me who's complaining about that. I am marrying the woman of my dreams sooner than I expected, after all."

And that was when my jaw dropped. Just momentarily. Just enough for the air to leave my lungs and my head to turn to look at my fiancé.

Matthew winked at me. As if he'd said nothing.

I swallowed, pacing myself. Right. Yes. *We don't get married but stay friends.* "Money is a great help, though," I said. "Money buys great wine, for one. Have you tried the merlot? It's from a winery in the South Mountains and they age it in oak."

"We could hire a proper wedding planner," Andrew offered.

"Besides Bobbi. You don't need to stress about the small things. And if you are, then you should let me know. Or Bobbi, or my assistant, who's also around."

"Or you could have asked us," Matthew countered. Simply. Nicely, even. Matter-of-fact. "At any point today, or any other time before this instant that I've brought it up myself."

It only hit me then that Andrew hadn't done that. Asked us. Asked me. And I hadn't expected him to. Not about the wedding, and not about how I was doing after the video came out.

"Cut them some slack, Andrew," Duncan said with a laugh, as if they were old friends. As if this was not my father whom he had just met. "These things are a nightmare. There's no bliss until the day all is said and done, so of course the man here is somewhat on edge." He directed that smile at us. Or perhaps, not really. Duncan had always seemed to gaze a little above my head. "Relax, Matthew. I don't think this one's going to slip between your fingers. She's clearly smitten."

Matthew's whole body stiffened against mine.

Just at the same time, I could see out of the corner of my eye, the entourage that Bobbi had mentioned assembled like a hive. It was a small group, but the cloud of cameras and electronics started moving behind Andrew and Duncan, devices buzzing, shifting closer.

A leather trench coat crowned by a blond bob popped into view, right in front of them. She stretched an arm, pointy black nails shining under one of the many garden lamps. I started breathing a little easier. Bobbi had this under control. Of course she did. She— The press hive swarmed her. Oh God, was she okay?

I tugged at Matthew's shirt. "Matt—"

A flash blinded me. I blinked, trying to make my eyes work. My vision flickered, but just as I started making sense of what was behind the buzz surrounding us, another bright, blinding light went off. Then another. Pop. Pop, pop, pop. Something moved in front of me. Someone. Matthew, because he was no longer at my side.

"Put that down," I heard him bark. And oh boy, he sounded so . . . angry. So absolutely unlike himself. This wasn't the plan. This hadn't been. I blinked the stars away, his back coming into focus with a realization, I'd miscalculated the situation. Matthew's words were calm. Low. "Put. That. Camera. Down."

I tried to move around him, but he stretched out an arm, stopping me. I peeked over it, watching Duncan approach, smiling. Relaxed. As if born for this. As if ready to collect some reward, even with a visibly annoyed Andrew by his side.

"Come on, gentlemen," Duncan said. Easy. Ever the Southern gentleman. Talking to Andrew and Matthew and disregarding me. "There's no reason to get all tense and stiff. This is a party. A great one, at that. I thought some of the local outlets would benefit from a little spice. It's not every day that Andrew Underwood visits. And we also have somewhat of a celebrity on our hands now. I'm sure she'll have her moment, too." He turned toward Andrew. "Now, let's take a picture together, Andrew. If you don't mind, of course. Then we can pick up our conversation somewhere else, away from curious eyes and ears."

I knew in that exact moment what Duncan was doing here.

"Andrew," I warned. And I didn't know what got into me, or why I said what I did, but the words left me before I could stop them. "Let's go back to the bar. The merlot really is excellent. We should try it."

Andrew frowned for a second. Duncan stepped closer to him, his arm already pointing at the spot where they should pose. My father hesitated for a long moment, and I really didn't want to, but I held my breath as I smiled at him. *Trust me,* I wanted to tell him with that smile. *Duncan just wants to take advantage of you, your status, your name, your money, probably.* I didn't. I just . . .

"Later," my father said.

Something in my chest halted. Fell. Or maybe all of me did. "Of course," I said with a chuckle meant to be light. Reassuring.

But Andrew didn't need my reassurance. He had already turned around.

I felt so dumb in that moment. So dumb and tiny.

It was laughable really, that I thought he'd somehow choose a glass of merlot over Duncan. Choose *me* over him. It was also laughable that a part of me had thought for an instant—even if short—that Duncan would be here for me. Of course he wasn't. Both Matthew and Bobbi had been so wrong to assume that. Duncan was here for my father. An endorsement? A photo op? Some of that somber muttering they both were so good at? God knew. I could all but picture the way his office must have somehow gotten ahold of someone and landed an invitation to this. We used to joke about that. How he could walk into a party and make it his. How his mama had raised him better than that, but good boys didn't get far without a trick up their sleeve.

The trick wasn't me. It never had been and it wasn't now. And my father seemed to agree.

"Josie?" Matthew asked.

I angled my body toward him but kept my gaze somewhere else. His shoulder. I smiled, hoping he wasn't realizing where my head had gone. I hoped he couldn't see how insignificant I was feeling and how much I hated that any of it was affecting me. But Matthew always managed to see a little more than I liked him to.

"Look at me," he demanded, and who was I to deny that? His expression was grim. His body exuding the kind of tension I didn't like. Coming off him in waves.

"Hey," I said, my eyes were stinging, and God, I hated that. "Should we go check out that gazebo? You promised me."

Matthew's face filled with something that told me that was off the table now. His lips parted, and I hoped it wasn't a no, because I didn't think I'd be able to take it. "I'm—"

A new flash went off.

Right in both our faces. I flinched, and when my vision returned, Matthew was cursing, shoulders turning around. I panicked. Not because I didn't trust him, but because I didn't want him to be angry over this. Do something he'd regret, like snatching away that camera that had been way too close to us. It wasn't worth it.

It really wasn't. Not for this. Not for me.

My hands closed around his arms.

Matthew's gaze bounced back to me, but not his attention. Not completely. That flash went off again, and his expression turned furious. He was really going after that camera. So I did the only thing I could think of to stop him.

I kissed my fiancé.

CHAPTER EIGHTEEN

In hindsight, I realized I shouldn't have used my lips to distract him.

We had agreed on a safe word that night.

So I could have used it. I could have punched his arm. Or pinched his side. Swatted at his ass. Broken into song. Pop, lock, drop it. Pretended to faint. Even screamed or yelped at everyone around me to stop.

But nope.

I'd kissed the man.

My fiancé.

Just a peck on the lips. A brush of my mouth against his.

And effectively shocked the bejesus out of him.

Because all Matthew did was stand there. Arms dangling. Looking all handsome, and tall, and ugh, so hot in that outfit I couldn't get off my mind, but so very stunned. I wasn't exaggerating. It's not like my head had taken one tiny sign of surprise and run with it. For a moment, I'd been sure I'd broken him.

That my kiss had.

I glanced down at the screen of my phone. It wasn't Page Nine for once. It was the *Six Hills Herald.* It had taken them a few days, but as Duncan had mentioned, they'd taken the opportunity to publish an article about Andrew and the party he'd thrown at the estate he was renting. I couldn't figure out why my father's presence in North Carolina, or the party he'd thrown for me and my *fiancé*, mattered, but it apparently did. Enough to fill what I was sure equated to several pages in the print edition. Along with more than a few pictures.

Among them, one of the impetuous kiss.

Because of course. How could that not end up there? The drama clearly loved me a little too much to miss out on the chance.

Was I a bad kisser? Had my breath been bad? Had I been the only one who'd felt that craving for his lips that night?

I locked my phone before I answered that and pushed it inside the pocket of my hoodie. Then I finally turned off the engine of the truck. I couldn't stay parked here any longer than I'd already been. What if Matthew came out the door? Or peeked out the window? It'd look weird. Like I was a stalker, prowling Lazy Elk's front yard.

I was stalking my fiancé. Thinking of ways I could attack him with my silly, disgusting lips.

I snorted at my own bitterness. Then I braced my hands on the steering wheel and said, out loud, just for me, "Get over it, Josie. So what if he didn't like you kissing him? The guy gave you an orgasm. And that's . . . relevant. Somehow."

I made no sense, and maybe, just maybe, the kiss had broken me, not him.

I threw open the door of my truck, grabbed the tote bag I had filled to the brim, hung it off my shoulder, and exited the vehicle.

Something on the right side of the property caught my attention.

Something that moved quickly and was small. Something

with brown and white feathers. *Sebastian?* No. We'd returned the Vasquezes' rooster to the farm. Months ago. For the seventh or eighth time after he'd escaped. But it was him. I was sure. I'd named the thing myself when it was nothing but a cockerel and I'd gotten him for the Vasquezes. As if in response, the runaway rooster cornered the cabin, head pecking and tiny chicken legs quick on the ground, moving past me.

Absolutely not, I thought. No. *No.* This was enough. If I could take control of something, it would be this. I'd see him back to the farm. I'd take him myself. There was so little in my control at the moment, but this was something I could do. A way to regain some sense of . . . balance. Power.

Without wasting more time, I dropped the bag on the ground and ran. Yes, I ran after Sebastian Stan. And dang, the rooster was wickedly fast.

Taking immediate notice of me, he doubled his pace with a loud cluck. But I was on a mission now, and I was going to see it succeed. So when he turned the next corner of the cabin, I followed him. And when he came to a slow stop, as if confused or distracted by something near a bush, I closed my hands around his sides and straightened up with a "HA!"

Victory, at last, I thought, turning around with a big vicious smile. Sebastian clucked in complaint, but this was our dance. This was our thing. He escaped and I retrieved him. He—

Something else was there. Someone.

My fiancé.

Shirtless. Skin glistening under the sun. Jumping rope. Wearing headphones over a backward hat.

A backward hat.

Matthew gripped the rope, making it skillfully fly over his head and under his feet. Head and feet. Head and feet. Arms strained. Muscles bunched. Mouth parted with quick puffs of air and face strained. Jaw clenching and unclenching to the rhythm of the rope. There were indents, too. On his hips.

A droplet trickled down his stomach, and I just wanted to move closer. Get a better look. But his body came to a stop, distracting me from that. Muscles still pulsed and flexed and shone and did things muscles do when they are worked to their limit. I wondered how they'd look if . . .

"Josie?"

My head sprung up. Matthew was panting, looking at me.

I blinked. Then I acted. Much like when I'd kissed him, only this time I had Sebastian Stan at hand. I lifted the rooster in the air, right in front of my face.

He batted his wings, clearly displeased.

"Josie?" Matthew repeated.

This was a new low.

"Heeeey," I said, dragging the word out for no reason other than to stall. I heard movement, then saw glimpses of golden, glistening skin approaching. *Distract. Deflect.* "Whatcha doin', lover?" I grimaced at myself. *Lover.* Lover? I cleared my throat. *"Brother.* Whatcha doing, brother?"

"Did you just call me *brother*?" he asked, and I could see over the batting of Sebastian's wings that Matthew had removed his headphones and wrapped them around his very deliciously sweaty—

"Were you watching me?" He sounded smug. Ugh. "I'm confused about the chicken, but I can go on, if you'd like."

"If I'd like?" I asked, for lack of a better thing to say.

"You were clearly interested," he announced. Now amused on top of smug. "It's all right. But putting that poor thing down might give you a better view."

"Ha," I deadpanned. But I left Sebastian exactly where he was. "So I'm a peeper, so what? You look really shirtless and very shiny and, honestly, hard not to look at when you're bouncing and—you know, flexing or whatever. And I am a woman. With functioning parts. Functioning eyes. Lady parts that like you, apparently."

There was a beat of silence, then an "Okay."

Okay. That was all?

I stretched my neck, glancing over Sebastian. Matthew was right there now. Right in front of me. Or us. So close I was pretty sure Sebastian could peck at his nipple if he wanted to. Maybe I should tell him. Or maybe I should let the rooster bring that grin Matthew was sporting down a notch or two.

"That smile is new," he said. "I wonder what it means." I smiled a little wider. He laughed. "You're cute. Are you plotting something mean? Is this why you're here? I'm up for it, either way."

I bit back a retort. The nerve of him, to call me "cute" and not like my lips on his. "You should move away," I told him. "Before Sebastian pecks at that shiny, glinting chest you love to flash me so much."

"I thought your lady parts liked it," he countered. That megawatt grin still there. "And I thought you were putting the bird down."

"No can do."

He stepped a little closer, and I lowered Sebastian in an attempt to save his chest. It was a nice one after all. "And why's that?"

"This is Sebastian Stan, and he's the Vasquezes' rooster. I'm returning him to the farm. He likes it here a little too much, it seems. Used to terrorize Adalyn and Cameron all the time. I just . . . seem to be struggling with logistics with you standing there."

"So that's what's been waking me up at dawn," he commented. My lips parted with a question. But his next words immediately shot that down. "Besides the idea of you, and that little sound you make, that is."

My cheeks flushed. I shook my head. "Smooth," I settled on. Unlike my word, that had come out a little wobbly. Was he talking about my moans? The moans I made on the phone while— "Funny thing to say, for someone who looks so absolutely appalled at me kissing him."

All amusement vanished from his face. "What?"

I tipped my chin up. Great. So he hadn't seen the *Herald* yet. "Nothing." I took a step to the side. "Not important. Now I'm leaving. Good day."

He blocked my way. "Put the chicken down, Josie."

"No," I said, moving Sebastian higher in front of me. I was being one-hundred-percent ridiculous. But if there was any time in life when I was going to allow myself to be petty, it was this one. After four engagements, I'd just found out I was a bad kisser. "No can do, sir. Bye-bye."

Matthew mirrored my sidestep. "Don't make me chase you," he warned. Calmly. Nonchalantly. "Because I'll run after that car."

I snorted at how serious he looked. "Don't be dramatic."

"Said the woman using a cockerel-shield."

My eyes narrowed at the gorgeous, gorgeous man in a backward hat. "If I put him down, he's going to come after us. He doesn't like to be picked up like this, in case you haven't noticed, Sparkles. As gentle as I've been. He'll peck at our heels. He's fast. Faster than us. Best thing to do at this point is call Robbie. Can you do that?"

"I think we can manage to outrun him." A shrug of one rounded naked shoulder. "And if you can't, then I promise not to leave you behind."

"You're being awfully smug for a city boy who's wearing little to no clothing. Do you think those abs of steel are going to protect you?"

Matthew was one-hundred-percent loving this now. He just was. I knew it.

"Fine," I said when he didn't answer. "You want to be smug. Then you'd better be smug while you run."

And before he could react, I lowered Sebastian to the ground and released him as gently as I could. A clucking battle cry left him, and right as I was breaking into a sprint, Matthew snatched my wrist.

We ran in the direction of the house, the squeal leaving me, thanks to the shot of adrenaline making me sound like a fool. As predicted, Sebastian chased us. Poor thing. I really needed to talk to Robbie to see if we should just let him pick his home. I glanced over my shoulder, my eyes getting a little distracted at the sight of Matthew by my side, roaming a little too low, a little too long. *And* totally missing a log lying somewhere around the backyard. I felt myself trip, cruising the air for a second that stretched, and just before I fell, Matthew's hands were there, swooping me up.

"That wasn't a kiss," he said, pushing up those porch steps with me in his arms, princess-style. "You weren't kissing me, Josie."

Brown eyes snatched mine just as we crossed the threshold of the door. He planted me right down. Chests heaving, my jean-clad hips pressed against his. Him. I audibly gulped. Those sweats did nothing to conceal him. The hard outline pressing against the softness of my lower belly. And I didn't want to acknowledge how good he felt against me like that, how solid, how enthralling or how thoroughly aroused I was, too, for no other reason than him touching me.

That wasn't a kiss. Hadn't it been?

My palms fell on his chest, making my breath catch with the sound that left him. A little growl. It made me move into him. I wanted to drag my fingers down. Up. All over him. He made me want so many things, this man. He made me breathless with things I thought I didn't need.

I stepped away.

Matthew's gaze flickered down, landing on my hands still splayed on his chest. He reached out for my left, brushing his fingers over my skin. Pausing for a heartbeat over the ring. His ring. My ring. He kept touching it. Looking at it. Making something tighten inside me.

"You weren't kissing me," Matthew repeated. "Not really. That wasn't our first kiss. You'd know if it was."

Our first kiss.

My heart jumped and plummeted to the ground. All the same. It had been, though. I'd kissed him, even if it had been just a peck.

"Don't worry." I retrieved my hands, let them fall to my sides. His eyes found mine again. "I didn't come here for a repeat. This is not about that. I came here for something else."

Matthew retrieved the tote bag from the spot beside my truck and returned to the cabin, leaving it with me before heading to the shower with a promise to be quick.

He hadn't been. Matthew was in that shower for a long time. But I was grateful anyway because I didn't think I could have done this with him looking all sweaty and shiny and . . . distracting, sitting across from me. So by the time he returned, I'd had enough time to get everything I'd brought with me neatly organized on the kitchen island, prepare coffee, and connect my phone to the speakers to play my deep-focus playlist. I'd return the rooster to the Vasquezes' tomorrow.

Today we had work to do.

Matthew's steps were heavy and slow as he approached again. He hadn't brushed his wet hair, the usually dirty blond locks darker and messy, some falling over his forehead. I wanted to sweep them back, see every crease in his forehead up close, ask him why he looked so serious, and thank him for discarding the contacts in favor of his glasses. It wasn't right. My brain was clearly still malfunctioning from that horrible kiss.

That wasn't our first kiss.

"I've prepared coffee," I told him with what I hoped was an easy smile.

Matthew's features softened briefly as he poured himself an Americano before coming to a stop at my left. A wave of peppermint and soap and *him* hit me right in the gut, and ugh, I wanted to lean into his chest so badly. Brush my cheek against the sweatshirt he was wearing. Just enough to feel him through the cotton. Maybe hear his heartbeat. Perched on a stool, I sat at the perfect height to do that.

"Those are your muffins."

My cheeks warmed the *tiniest* bit. We both knew that they were my apology muffins. But if I admitted it out loud, if I brought up that night at Andrew's estate, we'd talk about that kiss again. And I didn't think I could do it. The muffins weren't so much about that, they were more about me feeling responsible for Matthew getting so upset over the cameras. I was responsible for his picture being in the *Herald*, too. Both things could have been avoided if I'd listened to Bobbi. If I wasn't so naïve. Hence the muffins.

"I also brought the kale chips you love so much," I said, pointing at the pink container I kept them in. A breath left him, hitting me on the top of my head. The urge to turn and look at his face was strong, but I was stronger. "Please, take a seat. We have lots of ground to cover."

Matthew didn't sit. "What's all of this, Josie?"

"I want to help you," I told him. "With your job hunt. I know you might have seen most of these. But you said you'd let me know if you found something, and you haven't. So you can tell me where you're at with it, and we can take it from there." I reached out for one of the binders. "I've printed out job ads and classified them by state and field." I threw it open. "We have Illinois, and then positions that have to do with reporting or content or— Oh, there was an editor for creative ads and media that sounded so cool." I scanned the sleeves until I found it. "Here."

I glanced at Matthew and he looked . . . pensive. Quiet.

"Don't worry," I said, pulling at the section divider. "There's a section for Massachusetts. Most of the ads are for reporter positions. *Boston Guardian, Boston Globe,* a national media group I can't remember the name of . . . but that one's part-time." I stole a new glance at him. No change. "You have a nice face and can be very charming. I think you'd look great on camera if you're open to broadcast journalism?"

Matthew set the mug on the kitchen island. He scratched the back of his neck. "Is there a section for North Carolina?"

"Yes," I said, a jolt to my chest. "I thought you might want to be close to Adalyn and Cameron." I kept my gaze on the binder. "And there's one for Florida, too. I know you met Adalyn in Miami, so I thought you might want to go back?"

There was a long pause, only the slow beats of the music playing in the background filling the silence. Then Matthew moved. He grabbed a stool and planted it next to mine before plopping down. I seemed to hold my breath for a reason I didn't understand. As if I was waiting for something.

"When did you do all of this?" he asked. "This must have taken hours."

I swallowed, dragging my palms down the plastic sleeve in front of me. "A couple of nights ago."

Matthew's breath was deep and forceful and sounded like a complaint.

"I haven't been able sleep," I explained, keeping my voice up, happy. Normal. "Which is not rare for me. My head sometimes doesn't shut up. So I baked. Researched. Printed. Classified. Filed. It was very relaxing, and I was just glad I had something to keep myself busy."

Another of those exhales left him. "Look at me, Baby Blue."

I ignored the pressure in my throat, chest, belly, *everywhere*, and complied.

"Thank you," he said, and God, Matthew had never sounded or looked so . . . earnest. *Moved.* Like the two words were coming from someplace other than his mouth. Someplace deep inside him. His Adam's apple bobbed, and he turned my stool, angling my body toward him, as if he wanted all my attention. "I wish I could find the right words to tell you how fucking grateful, and blown away, I am right now. I wish . . ." He shook his head. "I wish I could show you."

Everything in me eased, taken aback by how much he meant that and how little I had done. "These are just printouts," I whispered. "It's the least I can do. You . . . You're looking for a job. And I wasn't doing anything for you. Not like you are for me. That wasn't right. It wasn't fair."

A muscle in his jaw jumped, and when he said, "That couldn't be further from the truth," I didn't ask what he referred to. His hand reached out, fingers tucking a strand of my hair behind my ear. It wasn't right how I could feel something so simple, so plain, so cliché if you will, so deep inside. "You're nothing I expected, Josie," he said softly. So softly it almost hurt. "I told you that night. But now I know you're nothing I deserve, either."

I frowned. "You deserve this," I told him. And I'd been doing such a good job at trying not to talk about something that made him uncomfortable. Something he'd never brought up but that I knew. "It's just help. It was unfair that they fired you because you refused to give them some scoop about Adalyn and Cameron. It's unfair that they're getting away with saying they were laying people off anyway. In fact, I'm sure there's a way we could sue them. We can look into that. I'll help you lawyer up. I have connections, I promise I can help with that."

Matthew smiled, but it didn't reach his eyes. "Do you know where I worked, Josie?"

"Some media and entertainment conglomerate," I told him. "They own newspapers and online outlets across the country, or something like that. I can't recall the specifics. I just know they don't have principles and were very dumb to let you go."

"They don't have them, no," Matthew agreed. "One of the outlets they own is Page Nine."

Oh. "I . . . I didn't know that. I probably should have asked."

"I should have told you." The corners of his mouth fell. "Page Nine is where I worked for the past year. My boss, Marissa, took me with her after a management change there. It's not rare to move people around. It was an adjustment, but I figured out soon enough how tabloids worked. News is news, no matter what the subject. It's more about who you know than anything else. And with social media, there's a lot more work in the tabloid industry than what most people think."

"So you wrote things like the stuff being said about me? And Andrew? Us?"

"I'm not proud of myself," he said. And I believed him. "I always thought I was somewhat fair, that everything I wrote was not crossing some imaginary line I'd drawn for myself. I checked sources, made sure everything was factual. But I could only control so much." A sigh left him. "*Filthy Reali-Tea* is scripted, to give you an example. But that doesn't mean you can predict what Sam and Nick will say. The whole thing is edited, but they occasionally get vicious, and people love that. It's big part of their success."

I processed that. All of it, really. I was surprised, it had obviously caught me off guard, but I . . . didn't feel betrayed. Just confused. *I should have told you.* "Why didn't you tell me this? When I asked you to help me that morning, here, in this kitchen?"

That muscle in his jaw jumped. "You said you needed me. Me."

The weight of his answer made my next breath a little harder. "Why didn't you say anything at any point after that?"

"I thought you'd break things off. That you wouldn't trust me."

Break things off.

Break what? I should have asked. What was between us was meant to be broken either way. But I wasn't an idiot. I wasn't blind. I could see, as much as I tried to deny it, that there was something else between Matthew and I. Something that had always made me gravitate toward him, and now had become this living, pulsing thing growing in the space we'd carefully put in place with those rules.

"Is that why they aren't talking about you? Because they know you?"

The quality of his gaze changed. "You're assuming that the reason is in part what made me keep this from you. I wish—" He stopped himself. "I wish I could have spared you all this ugliness, Josie."

"I'm not as naïve as you paint me to be, Matthew. I don't need to be sheltered—"

"You're not." He let out a hard breath. "And you don't need to be sheltered, no. Because you're smart. Way smarter than me. Fierce. Brave. Kind. You'll assume the best in people because that's who you are. You have a heart so fucking big, there's room for everyone there. And I love that about you. All of those things. That's what I wish I could protect."

I love that about you.

That's what I wish I could protect.

My heart tripped over itself.

I . . . was struggling to keep myself from . . . From what? From asking him to take all of that back? From asking him to expand, to tell me that he wants some of that space in my heart? From jumping in his lap and just . . .

"Then we'll find you something else," I told him. "Something as far away from gossip and tabloids and podcasts as we can go. You're incredibly smart, Matthew. Determined, too. And the fact that you have a moral compass is a good thing." Something flashed in his eyes. Was that hurt? I averted my gaze for a moment. "You tried to make the best out of a situation that was out of your control. You said no. You protected Adalyn and Cameron. And then you protected me too. Because I needed you. Like you said."

His gaze dipped to the space between us. And I realized I'd been fidgeting. No, shaking. My hands were shaking. He clasped them, gently but tightly, with that emotion I'd been seeing in his eyes. The one that made it impossible for me look away. I felt his thumb graze the ring. And I'd become so used to the weight, its presence, that him touching it felt as if he was touching a part of me.

"It was my grandma's engagement ring," he said, and I swore I stopped breathing. "My grandpa made a couple of modifications before proposing to her. The stone at the center was the color of her eyes. It's not that rare to have it there, but it usually is a solid heart."

Something thundered in my chest. I'd figured it was a family heirloom. Of course I had. But this? This I hadn't expected. "It's beautiful," I breathed out. "I wasn't lying when I said that."

"It's beautiful on you."

My heart fluttered. But I had to keep it down. I had to try not to ruin this. Us. Whatever that was. I didn't want whatever was in his eyes to go away. "The first thing I thought when you gave it to me was how hard it'll be to part with it."

Matthew's eyes held mine, intently, urgently, unsaid words that made me regret my own staring back at me. "You've been wearing it upside down," he said. He held my hand higher. Impossibly gently too. "According to my grandma, the heart should be facing toward you. To indicate you're taken. She said some people wait to be married to turn it around, but that Flanagans never did." My chest squeezed, a tide of emotion rising, flooding everything in its wake. "Not saying anything has been driving me insane."

Neither of us spoke.

I'd come here to help Matthew find a job, with the promise of making this afternoon about him, and I'd somehow ended up sitting under the weight of his gaze, more preoccupied with the way he was making *me* feel. The way my ears seemed to ring with something that demanded to be heard. The way my chest moved up and down.

We were engaged, but I wasn't his. He wasn't mine. We had rules and were not getting married.

It was us who were backward. Facing the other way. Not the ring.

Would he turn it, then? Make the heart point the right way? Would I turn this whole thing around? Could I?

Matthew's grasp changed. His thumb and index finger closed around my finger, gently, decisively. The air in my lungs seized. "Josie," he whispered, voice hushed. Low. "Christ," he cursed, huffing out a laugh. "The ring's facing the wrong way," he repeated. "Do you understand what I'm telling you?"

My heart cartwheeled, pirouetting around my chest. I wanted to nod yes, of course I understood, but I was overcome. This was all so backward I couldn't even breathe. I couldn't even make sense of how to speak. My lips parted.

A phone rang.

It wasn't loud, but it startled me.

Matthew's gaze remained on me. Set. Waiting.

"You should get that," I finally managed to say.

"It's my sister," he answered, body still, studying me. "Tay. She can wait. She's been calling all day."

All those questions I'd had about his family resurfaced, grounding me. Sobering me up. "It sounds important," I told him. It cost me a great deal, an intricate part of me, but I pulled my hand away. "I'll go."

Matthew frowned. "I don't want you to leave."

Once again, I forced myself to speak words I didn't want to say.

"They don't know about me, do they? About this being a lie? They think I'm the woman in the press, because I asked you to lie to them. I asked you to lie to everyone as much as you made me believe it was a call we were both making." I made myself smile, even though I felt horrible and ugly and undeserving of the way he looked at me. The ring on my finger. "It's okay. It really is. I just think I should go and you should talk to your sister. I'll leave all of this here, okay?"

His lips thinned. And he stared at me, deep in thought, that emotion still clear and bright in the brown of his eyes. My smile wavered, turning a little crooked in a way that couldn't be cute. I jumped off the stool and brushed a kiss on his cheek.

"New rule," he said, the words stopping me. "I kiss you."

My voice came out weakly, tired. I didn't want a new rule. I didn't want rules at all. "That's already one."

"No." His head gave a shake. "We don't just kiss if we must, from now on. *I kiss you.* I kiss you like I've wanted to do for weeks now. Not because we have to, but because I fucking need to." A breath heaved out of his chest. "Because you need me to. And because you know what it'll mean, no matter what's down the line."

"*Matthew,*" I started.

But he climbed off the stool and he stepped into me. He set his palm around the back of my neck and brought me to his chest. I realized the moment my cheek touched him, the moment I melted right into him, how much I'd needed it. This. Him.

"Yes or no?" he asked. "I'm not letting you leave until you answer me." His chest moved up and down. "Yes or no? I have no problem staying like this all day."

A strange laugh broke out of me, and I did all I could do in that moment.

I nodded my head.

"Yes."

CHAPTER NINETEEN

INTERIOR—*FILTHY REALI-TEA* STUDIO—DAY

SAM: So what did our polls say?

NICK: Whoa, impatient much?

SAM: I love a good poll. There's a very special kind of satisfaction in picking something and discovering whether it's validated in the results. Or in your case . . . in-validated? You always go with the odd choice.

NICK: I'm not sure that's the word you're looking for, Sammy. And you're talking about me like I love to pick the wrong side of a love triangle. I really don't. I—

SAM: The polls.

NICK: (sigh) All right, all right. So . . . for those of you catching up with all the developments in *The Underwood*

Affair. Much has happened. All of it you can find on our highlights, pause here and look them up, and before you ask in the comments, yes, the video had to be taken down.

SAM: I did feel a little bad for her, if I'm being honest? We were mere communicators but . . .

NICK: But you are so invested you're rooting for her. (gasps) Oh my God, you really are. Wow. Well, I'm collecting all that credit. I worked really hard on this series.

SAM: (sighs) So the polls?

NICK: Yes. Okay. So we asked you, our beautifully Filthy Reali-tiers, the following question. (pauses)

(Drumroll sound)

NICK: I do really love that, thanks. (clears throat) Will Small-Town Heiress walk down the aisle on December first?

SAM: (squeals with excitement)

NICK: And fifty-one percent of you said she won't.

SAM: (scoffs, outraged) I voted that she would. I believe in her. I believe in the power of healing.

NICK: I dunno, honestly. I'm as divided as our audience. I think it's because of that picture we talked about on Tuesday's ep. That kiss was a little . . .

SAM: Anticlimactic. Yeah. Maybe. I always thought he—

NICK: (laughs loudly and abruptly) That he looks like a man to grab a woman and just kiss the heck out of her? Yup. Blond guys in glasses, I'm telling ya. But on to our second poll now. Will Rich Daddy—oops, sorry, we can't address him as such anymore. Do you want *Andrew Underwood* to walk our real-life small-town princess down that aisle on December first? (drumroll sound) Poll said seventy-five percent yes.

SAM: (even more outraged) What? Why?

NICK: The power of Hollywood? Happily ever afters? The daddy issues everyone has? I did vote yes here. I'll admit that.

SAM: Ew. You're changing your tune awfully quick. Are you still fishing for that invite?

NICK: (feigning a dismayed gasp). I am better than fishing. But yes, yes I am. You really think there's no way I can get one, though? I know exactly what I'd wear.

SAM: (laughs) Of course you'd know. But the big day's in two weeks. I doubt that you will if it hasn't happened yet, bestie.

NICK: Ouch. I would have taken you as a plus-one but . . . alas. Oh. And for those of you filling up our comments with the most random requests: here's a little something . . . we are working on getting a very special guest on the pod. Soon.

Hopefully. Any guesses who that might be? Let us know! Until then, please stay tuned. And subscribe if you haven't! We also have mouths to feed.

SAM: You have three cats.

NICK: Exactly.

"Five more minutes?"

I turned my head to look at the man occupying the driver's seat of my truck. "Five more minutes."

Matthew smiled. "Yeah, I was thinking the same. Or maybe I need ten this time. I'll think about it. I'm sure you don't mind staying here a little longer, do you?"

I didn't. And he didn't need to think of anything. It was me who needed those five, maybe ten, minutes. Not him. But he was an incredibly sweet man, so he'd pretend otherwise if I let him.

We'd been parked here for a while now. Long enough for me to wonder if I'd ever work up the courage to open the door, exit the vehicle, cross the driveway, and knock on Adalyn and Cameron's door.

"What are you thinking?" I asked Matthew, dragging my gaze out the window.

"Karaoke."

"Karaoke?"

"Yeah," he said with a nod. "I was thinking whether you have a song. Cute girls always, always, have a karaoke song. I was wondering about yours."

Ugh. I couldn't with this man.

I couldn't deal with how full he made my chest with the silliest, most simple, things. "What songs were you considering?"

"I was still narrowing it down to genres and decades."

I pursed my lips just so I wouldn't smile like an idiot. "It sounds like a very efficient thought process. Do you want to share what genres and decades you think suit my karaoke choices?"

Matthew turned in his seat. The crewneck sweatshirt he was wearing stretched over his chest with the motion, momentarily dragging my eyes down. He looked great in green. It matched the specks in his eyes. "Country. Eighties."

I wrinkled my nose. "You got one right."

He made a thinking face. "It has to be the eighties, then."

"I do love a nice country tune but . . . yes. Karaoke and eighties go hand in hand for me." I smiled. "How did you know?"

"Because."

"That's not a reason."

His throat worked. And he looked at me in a way that told me his answer wouldn't be as trivial as our conversation. "Because it's my choice too."

I immediately lit up inside. As if he'd switched on a bulb with a simple click. I didn't need to ask what he meant. It simply made sense. That was the thing with us. It had always been. "You're a 'Careless Whisper' kind of guy," I told him. "You have to be. I bet you're a good singer, too. I bet you even put on a show."

The grin that tugged at his mouth was incredibly big. "Respectfully, but you give me a mic and I will make that stage my bitch."

That bright, overwhelming feeling expanded, pulling at my own lips. His words made it impossible not to forget everything for a few moments and imagine Matthew on a stage. Lit by a single spotlight, mic in hand, belting out those high notes with a naturalness he probably had no business having. It really wasn't right to be this handsome, funny, have those arms, *and* be able to sing. Or maybe, just maybe, it wasn't right how much I loved all those things about him.

My face started to fall. And just as quickly as it all had left—momentarily stretched out of my grasp by his smile, and the image of him—it came right back with a snap.

"I'm a little scared," I whispered. "To get out of the car."

Matthew nodded his head even though it was obvious that he already knew that. "Want to tell me why?"

I huffed out a bitter laugh. "The lies," I said.

He considered my answer, and I was aware that after what had happened back at Lazy Elk the other morning, after what he'd confessed and asked of me, after what was left unsaid, it was an unfair thing to say. *The lies.* It made it all sound fake. Like he didn't make my heart flutter with just a touch or a look. Like him distracting me with a silly conversation about karaoke wasn't worth anything. Like him in this car, making up excuses so I could work up some courage, didn't mean the world. It did. It all did. More than I could say. But it didn't change the fact I felt like a fraud going into Adalyn and Cameron's place.

"I voted yes," Matthew said. "On Page Nine's poll."

I frowned at him. I'd seen the polls on Page Nine's socials, as much as I tried not to look. It was becoming harder to ignore, the closer we got to December first. It was also difficult not to cave and allow what was being said to hold sway over me.

"I'm not trying to turn this around so we talk about us," Matthew said. "It's not the time, not right now, here in this truck. Not when your head is somewhere else. But I only voted on one of them, and I did with a yes. You will walk down that aisle, Josie. Not because you have to, or because you might want to, but because you can. That's also why you can walk across that driveway, hug Adalyn, and not ruin anything." His jaw set. "You can do anything. Understand?"

An overpowering, consuming wave of . . . emotion crashed into me.

I wanted to kiss Matthew. Now. So badly. I wanted to climb onto his lap and show him what his words, his faith in me, did to me. I didn't think I'd ever wanted to kiss him more than I did right this second.

There was a glint in his eye that told me he could see that in me, what I felt. There was a hardness in his face that also told me he was trying to stop himself from doing the same. Or from letting me. He deserved that, I decided. He deserved to have control over that kiss. Just like he'd asked with that new rule.

I kiss you.

I could give him that much.

I could give him things.

"No one's ever walked me down an aisle," I heard myself say. Because it was the least I could do. I wouldn't kiss him, but I could give him this. Something no one else had. "The other poll was about that."

He gave his head a nod, encouraging me.

"It was supposed to be Mom," I said. "*You and me against the world* kind of thing." Something clogged my windpipe, making it hard for me to continue speaking for an instant. "It was silly, I guess. And I always wondered if Grandpa Moe ever thought I didn't want him to walk me down. But I never dared ask him."

Matthew went still, so very still, then he reached out across the console. A palm wrapped around the side of my face. His thumb swiped across my cheek, and there was a desperation in his touch, one I understood—*felt*—deep within me. I'd never told that to anyone, as much as most must have assumed.

"I don't know—" I stumbled, continued, more truths coming out. "I don't know if that's why I couldn't do it. I don't know if that's why I tried so many times. I can't seem to get anything right. Does that make me a fool?"

Matthew leaned forward, his scent curling around me with

the air as he moved inside the car. I closed my eyes. His forehead pressed against mine. "Nah, Blue. It makes you the strongest woman I've ever met."

Blue. That was beautiful. It wasn't a kiss, but I liked how it hung in the space between our mouths. Touched my lips.

"Do you think you could get married, Matthew?" The words left me in a whisper. "Do you think our backwards can be straightened out?"

His whole body shuddered for an instant, right before he lifted his head. Brown eyes met mine when my eyelids fluttered open. My belly dropped. "We really are motherfucking backward, huh?" We really were. But before I could say as much, he was touching my forehead to his again. Just briefly this time, nothing more than a caress. He returned to his seat. "How about we get you a maid of honor first? Then we take it a day at a time."

A day at a time. There were fourteen of them left.

"Do you think she'll hate me?" I asked him. *For lying.* "For asking so late?"

There wasn't any hesitation in his words. "Not a chance in hell." He nodded his head at the sleeping, furry ball in the back seat. "Remember, we have Pedro. No one could ever be mad at someone holding a pig that tiny. Not even Cam."

I chuckled, even if a little strained. I knew what he was doing. Again. Distracting me. I didn't deserve a man like him. "Okay. You hold Pedro, though. I think I might throw myself at her when I see her, and I don't want him to get hurt."

"You got it," he said with a nod.

And in a matter of seconds, we'd exited my truck and were crossing the driveway to Adalyn and Cam's porch, with Pedro Pigscal in Matthew's arms.

I released a big gulp of air, squared my shoulders, and rang the doorbell. Matthew winked at me when I glanced quickly at him. It reassured me, but I still passed the sweaty palms of my hands down my denim skirt.

The door opened.

I held my breath.

Cameron's large frame filled up the space. There was a small pout framed by all that trimmed facial hair. "About fucking time," he murmured. He met my gaze. A smile broke through. Small, but it was there. "Saw you park ages ago. I'd hoped you weren't making out in my driveway, honestly."

"We really weren't," I said, voice soft. Too soft.

Cam let out a long sigh. "I know, darling," he admitted. "I know." Green eyes bounced to my side. He eyed Matthew up and down. "What in the bloody hell is that?"

"Hey," Matthew complained. And when I looked over, he was covering the pig's ears with a hand. "Don't talk like that about Pedro."

"We're babysitting for María—"

Something moved in front of me. And in a second flat, Cameron was shoved out the way and I was being hug-attacked.

"Ada—" I started, but a choking sound stopped me. It wasn't mine. I— Oh my God. Was Adalyn crying? After throwing herself at me? "Are you okay?" I asked, hearing my own voice crack. "Why are you crying?"

"Because she's the furthest thing from okay," Cameron answered.

My sister let out a little sob, making me immediately wrap my arms around her. "But you never cry. You— Oh my God, are you crying because of me? Did I make you cry?" My own eyes welled up. Emotion rose, flooding me. I squeezed her harder. Tighter. My sister never cried. She didn't tackle people with hugs. "I'm so sorry. I—I came here to ask you if you wanted to be my m—"

"Yes," she croaked. "Please. I'll be your maid of honor. And I'm not crying over that. I've just been so stressed. I thought you hated me because I wasn't there for you, and I am *veryemotionalandicannotholditin* . . ." A strange trail of words I couldn't make followed that.

But I didn't care too much.

Adalyn didn't hate me. I hadn't ruined this for us. At least not for now.

My eyes fluttered closed.

"All right." I heard Cameron say. "Let's move this inside. And stop looking at me like that. The pig can come in too."

Matthew let out a scoff. "As if I was going to leave Pedro outside."

CHAPTER TWENTY

Something got my attention from outside the window of Stu's.

Bobbi snapped her fingers, demanding I look back at her.

"Do you really need to do that?" I asked her as sweetly as I could. "Because I thought we'd turned a corner, and you were nice and encouraging and—"

"I'm a multifaceted PR strategist," she said. "And your attention should be on this steak tartare. Not outside the deli. Stuart closed up the shop for us."

I arched an eyebrow. Stuart? It didn't sound like Bobbi to care about some man closing his shop for us. "A wedding planner," I said, loading my fork and bringing it to my mouth. "Multifaceted wedding planner, in any case." Matthew huffed out a laugh from my side, making me puff out my chest with pride. Bobbi's eyes narrowed. "And no one serves steak tartare at a wedding. Raw eggs, raw meat, and unpasteurized cheese are very risky options. Everybody knows that."

Bobbi drummed her nails on the small table where we'd been

sitting. We were in a more private corner of the deli, although it was just us and Stu at the back. Stu's Beef Barn was in a neighboring town. Despite its name, it wasn't a big establishment, but it sourced everything locally and it had a few spaces for people inclined to grab a quick bite up front. Or for people like us, who were trying their offerings for an event. Bobbi had yapped about us going to a *real* caterer, as she had called it. But I'd checked this out on her master list, as much as I'd done so randomly. It had been an existing option, and I loved that fate had brought us here.

"We'll add it to the entrées—but for the rehearsal dinner, then," she finally announced. "I'll go check with Stuart to see if it's possible."

I opened my mouth to tell her that it made no difference, since the wedding and rehearsal dinner had exactly the same number of guests, but Bobbi was scurrying off her chair before I could.

"Who would have thought," Matthew said.

I knew exactly what he meant. "Not me. But I can't say I blame her."

Matthew's knee nudged mine. I also knew what that meant, so I glanced back at him. His smile was small, careful. "If you're into bald, bearded men in aprons surrounded by cuts of meat, you should have said something. I'm not opposed to trying out new looks."

I wasn't. Stu was nice, objectively speaking. Attractive, if you were into those things Matthew had just mentioned. "I don't know. Could you really pull off a bald head?"

"Absolutely I could," he said, bringing a hand to his chin. "And I could grow a beard, too." I cocked a brow in question. "I could learn how to broil things. Slice brisket. My biceps would flex really nicely while I do that, just the way you like."

Something a little too close to a giggle almost left me then, but I intercepted it in time. "You're pretty, but you're not bald-head pretty," I lied. I also loved his hair too much.

Matthew smiled. "So you think I'm pretty."

I shrugged. "You know I do." I turned back to the tartare and brought the plate closer to us. "I hope Stu stops Bobbi from adding this to the rehearsal dinner. I'd hate for half the town to get food poisoning. That happened at the last barbecue we held by the lake. And I ended up loading people on the bed of my truck and making collective runs to the ER." My eyes returned to him as I loaded my mouth with more tartare. I pointed at him with my fork. "If anyone ever offers you homemade ice cream in Green Oak, just say no."

Matthew watched me, as if waiting for something.

I didn't know what that could be. Specifically. There were one too many things hanging over our heads at the moment. And we'd been so caught up in the rehearsal *weekend,* not just dinner, as it had been executively decided by Bobbi, that it was hard to tell them apart. For me, it was that kiss. That was all I seemed to care about these days. And it was the one thing continuously escaping away from me. If we weren't with Bobbi, discussing something, Andrew was somehow there.

Matthew's words at the party had seemed to have an effect, and last time we'd sat down with my father, it had been to discuss his side of the guest list. He'd been very apologetic about it, and everything really, and went as far as asking whether I wanted him to do something about Duncan. Whatever that entailed. I'd declined, but I'd been able to tell that Matthew had been content at Andrew asking.

The memory of that meeting made me think of Matthew's family. He'd said they'd be there. But I couldn't know whether that was true, or something he was expected to say. I didn't dare to ask.

One day at a time, he'd said at my truck.

Yet here we were, trying out catering options for a—

"Will you sit on my lap?"

A half cough, half laugh toppled out of me. I sensed him move, and I stopped him, looking around even though I couldn't hear Stu or Bobbi. "What? *No.*"

Matthew looked so hurt it was almost comical. "Why not?"

"*Because.*"

"That's not a reason," he pointed out. "Come sit on my lap."

I couldn't believe this was a conversation we were having. I glanced back over my shoulder. No trace of them in the deli. "Where do you think they've gone? Maybe the kitchen?" I turned back around and found Matthew's pout in front of my face. "Are you serious right now?"

"I never joke about my lap."

A laugh puffed out of me. "I don't even know what to tell you."

"Tell me you'll sit on me, then."

"Give me a good reason," I said, fighting him. Because what if I didn't, huh? Then what? I'd be *really* sitting on his lap, with his face right there, up close, and then, God knew what I'd do. This man had the power to disarm me with a smile, no matter what experience I had with men or smiles. "A single reason why."

"Your head," he answered. "It was going places. Places I can't reach. Places I don't like, just based on how your brows curl right here." His finger touched a spot on his forehead. "I'd rather have you smiling. And I know you like my lap so . . ."

So he'd just managed to disarm me, then. Just like I knew he could. My hand, which had a mind of its own, reached out, falling on his forearm. I squeezed. "You're so—"

Matthew moved before I could finish. He somehow snatched my wrist and pulled, softly but firmly enough that I stumbled into his chest. His other arm slid around my waist and, boom, he'd maneuvered me into his lap.

"Am I not a much better choice than a chair?" he asked, voice smug.

I blew air through my lips in response, but yes. Yes, he was. So I didn't even try to complain, even though that special kind of warmth had climbed up my face at the closeness of his chest and . . . well. Everything else. I tipped my chin up, decidedly making the best out of this, and then I shifted my ass. I made myself at home, snuggling in his lap, just like he wanted, as if I wasn't sitting sideways on top of a man who had declared himself better than a chair.

"I'm sure this is something expected anyway," I murmured. He wanted to distract me? To stop my mind from wandering off? Okay. "Engaged couples are handsy. They get carried away in the honeymoon period and all that. Right?"

There was understanding in Matthew's hum. There was something else, too. Gratitude? Frustration? I couldn't tell those apart with my ass planted so close to his crotch. "We wouldn't want anyone in the deli to think we're not one of those couples."

It's just Stu and Bobbi in the deli, I thought. But I said, "We really, seriously, absolutely wouldn't want that."

Stu popped up in front of us with a big plate of beef cuts. "Here you go, guys." He set it on the table, not batting an eyelash at the fact that I was using my fiancé as a chair. "This is our chuck roast, and some of our London broil. Hope you enjoy."

"That looks incredible," Matthew said. "Thanks, Stu. I think that's the last?"

"That's correct." The bearded man gave him one satisfied nod. "I'll be in back nailing down all the details with Miss Shark if you need us," he added. "Pretty sure I'm about to haggle like I never have ever before, so please wish me luck."

We watched him leave, and only when I heard the swinging door lock into place did I say, "Do you think it's only details they'll be nailing? Should we go check?"

"Absolutely not," Matthew said. "Unless a scream comes from the back—and let's face it, it'll be Stu's—we're not going anywhere close to that door."

"Huh. You make a good point," I said, returning to the plate Stu'd just set before us, grabbing my fork and snatching a bite. *"Oh wow,"* I said through my mouthful. "This is incredible. Yes. I want this. Hundred times over."

Matthew let out a soft chuckle before rearranging me in his lap so he could have a better look over my shoulder. He sniffed, reminding me of a hungry animal.

I chuckled, and when I loaded the fork with a new bite and turned to offer it to him, it was purely out of reflex. Surprise registered on Matthew's face, as if he thought he'd have to beg me to do such a thing. As if I hadn't been reliving the evening with the wine over and over in my head. Men could be so blind sometimes. So— He closed his mouth around the fork.

"Good?" I asked, not breaking eye contact. The response he made was a groan. A groan. And it was so outrageously erotic that it made me squirm. I cleared my throat. "More?"

"Please."

My fork snagged some of the roast this time, and when I turned to look at him, he was leaning back in the chair. My breath caught a little at the sight of him, looking so brash and presumptuous like that. So in control. So unassumingly smug.

The fact that we were alone in the deli made it all the worse. Better. Dangerous probably.

I cupped his jaw with my free hand. The touch of his stubble prickled at my palm, the warmth of his skin sending tingles down my wrist. Matthew's eyelids fluttered closed. I brushed the pad of my thumb over his cheek, as if telling him that I, too, loved the feel of him. That I had missed this version of us. The version of something we'd never fully been. The realization of the latter, so powerful that it made my palm move, encouraged, hungry, trailing my fingers with it, until my thumb reached the corner of his mouth. What beautiful lips, I thought. I couldn't even remember them on mine.

Matthew's eyes reopened, and he parted his lips, demanding more attention. I obliged, grazing my finger across his bottom lip. Just a kiss of the pad of my finger against it. Just enough to make the brown in his eyes swirl with the same feeling I was sure mine did. Blood pumping, I wondered what I could get away with without breaking any of my rules. Or breaking all of them, except for his. I leaned a little closer, fork in the air again. Fingers wrapped around my wrist.

His head gave a shake. "Use your fingers."

My eyes widened with surprise and . . . excitement. Yes. And it was pouring down my body now, making my skin tingle with the possibility, my words barely whispered, "My fingers?"

"Your fiancé is a handsy man," he said, and ba-boom went my chest. "What's anyone going to say? I'm yours to do with as you want."

An overwhelming sense of . . . need swept me. Head to toes. Toes to head. *What's anyone going to say?* I snatched the greasy cut of meat between my index finger and thumb. Matthew's thighs bounced, impatient, determined, still sitting like a king waiting to be fed, and bringing my whole body toward his chest. My hip was sealed against his gut. Only I didn't just feel that. I also felt him. And boy. Matthew was hard, so much I could feel him pulsing against me, only the fabric of my dress and his jeans separating him from me.

He let out a curt grunt. "What are you going to do about that, Josie? Give me what I want? Or make me beg a little more?"

Beg. I wondered if the sharp pang of victory at feeling him had to do with that. I pushed my hand closer to his lips, and when Matthew closed them around my fingers, he did it in silence this time. Keeping his eyes on me. I leaned closer, not wanting to miss a single second of him. Matthew snatched my wrist.

A short gasp escaped me. And before I could manage to get my breathing under control, he was bringing my hand to his lips, slipping the pad of my thumb into the warmth of his mouth.

All the air left me in one single swoosh. My whole body shook as I felt his tongue against my skin. Need swirled, and I imagined how that would feel somewhere else. My lips? My tongue? My skin? Anywhere would do. Matthew pulled my finger out of his mouth with a pop. I pulsed. All of me. All around. Need pooled between my legs.

"Tried to warn you, Baby Blue," he said, and I swore I could hear the hint of that Boston cadence there. Oh God, I was already ready to combust. The weight of his palm at my waist shifted. It moved down. "I knew this would happen. That I'd taste an inch of you and I'd want more. Everything." My eyelids fluttered closed. His touch drifted around my hip, landing on my thigh. Fingers closed around the fabric of my skirt, dragging it across my thigh. "Now I want it all." My skirt kept riding up, shivers curling around my legs, pooling between my thighs. "Can I slip my hand under this?"

A breath escaped me, broken, needy. *Now I want it all. Everything.* I gave him a nod.

Skin clashed against skin. Mine warm, tingly, ready to burn under his. Matthew's greedy, aflame. His palm dragged up. Matthew hummed. "Can you feel me against your hip, Josie?"

"Yes," I whispered. I was defenseless under his touch. Effectively disarmed. And he was so hard. It was impossible to ignore.

His lips brushed the shell of my ear, the advances of his hand coming to a stop. "Do you trust me to keep you safe?"

"Yes."

Matthew moved us, dragging the chair with one push of his body and legs, tucking us further into the corner, out of direct view from anyone coming in from the kitchen at the back of the deli, if I had to guess.

My heart tripped at the realization. The possibility of what he—we—was going to do. "Everyone's in the back," he said. The flickering of his fingers across my skin resumed, reassuring, encouraging. "It's just us here."

"That's good," I whispered. And at the same time, a part of me wanted to acknowledge that it was also bad. That I'd never done such a thing and it . . . excited me.

Matthew hummed in understanding, as if I'd always been his to read. His thumb tickled around my inner thigh. Just a little. Just slightly. Just an inch. I shivered. "Anyone could come back at any given minute. See me with my fiancée in my lap, food forgotten. Hand up her skirt."

All the air in my lungs escaped me. I couldn't believe we were doing this. I couldn't believe we never had. "Your hand's not high enough."

Matthew's chuckle was surprised. Delighted. Dark. His palm was splayed around my inner thigh in one single motion of his hand. "What else?"

"You're . . ." I swallowed. Overcome. "Not touching me."

His fingers pushed upward, reaching the elastic of my panties. My whole body clenched. "Touching what?"

I met his gaze. "Me."

His smile was as beautiful as it was sinful. Fingers tugged at the fabric, one rough, determined tug, letting it snag back against my skin. His voice lowered, hard as concrete. "I've been wondering how wet you'd feel against my fingers ever since that night on the phone." My eyelids fluttered closed. *Oh God.* I was— "No. Look at me."

Not without effort, I reopened my eyes.

"I want to watch your face when I touch you. I want you to see what it does to me."

There was a question in his eyes. Last chance to tell him no.

This was insane. We were in an empty deli, but it was a public place. I'd never done something like this in a place where I could get caught. The words left me in a rush. "Please, Matthew."

Matthew's jaw clamped down in response. There was a kind of urge on his face, in his eyes, that I'd never seen before. That I wanted to touch, but just as I reached out, his fingers moved. He tucked my panties aside. What had to be his thumb grazed me. My mouth parted with a gasp. And in response, he gave one determined stroke.

A low moan escaped.

His chest rumbled with a grunt.

"More," I whispered.

Matthew cursed, hand moving again. Against me. A second stroke. "You're going to come," he rasped against my ear. "Here, on my lap. You're going to watch me. And when that scream rises, you're going to press your face into my neck and you're going to come for me. Say you understand."

My lips parted over the word *yes.*

He stroked a rough circle over me, higher this time, over my clit, showing me exactly what he meant. "You want to hear why?"

My head fell back, only slightly, only enough. But I couldn't function with him gliding over me like that.

"Because those moans are mine," he all but growled. A whimper rose up my throat, and I turned my face over his chest. This was crazy. This was so inappropriate. It was insane. His fingers slid further down, slightly in. Goodness me. "Are you going to give me what I want?"

I had no doubt, but I was too overwhelmed.

His mouth descended again, finding my ear. "Say *yes, Matthew.*" Another brisk motion of his hand over my folds demanded I did. But I couldn't speak when his index and middle fingers were stroking me up and down, up and down, up and down, making me grow slick, restless, needy with release. His thumb circled my clit again. I threw my arm over his neck and slipped my hand into his hair, holding on to him before I flew away. "I didn't hear you, Blue."

"Yes, Matthew," I expelled with a breath.

The laugh that left him was the kind you brought with you into a fantasy. My thighs pressed together, engulfing his wrist as he moved.

I felt his body strain with mine, growing harder still, pulsing against me. "You feel how hard you're making me? I'd be turning you over this table and fucking you in a heartbeat if we were truly alone."

My head started spinning. All sense leaving me. All that existed was Matthew's fingers, now back to tracing circles over my clit. His body under mine, now shaking. His scent, all around. His voice. Just him. I tugged on his hair, squirmed in his lap, I wanted more of everything. I wanted the tension to snap.

"This is all I've been picturing," he told me, his wrist flicking. My body spasmed. "Since you came over the phone, saying my name." The memory led him right to the spot I'd touched that night, imagining it was his hand. He circled, rubbed it back and forth. God, I couldn't believe I was going to come like this. I— "Give me what I want. Let me have you to myself."

I brought my free hand down, over the fabric bunched at the top of my thighs. Covering us. I placed my palm over his. Matthew hissed a breath, as if caught off guard. I whispered, "I want to know it's you."

"Fuck," he cursed with a grunt. "Come. Now." He pushed forward, moving us against the edge of the table. As if he was about to buck. I started throbbing. Pulsing. Leaving my body. I clasped his hand. "*Josie.* Now."

I went off. No cry, no whimper, no name off my lips. I just spasmed against Matthew as I rode the highest of highs, feeling hot and cold and full and empty all at once. He continued moving, drawing it out, pressing his mouth against the top of my head. It was like a soundless kiss, and he did it several times, as if once or twice wasn't enough. The smile parting my face was sated and happy and wide. And when I noticed his hand was still sandwiched between my thighs, it turned greedy. I wanted it there. It didn't matter where we were. What we were.

A hum left me.

It made Matthew laugh. "That was a beautiful sound. And I think you love the shit out of this chair."

"I think I might," I admitted. I let out another content sigh. "I can't believe you've made me come twice. It doesn't seem right."

"Why the hell not?" Matthew asked. The reluctant retrieval of his hand leaving me . . . a little less content. "I love my tally," he continued, the sight of the mess I'd made out of his fingers distracting me. I brought them to my lap and cleaned them with the fabric of my dress. Matthew huffed out a laugh. "Fuck, Josie. *Christ.* You're going to make it impossible for me to stand up."

Which reminded me . . . "Were you touching yourself? When we were on the phone?"

His smile was lopsided. "Absolutely. Until the line went dead. Killed my hard-on on the spot."

I straightened, meeting his gaze. "Why didn't you say?"

"It didn't seem important. Not when you weren't talking to me."

My cheeks flushed.

He nudged me with his nose before pulling back to look at me. "Don't get shy on me when you just used your dress to wipe my fingers off. Not right after I had them deep inside your—"

Matthew's eyes were no longer on my face. They were somewhere behind me.

"Matthew?"

His brow set. All that lightness gone.

"Hey," I insisted, trying to turn, but finding my body trapped between his chest and the table. "You're scaring me. What's wrong?"

Matthew's body moved back, making the chair scrape on the floor. He set me on the ground gently, still not looking at me. Then he came to his feet. Blocked me with his body.

"Where's Bobbi?" he barked. Then louder, *"Shark!"*

I peeked over his shoulder, scanned the section of street across the window. Something stood out. A guy. Leaning on a car. A backpack at his feet. "Why do you need Bobbi?"

Matthew finally turned, eyes meeting mine, and it was as if his body gravitated toward mine. His arm snaked around my shoulders, and he held me to his chest. "Can you wrap your arms around me?"

I immediately did. "What's happening?"

"There's a fucking pap outside," he said. "And if Bobbi doesn't deal with him, I swear to God, I'm going to walk out that door and—"

Noise sounded behind us, then Bobbi dashed past. "Stay put!" She barked back, leaving us behind. "You're not getting your hands on anyone else today, understand? I'm dealing with that!"

Anyone else?

Oh boy.

I didn't know what was worse. The possibility of that pap having caught me dry humping Matthew's lap, or the fact that Bobbi knew what we'd been doing up front.

CHAPTER TWENTY-ONE

It was rehearsal weekend—*R. W.* as Bobbi had been consistently referring to it in emails, texts, calls, and conversation—and the Vasquez Farm was brimming with people.

Last time I'd seen so many workers buzzing around had been last year at our first frost event. The magic—and doom—of the whole thing was that the celebration would culminate with a big party on the day after the frost. Only it never came. Days turned into weeks and much like this year, the temperatures never seemed to drop enough for that day to arrive. The festival stretched for over a month, and by the time we rolled into the fifth week without a nice and crisp layer of ice, it all had gone off the rails. Before I could do anything about it, Green Oak had turned into a betting house, and people argued and wagered scary amounts of money over this whole first frost business.

I told myself never again. You live and you learn, and you don't let a war erupt in your town.

Only maybe I didn't learn.

Because here we were. New polls were running on Page Nine on whether I would wear white, or whether it'd be the groom who ran this time, and I was inflicting yet another spectacle on Green Oak.

If Bobbi heard me call this a spectacle, she'd probably burst a blood vessel. She was oddly happy with how everything was turning out, despite my picking most things at random.

Maybe Matthew had been right all along. Beautiful things shouldn't be boxed.

I smiled at the thought, at the idea of him, my gaze drifting away from the clipboard I had propped against my hip. I'd been signing off on things all morning, barely allowed to move from my spot at what Bobbi had called a *safe area.* Because *we couldn't have the bride breaking a leg or an arm or her neck on R.W.,* apparently. *Not a week before W-Day,* like she also said. So I'd been demoted to logistics, which meant that I signed a slip while stuff was loaded off a truck.

I was bored, frankly. Restless too.

I wanted to talk to Matthew. Be with him. Study his face. The brown of his eyes. Look for any signs of panic because . . . we were a week out. From W-Day. And neither of us was making the other talk about what that could mean.

I looked behind me, making sure Bobbi wasn't around. Then I gave the delivery guy in front of me a nod. "I'll be right back," I told him with a smile. He cocked a brow. Understandable. Bobbi had been terrorizing everyone, including him. "I promise. Ten minutes tops. Please?"

The guy gave his head a quick shake. "Yeah, okay. But if she—"

"I'll take the blame!" I exclaimed, turning immediately around.

I hadn't seen Matthew since we'd parted ways after driving here. He'd picked me up at the house, just like every time we'd had to run errands. My cheeks heated at the memory of how he'd looked at me this morning when I'd walked through the door. Matthew never waited inside the car. He always, always leaned on the passenger door and watched me make my way to him, opening the door for me without breaking eye contact. A beat-up Prius had never made me blush like his did.

Like Matthew did.

Flashes of that day at Fairhill, in Stu's deli, crowded my mind, making my breathing a little too labored for someone strolling around a farm. I doubled my pace, as an excuse to justify it, or as a result of the urgency and excitement bubbling in my belly. I . . . wanted Matthew. It'd be idiotic to deny it at this point. I wanted his hands on me. Again. I wanted *him* on me, honestly. I wanted that kiss he wasn't giving me. I—

I spotted the back of his head, right by the grassy section of farmland where the long tables for the rehearsal dinner would be installed. A tent to cover supplies and crates from the weather had been set up, and he was sitting there, next to it with someone else. A smaller head of messy brown hair barely contained by a French braid. *María.* I smiled to myself just as she moved, allowing me a glimpse of Pedro Pigscal.

Those two were totally hiding here, sneaking away from Bobbi, I was sure, and neglecting the long lists of tasks I knew she'd handed them, too. I chuckled to myself and approached slowly, wanting to catch them by surprise.

"Trust me on this, Mr. Matthew," I heard María say in the distance. "I ran both your astral charts. She's a gemini sun *and* moon. And virgo ascendant. I'm very thorough with my work."

Matthew's laugh followed, the sound making my stomach swirl. "How old are you again?"

"Old enough for you to be smart and listen to me," María answered.

Another chuckle traveled through the wind. "I like you, kid."

"I kinda like you too, I guess," María answered. "And it's not because you have soul-mate compatibility with Miss Josie."

María's words brought my body to a stop. I hadn't been planning on eavesdropping, but when María continued I couldn't make myself move. "I'm only doing this because I think you can make her happy. And she deserves happy. So just listen to me, 'kay?"

Matthew's answer was solemn, "Okay, hit me. I'm listening."

"Miss Josie loves all kinds of stuff," María said. "But unlike most grown-ups, she thinks magic is real. Like me. And no, I'm not talking about Santa. I'm talking about real magic. Like witchy things, but also manifestation and all of that. We watch videos and talk about it all the time. Miss Adalyn doesn't believe in that stuff, but that's okay. That's why she has us." A pause. "Anyway, what I mean is that this will be important to her. You should tell her that you're soul mates."

I swallowed, my heart pounding strangely as I waited for Matthew's answer.

"Why do you think she should know that?" Matthew asked, voice serious. "Besides her believing in magic."

"Because I'd like to know," María said, as if it was obvious. "You know, I was too little when Miss Josie was engaged to all these people everyone keeps talking about, but that doesn't mean I don't know what's going on. Adults think I don't pay attention when they gossip, but I have two ears, just like them. And it sounds to me like those men could have done something about it, you know?"

"Something like what?"

"Like not standing there like a dummy while she ran, I dunno." She blew air through her lips, the sound frustrated. "Maybe Miss Josie acted all strong after leaving those guys, but I'm sure she cries when she's alone. Not always. But sometimes. Just like my dad does sometimes too, when he misses my mom. Miss Josie lost her mom, too, just like me. So maybe she runs because she's scared. I guess I would if I'd had my heart broken. But I don't know, I'm eleven and I've never been in love."

My gaze fell to the ground, my feet itching to bolt if not for the fact I was rooted to the place, heart drumming in my ears.

Matthew's voice was low, almost hushed. "You're very insightful for an eleven-year-old, kiddo."

"I know," María said. "Here. Hold Pedro, it'll feel nice. He's warm. And you guys did a good job babysitting him the other day."

I heard Matthew clear his throat. "Hey María? Do you think I can mend it? Her heart?"

She hummed in thought. "I guess? But I'm only a kid, Mr. Matthew. Maybe you should ask her. Or tell her you want to. That way if she gets scared, she won't leave you too."

That way if she gets scared, she won't leave you too.

Before I could dissect how or why that made me so incredibly sad, or what followed those words, I was on the move.

My break probably hadn't been the best idea anyway.

I set the last folding chair in its place with a shaky breath.

María's overheard words had left me . . . a little rattled, to say the least.

I was also never folding or unfolding chairs ever again. In fact, I was getting rid of them after all of this was over. I'd ask Robbie to help me organize a nice bonfire, and we'd chuck them all into the fire and watch them burn.

That's what three hundred folding chairs did to you.

I patted my hands on my jeans and looked around, taking in my work. The sight made the dropping sensation from earlier return, but that was why I'd decided to indulge in a session of self-induced shock therapy. It wasn't exactly necessary that the bride personally checked and arranged line after line of chairs. Not when there was a tiny army of people around to do that and I'd caught some fire for leaving my spot at the front. But I didn't care.

These were just chairs.

And I needed something to do.

My phone buzzed in my back pocket. A message popped up in the group chat.

ADALYN: Do you need us to come help? We can head to Green Oak early and stay at Lazy Elk tonight. With Matthew staying with you.

With Matthew staying with you. We hadn't exactly told Adalyn and Cameron that Matthew was staying at my place, but they'd assumed it. Of course they had. We were engaged. To be married in a week. So that was what the housing situation should have been looking like. My belly loved the idea of Matthew staying with me. My head was set on reminding me that we were lying to Adalyn and Cameron. Although . . . were we? I couldn't tell anymore.

JOSIE: Everything's under control. No assistance is needed (or wanted, because Bobbi is unbearable). You can just drive up tomorrow for the big thing.

ADALYN: You're sure?

JOSIE: Positive, sis. Let's meet in the morning if you want and catch up before everything starts. 🙂

MATTHEW: You could stay over tomorrow night. After the dinner.

I swallowed. That meant . . . Matthew wouldn't sleep at Lazy Elk, then. He would stay at my place.

ADALYN: Oh. That's a good idea. That way we don't have to drive back so late at night.

CAMERON: Awfully nice to be invited to stay over at my own property, by the man I thought was my tenant, too. Cheers, mate.

MATTHEW: You're awfully welcome.

MATTHEW: You're awfully cranky lately, too.

MATTHEW: And awfully hard to love right now. But I'm not discouraged. Do you want to meet for breakfast while Josie and Adalyn catch up?

CAMERON: Yes.

ADALYN: Ignore him. Please. He's just stressed out. We told you to make yourself at home and we meant it.

CAMERON: I'm sorry, love.

MATTHEW: I forgive you, sweetheart.

MATTHEW: And all it takes is for me to swing my schlong once around a place to make it mine. 🙂 You need to love me as I am.

The gulp of air I'd been apparently holding throughout Cameron and Matthew's exchange escaped me. It was a snort.

"There it is," a deep voice I knew well said. "It took me *swinging my schlong* for you to let go of that frown."

My gaze lifted off my screen and was immediately snatched by Matthew's, who stood a few rows of chairs away from me. He was smiling at me in a way that made that special place in my belly flutter. The man looked so handsome when he smiled like that. All tall and wide and happy. And way too wholesome for his own good, in his glasses and that cream knit sweater he was wearing today. The color brought out the streaks of blond in his hair, and now that I could see his sleeves rolled up, I wished I'd caught sight of him working.

He started moving, crossing the distance to where I was. "You're staring," he said through his smile.

"You're wearing your glasses."

He came to a stop in front of me. "I have a little wager going on," he admitted with a shrug. "Wanna hear about it?"

I gave him a nod, and he moved a little closer.

"You always point out when I wear them," he said, brushing some hair off my forehead. Goose bumps broke out across my skin. "So every time I leave home, I take a guess at whether you'll say something that day."

That was so silly. And I loved it so much. "Did you guess today?"

The back of his fingers grazed my jaw, his gaze down, fixated on my mouth. "Yes."

"And what did you win?"

His other hand rose, and he cupped my face. "This," he said, the pads of his thumbs skimming over my cheeks. "This blush." I tingled. All over. My feet moved closer, the tips of my sneakers touching the toes of his boots. "It makes a little boy who used to get called four-eyes puff his chest with pride."

I felt my face fall a little, and Matthew chuckled.

"Hey, none of that." Hands moved around the sides of my face before dropping to his sides. "Have you seen me now? I'm hot as shit."

The chortle that left me caught both of us off guard. Matthew's eyes glinted as they roamed around my face, whether pleased with himself or what he saw, I couldn't tell. Knowing him, probably both. I loved that about him. He was so shamelessly smug where I was concerned. The thought gave me pause. I was quickly realizing I probably loved one too many things about this man. And maybe . . . maybe I should linger on that thought.

Do you think I can mend it? Her heart?

Maybe you should ask her. Or tell her you want to.

"Matthew," I started. "Earlier . . ."

Before I could finish that statement, he pulled something from his back pocket and any confession I might have had died at the sight of what he was holding.

A blue thimble.

"Last of the season," Matthew said, my gaze on that stunning violet I'd always loved so much. "They should stop blooming around August, but this one had extra defiance." I looked up at him. His expression was soft. Incredibly so. "It's what makes it so beautiful. So unique. She's brave and resilient and can overcome anything."

My throat went dry, and when he slipped it in my hair, just like he'd done with that daisy two, three weeks, or what felt like an eternity ago, something solidified in my gut. Deep inside me. Something scary, something beautiful, something that was impossible to push aside.

"They remind me of Mom." Matthew's expression sobered, as if he knew I was about to tell him something I didn't admit readily. "That's why they're my favorite. She had a handkerchief embroidered with blue thimbles. She'd done it herself, and she always told me it'd be my . . ." I trailed off, short of breath. He clasped my hand. "My something borrowed and something blue." That void I'd learned to live with expanded for a moment, opening a hole. "Remember what I told you a few days ago? In my truck? She would tie it around my wrist, and we would walk down the hallway." A smile blossomed, it wasn't sad or happy, just something in between. "But I've never taken it out of the drawer. Never felt . . . right. As if it was too violet for something that was supposed to be blue, and no longer borrowed now that she's gone."

Matthew stepped into me, his body providing the warmth that had left me at some point during my speech. And when his hands cupped my face, it didn't feel like when he had done it a few moments ago. It felt like so much more. It felt like if I told him that some nights I cried myself to sleep because I missed Mom so much, he'd have a way to make it better. It felt like if I told him that I'd been flying on autopilot ever since he arrived in town and I wasn't brave enough to admit that I was lost and truly terrified and had no idea where I was going, he'd just be able to find me. Take me somewhere safe. It felt like if I ever felt the urge to run, he'd come after me.

"Can I be blunt?" Matthew whispered, peppermint tickling the tip of my nose.

I gave him a nod.

"There's nothing I want more than to kiss you," he said, voice hard. With the same fierceness I felt in the grasp of his hands. My heart cartwheeled, eyelids fluttering closed. "Wipe that sadness off your face with my mouth."

"What's stopping you?"

"I told myself to make it count." His fingers slipped into my hair. "Remember my rule? I kiss you because you know what it'll mean, no matter what's down the line."

My eyes blinked open. I remembered that. It was all I'd been thinking of lately. "And what would it mean? If you kissed me now."

Surprise registered in his gaze. The corners of his lips twitched.

"That's exactly what I mean, Baby Blue. You shouldn't be asking me." His forehead pressed against mine, just like he had that day in my truck. "You shouldn't be asking me."

Something fizzled inside me. It wasn't rejection. It was . . . determination. Curiosity. *Defiance.* "I do remember there being a part about you kissing me because you fucking need to. And another one about me needing you to. What if I do?"

A laugh escaped his lips, falling right on mine. And it wasn't a kiss, but it was pretty sweet, too.

Then the grip of his hand around my face changed. He tipped my head back, and when I met his gaze, I swallowed. Hard. He licked his lips, mine parting in response. His eyes dipped to my mouth, just the once, making my heart thrum.

His jaw clenched and he—started humming a song. Just under his breath, soft but loud enough for me to pick up the tune. It was a country song I knew well, and it talked about a girl who had roped in a man from a country mile and tangled him up. Just like one big ball of Grandma's yarn.

Grandma's yarn.

That had been my answer to his question about whether I had him wrapped around my finger. That night that seemed like eons ago. In my kitchen.

I smiled. And Matthew did too, even through the prayer in his eyes.

I wasn't going to get my kiss today. And as much as I was a touch disappointed, I was also in awe of the man. He had a willpower I lacked, and we were so backward it wasn't even funny anymore. "If you're going to ask me to dance, the least you can do is sing a little louder than that."

His eyes lit up, and his voice grew louder as we twirled between the rows of chairs. Soon, the earlier heaviness in my mind started to recede, and it was just us. Me and Matthew's voice and Matthew's goofiness and the promise of that kiss. By the time we were hitting the verse, I was laughing, and he was turning around.

He stuck his ass up in the air. And he—

"Are you twerking?" I asked him. "To an a cappella country song?"

Matthew caught my eye over his shoulder, still moving. "Absolutely I am." He winked. "And you can give me a nice pat. You know, test the horse before you buy it. Go on, country girl. It's a nice butt."

My smile turned so big I was afraid it'd hurt. He really had a nice ass. And maybe—

A throat cleared.

I froze. Matthew did, too, perky butt sticking out.

We turned, finding Andrew standing awkwardly at the end of the rows of chairs I'd unfolded.

"Sorry to, uh, interrupt?" he said. "Bobbi's asking for you. The two of you. If you can spare a minute."

There was a moment of silence. Matthew was probably letting me decide whether we immediately left or stayed to make small talk. Or how to respond to Andrew's request. I stayed put. I'd never seen Andrew look so sheepish. So shy.

"I could make an excuse," Andrew offered, making my brows arch with more surprise. "If you'd like me to. While you . . . finish here?"

My chest warmed. And maybe it was stupid of me, but it felt so nice that I couldn't stop myself from smiling at him.

"I think we're finished," I told him. I sounded happy. Way too happy. "But that's so nice of you. Thank you."

For a moment, I wondered what it'd be like to add a *Dad* at the end of those words. To have him smiling back at me the way I did at him. But that would be silly. That's what would make me naïve. Just like back at the party that night, when Andrew had chosen a picture with Duncan over me. But that was fine. It was all right. I didn't need things that were realistically out of my reach. I wanted simple things. Things that sometimes came easy, and things that you oftentimes had to put a little work in. And I wanted to believe this was him trying.

Matthew pressed a kiss on my temple. As if sensing the strange cloud hovering above my head. "Let's go, Baby Blue," he said. "See what Bobbi wants. Then I'll drive us home."

"That sounds nice," escaped my lips. *Us.* I didn't think he'd said it for my father's benefit, and I'd take a win where I saw one. "We should be rested for tomorrow."

Andrew nodded, his eyes bouncing between the two of us, as if he was noticing something he hadn't before. I couldn't imagine what. Matthew had always been like this. At least around me. The realization seemed important, but just as I was grasping it, Andrew spoke.

"Josephine?"

The thought fled. "Yeah?"

"I was wondering," he started, with a little pause. "If you'd like me to be there. For you. Next Saturday."

Next Saturday was December first.

Matthew stilled by my side. The hold of his hand tightening around mine.

"What do you mean?" I asked, even though I knew what Andrew was referring to. I was also very aware of what I'd just shared with Matthew. Of what I'd told him that day in my truck. About Mom.

"I am your father," Andrew stated. His throat tripped over something. Air? Words? Then he said, "I could walk you down the aisle. If you'd like me to."

It was my turn to stall. Although I'd known he was referring to this. I'd known and I'd asked. I'd pushed, made him say the words. "Is that something you would like?" I heard myself ask.

His face did a weird thing. Or maybe it wasn't weird. Maybe it was just something Andrew's expression did. I couldn't really know. "Yes."

I tried to stop the burst of emotion in the middle of my chest. I really tried.

It made me feel so tiny again, like a child. It made me happy and sad, too, all at once. I couldn't believe that one word from him could cause that reaction in me. Clearly, I had those issues the world accused me of having.

Clearly, I shouldn't smile.

Clearly, I shouldn't agree. Say yes. *Of course. I'd love that too.*

I should ask him why. *Is that because you want a relationship with me? Is it because you see me trying? Are you meeting me halfway*? This man couldn't be all bad. Not when his relationship with Adalyn had been somewhat salvaged after him admitting to his mistakes. Not when such a wonderful woman like Adalyn's mother had loved him. Not when Mom had seen something in him. Mom wouldn't just sleep with someone she met at a bar. Or with someone she just knew from town. Just because. Me and Mom had always been hopeless romantics. We believed in things like promises, vows, love.

I should ask Andrew if he was only doing this because there was a poll online. If it was the thousands of people voting, the ones who had decided who walked me down the aisle, and not him. Me. Us.

But the words that left me were, "Yes. Of course. I'd love that too."

Because when under pressure, not only did I make rash decisions.

I sometimes caved, too.

CHAPTER TWENTY-TWO

The knock on the door of my bedroom came just as I secured the strap of my right shoe around my ankle.

Belly fluttering, I made my way to the door, racing across my bedroom.

A pair of brown eyes lit up.

"Fuck me," Matthew breathed out. Then huffed out a laugh. "Seriously." He swallowed. "Fuck me. Please."

I pursed my lips. "That's sweet."

Although the way his eyes roamed hungrily, bringing heat to my skin everywhere they went—collarbones, hips, breasts, ankles, toes, breasts, face—was something a little more than just sweet.

"I wonder how many girls you've won over with that exact line."

He clasped my left hand and brought it to his mouth, kissing my ring finger. A shiver curled down my spine. "None," he said, matter-of-factly. "None who mattered."

"Now that's a little unfair," I whispered.

Matthew pressed into me, walking me backward into my room.

"It's the truth," he said, peppermint breath fresh on my lips. I wondered if he'd kiss me. Tonight. Soon. Now. The wedding was in less than a week. "Ask Adalyn. Ask anyone. Ask my mom when she gets here for Saturday."

The reminder of that made most of the fluttering sensation flee.

We hadn't talked about this. Not since that day in his kitchen. Lazy Elk's. It was inexcusable that I hadn't asked or pushed for more, but not only did I not know how, we'd also been so incredibly busy. And so . . . overwhelmed. In the best and scariest way possible. So absolutely backward we were. I couldn't quite believe how any of this was happening.

Matthew watched my face for a moment, then dipped and kissed my jaw. Wickedly fast and impossibly soft. Not enough. "My sisters think you're too pretty for me. They always have. They're not wrong."

"They always have?"

His smile was lopsided when he released my hand. He tugged at the lapel of his suit jacket, throwing it open. The fabric of his dress shirt was snug against his torso, displaying every plane and valley I hadn't really touched. Kissed. Memorized. Lord, this was my fiancé. And—

A phone appeared in front of me. Matthew's.

I frowned at the screen. There were messages. On a group chat. *The Flannies.* And there was a picture, too. Of us, Matthew and me. From the day at the farm, after yoga. I swallowed. I loved that picture. I loved all the selfies we'd taken that day. The only selfies we had.

"You don't need to prove anything," I told him. I wasn't reading the texts. He really had nothing to prove. "I'm not getting my feelings hurt."

"I'm not doing that," he said. So soft and gentle. So understanding that it made me feel a little worse. Because I really was getting my feelings hurt. But it had nothing to do with him. And all of it with me. "Check the date. Check the day I sent that."

With a sigh, I snatched the phone from his hands and scanned the screen.

The message was dated from that day. I remembered because I knew Green Oak's activity brochure by heart, I knew what day I did what. He'd sent that picture later that night.

"Why?" I asked, my voice coming out weird. The question too misplaced.

Why . . . what exactly? he should have replied.

"Check what I wrote," he said instead.

I glanced at him. Chest swelling. He made a face, as if he wasn't backing down until I looked. As if we had all night. I returned my eyes to the phone.

"I'm marrying this girl," I read out loud.

Something inside me stumbled at my words.

Something crystallized in his eyes in return. Something I didn't want to acknowledge. I shouldn't need to read anything into it. We'd been *engaged* by then. This was his soft launch text. *Hey, here's the girl. And by the way? I'm marrying her.*

His family was coming to Green Oak, and he was marrying me, if the setup at the Vasquezes' Farm was any indication. If the last weeks were too. If this whole thing none of us was stopping was.

Matthew cleared his throat. "My sisters have been, respectfully, worried I kidnapped the beautiful girl in the picture and tricked—or paid—her into smiling for the camera. They requested video proof, the *blink once for yes and twice for also yes* kind. You can see. It's all there."

I wasn't going to check. I didn't need receipts. He didn't owe me anything. But I appreciated him immensely for trying to convince me that I had any right. So I brought the device up. And instead of reading the messages, I studied the picture again. We looked so . . . genuine. We always had. "I think it's because you're staring at my boobs like you haven't had a meal in a week."

"They're great boobs."

"It's the yoga top."

"It's definitely the boobs. I'm a tits-and-ass man. And yours are beautiful. You are. I would—"

"I digress." A small smile parted my two growingly heated cheeks. "Why didn't you say something that day at the lodge?"

Matthew let out a strange breath. "Sit with me? I know we're already pushing the clock, but I want you to enjoy tonight. I don't want you to be thinking about shit that's weighing you down because I made a selfish decision. Otherwise I'll never get that first kiss that keeps eluding me."

"We already kissed," I countered.

"I thought I was clear when I said that wasn't our first kiss," he said, and when he tugged at my hand, I went with him without a complaint.

Soon, it was me guiding him, leading him to my bed. And I realized in that moment, that it was the first time he'd been here. The first time he was seeing where I slept, the dresser at the corner, the wallpaper on one wall, and a big yellow sun on the opposite one. It was the first time he saw me, sitting on my light-blue duvet in a dress I'd picked thinking of him.

I angled my body toward him.

I like him in my space. I love the way he looks at me from his spot on my bed.

"You look very handsome tonight," I said. And I could tell from his smile that he hadn't expected that. "I didn't say anything before, and I should have. I got caught up in you being silly, because I like it a little too much. I like *you* a little too much."

Even though *like* didn't seem the right word.

Matthew made a face. One that told me he was changing his mind. No talking. More touching. I clasped his hands.

"I'm sitting," I told him. "Like you asked. And I don't mind being late. But you should start talking because I really like you here, in my room. And if you don't distract me from that thought, we might be *super* late. Instead of fashionably so."

He was frowning now. Debating. I tugged at his sleeve with my fingers. "My family doesn't know about my job," he let out with an exhale. "My parents don't know I was fired. Or that I moved here to Green Oak. They think I am still in Chicago, and everything's the same."

I nodded, processing his words.

"My sisters think I'm using up vacation days and finally 'frolicking' like I used to. I don't know what Eve means most of the time, by the way. I never frolicked. Not since college, at least."

I didn't doubt that for a second. Matthew was thoughtful and dedicated. He could be far more serious than most people gave him credit for, me included. It made me wonder if he was maybe trying to keep that side of him from his sisters. Maybe even from his parents. His friends. The world. "Why didn't you tell them?" I asked him. "It sounds like you have a good relationship with them."

"Would you believe it if I said that I don't know? I . . ." he trailed off, eyes leaving mine and falling somewhere to his left. "A part of me didn't want them to worry or make a fuss. I've always had a job, even in high school. College. I accepted the first good offer that fell on my lap fresh off graduation day."

That sounded like him. He was a worrier as much as he tried not to appear as one. "Maybe that was why," I offered. "You were always independent. And perhaps you didn't like losing that too."

"Maybe," he admitted. "Or maybe I felt like I was failing everyone. That I was disappointing them." He sighed. "Fuck, maybe it's all the same thing."

"But you did a good thing, Matthew," I insisted, not liking the way his mouth had turned down. "You stood up for your friends. How could they not be proud of you for that?"

His palm fell on my thigh. Nothing but a reflex. Only this time, it felt like he was the one hanging on to me.

His eyebrows dipped in thought. "I guess they wouldn't know."

"What do you mean?"

"My parents . . . They never cared too much for my job. It's not like I worked at some newspaper with a big name. And that's fine. I never minded. It's okay that they don't care for gossip. Entertainment. The internet. Smartphones." He snorted. "They are proud of me. But they are simple, hardworking people, and I say that with all my respect and love. I'd do anything for them. They raised me to work hard, and once I was on my two feet . . . it gave them just enough peace. So why would I disrupt that? They're already struggling with Tay's choice to leave and follow a dream they're scared is too big for her. That's why I never told them the truth about what we were doing, Josie. Because I was already keeping things from them."

The truth about what we were doing. That this was fake. A PR device. "So they haven't seen anything about us, me or Andrew. Online or otherwise."

Matthew gave a curt shake. "Not in detail, no. They know there's some stuff being said. But they already knew Adalyn and who her—your—father is. They love Adalyn, so they were not surprised to hear I fell in love with her sister and didn't want to wait. A supersonic engagement? Just Matthew, doing Matthew things."

I fell in love with her sister.

My chest drummed in my chest. "Is going down on one knee and getting married in a little under two months a Matthew thing to do?"

"It can be." His grip tightened, and I could feel the gentle imprint of the flowers on my skin. "It could be. That's why they didn't make a big fuss. Why they're on their way here for the wedding, no questions asked. And why my sisters have been giving me so much shit. Tay is devastated she won't make it. Eve wanted to come earlier but didn't manage to on such short notice. My mom . . . She keeps asking me if you're sure." Matthew's head shook. "They might really think I kidnapped you, Baby Blue."

I smiled at him. I couldn't not smile. Meeting his family . . . made me happy. The fact that they didn't think I was a liar or a deceiver was a relief. But it felt strange, as if we were still under a pretense.

"So that's why you came to Green Oak?" I asked, trying not to think of that.

"Remember what I said about retirement and an RV?" I gave him a nod. "They deserved to get to enjoy that, free of burdens. Financial or otherwise. I'm their eldest, out of the three of us, I should have my shit together. I shouldn't be unemployed, or breaking the lease on an apartment I can no longer afford. I am also helping with Tay's expenses in England. If they'd known, they would have taken that off my plate and had me move back home."

They wouldn't have realized their dream.

He didn't need to say that. I read it on his face. In the way that same cloud that had hovered over my head yesterday was moving around his now. He was so selfless. So incredibly kind. He didn't deserve to look so forlorn.

"Can I sit on your lap?"

His brows shot up, and when he didn't answer, I scrambled onto him and threw my arms around his neck. He hissed out a breath, sounding like a balloon deflating. A happy balloon, though.

"You're an incredible son," I told him, feeling his arm sliding around me. He pulled me to him with one hand. "And an incredible man."

He breathed me in, nose in the nook of my neck. A hum left him.

It made my toes curl. "Now, don't get ideas," I said, more for me than him. "This is a very PG utilization of your lap. Purely for distraction purposes. We're running late as it is. If we don't get there, everyone's going to think we were really *frolicking* like your sisters said."

We both laughed at that, and when I pushed back, he let me go. Even if with a little resistance. I could be strong for him, just this once.

I stood up, grabbing his hands and pulling him to his feet. The sight of him standing in the middle of my room, smiling, was like a punch to the heart. He looked so right. So very mine.

"You have a sun on your wall," he said.

"I painted it years ago." My lips tipped higher. "It always makes me smile."

His eyes darkened in a way that told me his mind had drifted away. To a place that made my belly tight and my chest short of breath. A place that had me itching for that kiss he wasn't giving me.

When Matthew spoke it was quiet, just for us. "Those are the best things."

Those are the best things.

Once again, I recognized his words as mine. I'd told him that, when this whole thing had started. Only it hadn't been about smiles, but about something far bigger than that.

Something as big as the sun painted on the wall behind me.

Rehearsal dinners often went one of two ways.

They either went by in a flash, or they stretched on for so long that you had time to think of stuff like time and space being a construct of society or whether your butt was now shaped like a chair. A folding chair in this case. Thanks to Andrew's generously opening the invitation to all of Green Oak, we'd resorted to using them for all of the seating. And I would be throwing them into a pyre first thing Monday, the moment *R. W.* was over, if not because we'd need them for next Saturday.

The wedding.

Usually one thing followed the other. But this had never been a usual affair.

My gaze drifted away from my empty plate, toward my sister.

She immediately caught my eye and gave me a smile.

God, I hugged her so long and so hard when I'd seen her that Cam patted my shoulder with alarm. I'd missed them so much, even though I was still relieved after our visit to their place.

Witnessing Andrew and Adalyn's reunion had made some of that relief fade. They never had the easiest relationship, but I'd seen something in the way they hugged, even if awkwardly. I saw intention. Effort. And I hated myself for thinking of it, but I hadn't even gotten that. A hug from my father.

Before this wedding took the reins of my life, Adalyn and I had talked about Andrew's desire to make amends. She'd told me the ways he'd tried to build that bridge for her, and that as skeptical as she was, she still was open to seeing him try.

I'd been open too. But things between me and Andrew were simply . . . different. For one too many reasons. And it was strange to be here, sharing a table, and having to see that, although their relationship wasn't great, it still was worlds ahead of mine.

And on Saturday, he was walking me down the aisle to the man sitting by my side.

Andrew commented something about the wine, or dessert, or the weather. I couldn't know, really. But Cam straightened in his chair and grabbed Adalyn's hand from where it rested on the table and brought it to his lips before releasing it and filling up her glass with water. Then he passed the carafe to Andrew with a curt nod.

I wondered when Cam and Adalyn would get married. *I knew they both wanted to but weren't in a rush. They were busy with work. The club. Would she ask me to be her maid of honor?* It had taken me so long to do that. Oh God, I was really doing this. We were.

My knee started bouncing at the thought. Matthew squeezed, very gently, just like he had a dozen times tonight. It wasn't a *stop that.* It was more of an *I'm here, I've got you.*

I shifted on the outrageous folding chair.

I lowered my voice. "If I asked you to meet me somewhere at midnight and bring a big pack of matches with you, what would you do?"

Matthew's answer was quick and serious. "I'd say we better dress in black. Ash stains are a motherfucker to remove."

This man.

He was so perfect I couldn't even breathe. I turned to look at him, realizing my eyes were starting to well up.

Concern filled his expression. "Wrong answer?"

Far from it. I didn't think his answer could have been more perfect. I didn't think I'd ever loved an answer like I did that one. I didn't think I'd ever loved—

"Rubbing alcohol," I croaked. "If nothing works, that'll do the trick." I shrugged, attempting to be casual. "One too many campfires gone wrong."

Matthew's frown didn't go away; if anything, he looked like he wanted to press on whatever I had just shoved aside. Thankfully, the swiftly changing weather decided to give me a hand.

Thunder echoed in the distance.

"See?" Otto Higgings said with a clap, making Grandpa Moe flinch by his side. "I told you that storm was heading this way. I've been waking up to aching knees for three days straight."

"That's because you're old," Grandpa Moe muttered. "And why are you here? Shouldn't you be all the way there, on the other side of the farm? Or I don't know, in your house?"

I rolled my eyes, although Grandpa had a point. Somehow Otto had squeezed himself there, at this table of the many we'd set. I wondered whose seat he'd stolen or why Bobbi hadn't made a fuss over my neighbor breaking the seat arrangements she'd so carefully prepared.

"I'm two years younger than you," Otto countered, shifting his attention back to Andrew, where it had been most of the time. "So Andrew, you were telling us about the soccer club. The franchise. How did that come about? I remember you playing ball when you were *yea* big, but it was football, wasn't it?"

Cameron muttered something into Adalyn's ear as he retrieved the pitcher of water and filled Adalyn's glass again. She smiled.

"What do you think he just said?" Matthew murmured in mine.

A shiver raced down my arms at having his lips so close. *"Soccer's not a real word,"* I said, my voice low. *"Football's the name of the bloody sport."*

Matthew's chuckle warmed my skin. "Uncanny," he said. "It really is like I'm sitting right next to him." His hand drifted a little upward, to the middle of my thigh. My breath caught. "Good thing I'm not. I don't think he'd be appreciative of my table manners."

Something swirled in my belly. Lust. Or need. Probably both, considering the images my brain was pulling up and flashing behind my eyes. Me, on Matthew's lap. Us, at Stu's. His hand, up my skirt.

I closed my eyes, putting a stop to that.

"We have a safe word," he said now, softly. "Use it."

Use it. I turned my face toward him. Brown eyes burned with need. And something else. *Give us an excuse.* "Will you reward me, then?"

Matthew's jaw clenched. That emotion in his eyes flared. "You'll be the reward."

I pressed my lips so I wouldn't smile like an absolute fool, or worse, beg him to whisk me away. Now. Right now. Why hadn't he five, ten, fifteen, an hour ago?

My sister's words distracted me from the thought. "That's . . ." Adalyn trailed off, struggling with her words. Cameron threw an arm around her shoulders. "Thank you for saying that, Dad. I appreciate it."

"It's nothing but the truth," Andrew conceded with a nod. "You know I've been working hard at mending your trust after how things transpired with the transfer of the Flames."

I brought my hands under the table and flexed them against my lap. Matthew wrapped them in one hand.

"You must be so proud of them both, huh?" Otto said, that *them both* making me look his way. *Adalyn and me?* "The soccer youth club they started is everything everyone's been talking about since they cut the ribbon and had that big party. About time someone does something this special for the community."

Adalyn and Cameron.

"Oh, absolutely," Andrew agreed. "I've been pestering them about letting me donate to or fund it in any way I can, but they refuse. Can't say I wouldn't be the same, though. Maybe I instilled that in Adalyn. Or maybe it's just Cameron who hasn't come around yet. Either way," he said, raising his wineglass in front of him. "Cheers to that."

Purely on automatic, I retrieved one of my hands and snatched my glass, raising it like everyone else. Adalyn seemed so unsure that it made me clink my glass against hers and tell her. "So proud of you." She beamed then, and that brought me such comfort that when I turned to Matthew, it was with a smile. "Cheers—" I started.

But he was already downing his glass.

I frowned a little, then had a sip and put the wine down.

"So how did you two meet?" Otto asked, turning his attention to me and Matthew. "I don't think we ever covered that."

Matthew's chuckle was strained. "No, we haven't covered that." His calm tone set off a strange alarm in my head. "We were a little busy covering everything else."

"Dinner has been so wonderful, Josie," Adalyn rushed. "Just like everything you ever put your mind to. Seriously outstanding. I wish— We wish we'd been around to help. It's just so . . . busy. With everything."

"I know," I told her reassuringly. "You two are under a lot of stress, and that's completely understandable. I shouldn't take the credit, either. Bobbi's been in charge of most things. And Matthew's done as much as I have." Matthew's thumb caressed the back of my hand. I glanced at my father. "Andrew also made all of this possible."

Andrew cleared his throat. "Of course. I—"

"So Otto," Matthew interjected. "Before we somehow end up magically drifting away from the topic, you were asking how Josie and I met."

"Right," my neighbor said. "But if—"

Grandpa smacked him in the arm. "Let the boy talk, Christ. You've been yapping about nonsense since you sat on that chair."

"Thank you, Maurice," Matthew said with a nod that Grandpa returned. He squeezed my hand. "The first time I heard about Josie was through a text." I turned my head to look at him, finding his gaze on me. "It was from Adalyn, and it read: *I think I've just met your soul mate.*"

Something in the middle of my chest bucked.

Soul mate.

Adalyn laughed from her seat. "I'd forgotten about that."

"I haven't," Matthew said, his eyes still on me. "Do you remember what I texted back, Ads?"

There was a strange pause, and then Adalyn said in a soft, baffled voice, "You asked for a picture. Of your future wife."

All the air in my lungs left me, and I could only sit there, on that chair, staring at Matthew as his smile widened and widened, making a spot in my chest swell, taking up all the space.

"That's right," he confirmed. "And all I got was a laughing emoji. I was genuinely curious, and I wanted to press for more information. What did she look like? Would she laugh at my shitty jokes? What color were her eyes? How did she smell? Did I stand a chance?"

My lips parted, and I swallowed, trying to push down the emotion clogging my throat, chest, head.

Matthew's fingers, still around my hand, still on my lap, intertwined with mine. "But most of all, I wanted to ask my very pragmatic best friend what had brought her to make such a statement." His features sobered up. "*Soul mates* isn't a term one throws around lightly."

"And what did you do?" Otto asked.

Matthew's gaze dipped down to my mouth, before returning to my eyes. "Bided my time." He swallowed. "Prayed to God." The hand clasping mine rose, moving from under the table. Lips brushed my skin. "Believed in magic."

My mouth parted, the pounding organ inside my rib cage demanding to be let out. I wanted to ask him if he meant that more than I'd ever wanted to ask anything in my life. I wanted his answer to change things, to make him kiss me, to push every worry out of my head and just . . . fill me up.

His dream should have been getting married to you.

I could swear I could hear those words, from his lips, in my head. I could see them in his eyes right now. Waiting for me.

A glass clinking aggressively sliced right through the moment. My ears caught the sound of sniffling, female. Was Adalyn crying?

There was a muffled baritone voice, too. Soothing. Hushed. I sensed people moving, rearranging their seats. Surprised murmurs. But I still kept my eyes on Matthew. Just like he did on me.

Bobbi was talking. Announcing a speech that had Matthew's face shifting, that emotion that was making the brown in his gaze warm, intense, more beautiful than ever, slipping away. A deeper voice took over in the background. Andrew's. Matthew's brows furrowed. I heard my name.

I turned around then. Ripped my eyes off the man by my side and let them fall on my father.

Andrew stood at the end of our table. There was silence. Everyone listened. Watched. His voice was deep, his posture commanding, his presence meant to fill the room. This farmland. To travel further than the dark slopes behind us.

". . . And I couldn't be happier to be here to celebrate their union." Eyes a blue as light as mine found me, brows pressing down. "Here in Green Oak. In fact, it was Josephine's heartfelt speech back at the welcome gathering a few weeks back that made me see something I had somehow missed." Matthew's body was suddenly there, his chest against my back. Stiff, solid, as if bracing. Preparing. For what? "I've missed this. Green Oak. My daughters. Everything."

The air in my lungs seized. I was still so dazed from Matthew's words. From what they meant. So raw. So . . . exposed. That I didn't even think I could process what my father's conveyed.

"And that is why," Andrew continued, "I've decided to move back here."

My ears rang.

There was more following that. Something about not wanting to blindside anyone. Something about the book deal and Willa Wang. I was somewhat aware of Adalyn standing up and saying something too, something about Andrew not learning from his mistakes, making this about himself, but I . . . I didn't know.

God. I didn't think I cared.

Had my father just announced such huge, personal news at a rehearsal dinner? Mine. News he'd decided without checking in with Adalyn or me. This was Green Oak. It was my home. Shouldn't I know? Shouldn't I . . .

A ripple of laughter reached me. Mine. I was laughing.

Every head turned to me. "Well, that's just so darn *bootylicious.* Isn't it?"

Everyone blinked.

Matthew was immediately pulling me up from that horrible, horrible chair. "I'd love to stay and witness how Adalyn hands Andrew his own ass, but I'd rather spend my rehearsal dinner in a more pleasurable way." He threw the napkin that had been on his lap on the table. "And yes, that's a nice way to say: I'm making my woman scream until she forgets her father thinks so highly of himself, he decided to make this night about him."

There was a beat of silence. Then Adalyn snorted, Cameron laughed, and to my utter and complete shock, Grandpa Moe said, "Attaboy."

And with that very bright green light Grandpa had just given Matthew to make me scream, my fiancé turned around and led me away from the table with a smile.

CHAPTER TWENTY-THREE

Matthew was no longer smiling by the time we pulled into my driveway.

He killed the engine of my truck, the kind of silence that preceded a storm pouring into the vehicle, making the air thick with the smell of rain, the anticipation of what was coming, making my heart pound.

"Matthew?" I called softly. Making sure he didn't miss my question. "Are you going to kiss me?"

"Yes."

A flutter broke on my chest. "When?"

"The second I'm sure I won't end up fucking you inside this truck."

My belly dropped, that delicious anticipation building up. "Why?"

Matthew's eyelids shut.

"My truck is big enough," I continued, leaning toward him. Just a little, just enough. He made a sound in his throat. "And I don't think

I've ever done it in a back seat." His hands moved to the steering wheel, fingers clasping around it, leather squeaking. "What if I want to? With you. What if I want you to kiss me, then fuck me here?"

His eyes reopened, jaw clamping down. "What if I want to give you something better than that?" He glanced at me, the brown in his eyes seemingly darkening, the creases of tension around his mouth pleading with me. "What if I feel like I've already gotten carried away? What if I don't like that the first time I made you come I wasn't touching you? What if I *hate* that the first time I touched you, I wasn't able to hear or see your mouth move around my name? What if I wasn't planning on doing this tonight, and now I'm wondering if it's the right time?"

There was a moment. A pause.

I didn't breathe.

Then he spoke, "What if I can't give you any fucking firsts, so I want to make sure I get a chance at being your last?"

My chest expanded. That emotion I'd held throughout the day swelled, making it hard to contain. My hand reached out to cup his jaw. Matthew leaned into my touch. My smile made his eyes light up. "Come inside?" I said. "Please."

He frowned, but I didn't waste time. I turned in my seat, determined to make it okay for him, to make it possible for him to give me all those things, even when all I wanted was him.

When I pushed the passenger door open and my feet hit the ground, Matthew was somehow there. The dazed look on his face made my smile even bigger. Even more determined. He offered me his hand, and when I clasped it in mine it was me who pulled. I led him inside the house. Then up the stairs. Then down the hallway. Then inside my room. I ignored all the tingles spreading all the way across my body from that hand held so tightly, and led him where he'd stood earlier tonight, right before we left for that disastrous dinner.

"Here," I finally said, watching his eyes go crazy as they bounced between me and what was behind my back. His expression turned fierce, devastated, almost as if he wanted to scream or fall on his knees. "You once told me that perfection is subjective. Remember?" He didn't nod or shake his head, but I continued anyway. "This moment, right here, right now, is perfect for me." My lips fell, all that wrangle of emotion and tingles and anticipation came to a soft stall. "And that's because you're in it. That's because it's you. Only you. I don't care about firsts when I have you."

Time seemed to halt for a moment, it was less than a heartbeat, nothing more than a fraction of a second.

Then Matthew's mouth was on mine. Hungry. Desperate. Hands clasping both sides of my face, holding me to him, as if I was going to run away or disappear. I moaned into the kiss, melting, feeling like I was going to slip away, right between his fingers.

The thought had me bringing my arms around his neck, slipping my hands into his hair, fisting those locks that reminded me so much of the sun painted on my wall. Joy and need surged, meshing in my belly, making me slant my lips, changing the kiss, making it greedy. Our tongues touched and I pulled at his hair. Matthew groaned in response, deep in his throat. The only warning before his arms shifted and we were moving.

My back clashed against the wall.

One of his hands remained along my face, the other one pushing down, over the fabric of my dress. Collarbone, breast, ribs, waist, hip, it went, the roughness of its weight pulling at the sateen. I wanted out of it, the dress, I wanted that touch on my skin, on me. His fingers moved, traveling down my backside, over my ass. Setting up camp right under my thigh.

He pulled my leg up in a brisk motion, then rested his weight against my hips.

I moaned into his mouth, making him come up for air just so he could say, "Fuck."

"Yes," I agreed, panting. Breathing all over the place.

Matthew's hum was appraising, content, eager. And when his teeth closed over my bottom lip, my eyelids fluttered shut with a shudder.

His mouth returned, this time softer, slower, but making the kiss more intent. Making sure it stayed with him. Me. Tattooing himself on my lips.

"You think I make this moment perfect?" he asked, mouth moving away, words falling on my jaw. I started to nod, but his grip on my leg changed, fingers spreading. He opened me wider, pushing his hips further in. A loud moan escaped. "You think you can be all sweet and soft and call *me* perfect?"

I reopened my eyes, just so I could see him when I said, "Yes."

Matthew smiled, and it was big and cocky and dark, all swollen lips and lipstick smudged over his skin. I knew in that moment. I simply knew. I'd never wanted a smile—a man—more than I did him. I'd never loved like I did him.

The thought made me so breathless I gasped for the air eluding me.

Matthew's expression darkened, reading me. He kissed me again. Hard. Harder than earlier. Harder than I'd ever been kissed.

In the next beat, his hands were releasing my leg and face, and I was flipped around.

My palms fell flat on the wall.

Matthew's chuckle brushed the skin on my temple. I shuddered, blood swirling downward, pooling. "I love this dress on you, did I say that?" My eyes shut again, senses shorting, overwhelmed. I nodded, and his hands slipped between my hair and the back of my neck. I felt him push it aside, gently, the gesture almost reverent. His fingers returned to the top of my spine, then trailed down the buttons lining the seam. "I do love it on you, Josie," he continued. "But I hope you're not too attached to it, because I have no patience for these."

The rip of the buttons echoed in the room.

My lips parted with a silent plea. *Just take it off. I need you now.*

"Was that too rough, Baby Blue?" Matthew asked me, voice low and serious, hands bracing on both sides of my head as my cheek rested on the wall. "Am I being too much?"

I was panting too hard to speak, the need gathering between my legs, too overwhelming as it pulsed to the beat of the pounding of my heart. Where were his hands? I wanted them on me again. I wanted Matthew on me. In me. I—

"Josie?" My name, off Matthew's lips, fell on my hair, followed by a press of his mouth. It was so distracting. He was so distracting. All of him overruled all of me. I was at his mercy and I didn't even care. His hands clasped my wrists, softly, slowly dragging my palms down the wall and lowering my arms. He pulled at the fabric of my dress, just enough that I felt the sleeves pool around my elbows, the opening at the back letting the air in the room kiss my back. The fabric of my panties cooled against my skin. "Am I too rough? Am I too blunt? Is this too much?"

"No," I finally managed to say. My dress slipped even lower, the opening exposing the backs of my thighs too. "Rough is good. It feels good. You're perfect."

"Wrong." He swatted at my ass. "I'm perfect *for you.*"

A moan fell from my lips. Followed by a broken, "Oh my God." He'd really done that. And I— That had been so good, so—

"Say it for me, Josie," he whispered, arms snaking around my waist gently, softly, bringing me into his chest. He placed a kiss on the side of my neck. "Let me hear the words."

"You're perfect for me," I whispered.

I felt his approval on my back, his grunt pleased, satiated, and so fucking happy that it made my insides melt.

His palms descended. "This is what I wanted to do the moment I saw you in front of this wall." I dipped my chin, watching his hands as they dragged the dress hanging off my elbows down. "My sweet fucking girl," he said against my cheek as I let my arms fall. The material pooled at our feet. "So fucking beautiful."

Before I could make sense of how his words made me feel, or how he should be touching me now that I stood there in my bra and panties, Matthew's body was descending.

"Let's see if I can make you smile a little wider still," he said, hands landing on my hips. His breath fell at the small of my back. The warmth of his palms on my skin, finally, making me gasp for air. Fingers tugged at the waistband, just slightly, just enough. I felt the flicker of a touch, dragging down the curve of my ass. What a tease this man was. What a—

Matthew's palms closed around my inner thighs, opening my stance wider from his spot on the floor behind me.

"Hands back on the wall," he grunted.

My palms pressed against the wall. He pressed his lips over the silk. One gentle kiss right on the spot that barely stung from his hand anymore. My body arched. I started shaking. All over. "Matthew?" I panted. "I'm so wet right now. I'm so—"

He turned me back around. I didn't even know how. And I didn't really care.

I glanced down.

Matthew was on his knees, hands braced on my thighs, looking up at me through those goddamn glasses I loved so much. And I— He looked at me so reverently, so hungrily, like he'd been in the dark for ages and he couldn't get enough warmth and sunlight on his skin. It made me want to burn in return. Burn as I stood here, under his gaze.

"I can't decide," Matthew said. "I can't decide how I want to have you." His voice strained. "Eat you. Fuck you against this wall. Have you ride my face. Take you on the bed. Fill that tub up and beg you to let me come all over your back?"

My throat worked around the plea tearing at me. God, yes. Please. "Have me every way," I said. And when his jaw clamped down and his eyes darkened, it emboldened me. I planted the sole of the heel I was still wearing on his knee, opening up. Inviting him. Offering him a place to start. "We have all the time."

Matthew's hesitation was immediately gone. His expression turned feral. Then he surged with a grunt, flexing my leg and opening me even wider. I felt this breath through the fabric, making more need pool down, raising the pulsing between my thighs, pushing my heart faster. He tucked the fabric to the side with a labored exhale, as if he was battling whether to waste time taking them off. Air hit me, making all that urgency ring louder. Right into a high pitch. Then he pressed a kiss. I moaned, melting against him.

His mouth was slow at first, determined but tentative, exerting little moans from me. "You're drenched," he said. Rasped. Growled. I wasn't sure.

Because Matthew's caution was gone and now he was devouring me. My knee wobbled, and he used a palm to stabilize me. To secure me against the wall as he grunted against my folds, tongue dipping, lips closing around—

"Oh God, Matthew," I whimpered. I was already spasming. Tipping over the edge. "I'm so close. I can't believe—"

His hand joined in, thumb closing over my clit.

My hands braced on his head, searching for support and . . . and release. My fingers closed around his hair and I pulled him closer. Sensation twirling. Swinging. *"Matthew?"*

His tongue dipped inside me, mouth still moving, hand working around the sensitive nub that was sending wave after wave of delicious pressure up my body. He did something with his lips, and I moaned loudly, dipping my chin so I could see him. Brown eyes met me as he came up for air, mouth glinting with the mess I was making of him. "You're going to come?"

I nodded my head, barely able to breathe with his hand still moving and him looking at me like I was making his life for letting him kneel in front of me.

"Then come, sweet Josie," he said, the motions of his wrist changing. "Ride my face a little harder." His other hand joined, big fingers poking at my entrance. "Give me a little scream so I can fuck you."

His mouth descended, replacing those fingers with his tongue and I—

Screamed. Just like he asked. Although it wasn't little, and it was three words, *"Oh shit, Matthew."* I was sure they'd been heard all over town. But I couldn't give a damn when my knees were buckling, my back arching, and all of me ceasing to exist. *The world* ceased to exist, dragged by wave after wave of pleasure and . . . happiness.

Joy. Love. Release.

It was Matthew's laugh on my temple that made me realize I was in his arms and we were moving. He placed me on the bed, and I looked up, finding him taking a step back, eyes never leaving me.

"That's my new favorite," he said, softness and lust tugging at his voice. "You're *Oh, shit, Matthew* smile." My lips went even higher. His gaze kept doing passes up and down my body. "Never seen something so beautiful."

I went up on my elbows, pursed my lips in a pout I hoped he found cute. "Are you talking about my boobs again? I know you like 'em, but I have a face."

His eyes creased at the corners with amusement, but when he spoke, his voice was serious. "Smug looks pretty on you." The way he met my gaze made my belly flutter again. The flapping doubling when he started making quick work of the buttons of his shirt. I didn't even know when he'd gotten rid of the blazer. "Let's see how smug you are when I have you on your back." Pop. Pop. Pop. The shirt opened, revealing all hard planes of golden skin. Hard stomach. Those dents on his hips. My heart raced. "Or when I flip you on your belly and you feel my weight over you."

My throat dried at the sight of him, the words, the need resurfacing in my bloodstream. I scrambled to my knees, coming to a sitting position. Matthew tilted his head and he smirked. I really loved that smirk. I loved the words that came out of him. I'd always liked a sprinkle of dirty talk, but Matthew was filthy. And I loved what it did to me. I loved that he knew exactly what to say, exactly how to say it. I loved that he was able to make sure I wanted his touch and his words without me having to say a word. I loved that he was sweet and funny and clever and the way he never thought there was something wrong with me. I loved that he'd waited this long to kiss me. I loved that he wanted to give me things he couldn't. And God, I loved his smiles almost as much as I loved that he was obsessed with mine.

I . . . I loved all of him.

I'd fallen in love with Matthew.

And I didn't think it was new, born of this moment. I knew I already had before leading him upstairs.

"Matthew?" I called, as if he wasn't in front of me. My voice was odd, rocky, filled with emotion and realization and the enormity of what I just allowed myself to finally admit. *Finally.* Because it wasn't new. I'd had clues. Hints. I'd known I was falling. This is what I always did. I fell fast. *Had this been too fast?* Matthew's body froze, the shirt falling to the floor.

His gaze sharpened.

"Get over here," he said. "Now, Josie."

I moved to the edge of the bed, where he stood bare-chested in his dress pants. His hands clasped my face the moment I got there. He pulled me up, so our faces lined up. "I know," he murmured on my mouth. He brushed his lips on my jaw. Chin. Cheek. "I know."

His teeth grazed my bottom lip, then he kissed me. "I got you, okay? I'm not going anywhere."

I'm not going anywhere.

I couldn't figure out why, but the words rang inside me, making me want to cling to him. Just to make sure he stayed. I was the one who kissed him then, pulling at his shoulders and dragging him down with me. We both fell on the bed, his weight heavenly on top of me, making me feel so alive, so secure, so safe. My hands traveled down his arms, wandering, struggling to find a place to set up camp. Shoulders, arms, chest, stomach. I wanted to touch all of him. I pulled at his belt, greedily, and he moaned into my mouth. His hands braced on both sides of my head as he pulled himself up. He panted into my mouth.

Selfishly, I pulled at the buckle of his belt, studying his face as I worked it loose, taking pleasure in how his eyes went half-mast when I let my pinkies brush the hardness pressing against the dark fabric of his pants. Once undone, I unbuttoned him. God, I could already feel his heat in my hands, I could tell he was already so big just based on the bulge.

I unzipped him in one motion, and his jaw clamped down. My hands tugged at his pants, almost forcefully, almost out of control, revealing dark briefs. Biting my lip, I slipped my fingers into the elastic, slowly, dragging my nails over the skin of his lower stomach. Just a little. Just enough to tease.

Matthew hissed a breath.

I let my nails brush over his length, emboldened. Coming out of my skin with how good it felt to hold this much power over him.

"You're going to get a nice spank on that ass if you don't stop being mean," he told me, a promise in his voice.

My blood swooshed down with excitement, the ring of his words making me want to be meaner still. But I was too on edge already. I was too impatient and I needed him too much. As soon as possible wasn't soon enough. So I gave him my sweetest smile and finally got his briefs out of the way. A breath caught at the sight of him springing free.

"Give me a stroke, baby," he whispered. Pleaded with me. "Just one, before I lose myself."

My hands were immediately around his length, hard, scorching hot, bigger than I'd ever had, and I was giving him what he asked for. We whimpered at the same time, mouths clashing with the same selfish urge. I gave him a second one, and when he grunted, I stroked him a third time. His arms flexed, his hips thrusting into my fist.

"Need you," I told him, demand lacing my voice. "Inside. Now."

Matthew's body was ripped away from me, and suddenly he was on his haunches. "Condom," he said. "Where?"

"Birth control," I shot back, realizing we weren't wasting time on words. Realizing my underwear was still on. I tugged at the clasp of my bra. "I want you." My attempt didn't work. "I want you inside. I—"

I was flipped on my belly.

Matthew's body came over me, his mouth at my ear, his length nestled in my ass. "You'll want what I give you."

The moan that left me was outrageously loud.

His arms closed around my waist, pulling my ass up. "I haven't been with anyone in a long while. Are you sure about not using a condom?"

"Good," I whispered, a bite of jealousy in my voice. "You're my fiancé."

The sound that left him was halfway between a growl and a laugh. I felt him stroking himself, his fist brushing my skin as he let out a little grunt. "And you're mine to do with as I please."

"Yes."

He removed my panties, planting kisses on my spine, then positioned himself at my back. His hand clasped one of mine, bringing it between my thighs. "Keep your hand there. I want you to feel me."

Before I could know what he meant, Matthew was entering me in one swift, hard thrust that flattened me into the mattress. A loud whimper ricocheted. Mine, his. Probably both.

"How does that feel, baby?" he asked me, pulling back slowly before thrusting back in.

I closed my free hand around the duvet. "So full. So—"

"Perfect," he finished for me, his hips pistoning in one more time. "For you. Say it."

"For me," I breathed out. I squeezed his hand, the one still between my thighs. My nails dug at his skin, the pleasure swirling inside me becoming too much, more powerful, more overwhelming, dizzying, more perfect still. "Just for me."

I felt him pull out of me, turning my body slowly this time. With a cadence that made my chest tight. When he lowered himself over my body, slipping back inside me with one slow, torturous thrust, he was looking into my eyes. I swallowed a moan. "Look at you," he whispered in my mouth, his next thrust harder than the last. "Taking me so beautifully. Can't wait to see this every fucking day of my life."

The words triggered an explosion inside me. My eyes shut, and I started spiraling. My bra was pulled down, and his lips were closing around a nipple. I croaked something, a word, something like yes, or please, or— He nipped at the peak again, following it with a rough push of his hips.

"Let go, Josie," he demanded. Another thrust. "Let go so I can make a mess of you."

My lips popped open, but before anything left them, Matthew was pulling my hips up with one hand while the other one flew to my clit. I opened my eyes and it was the sight of him, with everything else, that made it for me. Pleasure rose, peaking, propelling me into the sun. “Matthew,” I whimpered, burning, an emotion filling my chest as I rode the crest.

Matthew slipping out was the only thing anchoring me back. “I’m pulling out, baby.” He fisted himself. “I’m making that mess.” His words were nothing but a growl, and his hand barely had a chance to move before he was coming all over me.

“Mine, Josie. You’re mine. Say you’ll have me.”

I didn’t know how my brain was computing anything at all, but I knew I’d never heard or seen anything more erotic than Matthew on his knees, panting, his hardness wet from being inside me, hand on my hip, and his spent covering my skin.

I reached out, pulling him back on top of me, basking in the way his weight felt against me. Matthew’s arms went around my body, and when he rolled us on our sides, I pressed my mouth into his skin, right above his heart.

“I don’t think I’ll ever be able to have anyone else but you,” I told him.

And I meant it. With every ounce of my soul.

What worried me was whether I’d be able to show him.

CHAPTER TWENTY-FOUR

I was awakened by a trail of soft, open-mouthed kisses placed between my shoulder blades.

My toes curled with the goose bumps traveling down my back, and I felt myself smile. "Matthew?"

He huffed a breath out against my skin. "Were you expecting to wake up and find someone else in your bed?"

I bit back a laugh and said as seriously as I could. "Hm . . . I dunno. What was your last name again?"

Matthew's arms went around my body, and he jerked me against his chest in one swift motion, rolling us on our backs. I squealed out the laugh I'd been holding, his breath tickling my ear. It was deep and rowdy and it made me feel the kind of happy I hadn't been in a while.

He tickled my sides, and I rushed out, *"Okayokayokayokay."* But Matthew didn't stop, and so I squealed some more, wiggling my body on top of his to free myself and—I felt him. Hard and long and very naked at my back.

My laughter died off, immediately replaced by a powerful wave of awareness. Need. Sultry and warm.

I felt his smile when he kissed my shoulder from behind me. "Can I ask you something?" he asked and I nodded my head, squirming, moving my ass against him. We both let out a hitched breath. "Why are you wearing so many layers of clothing? Don't get me wrong, I want you warm, cozy, and happy. But I don't even know when you left my side to suit up like this."

I breathed out a laugh, although it sounded strained, still very aware of the heat at my back. God, I wanted him again. Several times. All day? All the time. Yes. I—

"Blue," Matthew insisted. And to make a point he rearranged me, nestling himself right against my ass cheeks.

A shudder rocked me. Stupid pajamas. "I can't sleep naked," I confessed. "I feel . . . too exposed." I swallowed at the way his hold changed, I knew he was going to do something. Hopefully. "What if a monster comes and gets me? What if there's a fire and I need to climb out the window without clothes?"

There was a pause.

Then I was being rolled to the side, and as anticipated, Matthew turned me so I'd face him. He kissed the tip of my nose. I frowned at the tameness of that, and he chuckled in return. "I'd protect you," he told me. "From the monsters."

"You don't think my explanation is silly? I'm closer to thirty than thirteen."

"Nah," he said quickly. Easily. His arm came around my waist and he pulled me in. Secured me against him. "You're smarter than me. It never occurred to me that I might end up flashing my junk to a firefighter."

The corners of my lips inched up. "Would you even care if you did?"

"Not really, no." He shrugged. "I have great junk."

I tried to stop it from coming out, but boy, I couldn't not laugh. His eyes lit up, gaze going a little crazy, as if he couldn't decide where to look. "You kinda do, I guess. Maybe."

He brought me closer still. "He's not hurt by your reluctance." His chin dipped before adding, "He was there last night. For the moaning, the screaming, the coming, the *Oh shit, Matt—*"

I punched him in the stomach. Softly. A chuckle left him, unbothered. "I just *knew* you would be the kind of man who would talk about his penis in third person."

He grasped my fist with one hand, bringing it up between us. It was my left. "And I knew you'd love that about me." Matthew's gaze lowered, and as much as that happy glow didn't go away, something else entered his expression too. "Do you?" He swallowed. "Do you love that about me?"

I looked down at what had captured his attention. My ring finger. His grandma's Claddagh ring. Mine, for the last few weeks. "I do," I said, the words squeezing out of me. His eyes climbed up to mine. "I love that about you."

I love every single thing about you.

"Are we really doing this, Matthew?"

He inched closer, not letting go of my hand when it pressed between his chest and the flannel of my top. "We'll do anything we want. Anything we decide."

We.

My chest expanded with . . . hope. It was fuzzy and overpowering. The kind that filled you up, bringing bubbles to your head. "I think I could really marry you."

His laughter was soft, intimate, and it fell on my lips. "Flattery, meet Josie."

"You know what I mean," I told him. I was talking about walking down the aisle to him. Like it had been planned. I never thought it would really happen. "Do you think it's going to make any difference? Outside of us."

"I think I don't give a shit what it does for Andrew if that's what you're asking me. I only care about you."

I shot him a glance, even though I couldn't blame him. Not after last night. "I have a reputation, too. Which is kind of justified by real facts, you know?"

"You have a life," he told me. His mouth pressed against mine. "You don't have a *reputation.* You have a heart that chose to believe in love. A beautiful mind that singled out every bad or ugly thing that came at you and stayed hopeful. You have the kindness to give second and third and fourth chances. You'd rather lose hours of sleep baking so someone can feel a little better the next day than take care of yourself. You showed up on some guy's doorstep with a folder filled with printed job ads that you'd color coded. You have a fucking sun painted on the wall because it makes you smile. If someone fails to see all of that, or who you really are, then good." A throaty sound left him. "More of you that's just for me."

My smile was slow, but I knew it was there, parting my face. Mirroring the butterflies filling every gap inside my chest. Even the hole that Mom had left, even if just for a little while. "Those should be your vows," I told him, before doing the same and planting a hard kiss on his mouth. "Then you can pat your chest with your fist and growl a loud, *Josie, woman. Mine. Just for me.*"

His gaze darkening was the only warning before he rolled me on my back. Arms caged my head. "Poke fun at me, Baby Blue," he rasped. "The truth is scary sometimes, but it doesn't make it any less real." I swallowed, and Matthew licked his lips. "That doesn't mean you're not getting that ass s—"

The doorbell rang.

My chest heaved with the words that had just been left unsaid.

Matthew's nose flared. "Ignore it."

It rang again.

Matthew's jaw clamped, eyes filling up with an irritation I shared.

"You look so cute when you're grumpy," I told him before slipping under his arms. I snagged my robe and watched him as he let himself fall on his back with a curse. "Grumpy and horny. Yummy, even better now." I tilted my head, watching how nice Matthew looked in my bed. Hunger rekindled in my belly. "Actually? Don't move. Just stay there. I'll see who it is, shoo them away, and be right back."

And with that promise I sprinted out the door of my bedroom and down the stairs. The realization that Grandpa Moe had beat me to the door made me come to a slow stop before reaching the end of the staircase. Adalyn and Cameron stood there, bringing a smile to my face.

"Hi, guys," I said with a wave. "To what do I owe the honor?"

My sister returned the smile. Then her gaze flickered behind me. "Morning. And hey, at least you're not completely naked. Thanks."

I looked over my shoulder to find Matthew in his briefs. No shirt, no pants, no nothing. Just the briefs, ruffled hair, his glasses, and a smile. I braced myself on the railing, and he was somehow immediately behind me. An arm snaked around my shoulders, pulling me to his chest. "I don't like this extra layer of clothing here," he murmured into my ear.

A chuckle escaped me. Fine, a giggle. It was a giggle.

"Can we speed things along?" a bored voice said. Bobbi popped in from behind Cameron, sending the man an unimpressed glance when he glared at her. "Small talk makes me uncomfy, and we have things to say."

My lips popped open, but Adalyn beat me to it. "We want to make sure you're okay," my sister said, ignoring the other woman.

"Last night was a lot, and Andrew . . . it wasn't right. He overshadowed what the dinner should have been about. Which was the two of you, not him. Believe me, I talked to him. He wanted to come today, but we asked him to sit this one out."

My hands had wrapped around Matthew's forearm at some point. "Sit what out?"

"We're pampering the bride-to-be," Adalyn said, eyes shining with emotion.

Cameron brought her to his side with an arm. "I'm apparently also pampering." His green eyes flicked to Matthew. "You'll need to be clothed for that, by the way."

"Pity," Matthew muttered. He lowered his voice, just for me, "Is Adalyn about to start crying again? I think she might."

I was pretty sure she might, in fact. Which was . . . strange, to say the least. I never knew weddings made Adalyn this emotional. But I wasn't about to do my sister dirty and point that out. "Yay!" I exclaimed. "Totally unnecessary, but I'd absolutely love to be pampered and hang out. What's the plan?"

"It's a surprise," Adalyn managed out. Barely.

I blinked at her. "Adalyn, are you sure you're o—"

"She's fine," Bobbi interjected. "Can we go now? Time's of the essence and we have places to be. And just like I told Burly Brit here, no men allowed. *Especially* not Blondie. Oh, and no. This is not a bachelorette, so there's no need to get your singles out or wear your good underwear, yes? Now, move." She clapped her hands, looking straight at us. "Let's go. Come on. Oh, Maurice? Do you mind showing me to the coffee machine while we wait?"

The moment I jumped out of Adalyn's car, I knew things were about to take a turn.

I should have predicted that this was where we were headed when we got on the interstate.

The white and baby pink sign crowning the door stared back, as if pointing a finger at me, poking fun. *Always a Bride,* it read. The irony was like a bucket of cold water to the face.

"Come on," Bobbi said, ushering me forward with a hand. "Charleene is waiting for us."

Charleene.

I remembered her. Kind face, a little uptight, well-intentioned. She'd tailored the gown I'd made a run in. One of them. Greg's.

"I—"

"Nonsense," Bobbi interjected. "I know you said you would take care of it, but you're not walking down the aisle in something plain so . . . we're splurging. If this was a normal wedding, it'd be months too late for any of this, but it's Bobbi Shark organizing it, and Charleene and I have come to an understanding." Bobbi's hand rose and she rubbed her finger and thumb in a gesture. "Some lady with a perm helped me get your measurements from some costume for a Thanksgiving parade? We should just need to make some small adjustments. As you see, there's nothing Bobbi Shark can't do. Now, shall we?"

Bobbi didn't wait for my response, so I watched her make her way inside the shop, remaining rooted in place.

Adalyn popped by my side. She hooked our arms together and gave me a smile. "If you want me to take her down, you just say the word, okay? You should be enjoying this." Her eyes sparkled again, emotion welling. "I know I will. I never thought I'd get to do this with someone. Be there for my sister."

Be there for my sister.

I swallowed the sudden lump in my throat and squeezed her arm. "Let's try to keep the *taking Bobbi down* to a minimum." I made my mouth return the gesture. Back up my words. "This'll be so much fun. I'm so excited."

The moment I stepped inside Charleene's Always a Bride bridal shop, I realized how much of a lie that was. The middle-aged, red-haired woman handed us one flute of champagne each, and before I could so much as take a sip, I was being yanked into a vortex of tulle, lace, silk, and organza. As if I was watching the scene unravel from above, I found myself in my underwear, inside a spacious dressing room, with Charleene fastening a gown around my torso.

"Hold your breath for me, honey," I thought she said.

My lungs didn't react. My brain couldn't even process whether I was breathing. Was there air in my lungs?

She tugged at the fabric, making me brace a hand on the back of a Chesterfield sofa. God, who had a sofa inside a dressing room? *Charleene,* my mind answered. *Which you knew because you've been here already. You're always the bride.* A second tug. *Never the wife.*

"All right," Charleene muttered with a third and final pull. "I think this'll do."

My head dipped, appraising the gown. White. A layered skirt covered in tiny flowers. I swallowed. "I don't have shoes," I heard myself say.

"Don't worry," Charleene responded, clasping my arm and leading me out the door of the dressing room. "I have a pair out here. A six and a half, right?"

I stumbled down a narrow hallway, walking beside the woman for what seemed an eternity. Was the dressing room that far? She smelled like peonies and bergamot. The whole shop did. It had all those years ago, so some things never changed. "My feet," I mumbled. Every step felt like I was putting weight on a twisted ankle. Blood pumping in joints and odd locations of my body. "My ankles feel a little weird. I don't think the shoes will fit."

All Charleene did was laugh. I didn't know why. It was strained and strange and the sound was the last thing I heard before somehow being shoved onto a platform.

Bobbi and Adalyn materialized in front of me.

My sister's brown eyes welled up, and a tear slipped down her cheek. She mumbled something before whispering, "Oh my God, Josie."

"Well, that was quick," Bobbi said from her side. I looked at her in time to see her down her glass of champagne. "I don't think there's a point in trying anything else, Josephine. You look perfect."

Perfect.

I blinked at them, my brain struggling to sieve through words and my body feeling like one big pounding bell. Being hit by a hammer with every beat of my heart. Hands fell on my shoulders, turning me around.

My reflection crystallized before my eyes, blue eyes staring back at me wide and . . . void.

"I'll get the shoes," Charleene said, her voice sounding distant. Away. "Be right back."

For the fifth time in my life, I stood in front of a mirror, dressed in all white. Ironically, this time, the dress was something I would really choose. Something that had nobody else's interest at heart when hanging off a rack. Scoop neckline, thin straps, cummerbund-style waist. It was simple, if not for the intricate top layer of the skirt, covered in tiny, beautiful, embroidered flowers. It was perfect. Although perhaps . . . perhaps I was wrong.

Maybe it wasn't perfect. Maybe it didn't have my interests at heart. Maybe it was wrong. Maybe I was. The woman inside. Beneath. Inside the gown. I flexed my hands, feeling funny.

Images of what Saturday was supposed to be, to look like, with me in this dress, started taking form. Matthew standing there at the end of an aisle lined with rows of chairs. Smiling at me like he had this morning before we left. Like he had last night. Like every other time before. Everyone I loved was there. Grandpa Moe, Adalyn, Cameron. Everyone from town. Matthew's parents, who believed . . . believed we'd fallen in love. Weeks ago. Months. Andrew, who'd asked to walk me down that stretch of carpet that would be rolled at our feet. Andrew who I . . . Who I'd said yes to. I would love that, my father walking me down the aisle. Of course. But would I? Did I love that when I didn't even know why he was doing this? Whether he wanted me or not?

Whether he'd get this and disappear all over again?

Would Matthew do the same if that happened? Would he leave if he discovered all the ugliness beneath the dress? Every single emotion I'd ignored all these weeks? Every accusation, every single thing that had been broken. By me or somebody else.

We were backward after all. My ring— Dear God. My ring wasn't even turned around. How could Matthew accept that? How could he accept me? How could I let Andrew walk me to the man I loved when he wasn't even supposed to? It should never have been Andrew. Not like this.

I looked down. Brought my hand up. Pulled at my finger, trying to make this one wrong right. At least one. Just the one. It was the least I could do.

"Josie?" Adalyn's voice slipped in. Pushing through the ringing I hadn't noticed in my ears. "Josie, breathe."

My head turned. Was I not breathing?

Adalyn paled. "I think she's having a panic attack."

Was I? Hands moved, traveling to my chest. I noticed it was heaving, the sound of the air as it barely went in or out reaching my ears. But that wasn't important now. My ring was. Matthew's ring. So beautiful, so unique. And I couldn't get it off. Make it right for him.

"I can't," I heard myself mumble. My hands clashed, fingers fumbling against each other, fighting for control. Something was stuck. Something always was. "I need— I can't— I don't—" Air erupting out of me stopped my words.

Out of the corner of my eye, I saw a blond bob approaching, before being intercepted by someone. My sister. Soft hands were on me. "Josie." Adalyn's face. Her eyes. Sharp and filled with concern. I pulled away, feeling too overwhelmed. Feeling like I was going to implode. "Josie, you're scaring me. You're crying, and you need to breathe, please. *Please.* Do that for me? I know it feels too big right now, too hard, but you can do it. You can do this."

I can't.

I couldn't.

I couldn't do this.

I was always a bride.

"Matthew," came out of me with a sob. I pulled at my hand, as if my body had gone on automatic. Nothing was coming out, but something had to. Something must. "I want Matthew. I need—I need Matthew."

Adalyn stood up, and without her support I felt myself curl into a ball.

"Someone get Matthew," she shouted. *"Now."*

CHAPTER TWENTY-FIVE

"Where is she?"

Matthew's voice came from outside the dressing room.

I didn't know how much time had passed. Seconds, minutes? It didn't seem long enough for me to collect myself enough to make it out and face everyone. *Anyone who isn't him.* It didn't seem long enough for my voice not to betray me if I called for him again.

"If you just let me—" Charleene started.

"Where's Josie?" Matthew asked in that deep, seemingly calm tone that made his face look unnaturally hard. "I don't fucking care about some bullshit tradition." His voice broke. "She asked for me."

"But sir, she's only a little overwhelmed. It happens all the time. I'll help her out of the gown—"

"Where is my fiancée?"

Matthew's voice had me scrambling off the couch where I'd curled up. I braced a hand on the back, standing up, but a new voice stopped me.

"I'm sure everything's fine, Matthew." Andrew was here? How? I became very still. "Let's not be dramatic and cause more of a scene. There are enough people outside now and they can see everything through the window. If Josie—"

"Excuse me, Andrew, but you don't know shit," Matthew answered. "You haven't made the effort to know. You haven't earned the right to reassure anyone. So move *aside.*"

There was a beat of silence.

"Dad," a voice warned. *Adalyn.* "Just let him through. What are you even doing? Let him pass and let's go wait somewhere else."

Steps followed my sister's question, then the door in front of me flew open.

I felt my heart stop for a second before resuming that overwhelming pace.

"Josie," Matthew murmured under his breath, frozen, except for his eyes, which bounced all over me. He looked so immediately heartbroken, so devastated, for just an instant. Then gone. "Josie, baby."

A sob exploded out of me. As if yanked by those two words. Him, being with me.

There was a click of a door and then Matthew was suddenly with me. He picked me up, placing me against his chest. The kind of warmth that only he could provide blanketed over me, soaking my skin, body, making more tears trickle down. More sobs come out. More hurt break and burst out.

"I'm here, baby," Matthew's words were murmured into my ear. "I'm here now. I'm here with you. I'm not going anywhere." His words only made me cry harder, struggle for more air. Matthew's body was rocked by a shiver. A tremor. Or maybe it was just me. "You need to tell me what to do," he whispered. That soothing murmur turning into a desperate plea. "Tell me what to do to make this better."

My right hand was clasped around the fingers of my left, unknowingly pulling and tugging, and if the sight hadn't shattered my heart the way it did, my words would. "I can't—" I stuttered. "Can't do this, Matthew." A new wave of hurt and tears made me breathless for a second. I raised my hands, showing him my left hand. The skin was red, swollen. He made a strange sound. "It's all backward. I can't get it off. It's hurting."

A pained expression crossed Matthew's face. One moment it was there and then it was gone.

But God, I hated myself all the same.

Then something else was replacing that. I didn't know what, but slowly, gently, he wrapped his fingers around my wrist. He brought my hand up, until the tips of my fingers brushed his lips. My crying subsided, my breath easing at the contact. He pressed a kiss on my palm, his eyes closing for a moment. Then another one on my knuckles. Then a third, right above the beautiful ring that was making me hurt so bad and hurting him in return. His head lowered, chin touching his chest and gaze meeting mine again. There was a storm behind that beautiful shade of brown as he let his lips close around my finger. A whimper left me, and Matthew's whole body shuddered in response. I felt his tongue on my skin, then gently, firmly, his teeth were locking around the band.

He pulled.

A strange and powerful tide rolled over me as I felt the ring being dragged along my finger with his teeth. And even as his eyes flared with an emotion I didn't want to look at too closely. I felt . . . relief.

Matthew spat the ring into his palm, his eyes not leaving me.

Something broke at the sight. Whatever had been put together a heartbeat ago, crumbling down again.

I felt my lip quiver. My whole body did. "I don't want to hurt you," I told him.

"That's all right, Baby Blue," he murmured before kissing my temple. His voice sounded broken, his arms solid and tight around me. "So what if it hurts a little? I'll hurt if it makes you better."

But that wasn't all right.

It really wasn't.

I moved in his lap, that ugliness in me festering. My hands fisted the fabric of his shirt. "You shouldn't say that," I told him. "You should be mad."

A muscle in his jaw jumped. "No, I shouldn't."

My hold on his clothes tightened. My voice coming out coarse. Mean. "I just told you I can't do this. I can't walk down that aisle. I can't make vows. I can't say I do. I—I can't wear your ring. This is what I always do, don't you see?" I let out a breath, emotion overtaking my voice. "Last night changed everything. I know you feel the same. How can you not be mad? How are you not leaving me?"

Matthew's hands closed around my waist, and he rearranged me so I was straddling him. My gown moved around me, over him, and I felt so . . . bizarre. So strange. So out of place. This was the gown I'd never wear, the man I wasn't marrying, this position fitting a wedding night we'd never have.

"Because I only ever wanted you, Josie," he said, meeting my eyes. "Not the wedding, not the big party. You."

I gave my head one sharp shake. "I don't understand. Why would you want me after this?"

"Why would I not?"

The thrumming doubled. "Because I made you tag along. Because I just pushed you away. Because I want to turn around your ring but I can't. I— Because I knew it'd hurt you, and I still asked you to take it off my finger."

"Yet I'm here. With my arms around you, not going anywhere. What else?"

What else? "Because I'm a mess. I broke down at my reflection in a wedding dress. I have a reputation, baggage, issues. I complicate things unnecessarily. I might be incapable of ever getting married. I—" I shook my head. "Haven't you heard? I might break your heart, Matthew. Polls say more than fifty percent chance."

"You can try. Won't work, though."

Indignation bubbled up. "Why not?"

"Because with you, I'm unbreakable."

A strange sob climbed up my throat.

"Because you can't push me away." His arms pulled my body even closer to him, and when his palm closed around the side of my face, his gaze sharpened with something that danced between anger and need. "Not this easily." His throat worked before kissing me. The press of his lips was hard and fast. "Certainly not without a fight."

I returned his kiss, my lips now rough against his. I parted his mouth and brushed his tongue with mine. "Prove it," I whispered, tugging at his shirt, bringing myself closer into his chest. "Show me you mean this. Show me that you'll stay."

The quality of Matthew's eyes changed, darkening. His voice lowered. "Don't ask for things you don't really mean."

I brought myself up on my knees, pulling at the layers of the skirt until I moved them all out of the way. Then I made sure I was staring right into his eyes when I let my hips roll against his before dropping my weight against the pulsing length I could feel through his pants.

Matthew hissed a breath. "You're upset."

I rolled my hips a second time, the violent shudder rocking my body, making me struggle for words. "I am. Over the idea of losing you."

There was a moment of hesitation, then his hands were sneaking under the gown, his fingers digging into my skin with barely there restraint. He locked me in place. "You want me to fuck you in this dress, Josie? Is that how you want me to show you?"

I nodded my head.

I could see it in his eyes then. I could see that he was going to do this for me, despite the thing that had gone unsaid.

"I love you, Matthew," I whispered. Or maybe the words burst out of me. "I'm so in love with you. And this is not the moment, but God, I'm so goddamn terrified to—"

His mouth clashed against mine, taking my lips in his, and for a moment, God, for just an instant I swore I could have dissolved from the impact of that kiss. But I didn't. Couldn't, when all my body lit up, electricity flickering beneath my skin, a dazzling sensation sweeping me head to toes. My eyes closed, blinding me to the world, to everything around except for him, and I surged up, parting my mouth against his once more. Matthew groaned and my hands closed around his face, locking him against me.

There was a rip of fabric. My panties. Then I was bare, roughly pushed against the hard length in his pants. Matthew's hands guided me, up and down, up and down, up and down until I was breathless, panting, both of us gasping for air.

Brown eyes, dark like I'd never seen them, met mine. "You want me to show you how much I fucking love you, then all you need to do is ask." The sound of a belt followed by a zipper made my ears ring, stomach dropping with delight. "The only thing broken here is my restraint." He pulled me down, nestling himself between my folds and making us both hitch a breath. "You're drenched, Josie. Do you need me this bad?"

I gave my head a nod.

Matthew pressed a kiss to the corner of my lips as a reward, but instead of moving, he dragged his mouth across my cheek, all the way to my ear. "Beg me for it," he rasped. "Say *please, Matthew.*"

"Please, Matthew."

His palms shifted, hands digging into my skin as he squeezed my ass. "Good fucking girl," he whispered in my ear. "All mine. Now sit on me."

My hands grasped his shoulders as I lowered myself. I felt him at my entrance, my eyelids fluttering shut at how much I needed him. How good he felt. How much peace it brought me to be filled. My knees gave in, making my body fall.

A whimper rose inside me, and Matthew captured it with his mouth.

Lips moving against mine, his hands guided me upward before letting me fall again. Stars prickled my eyes. Electricity surged, stronger, overpowering, all across my body. The position, the urgency, the need to be reassured in any way I could by this beautiful man who I didn't want to lose, edging me closer, swifter, wickedly fast.

"I love you, Josephine Moore," Matthew said against my mouth. My heart stopped, then doubled, tripled its pace. "I don't care how I have you as long as you're mine."

A new sound climbed out of me, but this time Matthew let it topple, falling between us. The pace of my hips increased, encouraged by his words, the way he looked at me, the way his hands encompassed me, the way he made me feel so full, so right, so whole.

"My heart is not broken," he said, low, voice rocky in a way that told me he was so close. As close as me. "And I'm not leaving you. Hear me?" He thrust upward, impaling me before I let myself fall. A wave of bliss rocked me. "You're mine to keep. Now say it."

My fingers closed around his hair just so I'd hold on to something. "I'm yours," I whispered. "I'm yours. I'm yours. I'm yours."

The words encouraged the motions of his hips, his cock slipping in and out of me at a punishing speed. "Call out my name, Josie." His mouth took mine, teeth closing over my bottom lip before letting go. "Let them hear. I don't care. I never did. Let it rock you while I come inside you."

My eyes closed just as Matthew's hips rolled, his thrust somehow deeper, somehow closer, sharper, tipping me over the edge with a gasped, *"Matthew."* Before feeling him pulse inside me with a growl.

He pulled me against his chest. "You're not running, Josie," he said, planting kisses all over the side of my face, hips rocking, slowing down. "I'm not them. I'm not anyone. I'm not fucking letting you."

I closed my eyes, as tightly as I could, letting those words soothe me. Letting the feel of Matthew's body under mine soothe me too. He felt so solid, so certain and sure and safe. Unlike anything I'd ever had. Unlike anyone.

He really felt like mine.

And I loved him, I loved Matthew in a way that made me wonder if I'd ever known how love felt before him. It was so scary, it made me feel so vulnerable, so frail, and perhaps . . . perhaps that was how this was supposed to feel. Perhaps that was fine. Perhaps, *I love you*s were meant to feel this big. To make you feel this naked. This exposed. So big you were terrified to hurt. So safe no one could touch you.

Perhaps to love was to leave a mark.

And perhaps I no longer wanted to run from that.

It took us a long time to come out of that dressing room.

When Matthew slipped out of me, he was still hard. The chuckle that left him when I looked at him with a spark in my eye was strained and pleading. Enough for me to let it go and make him promise we'd revisit the topic back at home. *Home.* The thought made a spot in the middle of my chest tender to the touch. But those were questions that had to take a back seat when there was a bridal shop filled with people to whom I owed an explanation.

Once back in my clothes, which Matthew helped me put on, placing a kiss on my skin as a reward for every item that I slipped on, I took his hand in mine.

"Ready?"

I gave him a nod.

We walked along the hallway that led to the front of the shop, and the moment we got there, all heads and eyes turned.

All words, plans, explanations fled my mind. "I . . ."

"I'm calling off the wedding," Matthew said.

Every single person in the bridal shop froze.

Then Cameron—who I assumed must have gotten here with Matthew—stood up from some bench he'd been perched on. His jaw clenched.

"Calm down," Matthew said, fingers squeezing mine. "She's holding my hand."

"We're . . ." I trailed off. Again. "We're together. It's just—"

A sob broke free from Adalyn. Everyone turned toward her.

"It's all okay," I rushed out. "We're okay. We're not breaking up." I kept my eyes on my sister, avoiding Andrew's as he stood on one side. Avoiding Bobbi's, too, that I could feel on my profile. "It's all so complicated. But we're just not getting married. I—I can't. I don't think I ever wanted to." I searched for Charleene's gaze, finding her pale. "Don't worry, I'll pay for the dress. I promise."

"You better believe that gown is being paid for," Bobbi intervened. She walked closer to where we stood. "You have no idea how hard it was to keep everyone from going to check on you while you were in that dressing room."

My cheeks flushed slightly, but it wasn't with embarrassment. It was with the memory of Matthew's words. *Let them hear.* My hand was squeezed, and I squeezed back. "Thank you. We had much to discuss."

Bobbi rolled her eyes. "You're lucky the commotion outside

was distracting enough." She sent Matthew a glance. "I might have underestimated you, Blondie."

"What commotion?" I asked, before Matthew could say whatever had him smirking like that. "There was a commotion outside?"

Bobbi spared a look at my father, who stood in the exact same spot, still silent. "Andrew decided to show up," she explained. "Unlike we'd agreed. Someone must have caught wind of it and there were a few people with iPhones outside. Everything's so low-effort these days. Regardless, the photographers attracted people. A crowd. And they were interested enough in you to stick around. Especially after your boo here entered the shop like we were keeping you hostage."

Matthew's exhale was so forceful that I glanced over at him. He met my gaze, a muscle in his jaw jumping. "Cam told me where they were taking you and I asked him to turn around and drive here instead. We were already on our way when Bobbi called." So that was how he'd gotten here so fast. Slowly, every piece started coming together. His attention returned to Bobbi. "Now that you've had a chance to get your word in, we're leaving." He took a step forward. "I'm taking Josie home. Cam, Ada, let's—"

The woman's hand fell on Matthew's shoulder. "Nuh-uh. Not so fast. We need to talk. The wedding—"

"Is not happening," Matthew interjected.

Bobbi's eyes narrowed before turning to me. "The dress," she said, softly but stubbornly enough for me to stiffen. "Is it still wearable?"

My voice was apologetic but firm. "I'm not wearing it. I can't. I'm sorry, Bobbi."

"Pick another one."

"Don't make me repeat myself, Shark," Matthew intervened.

Bobbi huffed a laugh. "Well, I'm afraid you'll have to. Because this is ridiculous. You can't cancel a wedding just based on a few tears and a quickie in a dressing room. This—"

"It was all a hoax," I rushed out. "We were never engaged."

Silence fell. Thick and sudden.

I inhaled. Deep. Then out. Matthew's hold of my hand unmovable. "We—I convinced Matthew to do this with me. For me. To pretend we were engaged to be married until all of this went away. It wasn't supposed to escalate this fast or this far. I didn't want to become an issue, to be a problem. I didn't want to be a bigger problem than I already was. A misstep that came to bite you in the ass. It was stupid, and reckless, and over-the-top for something that started as a harmless way for me to make Bobbi leave my porch. I . . ." A big gulp of air left me. "I'm so sorry."

There was a long moment in which I could only hear my heart drumming in my temples. Feeling disoriented, I looked around. Bobbi was shaking her head in denial. Adalyn and Cameron were blinking at us, eyes wide, wider than I'd ever seen. Charleene was gone, probably to scream into one of the velvet pillows I'd defiled on her couch. And Andrew . . . paled.

"I'm not sorry," Matthew said. "About a single fucking thing."

"Matthew," I warned. But it came out half-heartedly. God, I loved him so much for saying that just to break the strange silence. "We are sorry. This was stupid. It was my idea."

"I'm not sorry, Josie," he repeated, and turned to look at me, as if we weren't standing in the middle of a room filled with people, giving them news that would alter big plans already in place. As if our coming clean wouldn't have consequences. He brought our hands up, to his chest, and mine felt so, so empty without his ring. "Be sorry if you have to, but I won't pretend I am. I'm not sorry I stumbled upon your driveway that night. I'm not sorry you thought this was your way to fix a mess that wasn't yours. I'm not sorry I played fiancé when I *knew* I'd end up falling ridiculously in love with you. And I'm not fucking sorry we're calling off a wedding you don't want."

I stared up at him, at a loss for words. I . . . "I love you." I really did.

His smile was as big as it had ever gotten.

"Okay, but listen," Bobbi said from our side. "I know this feels like the right thing to do. I know you're honorable and want to come clean or whatever. But you're not great liars. Just FYI. And no one seemed to care. Ah, wait. Someone does care. The whole freaking internet. So how about we—"

"The wedding is off, Shark."

This time, the words hadn't left Matthew.

Andrew had said that.

I turned to glance back at my father, finding his eyes already on me. For a moment, I'd thought he would say something to me. Anything.

He glanced at the PR strategist. "Do whatever is necessary to do your job without using my daughter as a prop. Either of my daughters. Did I not say that?" His face changed in a way I didn't comprehend. "You had a task, and it wasn't this. Yet you still lied to me? Knowing she was doing this?"

"But—" Bobbi said.

"We'll talk about this later." His frame whirled around, but before setting off he shook his head. "I'm so genuinely sorry, Josie. Now if you'll excuse me, I need to go handle things. Just like I should have done from the beginning."

Bobbi cursed under her breath when Andrew left and for a second she remained rooted to the pink carpet covering the shop's floor before shooting after him.

Matthew's arm slid around my shoulders, pulling me into his side. "You good?" he murmured against my hair. I nodded my head. "That was a lot, and you were so brave."

My lips popped open with an answer, but it was silenced by a cry.

We both turned in time to see Cameron pulling my sister into his chest much like Matthew had with me. She cried harder still, the occurrence so unlike her, so out of the blue, that it froze both Matthew and me.

"Oh, for fuck's sake," Cameron muttered, squeezing another sob out of her. "You're killing me, love. Just tell them already. Not saying a word is hurting you. And it's killing me seeing you like this."

"Tell us?" Matthew asked. "Tell us what?"

It was Adalyn's face that made my stomach drop with a realization I had been too blind to see.

"I'm so sorry," Adalyn said against Cameron's chest before extricating herself out of the man's body so she could speak. "I wanted to tell you, but I didn't know how without making everything about me. And I didn't want to intrude or steal anyone's thunder, so I stayed away." Her eyes snatched mine. "But you weren't talking to me like you used to, and I just didn't know what to do because I was lying and keeping things from you too."

"Love," Cameron murmured, placing a kiss on her temple. "You're not saying the words."

Adalyn huffed out a strange laugh, tears welling up in her eyes. "I'm pregnant. And I—I—I'm so overwhelmed with happiness and hormones that I seem to be crying all the time."

CHAPTER TWENTY-SIX

Adalyn and Cameron stayed the night in Green Oak.

We all bunked at my place. Grandpa Moe included, only he stayed in his room, and this wasn't anything like the girls' sleepovers we'd done in the past. Adalyn and I shared my bed. And Cameron and Matthew spent the night camping out in my living room.

Telling the whole story to Adalyn wasn't easy, especially not when the poor woman was so ridden by her hormones that she seemed to go from happy to sad and back in the blink of an eye. She'd also told me everything I'd missed about her pregnancy, from the moment she'd been late and suspected, to the doctor's visit when they'd been told the pregnancy was free of risk.

We both cried, though. That strange coincidence—our misguided senses to protect each other by lying—had taken a toll on us both.

Maybe we weren't particularly good at having a sibling. Good thing was, there was nothing in the world we couldn't learn to do. At least not when people were as stubborn as we were.

"Are you awake?" she asked.

"Yup," I answered, rolling on my side so I could face her. She smiled just as a ray of sunshine poured into the room between the blinds. "Pfft, you look so pretty right now it's almost insulting. I don't think it's just the pregnancy, but . . . happiness. It looks really nice on you."

"Both you and Cam are full of B.S." she said, but her eyes betrayed her. "My skin is not glowing any more than it used to."

I chuckled. "Please. I'm the worst liar in the county. Possibly all of North Carolina. And Cam's not better. Don't you remember when he signed both of you up for all of our fall activity brochure and pretended it was some ploy to get revenge? Obvious lie. The man had it *so* bad."

Adalyn's laughter was lighthearted and twice as happy. "I still can't believe he did that." A small frown took shape. "And I can't believe I showed up to goat yoga in heels."

A chortle escaped. "In your defense, they were very nice stilettos."

Adalyn's smile remained for a few more seconds. She swallowed.

"We're not doing that anymore," I reminded her. "Keeping stuff in for fear of bruising each other's feelings. So speak up."

"Matthew's in love with you," she said, and her words brought me pause as much as we'd talked long and hard about it. "He really is. And I know I had weeks to process this, but it feels like I'm hearing it for the first time. Like I finally get to ask you questions I couldn't because we were both being silly."

I scooted a little closer to her still. "I know he is," I whispered. "And I love him too. So much it terrifies me. So much I want to give him things I can't. Things I don't know I'll ever be able to give him." Adalyn frowned in question, and I clarified. "He gave me his ring. His grandmother's." My voice lowered. "He would have married me Saturday. I know he would have."

My sister processed my words for an instant. Then she smiled. "He's just . . ." She laughed. "He wasn't joking, you know? The story about the text wasn't made up. He asked me a couple of times how his future wife was doing before I created that group chat with the four of us."

A flutter took flight in my chest, but it was short-lived. "Future wife. When I saw myself in that dress I wanted to crawl out of my skin, which is horribly ironic for someone who has been engaged so many times. But I—I wanted to run, Adalyn."

"Not without him," she said, her hand clasping mine. "You aren't scared of a life or a commitment to him. It's something else that's missing. But I don't know . . . Maybe nothing's missing. Or maybe we don't need to be whole to function, you know? Maybe we just need to learn to love who we are and let people around us love us for that, too."

Maybe nothing's missing.

I didn't feel like something was with him. "I can't believe I'm about to say this, but I think Bobbi was right. It's very likely that I have abandonment *and* daddy issues. Probably other stuff too."

"I think you tried your best, Josie," Adalyn told me, voice hardening.

I frowned. "I think I could have done better than wrangling the whole town into this."

"It's okay to be hurt," she continued with a fierce expression. "It's okay to have issues. It's fine for life to bruise you and leave a mark. That only means you're living, you know? It means you're trying. It doesn't really matter what the world or anyone says about that. It doesn't matter that you get to experience love in a way that's different from what you expected. We were both raised by our mothers and in one way or another Andrew wasn't there for us. For me, he was the man I mimicked but never seemed to impress, to be good enough for. And for you he wasn't much more than a name. Before he came into your life, you didn't think there was anything wrong with how you approached love, or life, so why start now?"

I smiled. "Matthew said a similar thing."

"Well, he's a great man," she answered. "He's my best friend. And he loves to pretend he's silly, but he's not. He will occasionally say some things that blow my mind."

I agreed. I loved Adalyn. I always had. From the moment I saw her standing at the entrance of what today was Warriors Park, looking very fashionable and completely out of place. I . . . I threw my arms around her and hugged her to my chest. "You're going to be an incredible mom, and I'm going to spoil my niece or nephew so absolutely rotten it's not even right. I'm going to be their favorite person in the world."

Adalyn chuckled, and this time, she wasn't even crying when she released me. "That's exactly what Matthew—"

The door flew open and two figures ran through it.

"Jesus Christ," someone grumbled from the foot of the bed, right before I was tackled from the side by a big ball of warmth. "You're like a child. I give up."

Matthew's chuckle fell against my ear. "Stop growling and get over here." He hummed. "It's as cozy and nice as I expected."

Adalyn snorted, and I couldn't help but laugh. "See?" she said from her spot on the bed, bringing herself up. "I told you. He was never really good with personal space. I've been telling him that it'd get him into trouble."

Matthew snuggled further into me. "My most predominant love language is physical touch. Tell that to your baby daddy, by the way. He punched me when I tried to climb onto the couch with him. He's lucky I still have a man crush on him and I refuse to give up on our bromance just yet."

Cameron grunted something before saying, "I apologized."

"And I forgive you," Matthew quipped, hands splaying over my sides. "If you take your woman and leave. I've been respectful of sister time, now it's Matthew time."

I huffed out his name, feigning that the implication of spending alone time with him hadn't just sent my belly twirling. "I was thinking it'd be nice to have breakfast. The four of us and Grandpa Moe."

"Matthew time has just been officially rescheduled," the man inappropriately but deliciously plastered at my back barked. "I'm starving for more than cuddles."

A laugh rolled out of me as I watched a smiling Adalyn being helped off the bed first, then led outside the room by Cameron. "We'll be downstairs."

Matthew's lips brushed a kiss on my jaw the moment we were alone. All goofiness gone. "Do you feel better this morning? After talking to Adalyn?"

I turned in his arms so I could look at him. "Yes. I feel a lot better."

He kissed the tip of my nose. "Good."

"Did you have a nice time with Cam?"

His smile was lopsided. "He gives me shit but I know he loves me." His voice lowered. "Don't tell him but I still can't believe I got to share a couch with one of my idols. It was really hard to keep it together and act cool. I deserve a reward. Even if small. Preferably from you. Ideas?"

My laughter was unstoppable. "You do know you *will* be their child's godfather, right?"

His eyes widened with the thought.

I kissed him then. There was a surprised tiny gasp, then he took over, deepening the kiss with a low hum.

"That's exactly what I was talking about," he murmured, coming up for breath. I arched my brows. "You're my reward, Baby Blue."

Matthew was wrong this time.

He was my reward.

We spent most of the day together before Adalyn and Cameron hugged us goodbye and returned to their place with the promise of coming by the following day.

Quickly after, Grandpa Moe retired to his room to watch a rerun from one of his favorite seasons of *The Bachelorette*, leaving us alone to *canoodle or whatever,* in his words. Judging from Matthew's face, I doubted Grandpa Moe's comment had left him exactly in the mood to canoodle so we were—innocently—curled up on the couch, while we ignored the unfolding consequences of everything that had gone down the day before.

I'd been trying not to think too much of it, or at the very least, not to speak of it so I wouldn't make it any more real than it was. But if I'd learned anything these past weeks, it was that keeping stuff from coming out usually meant it'd eventually make something burst.

"The town's going to be unbearable tomorrow," I whispered.

Matthew sat up on the couch, as if immediately ready to talk about why or how much, or anything I needed to, really. He appraised the space between us with a frown, then snatched my legs and placed them on his lap. "I'd offer to drive us fast and far away from here, but I don't think that's something you want to do. So how about I come with you to Josie's tomorrow? We'll open up together, and then you can set me on a stool at the counter and I'll take every question while you work."

I considered the plan with a smile. Perfection might be subjective, like Matthew loved to say, but to me there wasn't a thing about this man that I didn't think was perfect. Not after saying that. Not after everything.

"Driving away is tempting," I admitted. But having him with me at Josie's, just like he'd painted, not just tomorrow but every day, was even more so. It made my smile wider, although it also opened up questions. Like Matthew's job or where he'd live. Was now the moment to talk about that? I shook my head. "But you're right. I—"

He squeezed my ankle. "*We* should face everyone and get that out of the way. It won't be that bad. They were probably expecting me to blow it anyway."

Matthew's face hardened. "You haven't blown shit, Josie. And if anyone implies that tomorrow, no matter how well-intentioned, I'm kindly but firmly answering by leading them out of your establishment."

A chuckle escaped me. "I've always wondered what having a bodyguard would feel like. Will you pick me up, princess-style, and navigate the crowd of gossip-hungry customers as you pull me away?"

The corner of his mouth tipped up as he threw me a wink. "Absolutely."

I couldn't know if it was the goofiness in the wink, or the way he'd said that like it was nothing, or maybe the domesticity of the moment, but . . . "I love you."

My words seemed to catch Matthew off guard for a second, so I poked his stomach with my foot.

"Get used to it, mister," I said. And the surprise dissolved, giving way to his smile. Matthew's smile. Then something else. "Stop looking at me like that. I'm trying really hard to have a conversation with my—"

"With your what?"

"With my man. My Matthew. The man I love." His face softened impossibly. "The man whose parents are arriving in town for a wedding that's not taking place, too." I swallowed. "Do you think they will be mad?"

"They will be surprised," he answered, voice matching his face. "They'll want an explanation. But no, I don't think they'll be mad.

There's nothing to be mad about. Not where you—we—are concerned. As for myself, I'm most likely getting my ass whooped for lying about my job. But that's a different conversation I need to have with them."

"I could be there," I offered. "When you tell them about that. I can hold your hand. If you need me."

Matthew's gaze turned impossibly tender. Sweet. Also hungry.

Delicious heat climbed up my neck. I swallowed. "You look ridiculously horny, Matthew Flanagan."

"And you're making your smile."

He didn't need to say which one.

Matthew chuckled, and his mouth popped open with what I knew was a promise, but a ping from the coffee table distracted us. All amusement was snuffed out, and I knew from the way he looked at me that he wanted us to ignore it but wouldn't ask me to. We both knew what that message was most likely about, and we both had been ignoring the world—and the internet—long enough.

He stretched his arm and snatched my phone, handing it to me without peeking at the screen. I sat up, coming to his side so we could both see whatever had torn at the thin bubble I'd carefully blown around us. He brushed a kiss at my temple as I unlocked the screen.

BOBBI: I know I'm fired and I'm supposed to cut all contact with you, but I'm at the airport and I'm bored. So you're getting this from me. Consider it my breakup text.

I looked up at Matthew, eyes widening. "Andrew fired Bobbi?"

He clenched his jaw. "I'm surprised to agree with a decision that man made, but she should be fired. She played Andrew the moment she decided not to tell him the truth. And even after you broke down like that, she still tried to push you to—" His exhale was forceful. "You always come first, Josie. And I hated—hated—seeing you crying and hurting like that."

I kissed his cheek. Then his jaw. Then his lips. Matthew's tension eased away. "I'm all right now. I'm better than all right. I'm with you."

Another new text popped up, making us both glance down.

BOBBI: Andrew's way to handle things is paying Page Nine off. I'm saying this because he won't admit it. It won't work. That's why he hired me. They won't take the money. Page Nine makes their own rules. They're the twisted, Gen-Z targeted Robin Hood of gossip.

"They won't take the money," Matthew said. "She's right. They'll probably retaliate if Andrew tries to silence them that way."

BOBBI: They want Matthew on the podcast. They wanted Josephine at first, but now that she called off the wedding, they want groom number five. It's the big reveal they were working toward. Live thing, streamed, etc. They were sure he'd be left heartbroken, so they've been biding their time.

I blinked at the screen.

"Fuckers," Matthew murmured. "I should have known."

Another text came before I could speak.

BOBBI: They'll offer him big money. His job back (yes, I also knew about that, Blondie). A raise. Anything, really. My advice is to take it. Go on the thing, lie, and put out the fire once and for all. You're not getting married anyway. And it's not only for Andrew's sake but for the two of you. Blondie gets the money. Josephine becomes old news.

BOBBI: Yes. I used you to serve a purpose. But I always tried to protect you. Those two pretend to be righteous, cool, woke. But they forget all about it for the sake of a good story. When it's someone else's life on the screen of a device, we forget that it could be us or someone we care for.

BOBBI: You can't change that, just learn to live with it. Make the best out of it. Roll with the punches and take the money. Give them the conclusion to the story. Move on.

BOBBI: Oh, and it was Duncan who leaked the clip. Don't ask me how he got ahold of it, but I suggest you stop dating politicians.

BOBBI: It wasn't a pleasure working with you, but it wasn't as harrowing as I thought it would be. So call me if you ever need me. It'll be on the house for all the trouble I might have caused. Although you should probably be thanking me for giving you an excuse to bang. Bye.

That was . . . A lot. And it all swirled around my head, slowly but distinctly locking into place.

"Matthew?" I asked.

"I'm not doing that," Matthew said before I could follow that up. "I don't want their money. Job, a raise. None of that."

"I understand that." I swallowed. "They're horrible people. But I don't want you to turn that down because of me. I . . . I can't ask you to uproot your whole life to be with me. I've tried to do that in the past. With every man I've been with. I've molded myself and tried to fit, and sure, I fell in love with certain things that I made mine but . . . It's never worked. So I can't ask that of you."

"You're not asking me." Fingers clasped my chin gently, bringing my gaze up. "You're not uprooting my life, either. They did that. I did that. And I don't want any of that back. I only want you."

I only want you. "Well . . . there goes my plan."

"What plan?"

"Sending you off. Have you consider taking the job and go back to Chicago. Giving you space so you could have a choice." I smiled at him, even though a little weakly. Matthew kissed me and I felt the words on my lips. *You are my choice.* He was mine, too. "What if you take the money? Like Bobbi advised. We feed them a conclusion, and you cash in a check."

He snorted. "I'm not going on that thing to lie about the woman I love."

"Then don't. Don't lie. I'm so tired of that. So exhausted by the lies and the shame and . . . caring about what people think and say about anything."

His brows met, but I could see him piecing everything together. Where my head was going. What I meant. "That's your story to tell, Josie. Not mine. I would never dare."

"I don't think it is, though," I murmured. And when I heard the words, it solidified something in my head. I twisted my body so I could fully face him. So he could see my face. That I wasn't sending him off, or running, but the opposite. "I think it stopped being mine the moment all of this started. And they want you, not me."

Matthew's arms came around my waist, and he pulled me closer, encouraging, providing the safety I always felt slip through my fingers whenever this whole PR mess was brought up. "What are you saying, Blue?"

"I'm saying that I'm a little tired of having strangers treat my life like it's theirs to discuss. I'm saying that I trust you and I love you and I can't think of anyone better to tell everyone the truth. I'm saying it's no longer my story, that I'm no longer on my own when I'm with you because it's *us* now. I'm saying Bobbi is partly right maybe, and this is the only way it'll all be put to rest. And I'm also saying that I've already asked way too much of you, and I keep asking more, so if you don't want to do this, I understand."

Matthew kissed me again, a bruising press of his mouth against mine this time. "So you're not pushing me away."

"I don't think I'm capable of that."

His arms tightened around my back. "What do you suggest we do, then?"

We.

"We didn't start this," I said. "But we can decide how it ends."

CHAPTER TWENTY-SEVEN

Matthew left North Carolina at dawn.

Cameron had dropped Adalyn off with Grandpa and me, and then booked himself on the same flight as Matthew.

The thought of him tagging along eased me. It made me a little less anxious as I counted down the hours to noon—when *Filthy Reali-Tea* would be on air with the man I loved and had asked to tell the world every secret we have shared.

Time had trickled slowly, and although Adalyn had been around, Josie's Joint remaining closed hadn't helped. Not that the alternative was an option. I couldn't face everyone without Matthew. It didn't feel right. And he'd made me promise I wouldn't. So I'd hung a sign and let everyone believe we were working through our feelings.

We were, in a way.

Because Matthew was going on that podcast to tell my story. Ours. And it filled me with as much relief as anxiety. I also had this gut-feeling, my gut-tummy-drop feeling, that something was about to go down. That whatever plans we'd spent making that night wouldn't necessarily work. But it could be just my insecurities or fear talking. It could be just me.

Because I did believe that sometimes love was enough.

And some other times it conquered the world.

It depended on how much magic was in the air that day.

"Do you have any of those kale chips around?" Adalyn asked from the threshold of the kitchen. "I'm craving something green."

"Huh. Matthew finished them." Adalyn's mouth fell. "But I have olives. Peas. Brussels sprouts?"

She sighed. "I'll take the olives I think." Her expression turned hesitant. "Are you doing good?"

"Yes. Absolutely. Just a little anxious. I wish I'd gone with him. He got all gruffy and scowly when I suggested it, and I conceded because I think a part of me was scared to go. But that was probably selfish."

She padded the distance between us and gave me a squeeze. "You're the best person I know," she whispered before releasing me. "You're not selfish. And there's no way on earth that Matthew would have let you board that flight. Neither would Cam, actually. It's been incredibly hard to keep him from stomping into Page Nine to take matters into his own hands all this time. I'm a little worried they secretly plotted doing that in fact." She sighed. "So let's just hope we don't need to bail them out for something stupid tomorrow. Now tell me where the olives are, I'm getting cranky."

I chuckled, although it came out a little strained. "Top cabinet, left."

The doorbell rang and we separated, her disappearing into the kitchen and me jogging over to the door.

A set of blue eyes behind a stern expression welcomed me. "Oh," I mumbled, surprised. "Hi, A—"

"I'm sorry," he said. Or more like the words left him.

My body stumbled back a little, the weight of those two simple words hitting me harder than I expected. "That's . . ." I swallowed. "Thank you."

"You shouldn't be thanking me." Andrew shook his head. "Listen, I . . ." he trailed off for an instant, hesitating. "I don't know how to do this. Any of this. I think it's clear from the way I've acted. The truth is that I don't know how to be around you. I don't know whether you hate me or are skittish because you don't trust me. But I do know I've done enough to deserve both. That's why I'm here."

I frowned, not really understanding what he referred to. There was so much to unpack. So much to ask and to say and to discuss. "I don't hate you," I told him. "But you're right, I don't trust you, either. Trust is something you earn. Not through video calls or turning a person into an agenda item, or unilaterally deciding you're moving closer to them. And I . . . I wasn't brave enough to say that earlier. But I am now."

His expression opened up, as if finally receptive to what I was saying. Receptive to who I was.

"I wanted a relationship with you," I continued. Embracing that surge of courage I'd found in my words. "I don't blame you for the mess I made, and I also owe you an apology for lying. I'd love to say that it's fine because it was well-intentioned. But it wasn't. It isn't fine, and while I have a lot of work to do on myself, I think you should also do that." Emotion rose, attempting to clog my throat. I pushed through. "I wanted you, Andrew. As my dad. But I'm realizing you don't owe me that. I'm wondering whether wanting that relationship was a mistake. I'm realizing I no longer want to bridge the gap to you. So until you decide to do that, I'm not sure I want to keep in touch with you. It's . . . too much. And I'm sorry. But—"

"But nothing," Andrew interjected, voice softer than ever. "You don't need an excuse or to justify yourself. The mistakes that have led us here are mine. Eloise wanted to protect you, and I can't say I blame her." His head shook, and my chest tightened at the mention of Mom. "You're not a misstep."

My lips parted, my emotion coming out in a single breath.

"You're not a regret, Josephine. I'd love to say that my biggest regret is allowing the circumstances to define how we met, but I'm the only one to blame for that. I see that now."

I pressed my lips, just so nothing would come out. Just so I would stay strong and not break the promise I made myself to give us space to grow. Whether that was in the same or different directions.

He pulled something out of his jacket.

"These are my responses," he said, gaze cast down on the stack of letters he held between us. "To the letters your mother sent me while you were growing up. I wish I could tell you some big tale about star-crossed lovers, but we were far more pragmatic than that. I never cheated on Adalyn's mother. It wasn't an affair. It was just two people feeling lonely one night." He sighed. "It all . . . unraveled quickly, and I was selfish enough to convince myself I had a say in more than just my life. It's all in the letters. I think that's why I never sent them." He took a step back. "Read them. Burn them. Feed them to the press if that's what you think I deserve. They're yours to do with as you please."

I blinked at him as I took the stack. At a complete loss for words.

Andrew continued, "I'll fly back to Miami today. This is not something you should care about, but the book is not happening. It's what started all of this, in a way. I was concerned with the tabloids smearing that. My name. My legacy. I suppose the dream had always been a byproduct of my ego, like Bobbi said a few times." He huffed out a laugh. "I don't really see how much wisdom I could impart any longer either way, don't you think?"

My lips fell open, but nothing came out. My brain was struggling to process all of that. To deal with the fact that this was the most

Andrew had ever told me. The most we'd ever talked. The most he'd shared.

"Thank you," I finally mumbled. "I . . ."

I won't burn the letters. Or publish them. I never could.

That was what I should have said.

But I didn't. "Matthew's telling everyone the truth. Today. He's landing in Chicago as we speak."

Andrew's mouth twitched and tipped up, gracing his face with a smile. It was an odd one. Small, and crooked, as if rusty from misuse. It was also a surprise. "Good," he said. "I won't bother you for a while. But I'd love to have the four of you over for Christmas. Doesn't need to be a holiday. Any day you can all spare will do."

My brows arched.

"Feel free to say no." He took a step back. Then another one. "I'll keep trying until you ask me to stop." His head dipped, giving me one stern nod. "Bye, Josephine. Bye, Adalyn."

I was watching him descend the porch steps in the direction of a black sedan, barely making sense of his last words, when a hand fell on my shoulder.

"You okay?" Adalyn said, squeezing. "You're barely blinking, and my brain is saying that's not necessarily bad, but my hormones are on high alert."

I shook my head, a strange laugh coming out. "I . . . I think I'm fine. Yeah, I think I'm starting to see how both our mothers weren't completely blind."

Adalyn snorted, but the amusement was short-lived. "He has his moments." A pause. "It's about to start."

My heart plundered, and I hugged the letters to my chest. I still didn't know whether I wanted to read them, but he'd given me the chance to. The choice.

"Let's go."

INTERIOR—*FILTHY REALI-TEA* STUDIO—DAY

SAM: Hi, hello. This is Sam.

NICK: And this is Nick.

SAM & NICK: And you're listening to *Filthy Reali-Tea.*

SAM: (laughs) Wow, look at us. Nailing that for the first time in *Filthy* history.

NICK: I know, who are we? (chuckles) It must be the pressure of having such a special guest with us today. And let me tell you, if you're not watching the video recording and are listening, yes, he's hella cute too. And he showed up with a man that had me gasping for—

SAM: Stop that, Nick. You said you'd stop flirting with our guests. And the guests of our guests.

NICK: I said I'd try.

SAM: Well, try a little harder than that before you derail this train. All right, let's all ignore Nick being Nick and give a warm welcome to our guest, Matthew Flanagan, who you know as Fiancé Number Five, if you've been following *The Underwood Affair.* Hi Matthew.

(Beat of silence)

MATTHEW: Hi.

NICK: I mean, I do love a man who makes us work for a laugh. So Matthew, hi again, and thank you for being here. You really love playing hard to get, and not just for that smile you're hiding. When The Boss, who you also had the pleasure of working under, told us you'd confirmed last-minute, it took me a moment to process.

SAM: We should tell our Reali-tiers that Matthew used to be a colleague until not long ago. He was the man you can't see behind the glass window, making sure everything ran smoothly and things like this podcast had—

MATTHEW: A script.

NICK: (awkward laugh) No need to throw us under the bus here. We like to call that script more of a . . . guideline. We bring the authenticity, right? There's no podcast without a good podcaster, and that's just fact.

SAM: Period. But for legal reasons, all jokes belong to the pod, not us.

NICK: So anyway. We're super excited to have you here, so we can finally get the real scoop, straight from the source. But first tell us, how are you?

SAM: Heartbreaking news. We were all rooting for you. Well, I was rooting for her, to be honest.

MATTHEW: You weren't rooting for her. You never were.

NICK: (laughs awkwardly) Hey, I would be touchy too. And don't worry, we are more than happy to be your emotional support blankie, just grab on to us and tell us how you feel. How did this start? How did it crash and burn? The wedding is clearly off now, but how is the news affecting you? Did you see it coming?

(Long silence)

MATTHEW: I don't really want to be here.

NICK: Gee. (chuckles) Don't go around being so mean, Matthew, or I might fall in love with you.

MATTHEW: We had a plan. She asked me to do this. To come onto this and tell her story. Our story. That it all started as a PR issue that wasn't hers to deal with.

SAM: (gasps loudly)

NICK: I'm sorry, what? Hold on—Are we getting some tea on Rich Daddy? Sorry—Andrew Underwood? Did he hire one of those PR teams and have you guys trained or something? You can tell us. You—

MATTHEW: But there was never an issue. She was never an issue. And hers is not my story to tell. (laughs to himself) I'm fucking done with hearing her name in your mouth. Anyone's mouth. So you're going to hear my side.

SAM: (murmured) What is going on right now?

NICK: I don't know. (muttered, then clearer) But let's hear it, then. This is all we've ever wanted, by bringing you on. The story beneath the story. The wedding is off now, you clearly are hurt by that. So tell us about that. Tell us your story, Matthew. How everything unraveled.

(Thick silence)

MATTHEW: Josie's the love of my life. Plain and simple.

SAM: (hesitant) Whoa. I feel you, I mean—

MATTHEW: You don't feel me, no. *Spare no details,* she asked me before I left. *Let's dictate how this ends.* She meant about her and her story, her reputation, as she loves to call it. As you've made her believe. Well, fuck that. I'm going to tell you about mine. I'm for the most part what you would call unserious. I never took much besides this job seriously. I joke about everything because I feel that's what's expected from me. There's one thing I'm always serious about, though. That's love. When I was little, my grandmother told me that a Flanagan man just *knows.* She gave me a ring and I kept it ever since. Decades later I got a text from my best friend saying she'd met my soul mate. (laughs with disbelief) This is the second time in a few days that I'm talking about that damn text, but the truth is that I have been thinking of it for a long time. (pauses) It was meant as a joke, a comment you made in passing. But I immediately remembered Gran. I had the suspicion, the inkling of a feeling, that my best friend might be right. Months later, I was fired. From Page Nine, yes. Just because I refused to be a complete hypocrite. Josie thinks it's because I wanted to protect my friends. But I also wanted to protect her. I knew she'd be dragged into it. It'd be a matter of time.

NICK: (in a low voice) Ah. Can that be cut? I don't think—

MATTHEW: Life uprooted. My gut immediately screamed at me. A part of me knew where I wanted to go. To her. Before I knew what I was doing, I was calling my best friend. Asking for a favor. (brief pause) The ten hours of driving I spent convincing myself that I was being an idiot. A fool. What was I even doing? Then I finally saw her. In the flesh. And as much as I tried not to build her up in my head, as much as I'd told myself not to be a fool, that there aren't such things as soul mates, or fate, or love at first sight, there she was. In a fucking face mask, a towel wrapped around her hair and a robe covered in strawberry jam, while she stood in the middle of the strangest fucking situation I'd ever stumbled upon. And I kept looking at her eyes, gut telling me something I couldn't understand, something I couldn't quite piece together. I was so fucking tired that night. Dead on my feet. And I hadn't recognized her, you see. Not right away. I hadn't immediately known it was her. I was so furious at myself. You have no idea. In an instant I'd gone from having a chance, a clean slate to see if my grandmother's words were a fantasy or nothing more than words an old woman brought with her from a past life, to having none of that. She was asking me to play her fiancé. To act like we were in love to make some PR shit go away. But the moment I agreed, I knew she'd think all I did was pretend.

I knew she'd push me away. Eventually. I've watched enough movies and read enough books to know everything would get too complicated. Too hard to discern what was true from what was fake. Hell, I worked in a world that profited from that. By some miracle, I managed to make her see past that and fall in love with me. I showed her I'm giving chase, I'm not letting her run on me, or push me away. And yet, when she heard that you would tempt me with money or job offers or a raise, I saw it right there. In her eyes. The doubt.

That's why I'm really here. Not because she asked me to tell the truth and put all of this to rest. But to tell you to show the decency you love to brag about. To tell her, the world, to show her that there's nothing to choose. There's no settling, sacrificing, or molding myself to anything. Dear God, this is what those men, what Andrew Underwood, what you two with this bullshit you call entertainment, have led her to believe. That she's either meant to leave or be left. Goddamn fools, all of them. I'd personally thank them if I didn't want to break their teeth for not seeing what was in front of them.

Luckily for me, I'm not them. I'm not changing my life for her. I'm not settling. I'm not sitting here and telling you anyone's story over mine. I'm not choosing her over something else. I can't because there was never a choice. I don't give a shit how corny or cliché this sounds, but I knew when I saw her, and I know now more than ever before. I don't need her to walk down an aisle, wear my ring, or sign her name on a dotted line. She's my happy. The rest is only important when you need it and everyone should fucking know that.

I only need her. Jobs are replaceable. Careers are fickle. Roots grow anywhere there's ground. Commitment and love are shown with actions. And I plan on doing that every fucking day of my life as long as I have her.

Easy as that.

(Long moment of silence)

NICK: I . . . Wow.

SAM: (clears throat) Holy shit. I— That was not planned.

NICK: I did not expect that, no. I— Wait. Matthew. Matthew? Where are you going? We're not done. We—

MATTHEW: (muffled, then clearer) Josie won't be happy with me after I get this one last thing out, but as I've said many times, she has a class I lack. Duncan Aguirre? If you ever so much as think to use my woman or anyone in our circle in the future for your own benefit, I'll tell the world where you were on September 15. And who you were with. And yes, I'm talking about her mama, too. I might have principles sometimes, but I'm still a petty man. That's it. I have a flight back home to catch.

CHAPTER TWENTY-EIGHT

Matthew

Irony had a sick sense of humor sometimes.

Or maybe it always did.

Either way, something had to explain why the only structure still set up on the farm was the arched arbor. The one at the end of what should have been the aisle Josie would have walked down.

There was no grief in the sight or the thought of something she wouldn't do. I would have loved to watch her make her way down to me, dressed in a gown, a veil hanging delicately off her head. But I never needed that dream.

And Josie had always been Technicolor in my head. Not white.

The only reason I was here was because Josie hadn't been home when we'd pulled up to her place. She'd been here, surely trying to help finalize clearing the farm. So I'd asked Cam to drive me here instead of waiting for her.

My own words were still whirling around my head. I'd always suspected I was a hopeless romantic. Mostly because that would explain why I was so good at looking at everyone else's love affairs under a clinical lens. One needed to really know about a topic to be able to pick it apart. It was either that, or the fact I was incapable of taking shit seriously. Serious people didn't believe in the things I did or go on a podcast with national reach and swear a total of seven times, then threaten a senator and walk off.

Ma wasn't impressed with me in that regard. I'd been saved by the fact I'd asked them to tune in and she somehow believed my words had been the first real thing I'd said in a long time. *Years.* They would be getting to Green Oak tomorrow instead of today, after my father's suggestion to give everyone a little room to breathe. I didn't regret lying to them, but I regretted not giving them more grace. A little more credit. I owed them everything, and now that included an apology. But I didn't even mind catching some heat. They were meeting Josie. And I couldn't fucking wait for them to meet her.

There was something I'd kept from someone else, too. I'd always been looking for jobs in the Charlotte area. From the moment I was laid off. It hadn't been just about Josie, although I'd be a fool and a liar to deny that, after going on air and saying all of that. It partly was. But there was always more. Ever since Adalyn had found a home here, it had made me see things differently. Wonder what the fuck I was doing with my life. Josie hadn't been wrong to ask me why I wasn't doing something I loved. Something in sports. That was a dream I snuffed out a long time ago in favor of being pragmatic. Comfortable. Content.

The only reason I hadn't told her that was fear. Fear of chasing a dream I wasn't sure was for me, and fear of scaring her away. It had always been difficult not to come off too strong around Josie. And it had never been like I'd decided she'd have me in her life, whether she wanted me or not. I would have settled for being her friend. I simply hoped for the possibility of becoming more than that to her.

Steps sounded behind me, and I immediately knew who was

there at the other end of what could hardly be called an aisle anymore.

Blue eyes met mine when I turned, and man. She was so beautiful standing there, looking at me like that. Watching her smile had always overwhelmed me.

"You knew I'd be here," she said. Her lips were pink today, and the idea of kissing that lipstick off them made my chest flare. "You also went rogue."

"I did."

"We had a plan," she added.

"I'd hoped you wouldn't mind me changing it."

Her frown was small, but it was one. "I minded."

I took one step forward. It was small, too, and it made her raise a hand to stop me.

"I also made plans on my own," she said, voice going breathless in that way that told me she was also overwhelmed at the sight of me, walking toward her. "They were great romantic plans. To reward you."

"You are my reward."

She nodded her head, her gaze going a little crazy for a second. Taking in every inch of my expression. Then all of me. Head to toes. Toes to head, stopping at my chest, shoulders, then eyes. I loved the way her face went hazy when she did that. "I found your ring. Your grandma's. In my box. It doesn't belong there."

My words barely made it out. "It's yours. It always was."

"I'd like you to put it back on my finger, facing the right way. Knowing it's there for us. Not for anybody else." She took a tiny step forward before eyeing what was behind me. The arch adorned with colorful flowers. Her attention returned to me. "I wanted you to before you went on air like that and said all those beautiful things, though."

"How about you come here," I said. My tongue peeked out,

wetting my lips. I was dying to kiss her. "Tell me more about it. All about these plans."

"You're standing at the altar."

My smile was unstoppable, my words a plea. "I know."

I saw how my words affected her in the way her lips parted, that light pink flush I'd grown so familiar with covering her cheeks. "Have you not learned anything?" she said, recovering. She took a second step forward. Smaller this time. "I don't do this part."

"You do when it's me on the other side."

Josie's bottom lip shook for an instant. She didn't move, but a smile broke through. "Did you mean that? What you said?"

"Every fucking word."

A breath left her. "So you do believe in magic. Fate. Gut-feelings. Soul mates."

"That's a part of it," I answered, widening my stance. It was physically difficult to restrain myself from going to her. But she wanted to do this. I could see it in her eyes. In the beautiful way she was stalling. And I wanted her to do it. I'd wait as long as she needed, too. "I also believe in compatibility. In falling in love. In two people finding each other because perhaps they were meant to, but in them also making it work when they do."

"You should have told me," she said after a beat, a beautiful emotion clogging her voice. She shifted her feet, moving. "That night. You should have said all those things. Preferably, in my ear. It would have saved us a whole lot of trouble."

Something caught my eye as she took a new step. Larger this time. It was on her wrist. Her mom's handkerchief. My restraint broke then. God, I was going to cherish this woman as long as she let me. As hard as I could. I returned my gaze to her eyes. She knew I'd seen it. And there were tears welling up. They weren't sad, but they broke me, punched me in the gut all the same. I wanted to kiss that away.

"Come here, Josie," I begged. I was done for. I always had been. "Get over here before I lose my mind. Walk this distance with that handkerchief tied around your wrist and let me show you how much I mean every promise I ever made you." Her whole body seemed to shake. Tremble. "Go on, Baby Blue. It's me you're running to."

A beautiful laugh left her as she ran, and when I caught her in my arms and lifted her up, I captured her laughter with my mouth. I kissed her, basking in the feel of her lips as they moved around mine. In how having her in my arms felt like one of the best things I'd ever get to have. Not simply enough, but everything. Right. Whether something had led me here, to this spot on this farmland, to this woman who had my heart, or whether there weren't things like luck, fate, or magic.

"I love you, Matthew Flanagan," she said against my mouth. "Even when you're really bad at following plans. And even when you've kept from me all these things that would have made me love you instantly."

"Say that again."

Her face softened. "I love you," she said. "You already knew that. I—"

I kissed her again, making sure she knew how grateful I was for getting the right. How deeply I'd fallen in love with her. And when I came up for air, I made sure she could see it in my eyes. All over my face. "That's my favorite," I said. "Out of all your smiles."

She was a little breathless when she asked, "Which one is it?"

"It's your *I've just walked down a goddamn aisle* smile," I said, before I placed her down on her feet. "And that's your *don't ever let me go* smile." I brought her hand up, the one with the handkerchief. I brushed the fabric over my cheek. "That's your *Mom would have loved you* smile." The breathtaking blue in her eyes turned watery. I kissed the corners of them. Then the tip of her nose. Then her lips.

"And this one's your *fuck, I love you so much, please take me somewhere I can show you* smile."

Josie laughed. And the sound felt like a bell, signaling the start of something.

It was the start of a life, with her.

And I had every intention of doing all those smiles justice. Every morning, evening, and night. Every dawn, every sunset, every time she frowned or laughed. Every time she saw me standing before her.

For the rest of my fucking life.

The End

ACKNOWLEDGMENTS

Hi, OMG wow. Here we are again and here I am once more in complete awe of you (the reader) for sticking with me one more time. I wish I could say every book gets easier but I'm slowly learning that writing is a lot like love. There're certain things you learn from experience, different relationships, heartbreak, and moments of pure, unfiltered joy; but the real magic is in how unpredictable the journey always is. Sometimes beautifully, and at times not so much. I'm happy to report, though, that unlike the matters of the heart, every book has led me to a Happily Ever After. With every story I've had the honor to give you, I've walked right into the sunset hand in hand with an array of characters I have fallen helplessly in love with, and with you, too. Hopefully. If you didn't completely hate it. And you know what? Also if you did. I am as sticky as I am relentless, and I vow to always try to make you fall in love. That's why you'll always come first in my acknowledgments. Because without you, this is all nothing but words on paper.

As always, Jess, my agent superhero: I really should get you a cape. Not so you can come flying through my window when I have a meltdown (although it would be nice, honestly), but because you really should have one. They're cute and you'd rock it. Thanks for always keeping me from bursting at the seams. I'd be a disarray of Elena parts scattered around the floor otherwise.

AC, Jenn, Nick, and everyone at Sandra Dijkstra, thank you for being the best agent team an author could ask for.

Kaitlin, Molly, thank you for everything. Every meeting, call, word of encouragement, praise, and every time you've protected me—even from myself. But overall, thank you for believing in me and cheering for me. I don't say that enough.

Megan, Morgan, Zakiya, Ife, and everyone at Atria, thank you for everything you do for me and my books. I'm so grateful for the incredible work you continuously do. (I'm still a little sore over that goat yoga session we never went on, but I'm delulu enough to believe I will eventually manifest it.)

Harriett, Sarah, and the rest of my fantastic UK team, thank you so much for the continuous support and wonderful work. It made me so happy to finally meet everyone in person last fall!

Mr. B. I'm not giving you shit for the flowers anymore. You've kept me together—and made sure I *survived*, which wasn't a small feat these past few months. Who wants flowers when I have you? (Fine, me. Also, a puppy. And a cat, too? But just a little bit.)

Hannah and Becs, thank you for putting up with me. I know you say you don't do that, but you really do, though. So thank you.

Lana, I'm so happy we're friends. I was never too good at making them, and you made it so very easy. I love how unhinged our conversations are, and I'm starting to believe you really don't mind me sending outrageously long voice notes.

María, gracias. Sabes lo afortunada que me considero de haberte encontrado :)

And as always, to those who have made it to this last paragraph:

thank you again. I hope you loved Matthew and Josie's story as much as I loved having their beautifully chaotic voices in my head. Theirs is a love that has filled my chest in a special kind of way. Ever since I started thinking of them. So I hope I managed to do that justice and you've felt that breathlessness that makes your heart skip a beat or two. If you did, you know my DMs are open for screaming, so come yell at me. Because like Chandler says: I'm hopeless and awkward and desperate for love.

ABOUT THE AUTHOR

ELENA ARMAS is a Spanish writer, self-confessed hopeless romantic, and proud book hoarder. Now she's also the author of the *New York Times* bestsellers *The Spanish Love Deception, The American Roommate Experiment,* and *The Long Game.* Her books are being translated into more than thirty languages—which is bananas, if you ask her.

Discover more swoony romances from

ELENA ARMAS!

NEW YORK TIMES BESTSELLER

THE SPANISH LOVE DECEPTION

Pretending to be in love never felt better.

NEW YORK TIMES BESTSELLER

THE AMERICAN ROOMMATE EXPERIMENT

A NOVEL

NEW YORK TIMES BESTSELLER

"Armas is an expert on what makes a romance reader's heart race." —TESSA BAILEY, #1 New York Times bestselling author

THE LONG GAME

A NOVEL

ELENA ARMAS

New York Times bestselling author of THE SPANISH LOVE DECEPTION

Available at **SimonandSchuster.com** or wherever books are sold.

98387